3

MURDER
ON LINE
ONE

Jeremy Vine is a journalist and broadcaster who reaches an audience of millions per week. He hosts a daily breakfast show on Channel 5 and a peak lunchtime slot on BBC Radio 2, presenting news, views, interviews and popular guests on Britain's most listened-to radio news programme. He has previously hosted *Eggheads* and *Points of View* among others.

He lives in London with his wife, two daughters and two cats. In his spare time, he rides a penny farthing.

𝕏 @theJeremyVine
⬚ @thejeremyvine
f @TheJeremyVine

Also by Jeremy Vine

The Diver and The Lover

Non-Fiction

It's All News to Me
Your Call: What My Listeners Say and Why We
Should Take Notice

Jeremy Vine

MURDER ON LINE ONE

HarperCollins*Publishers*

HarperCollins*Publishers* Ltd
1 London Bridge Street
London SE1 9GF

www.harpercollins.co.uk

HarperCollins*Publishers*
Macken House, 39/40 Mayor Street Upper
Dublin 1, D01 C9W8, Ireland

First published by HarperCollins*Publishers* Ltd 2025
1

A catalogue record for this book is available from the British Library.

ISBN: 978-0-00-870705-7 (HB)
ISBN: 978-0-00-870706-4 (TPB)

This novel is entirely a work of fiction.
The names, characters and incidents portrayed in it are
the work of the author's imagination. Any resemblance to
actual persons, living or dead, events or localities is
entirely coincidental.

Typeset in Sabon Lt Pro by HarperCollins*Publishers* India

Printed and bound in the UK using 100%
Renewable Electricity at CPI Group (UK) Ltd

MIX
Paper | Supporting
responsible forestry
FSC
www.fsc.org
FSC™ C007454

This book contains FSC™ certified paper and other controlled
sources to ensure responsible forest management.

For more information visit: www.harpercollins.co.uk/green

To my three Queens:
Rachel, Martha, Anna

'It's not true I had nothing on. I had the radio on.'
Marilyn Monroe

PART ONE

CHAPTER ONE

He could smell the lad. Smell his son on the field as he approached. The unquenchable, restless love of the parent, scanning the air like radar. The lion's nose – the wind always told you where your cub was. The February cold stung his cheeks as a slap would. In the distance he heard the teams shouting 'Pass! Here!' and strained for Matty's voice.

He could not wait to reach the touchline and call out his support. The mist rose from his mouth as thick as vaped cinnamon. Approaching the other parents, he felt a sudden cough leap in his chest and stifled it, hugging his overcoat. A cough at this moment might have sounded deliberate, a way of ensuring they turned and greeted him. He would rather be alone.

The sports field was on Pinn Lane, a former wheatfield halfway between the school in Cubitt St Clare and the coast at Sidmouth. The seaside was a four-mile drive from the school; the boys must have been disappointed when the coach stopped halfway, after the sharp left which put the River Otter behind them. A sign read SCHOOL SPORTS PRIVATE, suggesting a world shortage of colons. On the field, the occasional lopsided bounce of the football was a reminder of furrows here in years gone by, a memory of wheat grown. Some sheaves still sprouted behind the goalposts; once a wheatfield, always a wheatfield.

Edward Temmis hated that the kids did the trip from Cubitt by minibus even on the hottest summer days, all those youngsters seat-belted and cooped up behind toughened glass, but he guessed it was school insurance that made the protection of a vehicle necessary. Perhaps that could be an item for the show one day.

Avoiding the home supporters – the gaggle of parents on the far touchline who knew him – meant lifting his knees high to cut through the long grass and brambles at the back of the pavilion, which still showed the last cricket score of summer.

This was one of those days when you could not imagine going without an overcoat, much less wearing sunglasses or hearing the thwack of a cricket bat. He admired the boys for coming out in shorts on a day like this. They were twelve; some were thirteen already. At eleven, Matty was the youngest by a year. He admired his son for staying with the team; his boy was the best player by a country mile. No gloves on the pitch – which was, quite literally, 'old school'.

The shouting got louder. He felt the damp from the unkempt grass reach his shins, and cursed a bramble that caught the end of his trouser leg. No one heard his expletives. He could have been invisible.

Emerging from behind the pavilion, incognito, safely away from the other parents, he made for the left touchline and chose a spot where any action in the midfield would stop him being seen by the mothers and fathers on the line opposite. He began shouting for the team. Stupidly he had left the fixture list at home and had a sudden panic about where the visiting players had come from. This was the Devon and Cornwall Schools' League. Cubitt St Clare Boys were mid-table, punching above their weight, not least because of a couple of crackers Matty had scored from midfield. Matty's mother would have loved to hear about that.

An observer might have wondered about this tall, heavyset dad with a whiskery growth of beard and dark hair curling beyond his collar who joined the visiting team's parents and, rocking backwards and forwards in those big shoes, shouted for his child. They might have noticed the hearing aid when he reached behind his left ear once or twice. A boys' football game was not the sort where fans of opposing teams had to be kept separate, but the way he called his son's name and urged him to 'pass, Matty, double back, that's it!' or 'watch for the long ball, just run, it'll find you!' was a little hard on the ears. The parents around him – the away fans, visiting from Dittisham, he now remembered, forty-five miles distant – shot each other glances.

'Nice to have you with us,' said one of the mums eventually, as if she was the one the others insisted should speak. The woman was much shorter than Edward, with a smart, pea-green coat and matching driving gloves. He wondered if Dittisham was a private school.

'What's the score?' he asked. 'I was late.'

With that he adjusted the hearing aid. She might have thought he was trying to hear the answer, but Edward was actually trying to turn the world down. He was just here to shout for Matty. The woman turned and contemplated him. The calling of the boys on the pitch quietened, momentarily, for a throw-in. 'I know your voice,' she said. After a pause, as if she had tried and failed to place it, she turned to another woman next to her. 'The score, Chloe?'

'There isn't one,' said the woman. She was dressed all in muddy green, taller and altogether more imposing than her friend. Her jeans were streaked with oil. She kept her eyes on the pitch, as if refusing to be interested in the stranger.

Sensing that the two women desired some sort of acknowledgement, he wanted to say his name: 'I'm Edward Temmis,

Matty's father. Matty plays for Cubitt's.' He could have added in a raised voice, 'I don't have to explain why I didn't stand on the home line.' He was on the wrong side of the pitch because he did not want to stand with the parents from Matty's school, and there were good reasons for that, reasons he did not want to explain. So Edward sank into his overcoat, screwing up his eyes to find his son as he stared at the mob of boys around the ball.

There was a Dittisham lad who broke clear on the other side at that moment, trapping a loose ball that had been headed by one of the Cubitt's boys and, left toe killing the energy in the ball for a second, turned his body and completed a back-heeled pass to one of his team members.

'I know it now,' said the woman beside him. She tried again. 'I realize where I know your voice from.' Instead of turning to her left, where Edward stood, she angled her body right and spoke to the friend in the oil-encrusted jeans. 'The radio.'

That would have been the end of the conversation, which Edward had barely heard and had no desire to continue, except that the second taller woman suddenly said loudly, 'Oh! I know it too. I know it now. Oh goodness. Excuse me, Cheryl.'

And, while he focused on the pitch, she turned and walked off purposefully.

'I don't know what's got into her,' said Cheryl.

'Your friend?' he asked, sounding uninterested. He touched the hearing aid, realizing he was not going to be allowed to tune them out.

'We're Chloe and Cheryl,' said the shorter woman. 'So we sound like something halfway between a CBeebies cartoon and a porn movie.' She giggled at her joke, which he thought she must have made a dozen times before. He hadn't expected the words 'porn movie' from a woman in an immaculate coat with gold buttons, but his laughter caught in his throat and the cough he had stifled ten minutes ago emerged.

To counter it he raised his voice, spluttering: 'Matty! Matty! Pass here! East–west! This side! Now! Now!'

He had been too loud.

Something happened beside him, a fractal shift in the way the light curved. Cheryl shifted her weight from one foot to another and said softly, 'But aren't you . . .? Didn't you . . .? No, that can't be.'

The Dittisham boys had the ball again. They played in a mauve and white stripe. A fair-haired lad, about the same age as Matty but bigger and bulkier than Edward's son, tore down the left, and for a moment Edward worried that Matty would try to intercept him and get trampled. But he shouted anyway, 'Get over here, Matty!'

And then he felt the hand on his forearm.

'Oh, Edward,' said Cheryl. The tone was as far away as it was possible to be from her brisk and rather remote greeting not five minutes earlier. When he looked down at the woman, he could not take his eyes away from a dash of scarlet lipstick that had moved from her upper lip to one of her front teeth. It made him think of blood.

'Oh, Edward,' she said again, and he saw that she was crying. Her make-up ran. Her grip tightened.

At that point he could have hugged her and cried his eyes out, for reasons both of them would understand without speaking another word. But no, he was here to support his son and would not be distracted. A Dittisham beanpole with red hair brought the ball down. That must have been Matty who tackled him.

As he turned back to the pitch, his pride overcame him. Again and again, louder and louder, he called for Matty to pass it, bury it, lob it, lift it . . . *'Just walk it through to the goal!'*

Now he turned his hearing aid fully down so that, at least on his left side, there was no return path and no one could interrupt him with a clumsy question or the conversation he knew was coming. But he could no longer avoid the way the mums and dads on the opposite side of the pitch were huddled around Chloe, the denim-clad woman who must have walked two hundred yards of touchline to reach a group of perfect strangers.

He pulled his arm away from Cheryl by taking a step to the left. He was supporting Matty. That's what he was here for. He would not let Chloe or Cheryl or Clare or Carole or Chris or Clive or whoever these people were . . . No, he would not let them stop him. They had no right. He was here for his darling eleven-year-old, his Matty, who was so good at everything, so loving towards his father, so promising, so bright. And such a goal-scorer! Hey, was that him now, through on goal?

He grew hoarse as he called his son's name. But strangely, each time Edward shouted, his words seemed to stop a player on the pitch. One at a time, they halted their runs. They said something to each other. The ball went out of play and no one went to fetch it. Some of them stared at him. Two hugged each other.

Cheryl, the lady he had met less than half an hour before, put her arm around him and held him close. This time he did not resist. Chloe was walking back with some of the Cubitt's parents, at first hugging the touchline and then, with play apparently suspended, cutting across the pitch itself.

'What's happened?' he asked, the question directed at his shoes as the new arrivals gathered around him.

Cheryl pinched her nose. Her eyes narrowed. He turned on his hearing aid and it whistled.

'Lovely man, it doesn't help you if I mince my words.' She inhaled the winter air deeply, like a chain smoker drawing on her first cigarette after a long-haul flight. 'I am a business coach. Honesty is at the heart of what I do.'

Then she uttered three quick sentences.

'Edward, your son is not here. He is not on the pitch. Edward, your son is dead.'

CHAPTER TWO

'Remind me,' the controller had always said, 'why they put our radio station on a seafront?'

Edward sat alone on the bench facing the roaring water. The promenade was ten feet above the beach, the sky was darkening, and the waves were crumping against the sea wall.

Funny how time worked – he was five minutes from the front door of his workplace and fifteen minutes from the meeting. Two different measures of the same moment. Was that what Einstein was all about? The problem of distance measured by time? So how should he measure time since Matty? In months, or memories, or mornings lost in bed? What was the line in that old poem – should he count the days in coffee spoons?

The wooden shelters on the promenade at Sidmouth barely kept out the wet. Even the slightest breeze drove sea spray sideways onto the benches, with the result that the council had to repaint the shelters twice a year with dark brown Cuprinol.

Occupying two upper floors of an old hotel in the middle of the promenade, the radio station took the same public lashing as the shelters but without the protection of the council. Twelve months a year, just over his left shoulder, his employer's building had regular beatings from Devon's coastal climate – salt and storm and sun and sea all caned the rotten frontage like a 1970s headmaster attacking a long-hated pupil with barely a break between strokes. At least the bus stops got Cuprinol. The station did not have the money for fake tan.

Edward had fished a Sainsbury's bag out of his pocket and was sitting on it. A baseball cap hid his face. That was the mistake he had made at the football game, not wearing the cap, allowing the others to see him, allowing his loss to become their pity. The business coach had woken him from his dream; possibly that was what business coaches did. But what use to him was reality? All he had wanted was to go and shout for his son like he did before the accident. It did not mean he was mad, did not mean his son was not dead. It was the briefest escape and hurt no one.

The kids on the pitch had not noticed until that moment when the Dittisham beanpole snatched the ball from the air and he, Edward, had raised his voice to block out Cheryl's chirping, and everything around him had stopped.

He took solace in the waves. He had come to this mile of seafront every day for nearly twenty years. He had started at the radio station aged twenty-five and here he was, still presenting his 'show with a view of the sea'.

Except he wasn't. His compassionate leave had been months not weeks, and today the boss wanted to see him so they could talk about his return.

Beside him, he heard a rustle of plastic. The same shade of orange. Another Sainsbury's bag. He looked, and, to his surprise, it was Agnes Chan.

'It's dark, isn't it, but I saw you from my window,' she said. 'I learned this from you, of course.'

'Using a bag?'

'The bag for dryness. Sainsbury's is best. The orange is a water-repellent, I think.'

'I'm not sure that's scientifically proven.'

'I never know when you're joking, Edward. You're worse than me.'

He smiled, staring at the sea and the dank black clouds that had stolen the last hour of daylight, thinking how forced her banter sounded. The surface of the water was wild. 'Glamorous, aren't we, down here?'

She laughed at his effort.

A pause while they listened to the waves break.

Then, 'Good to see you, Edward.'

'You, too.'

'Some days I wish I was a fisherman,' she said, 'miles away from all this.'

He followed her gaze to a trawler in the distance. 'Don't we say "fisherperson" now?'

'Not in Devon we don't! Fisher*man*, please!'

He thought she tried too hard to sound like a local. Being offended by political correctness was a badge of honour, but she wore it without conviction.

'Remind me why we put our office on a seafront?'

'You always say that.'

'And I'm always thinking it,' the controller confirmed. 'I like that you now expect the comment from me, so I don't like to disappoint.'

Agnes Chan was six or seven years younger than him, in her thirties, a London hotshot brought in by the parent company after succeeding in places as varied as Milton Keynes and the Scottish Borders. They had posted her to Devon's Rock 'n' Talk Radio 92FM three years ago. He could not fail to notice how it had aged her. He vaguely remembered a slim, chatty, angular thing arriving in Devon, who talked a lot about badminton. The person who sat next to him now had no sharp corners. He felt guilty for noticing her weight had ballooned – there were rumours of fertility treatment, but no sign of a partner – and for casually assuming a badminton racket was gathering dust somewhere in her house. Adding to the sense that his boss was in some kind of personal struggle, she had taken to wearing thick spectacles with photosensitive lenses that darkened even in winter sun. They reminded him of the plastic fish you win in crackers, the ones that bend and darken in the palm of a person's hand according to their mood. She seemed guarded, unreadable, and when the glasses closed her off at odd moments, it amplified the impression.

He would have loved to believe that Agnes Chan was staying in Devon because its stress-free walks along the Jurassic Coast were the perfect tonic, but they both knew she was staying because she had failed.

The radio station – which everyone called Devon RTR, or sometimes RTR-92 – had an older audience and older present-ers, and here was a woman in her thirties coming down from London to shake it up. Her mission – the absolute inanity of this – was to 'bring in a younger audience', and the older DJs on the station – among them a local legend called Vic Turnbull who did the mid-mornings and ran a dairy farm, his jingles cho-rusing 'Pumping it out from 9 till 12' – had ganged up to make things difficult for her.

At first, Edward was a part of the antis. But he was only in his forties, a good twenty years younger than Turnbull, Wendy Goodenough and Brian Channon, the holdouts who were like the Viet Cong of the radio station, and he sensed there was something vicious and personal about their anger, which made him gradually more compassionate towards the situation his boss was in.

Then, one day, not long after Agnes had started, as he sat with half a dozen of the oldest presenters in the station canteen, including a man called 'Lord' Keith Wenn, who was still doing a weekly show at RTR-92 and was definitely not a lord, the con-versation turned to *that one*. Vic Turnbull, who had consumed two tins of Pinot Grigio, thumbed over to the glass box that passed as the controller's office, lowered his voice and hissed at the others, 'How do you suppose the bosses in London decided we should be run by a Jap?'

Without thinking Edward said, 'What the holy hell does that mean, exactly?'

Vic gestured at Brian Channon. 'I'd rather have a Channon than a Chan.'

Brian and Lord Wenn laughed. 'And I gather she's got one of them on the go, too.'

'What do you mean by that?' asked Edward.

'Some African.'

'Perhaps he's taken her up the Zambezi,' chuckled Lord Wenn. There was a roar of laughter.

As if stung, Edward jumped from his seat, possessed by an outrage that surprised him.

'I was married to *one of them*,' he said, furiously.

Caught on his sleeve, his fork had gone flying as he stepped back from the table. When it hit the canteen window, everyone turned from him to the point of impact as if something was happening out at sea. There was a moment of silence as the exchange sank in. Presenters might hate each other, but they never, ever argued in the open.

Edward left the room. Behind him Vic said, 'Ah, the younger generation!'

Wendy Goodenough added: 'Did he just throw a fork at you?' But there was no laughter.

So that had been it. Edward was no longer part of the old guard, nor part of the new. There was no more for him to say and no way back with his colleagues. Vic and Wendy never spoke to him again and pointedly left him off their leaving party invite lists. Agnes clumsily sidelined them as Edward watched. It was a bloody business and, exactly as they had warned, the listening figures slumped.

Perhaps Agnes Chan had heard the clatter of the fork from

her office and looked over. Perhaps she had discovered that, on account of her changing shape and Chinese heritage, the older presenters, thinking Japan and China were close enough to be the same country, had nicknamed her 'Sumo'. From that day, she treated Edward differently.

'You don't need to worry,' she had quietly told him one day. 'In the evenings, it's you. It's always been you. The Gammons wouldn't play new music. You don't have that issue.'

Gammons? So here she was attacking old white men, while he had defended her from attack as a young Asian woman.

'I can stay?'

'You can stay.'

But their relationship had never been perfect. He found her cagey – those spectacles incessantly shading and clearing. He would no more be able to guess what Agnes Chan did in her time outside work than he could describe activity on the seabed a mile down. So much of her life seemed hidden. She would never open up about the stress she must have felt when the old presenters left – Vic Turnbull managing a ferocious on-air denunciation on his final day of 'the malign forces at work in this building', which Edward suspected may have been Pinot-fuelled – or when the station's listeners reacted badly with angry calls and scratchy handwritten letters.

The mythical younger audience was not lured away from YouTube and TikTok by RTR-92's constant rotation of music by Harry Styles and Bz01nc (pronounced Ba-zoink), nor by its constant advertising of an online petition to BRING TAYLOR SWIFT TO SIDMOUTH, which garnered only 3,800 signatures. Edward sensed Agnes becoming embattled.

Then tragedy struck. He lost Matty. It was eleven months ago now; last March. She had been there for him, allowing 'as much paid time off as you need', but the moment was coming where he would need to come back. He wanted her to set a date for him to aim at. One year was the obvious moment.

'The sea is furious today,' she was saying.

'As angry as Brian Channon,' he said. The water rolled and spray was beginning to hit their faces. A thin rain had started, becoming mist as it fell on the water and mixing with the spray – a cold, rough, salted ghost of water that drifted upwards and sideways and drenched everything. Even on the most miserable day you might see a lone swimmer or layered-up holidaymaker, but today there was not a soul.

'Is it safe here?'

'*Ha!*' he laughed, but not unkindly. 'You are so . . . so London, boss. Yes, it's perfectly safe.'

She looked pained. 'I'm not London. I was brought up in Manchester. Grandparents lived in Manchuria. They left because Japan suddenly piled across the border. No room for Chans in Japanese Manchuria, but plenty in Manchester. So I was never really London until I started working, and even then I moved straight out to the radio stations. The whole London thing was spread by that farmer.' She couldn't bear to say Vic Turnbull's name.

'He used to spend his mornings muckspreading, then in the afternoons he would work on the farm.'

'Well, exactly.' She turned to him, a movement he saw at the periphery of his vision. 'How are you, Edward?'

'Sorry? It's so—'

'Loud? Yes. I was asking how you are.' She raised her voice above the roiling of the sea and brought her face so close to the hearing aid over his left ear that he could smell her perfume, even here, even with the wind whipping the wooden shelter. She shouted, 'Are you happy to chat out here, not in the station?'

'This'll be the loudest private conversation in history.' He shrugged and called back: 'It's fine, I guess.' They bundled themselves up and leant back into the shelter, which gave a little extra soundproofing. 'I'm fine.'

Still staring into his ear, she suddenly said: 'Look, I saw

Twitter yesterday,' she said. 'The football-match business. It was awful. I'm sorry.'

'Please don't be sorry about it. I was in my own world.'

'I don't mean "sorry" about that. I mean I'm sorry, but you can't come back to your show. The hashtag was #MentalHealthEpisode. I consider us to be friends.'

'Wait . . . I'm sacked?' He grabbed the edge of the wooden seat with both hands as if he was in danger of sliding off it. For the first time, he turned to face her properly. His face was slack, his mouth hanging open in shock, and the blast of sea wind he thought he'd just heard had been a gasp from his own lungs.

Now that he had turned to her, she wouldn't meet his eye. 'Maybe we can find you something less onerous.'

'The religious slot?'

She missed his irony. 'Would you like to?'

'Come off it! I haven't been to church in years.'

'Dan was a Satanist.'

'I live for my show,' he said. He turned back to face the sea, looking out blindly across the beating waves. 'It's all I've got now.'

'Oh, Edward.' He noticed, despite the low light, that her spectacles had darkened completely. 'Your listeners love you, *loved* you,' the change of tense was brutal, 'but I can't inflict your rage and grief on them.'

He knew he sounded desperate, but he wasn't ready for this. 'Hey, I'm not in pieces, I'm getting better.'

'It's great that you are. Maybe we—' A roar of sea cut her off, the heavy drop of wave on foreshore rocks. Still in shock, he moved his head closer to hers to hear better and thought how strange this was. He took in the texture of her skin, almost papery, the pores spotless as if the sea had washed them clear; there was a flash of pink dye in stray hairs projecting from underneath the beret she often wore. Again he caught a waft of expensive perfume in the salted air. Edward realized Agnes had

17

wanted to see him out here because no one would hear them, just as Moore and Connery always ran a bath in the old Bond films to stop conversations being overheard.

There was a muffled boom. Like a trussed-up body dropped from height on sand. The crump of a wave hitting the sea wall. Freezing spray from the impact hit them like a flood.

Agnes screamed. There was another scream from somewhere, more guttural, and he saw a mother trying to hold on to a pram drenched in water. The wind, having been calm, had suddenly come at them in gust after gust, like blasts from sawn-off shotgun barrels hitting everyone. The squall pinned them into the shelter and made Agnes grab his arm. He suddenly felt her fear and frailty.

'Jesus, let's make a move and get out of this,' he shouted.

But the sea stood up before they did. In a fraction of a second it turned from horizontal to vertical. It had been a churning surface; now it was a wall. And the wall fell on them. The wave, twenty feet above the promenade, broke in staggered sections from one end of it to the other, drenching them completely, both their exclamations lost in the roar of sound and water.

God, the woman with the pram. Was she in the sea?

The second wave was bigger than the first. Edward felt the air blown out of his lungs as it crashed onto the shelter and, in a scooping action, fired him legs-first over the sea wall.

Kicking, Edward surfaced into the heavy rain and waves. Above him, between waves bucking him wildly, their shelter on the promenade was still standing, incredibly. He panicked as he gulped sea water and cast about for a sight of the young mother or her pram. She was not on the pavement any more. If the child was strapped into it . . .

The sea was raging. It was almost over the top of the harbour wall. He shed his overcoat because its weight in the sea would have dragged him down, but his trousers were waterlogged too and he could not move his legs. Where was Agnes? Had she run for help? The wave had been enormous but the seafront was used to water. Traffic was moving on the road again. He shouted but the downpour and the surf cloaked and silenced him.

And then he saw the flare of fabric in the sea, the mound of wool containing a bubble of air and surely, *that was the child in the pram.* Face down. Floating, barely. He struck out, thrashing his arms. Water rushed into his nose and he gagged. Onto his back, then, for a moment. The child was only ten feet away, and no one had seen her go in. It was getting dark. He ripped at his trouser belt underwater, wrenched it out, spun and pulled the trousers off. Now he could kick. The waves spat him sideways, tumbling him against the brickwork of the wall, winding him. He burst into a flurry of movement, cutting the bitter sea with his arms. Now, closer, he lunged at the mound of coat and knew he had got the child.

But it was not the child. He pulled the coat towards him and the body was larger and heavier than anything he expected.

'*Agnes!*' he shouted. 'Agnes, I've got you!'

His yelling stopped a pedestrian, who looked down into the dark water and screamed. Others gathered under the street-lights, just flickering into life. Two teenagers started down the promenade steps and a wave soaked them in an instant. Edward turned and placed his arm under the neck of Agnes, who felt as heavy as a rock.

'Kick! Kick, Agnes, kick!' He could not feel her moving. He worried about wrenching her neck in his arm, but he had to move.

'This way, this way Agnes!'

Now everyone was screaming. The traffic had stopped and people were climbing out of their cars. A policeman arrived and started to wrench an inflatable ring from the locked safety box on the pavement. But as soon as he threw it, a wave took Edward and Agnes to the wall, splashing their bodies against the unyielding brick, stunning Edward, although he kept his hold on her. Now his shirt was grabbed by the first teenager, who stood waist-deep in the water. The yanking of the shirt tore buttons all down the front, but his arms stayed in. He found the steps with his feet. But Agnes was lifeless. He and the two teenagers dragged her up the staircase and laid her on the pavement. Edward was not letting go of her. He locked his lips on hers and gave mouth-to-mouth. Then he sat astride her and pumped her heart with his hands though he was exhausted and close to vomiting. The police officer, setting his radio aside, physically lifted Edward off and took his place. Edward stood there shivering. A man gave him his coat. Someone took a photo.

Edward turned and saw the mother with the pram. She had removed her child from the buggy and they were cuddling. The two were soaked through and the buggy was on its side, the baby screaming in its mother's arms. Edward walked up to them and hugged the mother, wordlessly.

CHAPTER THREE

Barbara Sinker had two pieces of news for her daughter. She laid out the newspaper with the astonishing front page – but there was something else. She giggled to herself. Something bigger. The second thing was sensitive, personal, and she would have to be careful how she raised the subject.

Her home was in Colaton Raleigh, west of Sidmouth, the last bungalow on Tremory Road, a long field sloping away at the back. She had just returned from the seafront. Most mornings she would drive there. A direct route would only have been three miles, but the River Otter had few crossings for cars so she had to follow it north from Colaton to Newton Poppleford, then take the right turn at Bowd to head past Woolbrook and through Bulverton. The area was lush green farmland. She could have been driving through the 1950s.

When Barbara got to Sidmouth she would stop in the big car park on Manor Road (cursing the app system they now used instead of Pay and Display), then walk for twenty minutes to reach Jacob's Ladder. The ladder was more a staircase, right angles of wood painted white. The Victorians had built it where erosion of the cliff face had washed away the path. It had taken a family of four dying in a plunge in 1850 – from what had become a steep drop rather than a walkway – for the reluctant Victorian authorities to decide that it was probably unsafe to let the public wander down a precipice in search of the beach. The name Jacob's Ladder was biblical, because in the Bible Jacob had a ladder that took him up to heaven. In Sidmouth they had a ladder that took them down to the beach.

'They' was just Barbara and the dogs. She would pop a pill and walk her two King Charles spaniels, Rascal and Roy, as the sun rose. They would start with a circuit of the field in Colaton to warm themselves up, then drive fifteen minutes to Jacob's Ladder. The ache in her hips was annoying; the doctors had said Avascular Necrosis, which she was sure was the name of a Greek pop star she had liked in the Seventies. Barbara's condition caused constriction in the blood vessels supplying certain joints. Pain relief medication kept her moving, but she was always worried about getting dependent on it; she had seen a horrible documentary about opioids in the States.

Despite the chronic pain, Barbara Sinker kept herself positive. Divorced for around twenty years, she would have considered herself, until recently, a happy singleton with interests all over Sidmouth – mainly catching up with her three children and their busy lives, but also a flower-arranging group attached to Colaton Raleigh's church; a birding club that met on the coast at Branscombe during the summer to spot the county's feathered visitors; Baileys-and-Canasta nights with her friend Phyllis, and the pub she visited at least three times a week for quizzing and where occasionally she could even be found volunteering behind the bar. And of course, her collection of automata with which she might admit to being just a little obsessed.

Automata? She told everyone who asked: 'Oh, they're not as modern as they sound. I have seven. Five from the 1800s. Just the most lovely pieces of intricate machinery. No screws. Painted wooden models a few inches high, with cogs and cables,

22

which move when you turn a handle.' Among her collection was a miniature bell-striker, for whom she preferred the posh name, Jacquemart. The six-inch imp with a hood would hit a bell, somewhat unconvincingly, when a handle was turned. Another ghoulish item, when operated, showed a blindfolded figure dropping through a trapdoor with a rope around its neck. She dreaded breaking one of her models, and despite her lack of funds was always looking out for another.

Barbara missed her profession, the home décor and decorating she had done for two decades after her divorce, but her hips meant she could not stand for long periods now. She *was* happy, but . . .

The last three weeks had taught her something was missing.

Kimberley Cobden walked up the garden path, breathing the village air deep into her lungs, betting herself that her mother would find the front door latch before she had even knocked. In fact she could fit together the sequence before it even happened: (1) Mum opens front door, (2) Mum says you're looking thin, (3) Mum asks where Anthony is.

Her hand was on the knocker when the door opened, pulling her with it.

'Darling. Now, promise me. Are you eating enough?'

Two out of three, thought Kimberley. She should have asked Bet365 to give her the odds. 'Mum – come on.'

The younger woman did what she always did, because it made her remember childhood. After hugging her mother carefully – always conscious of Barbara's hips and always a little worried her own genes might be lining her up for the same fate – she asked how her dad was. Roy lived amicably around the corner, her parents even taking walks together once in a blue moon, him having forgiven the naming of one of Barbara's dogs after him.

'Oh he's fine, love, fine. I haven't seen him in a few weeks, mind, but you know your dad.' Barbara turned away at this, making a show of bustling them both inside.

Formalities over, Kimberley followed her mother through the interior of the home until they got to the bay windows that faced the field out at the back.

As she walked, she felt the years fall away – thirty-something, twenty-something, teenager. By the time she saw the expanse of green beyond the window, like an airport runway, she was ten, remembering the neighbours' horses and her mummy and daddy calling her for dinner. She ached for childhood on days like this. Her brothers were delivered in the hospital in Exeter, but this was the house where she, the youngest, had been born. The view was some kind of miracle, as if the building was floating above the land and the whole planet was green. The garden stretched fifty feet from the back wall, sloping to a fifteen-foot drop into the closest field, and she remembered her parents' obsession with stopping her wandering out of sight when she was a little girl, in case she jumped or fell.

'Where's Anthony?'

There it was, number three, as predicted. 'He's in the car.' There was no point pretending.

'Why don't you bring him in? Oh, don't tell me,' her mother went on, answering her own question, 'he's working on something.'

'Well, he is.'

'And everything's all right now?'

'Why wouldn't it be?' Kimberley bridled. She knew she sounded defensive, but her mother's emotional radar was so powerful that you had to either hide completely or tell everything. She always wondered if Mum wanted to hear her daughter's marriage was in trouble so she could feel better about her own breakup, which happened when Kimberley was at the sensitive age of thirteen. Barbara Sinker was always so insistent, so curious; like a sparrow, jumping from one blade of grass to another, searching for worms. She would peck for any truth she felt was being covered.

'Anthony never seems to want to see me. Where is he parked?'

'Just around the corner – no, Mum! You can't hobble out there. You know he's just quiet.'

'It's being in the police,' said Barbara. 'You think the world revolves around you.'

A shocked laugh burst from Kimberley. 'I don't think he thinks that at all! He's just been different lately.' She was saying far less than she could.

'A couple of items to tell you. This first,' her mother said, as if convening a board meeting. 'Well, show you. Have a look at the *Gazette*.' Barbara scooped the newspaper from the dining-room table with a flourish.

'Wait. My glasses.'

'It's your friend. Mine, too.'

Kimberley was rustling in her handbag for her spectacles. 'I can't think of anyone who might fit that description.' Glasses on, she peered at an article about a local wrestler, which she read aloud: 'Local fighter, Denny Tajine, appealed to *Gazette* readers to give him a proper wrestler's name, and they chose Denting Machine.' Next to the piece was a photo of a tattooed and muscled teenager. She shot her mother a puzzled look.

'You're on the wrong page. Not the sport. Turn it over. The front page. Like I say, your friend and mine. And Björn Borg, of all things!'

Kimberley stared. The front of the paper was taken up with a dramatic photograph, underneath the masthead, *East Devon Gazette*. A man stood in a soaked shirt and underpants, his long legs bare and white. The shirt had ridden halfway up his torso. The underpants, being waterlogged, hung from his rear like a nappy that needed changing, and – yes, the brand name BJÖRN BORG was stitched into the waistband.

The man in the photo was hugging a drenched woman in

the street whose face was obscured. Behind him and slightly to the left, another woman lay on her back, the soles of her feet facing the camera. The flash bounced off the reflective trim of the shoes. From the photo it looked as if a kneeling police officer was pumping her chest.

'That's an amazing picture.'

'Yes,' said Barbara. 'But look who's in it!'

Kimberley stared. The headline read: SIDMOUTH 'TSUNAMI' COULD HAVE COST LIVES, SAYS MAYOR.

'It can't have been a tsunami because nobody died. With a tsunami, everyone's dead.'

'Don't be callous, Kimberley. You remember you sold him a house?'

'Are you talking about Edward Temmis?' Kimberley was still staring at the photo, and now saw the caption. *Pictured: popular local radio host, Edward Temmis, in aftermath of Sidmouth tsunami.* 'Of course I remember. I sold him a very strange house.'

'On the cliffs.'

'Almost over the edge of the cliffs.'

'Does he blame you for it? Are you still in touch? Darling, you're shivering. What *is* the matter?'

Kimberley was staring at the photo. Seeing something her mother could not see.

'Darling?'

Kimberley flinched and pushed the *Gazette* aside. She sounded suddenly professional. 'Yes, it was a strange thing. He bought that house because I think he liked the thrill of it, and he's quite . . . eccentric.'

'Surely not an *exhibitionist*?' Barbara used the word as if it was the label for a disgusting hobby, like nudism.

'No . . . well. Shy, really. Quite private. He used to be full of the joys. Positive. Quite funny. *Very* funny. At least, that's how he was before things went wrong for him.'

Her mother paused as if she was about to cry. 'He hasn't

been on the radio since that day. I read about it. The station played slow music for twenty-four hours. I thought he'd be back by now because . . . Oh, it's silly, I thought . . .' She trailed off.

'You thought . . .?'

'You'll laugh.'

'I won't, Mum.'

'I thought he needed us. Needed his listeners. He always called us his "crew". I liked feeling part of that.'

'I know you did. How many times did you call that show?'

Barbara forged ahead, ignoring the question. 'And they have a teenager on now.'

'I'm sure she's not a teenager!'

'Well, she keeps talking about Ed Sheeran and gin festivals. And she asked a question, "Which came first, Genesis or Genesis?" It's so disrespectful, the idea that Phil Collins might have existed before the Bible.'

Kimberley frowned. 'You don't even like Genesis. Either Genesis. Why would you mind?'

Her mother's tone did not lighten. 'I'm *of an age*. That's the phrase they use. I'm of an age where you get put on the same table as all the people who can't remember whose wedding they're at. I used to be with the teenagers, and they loved me sitting with them, and all the jokes and laughter we'd have! But look at the way I hobble, moving left and right when I walk, like a desperate belly dancer.'

Kimberley snorted with laughter despite herself.

'And the skin on my neck looks like a snake's, like a cobra that can't hood up any more. I'm one of those now – the *old dears*, we used to call them, laughing at the way they dribbled.'

'I think you hood up pretty well. I've seen you raging at the Pay and Display in Sidmouth. And you don't dribble at all.'

'I dye my hair. I keep fit. I walk every day, okay, slowly. The doctor said "Use it or lose it." I listen to the Sex Pistols, because no one can believe us Pistols fans are drawing our pensions now! I *haven't* started dribbling, I haven't complained about kids on buses playing music from their mobiles, and sports cars revving on the promenade like they're in some sort of movie—'

'This is quite a long list of things you're not angry about.'

'I don't complain about getting to the top of the stairs and forgetting why I climbed them.'

'You don't have stairs, Mum. This is a bungalow.'

'That had slipped my mind, to be fair.'

They roared with laughter together, both at the same pitch, mother and daughter in perfect sync, if just for an instant. Behind Barbara's head, Kimberley noticed the sun move between two clouds.

'All I'm saying,' her mother went on, 'is that I loved Wimbledon and I miss him.'

'What are we talking about now? Wimbledon?'

'Oh, some of us set up a Facebook page after Edward made a remark about his surname. Just a silly remark on the radio. He said every time he rings a call centre and says "Temmis", they always reply "Tennis as in Wimbledon?" So we called our Facebook group AS IN WIMBLEDON, but it's slightly lapsed now. What with the tragedy over his poor boy.'

Kimberley saw another look of profound sadness cross her mother's face. She wondered why the loss of this stranger's son had affected her so deeply. She guessed that, for Mum and her friends, it was because Edward was no stranger. He was the best friend they had never met. *Popular local radio host . . .*

The younger woman thought back to her first meeting with Mr Temmis, as she had called him, and the way he strode into the office with a torn coat and a shambling gait as if his legs were trying to walk in different directions. He was buying a house and she felt a beautifully disorganized humour roll off him. He needed the house cheap and he needed it slightly exciting, 'for my son.' She remembered his laugh in particular – like a stream; babbling, almost continuous.

'Cheap and slightly exciting?' she had repeated. 'That sounds like the cliff-edge place at Ladram Bay.'

'You have a house there?'

'Not for sale, too dangerous. Condemned.'

'I'd like to see it, Ms – er – I suddenly realize I don't—'

'My name is Cobden. Kim.'

He looked momentarily confused about which order the names were supposed to be in.

'First name Kim,' she said.

'Ms Cobden then.'

'Mrs.'

Her mother's voice brought Kimberley back. 'I just think it's so odd, Anthony staying in the car.'

'He knows I'm only here for an hour, and you know what the police are like, the paperwork.'

'He's doing paperwork in the car? What's he resting on?'

'His knees? I don't know.' Kimberley was sure her mother would know she was bluffing. It was difficult to explain what had happened to her husband this past year, difficult even to describe it. She had been married to a forthright, matter-of-fact, call-a-spade-a-spade Yorkshire cop, who was everybody's favourite gentle giant until the front door closed behind him and he became an angry brute. For years, Kimberley had been mocked and belittled, grabbed, pushed, and once even punched, until she eventually learned how to avoid the eruptions by offering nothing but compliance, almost hero-worship, to calm the smoking mountain of anger in her home.

Then, for reasons she could not fully understand but she suspected could be bracketed under the heading 'mid-life crisis', Anthony woke up one day in tears and had been crying ever since.

A psychologist friend had informally briefed her with all the possibilities a professional might look for – sudden life change (no), a so-called Serious Narcissistic Injury (possibly caused by that missed promotion to detective sergeant at work?), trauma and PTSD (but he had seen many murder scenes and never been bothered), religious conversion (this was getting madder and madder).

Whatever the reason, the tiger had turned into a rabbit. The bite was gone, the stripes were gone; the roar was now a squeak. Faced with nursing a broken husband when her husband had previously done all the breaking, some women might have left – it was like seeing a jailer fall asleep with the keys to your cell within arm's reach. But she had remained, because it was easier to deal with misery than violence. Anthony would wake in the morning in tears and take two hours to put his uniform on. She would help. She would comfort him. She would stay. And a part of her hated herself for doing it, because when had this marriage ever given her even a day of solid peace? She stayed when he hit her and she stayed when he stopped. When she asked herself why she was still in the marital home, she found herself coming up with stuff she had read in glossy magazines, headlines like WHY I ALWAYS BELIEVED I COULD CHANGE HIM that she had seen above readers' letters. Maybe she *had* changed him, though? He had gone from raging to weeping. She could not punish the broken man for the actions of the breaker.

There was a remote possibility, she thought. A possibility he had found out something about her that she did not want him or anyone else ever to know. And there she left the thought, boxed and tied up in the attic of her mind, somewhere no one would ever stumble upon it. That dangerous thought.

She came back into the present and realized Edward Temmis was once more the subject.

'You know how much I love his show. Such a tragedy, what he went through.' Barbara's voice started to break. 'How could any man absorb that?'

'Please don't take that pain on. It's not yours to suffer.'

'But imagine losing one of yours.'

Answering this would have required Kimberley to declare three miscarriages, so she said nothing.

'If you had one,' said her mother awkwardly.

'Still time,' said Kimberley.

'That day you introduced me – my, you'd never even said.'

'Introduced?' Kim remembered. 'OK. You mean when we bumped into each other.' She was suddenly finding the conversation tiring. She felt a headache coming on, and as she glanced around the house the pulsing in her temples worsened. Looking at your mum's knick-knacks could do that.

On the mantelpiece above the fire was a gilt-edged commemorative plate showing Charles and Diana on their wedding day. Barbara had never forgiven Charles for what he did to Diana, and Kimberley knew never to mention it. There was also a collection of old porcelain thimbles mounted next to the plate, and behind them the wallpaper was a sky-blue expanse peppered with green blobs that turned out, on closer inspection, to be flying turtles. Her headache was becoming a migraine.

'Let me go out and at least take Anthony a cuppa.'

'*No, Mum!*'

'Oh, love. Is it your head again? You've too much stress—'

'Where have your little wooden machines gone?' interrupted Kimberley.

'You're just trying to throw me off asking about Anthony.'

'Maybe a little.'

'They're automata. "Wooden machines" sounds like children's toys. They're in that room if you want to look.' She pointed. 'You've seen them a thousand times anyway. I heard *Antiques Roadshow* is coming to Tiverton in a couple of months, so I've been dusting them off in the lounge, where there's a brighter lamp. Perhaps I'll bring them along and let Fiona look.'

Kimberley raised her eyebrows, amazed that Barbara might show them to the TV programme, and Barbara read her thoughts. 'For valuing, of course. Just valuing. Not selling.

And,' she looked gleeful all of a sudden, her eyes shining, 'I might have another one soon, too.'

'Oh?' exclaimed Kimberley, who knew her mother had little in the way of spare cash.

Again, her mother read her mind. 'It's being ferried to me by . . . a friend, Kimberley. I'm not buying it.'

'Ferried, eh?'

As though she'd said too much, and knew she had to curb her desire to say even more, Barbara zigzagged off to the kitchen, chirping about cups of tea. Kimberley took a seat on the sofa. Elbows on her knees, she dropped her shoulders and allowed herself to relax. She got up, opened the window an inch and let the cool air and the smell of cut grass enter the room. Looking out towards the horizon she caught movement and saw, below the level of the window frame, her reflection moving in a small portrait mirror. It looked out of place, resting on the carpet and leaning against the wall. Why would her mother leave a mirror on the floor at that angle?

Kimberley contemplated her reflection. Her dark roots were showing, but generally she liked her look. Nose a little too angular, maybe. Compact around the hips. Narrow knees. Shoulders that suggested shoulder pads, even though she had never worn them. Her mother was short and squat; Kimberley was leggy, almost sporty. She had an athlete's metabolism even though she barely even ran for the bus. What she consumed seemed to burn straight off, while her mother often complained she was still trying to exercise away a doughnut she had eaten under the Thatcher government. ('It was a jam one with a glazed coating, I remember it well.')

Would Kim's life have been different had she not fallen in love with this corner of the country? What if, instead of staying in Devon, she had moved to London or Birmingham, or gone even further afield and sold houses in California or Cape Town? She knew she was good at what she did; she could find the soul in a property, make the buyer's heart beat in time with it. She had sold and sold and sold for others, and now she sold for herself, for her pleasure. Running her own company! Who would have thought it, when she had been the dunce of the siblings, leaving school with three Ds at A level while her two older brothers went to Oxford and Durham. Undiagnosed dyslexia could do that.

She stood up suddenly to go and look at the automata. But as she moved for the door she saw the newspaper, left on the table. She stared at the front page for a full minute.

The tea was made, finally. Barbara brought it slowly on a tray. Two cups, a china pot, Garibaldi biscuits fanned out on a plate like playing cards.

'You said a couple of things, Mum.'

'What?'

'You said you had a couple of things to tell me. The newspaper and . . . Something else bothering you?'

'Oh, not bothering! No, this is a good thing, darling. I think I'm in a relationship.'

Kim's eyes widened. She took a bite of biscuit and a sip of tea to buy time. She must measure her first response. 'Well! You've been on the scene, have you?'

'What? I don't know what scene you're talking about.'

'The dating . . . Mum, whatever scene it is. I assume it's not Tinder. Meeting people, getting out there, that's all I mean.'

'There's been no "getting out there", which I assume means the same as "putting it about". Darling, I do have some life in me. I brush up quite well so long as no one asks me to stand on my head or run the hundred yards. There's no need to look so surprised.'

'I don't think I was looking surprised at all. Where does he live, if I can ask? Is he local, or further afield? Exeter? Or are you going to tell me it's the Archbishop of Canterbury and make me drop my biscuit?'

'Local. I've said quite enough. Why all these questions? I don't want you dropping any biscuits on my carpet. Didn't you have an appointment?'

'A house viewing in half an hour in Newton Poppleford. Plenty of time. Twenty minutes' drive.'

'No, that's forty with the roadworks! You'd better get going.'

'Come on, Mum – you obviously want to tell me about him or you wouldn't have raised it.'

By this point Kim was halfway to being bustled out of the front door. 'I wanted to tell,' said Barbara. 'I didn't want you to *ask*.'

'This is like that time I was thrown out of a pub for swearing.'

'Forty with the roadworks! Off you go!'

The front door slammed, shutting off whatever it was Barbara simultaneously wanted to tell her daughter – and didn't want her daughter to know.

PART TWO

Three weeks after the wave

CHAPTER FOUR

Bowdham Garden Centre, twenty miles from the border with Cornwall, was the place everyone went for spring bargains. Even during Covid, older residents of the surrounding area had used it as a meeting place until it was shut during the worst of the pandemic. The chief medical officer for Devon had memorably complained about the way garden centres were initially exempted from the lockdown imposed on high-street stores, calling them 'rave venues for the halt and lame', so Bowdham and places like it had shut completely. But now it was thriving again. Garden tools, barbecues, outdoor furniture, plants big and small, seeds and flowers were all on sale. You could pick up a mini-pack of writhing maggots for fish bait or a Bosch workbench too heavy for one person to carry. Even cut flowers had their own section. No customer left with nothing.

The till nearest the cut-flower display had only three people queuing. Last in line was a young woman in an airman's jacket who seemed to have nothing to buy. When she arrived at the counter at last, she flashed a smile at the person serving.

'The Lord is my fucking shepherd,' she said.

The man behind the counter stiffened, unsure what to make of her.

'Many people wouldn't recognize you – Ted,' she said, peering at his name badge.

When the badges were assigned after the week-long induction, new staff simply chose a name they wanted. Any name, never their own. Clare and Tracey, firm friends, became Janet and Jane. A young man called William laughed when he pinned 'Dexter' to his apron. Everyone wanted the name 'Skill', which had been printed for a worker long since departed. But Edward Temmis was not allowed to join the name-badge game. The manager said it would make a mockery of the place if someone so well known in Devon had to go by Jeff or Wes or Bill or Clive. He had not put up a fight – why would he? – so he ended up with the 'Ted' badge, a contraction no one had ever used, which felt like a compromise. 'Ted as in Bundy,' the manager said.

He told himself he needed the job. The payoff from RTR-92 had been £62,500, equivalent to a year of his late-night shows. With a tiny mortgage on a falling-down house and no dependants, he could have lasted for a little while on the money. But there were back taxes to pay and he was worried his life might slow to a halt if he had no routine, so he jumped at the vacancy when he saw it advertised.

On the first day at the garden centre he had told himself: *Just make the best of it. Take joy where you can.* Because the alternative was to be swallowed by his sadness.

The sweary young woman in front of the counter was looking keenly at him. He was probably returning her gaze just as intensely. Her skin had the near-orange sheen of a *Love Island* contestant, and he wondered if she had had filler injected into her lips. From underneath a scarlet bucket hat her hair tumbled in gigantic gold curls.

She had short, muscled legs, the skin visible in snatches through two wide ladders which ran in parallel down the front of her tights. Below the thick jacket – faux leather, faux fleece; a fake zip too? – was a denim skirt cropped at the thigh. And, incredibly, she was on heels so high that they were almost forcing her knees to bend inwards. Without them she would have been barely five feet tall. Yet she stared at him with eyes so captivatingly blue that she seemed to freeze him to the spot.

At last she blinked.

'You'll have to forgive my bad language, Ted.'

He kept his voice level. 'What would you like to pay for, madam?'

'I'd like to pay for my rudeness,' said the young woman. 'I have a Tourette's thing. Vicar's daughter, but also a Glasgow gene. Long story, but when I'm stressed I either reach for Bible verses or profanities. Sometimes it goes wrong and I get sodding both, God. Happens when I'm nervous. Apologies.' She shook her shoulders and arms, like someone coming in from the rain.

He had the immediate thought – this was one of Tessa K's listeners, come to finish him off. The youngster would pull a knife and that would be it. But that was ridiculous. A Tessa K devotee would be more likely to pelt him with vegan croquettes. Feeling his age, he told the girl, 'We might have to calm the language down a little.'

'Actually,' she said in a voice that was husky and in which he now heard the trace of a Scottish accent, 'a little bit of your time is what I need. Forgive my manner, Mr Temmis, but you are quite a . . .' a sudden shake of the head, as if she was throwing off a memory . . . 'shite. Hmm. Sweet Jesus. I mean to say, you are quite a hard man to find.'

It was true. Agnes Chan had never announced his departure, and he had never complained publicly. The effect was of him simply vanishing into his own grief. The *East Devon Gazette* made an attempt to link it to that embarrassing business at the football game, but the radio station had given the paper a statement that said: 'Edward Temmis is pursuing opportunities in television.' That made him laugh, because his first posting in the garden centre had been in the Home Electricals section.

Occasionally, a customer would peer at his name-badge, like a passport officer glancing from passport photo to face and back down again. One or two had recognized his voice; he had never been on screen, and as a result many of his former listeners had no clue what he looked like. They would hear him speak, then jump slightly, frown, and maybe say something gracious like, 'I did love your show.' Or, 'My mother, bless her, always listened.' Or, more likely, 'I was so sorry to hear what happened to your son.' One customer had been the coach of the Dittisham boys' football team, which had been playing on the day of his famed meltdown. Either the man had not realized who was serving him, or he had disguised his embarrassment.

When there was recognition, Edward would always do the same thing. Smile, wink, tip his head to the right and say: 'New life for me. Now, how can I help you?'

He looked at the young woman in front of him, standing at the till with a conspicuous absence of anything she wanted to buy. Edward had assumed she was a teenager, but then he realized her height belied her age; she was probably in her twenties.

'Do you know how I found you in the end? Had to open a Facebook account.' The words came out of her mouth as if she was tasting something sour. 'It was like wandering into Jurassic Park.'

'I thought you were all on that,' said Edward. He added nervously: 'What are they saying about me?'

'You think the kids are on that trash? Forget it. Facebook and Twitter are like The 1975 – the band old people like because they think young people do.' She did something with her fingers, a quick movement, as if she was checking she still had sensation in her fingertips. 'As for what they're saying about you, I didn't get into it much but God, the boomer squadron have a whopping bulge for you!' She immediately dialled down the positive. 'Bear in mind, it's all the people alone in big houses thinking you filled their lives because they're as empty as wind. Anyway, someone posted that her brother swore you served him at the garden centre.'

'There's a guy works down the chip shop swears he's Elvis.'

For the first time, the young woman looked unsure. 'Riiiii-ight.' Edward's reference to the old hit record's title evidently made no sense to her. He was now conscious of what she could not see – the queue of three customers behind her, all carrying big bunches of flowers that hid their faces, quietly growling in frustration. Had they heard her bad language?

'Can I help you, anyway? I'm very aware of the customers waiting for . . .'

The young woman looked around, then made a waving motion with her left hand, as if the others could wait.

'I'm not good at this. Conversations. I'm not a . . . Not. A. Frigging. Diplomat.' She bared her teeth as if forcing the words to come out right. 'Edward, it's about my grandmother. She died suddenly. She was one of your listeners. She was a lovely woman. Arthritis, especially in her hands. Struggled to hold a knife and fork. Struggled generally with cooking and so on. But lovely. Lovely to me when I was . . . difficult. Greater love hath no man. And she died. And I think you might know why.'

'What?'

'I think. You. Might. Know why.'

Split up for emphasis, the staccato sentence rocked Edward. What could she possibly be implying? He took a quick step back and bumped into the shelving behind him. The bunches of flowers advanced slightly, all the other customers sensing the woman had had her moment and must now move on.

He felt his breathing quicken. 'I don't . . . I don't know what to say. What's your name?'

'Stef. But everyone calls me Stevie. My parents liked some dead old lady poet with that name.'

'Stevie Smith, maybe.'

'That's it, clever clogs.'

'I'm sure I have no knowledge of her death – your grand-ma's,' he added, in case they were still on the poet. 'Now, if I may just—'

'I think you might do. I'll tell you what happened.'

The middle bouquet – narcissus, lonicera, camellia – sud-denly shouted, 'We can't wait for ever here!'

Stevie took a wrap of chewing gum out of her jacket pocket and squeezed one into her mouth.

She turned and, with incredible enunciation, said: 'Shut. The Fuck. Up. Bonzo.' And added, 'God bless you.'

Edward tried, 'I'm sorry, you must move on if you're not buying anything.'

'When's your lunch break?'

Edward resented the idea that he must set aside his break time for this person, but then he saw she was biting her lip as if about to cry.

'It's taken me ages to find you,' she added, the accent stron-ger for a moment – 'you' was almost 'ye'.

'Okay. Okay. One thirty. What was your mother's name?'

From the bunch of flowers directly at her rear came a loud voice: 'Shall I put these down if this is going to take a while?'

'*Grandmother*. Her name was Rebecca,' said the young woman. 'Rebecca Mason.'

By the time they reached a spare table in the canteen with their bowls of soup and bread rolls, they had no more than twenty minutes before Edward had to return to his till. The pair sat down quickly, wordlessly, with lacquered trays. The area was open plan and they had accidentally picked a table where the low sun hit one of the places square on, so Stevie's first words seemed to come to Edward from within a whorl of blinding light.

'I seen you lost your job.'

Edward noted the Glaswegian – saw/seen interchangeable

– and politely raised his hand to fend off the sympathy. Most members of staff at the garden centre did not know him; their parents might do, or, more likely, grandparents. He'd dealt with the loss of his job by getting another. He was living again. At least, living the best he could. He pitied Matty for the years lost; he must never pity himself. Self-pity was a fifty-foot well, a plunge into narrow darkness no one ever emerged from. As for his son, missing him was not daily or hourly – it was cellular, as much a part of his existence as breathing.

The worst thing anyone said was, 'You'll be okay soon.' The most helpful, strangely, had been the bleakest. An old woman at the cemetery crept up behind him and, after saying she was 'visiting my teenage daughter', she had seen the date on Matty's gravestone and added quietly: 'You know something, my sweetheart, you never get over it.' Somehow the confirmation that he would never be released from his prison of sadness made it easier to be comfortable in the cell.

Stevie pulled off her bucket hat. 'Use this to block the sun, Ted.'

'Edward or Ed, honestly, is fine.' He shuffled his chair, got himself out of the direct light, saw her outline emerge like the image on an old TV when the aerial is moved into the correct position. She hesitated before she placed her hat on the tray, apparently checking the surface was clean. But then, seeing a smudge of encrusted sauce, she used the hat to wipe it off. His mouth twitched with the merest hint of a smile, which she did not see.

'So, okay, I'm Stevie – God, have I said my bloody name already? Mason. Stevie Mason. I didn't know you wore a hearing aid.'

'I didn't know it was obvious.'

'Loud headphones on the radio, I guess?'

'No,' he said tersely, 'an accident.'

She was still chewing gum even as she dipped her spoon into

the soup. With the table hiding her figure, Edward thought her face and hair were so perfectly arranged, the skin so luminous, she could have done make-up adverts in *Vogue*. The wrap-around fleece collar of the airman's jacket cupped her head like an egg and her blue eyes were like pools, deep enough for a person to dive into. He had never seen eyes so bright, suggesting a brain just as powerful. Yet she seemed to struggle to express herself, as if words were backing up in a tunnel behind her mouth, momentarily stopping and then arriving in a torrent.

'A bit about myself,' she said. 'Victim, at the start. Glasgow born and half-bred. Then the authorities got involved when I was six, parents up to their ears in crystal, and I got placed with a foster couple who moved down here latterly. Foster dad a vicar, which is why I'm always quoting the Bible. Parents – okay. Wired tae the moon. Start of my life – no good. Like Jonah, I guess I got vomited out of the whale. Yep, Mr and Mrs Vicar saved me. But Granny was Queen. Rebecca! She was my dad's mum. My dad the vicar's mum. She lived on the edge of Sidmouth. My parents still live round here, still have a church. So not far. Which was good, because they would see Granny three or four times a month. She—'

'Slow down, slow down.'

Stevie gazed at him. 'Of course. Sorry. You struggle to hear?'

Instinctively, he raised his hand to the device behind his left ear. 'Sometimes.'

'Must be awful.'

'It's life,' he said. 'It's not awful. There's very little that's truly awful.'

'Nobody died, my mum used to say.'

Those seven words infuriated him, but how was she to know? She was young, she would not have been his radio listener, she did not know about Matty. In his thoughts, he begged her to say nothing now to make it worse.

Suddenly, the details of Stevie's grandmother came gushing

44

out. 'Okay, so here goes. Granny was seventy-eight. She died in December very suddenly and the police say it was an accident. It was so bloody crap! A shitty, terrible, boggin' awful thing. She's asleep. Phone and keys on the bedside table. Book open at where she'd been reading it, half the pages burnt. There was a blaze downstairs. Everything fucking went – the fires of hell, brimstone – excuse my French. She tried to jump out of the window but hit the ground and . . . like a sodding watermelon . . .' Stevie choked back tears, gulping as if she could not breathe. 'She burst.' Her body was heaving with the memory. 'Jesus Christ alive. Excuse my language. You've got to understand, she was there for me.' She steadied herself. Grabbed her hat and squeezed it.

The next sentences were delivered softly, like a long sigh. 'She died when she landed. Two floors, no chance. Headfirst, who jumps like that? Burning in the air, the negligee just a thread of ashes! But then if she hadn't jumped the fire would have got her, so . . .'

'It's very sad.' He meant it.

'Is the name familiar to you? Rebecca Mason? Surely it must be!'

Edward reflected. There was something, but . . . no. It was a classic old-person's name, common in the Thirties and Forties. Rebecca Mason. He must have had several Rebeccas on the contacts database at the radio station.

'. . . listening every night,' Stevie was saying, her accent becoming more pronounced, or so it seemed to Edward. 'She seen you absolutely as her port of call.'

This was a part of the conversation Edward Temmis did not want. A reminder of the job he loved, the job he had lost. He felt a shiver pass over him, remembering Agnes Chan on the seafront: *I'm sorry but there it is.* But he was genuinely interested in anything that affected a listener of his, and the violent death; fire, a fall – he shuddered. It was just too awful. Stevie had also ordered soup, but she pulled a face every time she sipped from her spoon. Edward wanted to say, 'It will taste better without the gum.' Once again she fixed those bright blue eyes on him. But this time he saw something else in them – not sorrow, but steel.

'In the last two months before she died, something was going on with Granny. Like, she became quite bloody reclusive. She was furious with my dad for dropping in once. Wanted notice if anyone was visiting. Furious! That was unusual. Why would she be super-defensive? Why? Answer me!'

'I don't know.'

'I'm sorry. It's got me so riled up. My dad thought maybe she had taken a stranger in. She was churchy like him, and she was always saying the government didn't care, you know? She had a photo of Marcus Rashford in her bathroom. So we reckoned she'd taken pity on someone and taken them in for the winter, and she didn't want us to find out, because of course we'd worry about her being exploited.'

Edward nodded quietly. He was suddenly finding the story interesting, wanting an ending, wanting to know where he fitted in.

'So my dad chose a morning when she was at the shops and he sort of . . . broke in. Well, he did break in. Normally his key let him through the front door, but she had started using a second Yale lock that he had no key for. Again, why? What was she hiding? He got in through the upstairs loo window.'

'That really is a break-in.'

'With a ladder! A break-in by a vicar, can you imagine? Jesus. Imagine that in the *Gazette*!'

'Front page, for sure.'

'For sure. Luckily, he's quite a small man so he squidged himself through the window okay. He just wanted to see if the spare room was being used. He'd got a bit obsessed with the idea.'

'What if it was, I don't know, a Ukrainian refugee?'

'Surely she would have told us something like that – bleedin' hell! Okay, yes, that would have been lovely. But we were worried about something else – I don't know, you hear these stories of well-wishing people taking in a psycho.'

As she spoke she blinked a lot. Edward felt her nervousness. She was trusting him with a confidence. She pushed the soup to one side. 'I've no idea what flavour that was.'

'I think the label said cardboard.'

She met Edward's joke with puzzlement, and he realized her brain had a bias towards the literal: if he said cardboard, cardboard was the thing he was most likely to be talking about, even if it made no sense. He changed tack. 'I don't know if I would have broken in like your dad. What if she'd found out?'

'Well, as it happens . . . no, wait, I don't want to skip ahead—'

'I only have a few minutes.'

'She did find out. But that came later. What happened while Dad was in the house was really weird. She has a big place. She used to own a farm. Her husband died, she sold it. Pots of money. The house is ornate, you know? Was, before the fire. Old people's décor. Typical Devon. Estate agent's dream.'

'Worn carpets with flowers on, dust on the skirting board, cobwebs on cornices,' he suggested.

'How did you know? Yes. Nineties light bulbs, not the new LEDs, so orange light, a bit gloomy. What is it about old people and lampshades? And Dad found everything where it normally was, and no one was staying, so it was all fine. And he was about to leave. And then he looked in this room at the front, which he didn't think she ever used. A long narrow room. A funny shape. The curtains were drawn and the light bulb in the ceiling had gone. So he put a lamp on and it was pointing at the side wall. And there was this picture.'

'Right.'

'Really big. Not a painting, more like a collage. In fact more like a mural, made up of pieces of A4 paper, covering the whole wall, right up to the sodding corners, excuse my French.'

'A mural? Of what?'

'He didn't know how to describe it. An old house in black and white, he said. Like, an inside view – just a massive staircase made of wood, flowing down. And the viewpoint was onto the top of the stairs. The stairs led down from a wooden balcony. That's all he said.'

'And this picture was across the whole wall? Could it not just be wallpaper?'

'He said it was really badly done. She must have printed it out piece by piece. Like a collage. Glued to the wall. So that's weird, isn't it? Stuck to the wall? It looked, just bizarre.'

'And what did you say the picture was of?'

'A big sweeping wooden staircase, curved, like you'd see in an old movie. And then – sorry, there's more – he looks down at the floor, and the light isn't that good, and he sees something. He directs the table lamp downwards. Taking up so much space that he was almost standing on it, was a hugely expensive bright white dress. I mean – God – *hugely*.'

Edward was silent. 'White? A wedding dress?'

'More like a ball gown.' She reached for her phone. He was expecting a photo but she must have opened a text note, because she now read: '"Brand-new white ball gown, plunging neckline, fitted bodice with flowers, sash and ribbon, huge netted skirt, puffy sleeves, and then a big floppy hat."'

'Floppy hat? It sounds old-fashioned.'

'But brand-new. He took a photo. Then, you won't believe this, he couldn't get out.'

'The front door?'

'No. I don't know why. Maybe it's faulty, maybe it was deadlocked? And the loo window he got in through – it was always open – but that was up on the first floor, and the ladder had shifted, so he took one look and thought, "No way." Then he heard her coming back. Dad had to hide in the house until she was upstairs, creep down, unlock the front door with her key, post it back through the letterbox and run.'

'I can imagine the headline. "Vicar Breaks into Home of Own Mother Then Breaks Out, Say Police".'

'And guess what? Dad showed me the photo. I do the intranet for a council and a lot of that is computer stuff, so yes I'm a bloody geek. But I am aware of the world and the price of a dress. This one had a tag, a maker's tag. Do you know how much a Givenchy ball gown costs new?'

'Several hundred pounds.'

'Try five thousand. This one maybe seven. My dad said this thing was so white it glowed in the dark. It was a giant apparition, lying there on the floor. And next to it – we only saw this in the photo – was a wig.'

'A wig? So . . . A ball gown, a wig, a floppy hat, a mural. Are you expecting me just to give you the answer?'

'Can you just give me five more minutes, Ted?'

He didn't answer.

'My dad rang her two days later. And he makes it a normal conversation, our news, his news, my job, my boyfriend et cetera. I don't have a boyfriend, but sometimes I pretend to. And then he asks, "Mum, is there something going on in your life that we should know about?" He thought she would fly off the handle but she didn't. She said, very calmly, "I saw the ladder, Theo, and I know it was you." And while he blustered around, she said, "It's under control. I know where to go for help."'

'Help? Where did she go?' asked Edward.

The young woman paused. 'To you.'

'*No!*' Edward exclaimed.

Another pause.

He repeated: 'No. That didn't happen.'

'Did she email or write to you?'

'I-I don't know. I've been away. I've been on a long period of . . . leave, and then I didn't come back. Long story, but the radio station is a tricky place for me now. Okay, an urgent letter should have got to me. But an email – no.'

'Could you ask them?'

He was silent, reflecting on the question. Surely the ever-loyal Derrick, his former producer, might be able to help if a letter had arrived.

'I don't believe the fire was an accident,' said Stevie. 'I think Granny was so upset about something she took her own life. And I think, if I loved her, which I did, very much, the least I can do is to show interest.'

'Why would she have bought that dress? Why would she have put that mural up? And the wig? And then take her life?'

'But that's *it!* And what I can't understand is my dad's lack of curiosity. Something was going on, and he didn't understand it, and she ended up dead. Accident, suicide? That's the tribute I want to pay her, that I find out why she went, especially if she offed herself.'

The last phrase was blunt to the point of offensive. Edward tried, 'Look, it may have been an accident like the police say. Sometimes the obvious—'

'We think it might be dementia,' Stevie cut in. 'My father tried one more time to challenge her, and she burst into tears and said something like, "You can't know what's going on because it's so serious." And she said something had happened to "make it all harder" and she had written to you. "I have written to Edward Temmis and he will help me."'

Edward felt a sadness so real that it chilled him. 'I wish I could help, I really do. Maybe she rang my programme as a caller, do you think? Would she have used her own name?'

'I don't know.'

'I've got to go,' said Edward after a pause, hesitant to leave her in distress but acutely aware of the time. 'I'm so sorry I couldn't help.'

'At least let me give you my number,' said Stevie, and wrote a mobile number on the canteen napkin in felt tip. For the first time, she looked around the room. 'I like this place. Lots of light and air. Only let down by the multiple-choice soup.'

He grimaced when he probably should have laughed. He took the number. 'I'm afraid I don't have a phone at the moment, because mine fell in the sea. I've just got an old iPod thing.' A thought struck him. 'Did you say there were some nice messages online? I'm not on social media.'

'I had to wade through a lot of boomer energy to find you.'

'But, what you waded through – was it on Facebook? Was it nice?' Edward was trying not to sound desperate.

'Yes. Yes, it was nice.'

When Stevie stood, quicker than him, he saw that one of her legs bowed inwards at the hip, to the point where she almost seemed to trip over it. It would not take her weight and she needed the back of the chair for a moment. Now he could see her torso was askew, too, and guessed a zigzag in the spine. Her high heels were therefore likely physical extravagance, rebellion, and a profound feeling of empathy broke over him. An innocent blonde child with swimming-pool eyes who had been assaulted with whatever cruelty by . . . didn't she say her birth parents were on crystal meth? A body broken but not her spirit; then rescued by a well-meaning couple with a modest church ministry, whose devotion to her had gradually become claustrophobic. Yet she was the apple of their eye, this child who had grown into a strangely confident and fragile young woman, full of Bible verses and profanities. Perhaps it was the excess of his love for Matty that rose up in Edward Temmis, the unused part of what he felt for the son he had lost, because he suddenly felt protective of Stevie as he would of a daughter. Maybe he could help. Maybe he could try to find out what happened to Rebecca Mason.

He reached into his jacket pocket and showed her the slim rectangular object. 'Regarding Facebook – I think I had a login. Hey, could you . . .?'

'Could I what?'

'Log me in or whatever.'

51

'What's that, an old iPod Touch? I'll need your Facebook password.'

'I think my password fell in the sea.'

She raised her eyebrows.

'With my phone. It was on my phone. I got hit by that wave.'

'Show me that.' She grabbed it from him. 'This is an iPod Touch Fifth Gen! They don't even make them now!'

'My phone was swept away, and it's the only bit of tech I have. I just thought – if I saw some of the messages from my listeners, I might feel better.'

She shrugged. 'I thought you was late for work.'

'I am a bit.'

'Well. You go back to your till and, if I can, I'll sort this. You just need to give me the code for the device. So long as you have email on this I can reset your Facebook password. Hopefully I'll bring this back to you in ten minutes. And then you'll help me and ask about Granny's letter, yes? Ask at the radio station?'

He nodded, though the request was far more awkward than she would ever understand. And was he supposed to undo a suicide? The story of the death of Stevie's poor grandmother would most likely lead nowhere.

He had not the slightest inkling of how wrong he would turn out to be.

CHAPTER FIVE

He sat alone in the dark, the screen in his palm the only illumination.

The lights in the house had gone again. But the lights were the least of it. The property Edward Temmis had bought should not, really, have been sold to anyone. The last owners, a Polish couple called Jankowiak, had been pensioners when they were given advice that it would fall into the sea – not in the year 2300, as had been the original forecast, but possibly before their expected natural deaths. In a single afternoon, half the land behind the house had gone while the pair were on a day trip to Totnes. The story became international news as a dramatic sign of climate change. Mr Jankowiak told CNN he wanted to stay in this beautiful house 'and take my chances', but the reporter asked, 'What if the view becomes your tomb?'

Poor Mrs Jankowiak, already a bag of nerves, was admitted to hospital with a full-blown breakdown. Edward was the only bidder when they sold.

Tonight the electrics had gone, which they often did after heavy rain. He sat in the dark kitchen, hearing only his own breath and wondering again what possessed him to buy the place. The obvious reason was the combination of magically low price and dramatic location, and he even had the chance to give the same interviewers a second bite (CNN guy: 'What if the view becomes your tomb?' Edward Temmis: 'Aren't we all, as a civilization, living on the edge? This just makes it real.' The Americans had gone too far with their caption: I WILL DIE FOR THE PLANET, SAYS CLIFF BRIT).

It had made Matty popular at school. That was a bonus. All his friends wanted to come to the house and get as close to the edge of the garden as they could. When the youngsters got home, their parents were full of anxious questions.

'Did it creak? Could you see the edge?'

Those days were gone. Now he was here on his own. Edward felt the precipice closer than ever. The council had put sensors in the garden to warn of any landslip but they were registering nothing. Sometimes, as tonight, he sat without the lights on, the only sound the breathing of the sea.

When the landline rang, his heart banged. He watched the bulb on the handset flicker on the other side of the kitchen. Pulsing in the light was his favourite photo of Matty from when Tara and Edward had been together. Tara had taken the picture. Edward was lifting their toddler into the air, face aglow with laughter. He was singing 'Rocket Man' by Elton John. The Magic Kingdom was behind them, illuminated pink against the darkening Florida sky. That had been a good holiday. Tara and Edward – five years dating, four years living together, three years married, two with a baby and then nothing. Like a cancelled countdown: five, four, three, two, zero.

Tara had remarried and kept producing children. She now had two boys and a girl. Their custody battle over Matty had been bloodless, more a formality than anything: Matty split his time equally between his parents, one week here and one week with Tara in Exmouth. Edward began to look forward to the fortnightly Saturday arrival more than any other, weathering the sense of loss on alternate Saturdays when Matty left. It was, of course, one of Edward's Saturdays on which his boy had died.

Should he take the call? The ringing landline, now so rarely used in an age of mobiles, took him back to the day Matty's short life ended. A phone in the hospital had woken Edward from unconsciousness. Had he been an inattentive father that day? When Matty was hit, where was he? He racked his brain for the answers. He knew the place, the exact spot, because the police had taken him back there. The memories *must* be in his head. An image or even just a sound from the moment before impact. Perhaps if he went back . . .

He shuddered at the thought.

The phone – someone was persistent. He stood, body creaking like the house. In the near darkness he reached for the handset in its cradle.

'Hello?' the female voice at the other end said.

He felt his heart in his mouth.

'It's me,' she said. 'I couldn't get through on your mobile. It makes a strange noise.'

He was silent. Then he cleared his throat. 'I was hit by a wave and it was washed away.'

She paused at the other end. 'I saw the newspaper. I hope you're okay. How's the house?'

He chuckled softly. 'You're calling from the estate agency, Kim?'

'Strictly business.'

'Well, I've realized it's on a cliff edge, and I would like to complain.'

The silence suggested she might be taking him seriously. So he added, 'Service gets four stars.' Her gentle snort at the other end made him smile.

'Still standing?'

'It'll probably still be standing in two hundred years. But every time the ground moves, something is knocked out of alignment. The latest is that the front door won't close unless I put my shoulder to it.'

'The tremor sensors?'

'I keep wondering if the app works. Nothing registers for now.'

'The app doesn't work on the seabed.'

'Fair.'

'What about you?'

'Me?'

'Are *you* still standing, Edward?'

He felt for the edge of the kitchen counter in the dark and leant against it. There was no answer he could give. Despite himself, despite his promises not to cry over it, he let the emotion engulf him. Here in the dark kitchen, in the creaking house, Edward Temmis wept down the telephone line until he could barely hold the phone against his ear.

'Hey, hey,' Kim was saying. 'Hey. Come on.' But now he heard her weeping, too.

'I haven't been able to . . . you and me . . .' He trailed off.

'Process it?'

'No.'

'Nor have I – not since . . .'

He said, 'I wanted it.'

'It's totally my fault, what happened. I was in the wrong. I took advantage.'

'Don't beat up on yourself. Like I say, I wanted it.'

She said, 'I wanted it, too, Edward, but I knew I couldn't and shouldn't. I took it anyway.'

'Is this an apology? You don't need to. It wasn't written in the stars, I guess.'

'I needed to escape. Should we meet up to go through it all?'

'Kim, I don't think—'

She spoke quickly, cutting in. 'No, no, not like that. I've missed you terribly. But when you lost your son, I knew I couldn't help. I knew you would be too broken.'

It was hard for him even to think back to the time before Matty had died. But there it was, as clear as a bell in his memory – he had gone to an estate agent to buy a house and, on their first visit after the sale had gone through, they both knew what was going to happen and it did. As soon as they had gone through the front door, they were upon each other. Their hands moved quickly. He lost two buttons. Soon they were on the floor in the lounge, with the sea roaring disapproval at them through an open window. He did not feel guilty. Another man's wife? But she had bruises. He was taking what the other did not deserve to keep. And it was hardly taking – she had pulled him to the floor.

And then, barely two months later, his son was gone. Everything else faded away.

He said, 'I can't talk about Matty. But I'll just say, I knew that was the end for you and me. It was all too much, and it's too much for everyone I meet. And I became a bit reclusive.'

'They still haven't found the driver?'

'Have they even looked? Matty is still getting blamed on all the social media. Well, less so him. I get the blame. "No helmet". Then he gets the blame. Then someone might mention the person who hit us – ' *Was it a man, was it a woman?* – 'but okay, to be totally frank, I was relieved not to hear from you. I went to my cave.' He scratched the back of his neck, feeling a draught. 'At the end of the day,' he said, hating the phrase, 'you're married, it wouldn't be right.'

Her voice was steely. 'I'll be the judge of that.'

Since the day of the accident, they had not spoken. If he had thought of her after that, it was only for a millisecond amid the grief. His memory was the seafront shelter, blown away by the tsunami.

'Kim, I've wanted to ask again and again how you are.'

Her answer was a deflection. 'My dear mum is pining! She still remembers meeting you. "You introduced me to him by Zizzi, darling Kim, what an honour it was." She talks about it like she met King Charles.'

'Oh my God. And she didn't suspect anything?'

'She hates the new woman.'

'Tessa K is really good.' He had to say that.

57

'Tessa K is a witch, according to Mum. She completely went off on one about it. Said she'd disrespected Phil Collins.'

For the first time since he had been led away from the football pitch, Edward let out a roar of genuine laughter.

'Seriously now. Do you want to meet for coffee?' she asked. 'Just as friends. Just to talk. Tempt you out of your cave.'

'I don't know, Kim. When I lost Matty it buried everything, the whole of my life. I feel like I'm just waking up now and trying to work out what I have left. And your marriage – whatever you say, it was wrong, all that, from my point of view.'

Kim did not persist. 'Mum told me she had a Facebook page just based on one of your remarks, something about Wimbledon.'

'How is she?'

'Spending too much time online. She had a small mirror out last time I was round, leaning against the wall at a really weird angle. So I asked her what it was for and she said "a portrait picture". What kind of portrait pic is that? She thinks she's found love but she won't say who. I suspect someone in her church choir – that is one mucky unit.'

He laughed.

'I just hope to God she isn't going to be hurt by someone. She was very secretive about it. Anyway Edward,' Kim continued, 'I've been avoiding you in case your house had fallen off a cliff and you wanted a refund.'

'Don't worry. I chose this. But you – are you okay?' He remembered that bruise, along the line of the ribs.

'Yes. Business good, thank you.'

'Has he hurt you again?'

'No, not that.' Perhaps she meant: *I'll talk about anything but that.*

Edward collected himself. 'So you saw the news about the tidal surge?'

'My God. My God. You were hit by a bloody big wave last month. And the policeman reviving someone on the prom.'

'And my pants looking like a nappy.'

She giggled. 'Björn Borg pants. My mum was all over them.'

'It was my boss, Agnes Chan, who was being resuscitated. She sacked me and then got hit by that wave. Proves divine intervention doesn't work. The wave should have come before the sacking. She must be angry that I had to pull her out of the sea, because I haven't had a word from her since.'

'Did you give her the kiss of life?'

'She gave me the kiss of death.'

'How long have you been practising that line?'

'Ha. I was just waiting for your call.' Edward smiled to himself. Though his liaison with Kim had been brief, he had deeply missed their connection and camaraderie. 'Honestly, it's fine. I'm feeling okay about it now. I met this young woman today, a bit eccentric, on a mission, heart of gold, long story. She told me there was stuff on Facebook that might make me feel better about it all, the sacking, you know? Happy stuff. She sorted out my ancient iPod Touch, so I can read it. Social media isn't all bad.'

'What, conversations between strangers who love you?'

'Erm . . . I'm ashamed to say yes.'

'Is that what you were doing when I called?'

He had said too much to deny it, so he did not respond.

'Oh, Edward.' Kim paused at the other end as if winded, and he tut-tutted to fill the silence, but it just sounded like he was voicing his own disapproval: didn't they call that sort of internet surfing *glory hunting?*

'Well, like I say, Edward, my mum looks out for you, and earlier she rang me about your boss, Agnes Chan. Apparently, she's done an interview and it hasn't gone well.'

Kimberley's last few words coincided with a noise from the front of the house. As she said 'done an interview', the building creaked. The creak was not on the higher register he was used to – joists bowing as the building leant into the wind – but something deeper. A low howl, a yawning, as if the bones of the place were under strain. A floorboard. *A floorboard.* Wait – was someone there?

Kim said, 'Edward? Are you okay?'

'A floorboard just . . . hang on, I think there's someone in the house,' he whispered. 'God. Wait a sec.' He gently placed the receiver on the counter, and felt for a drawer in the dark. *These damn lights.* He took out a box of matches, struck one, lit a candle. He thought he heard Kim's voice in the receiver for a second, a tinny scratching, maybe a question he was missing.

Was there someone in the building? He picked up the candle. The flame flickered, painting luminous yellow across a six-foot circle around him, but plunging what was beyond it into even deeper darkness. Blinking in this strange, unsettling combination of light and dark – the candle working against him – he moved from the kitchen into the living room and stood in silence. He turned the handle of the living-room door and entered the hallway.

He saw the figure in the doorway only as a silhouette. It was a man, he could tell, from the height and the uneven line of bristle along the jaw. The person stood well over six feet, wore a hat, and appeared to have entered through the front door. He was now frozen just inside the hallway, as if remaining stock-still would prevent him being seen.

In the instant before any words passed between them, Edward Temmis contemplated the sadness of his solitary life. He imagined what the candlelight was doing to his face, how the intruder would see skin like yellow parchment rolled across the bone, the shadows flickering at his cheeks. Maybe he would think Edward was dead already, a ghost; he was seeing a face eaten by grief. If the visitor was about to bash his skull in, would he wonder if the skull was worth it? Edward would die, as he deserved, sad and lonely, buried in a blur of trying-to-say-something-nice obituaries. 'One of the outstanding figures of Devon's local radio scene.' 'Missed by thousands of pensioners across

Sidmouth.' In that millisecond, which opened like a shutter – a flash of light in the black expanse of time, in the literal waste of time – Edward Temmis resolved that if he survived this moment he would begin again and differently. He would put his loss and sadness behind him and become a different version of himself. He promised he would do something good for Matty. There would be no more waste. He would live again.

Then the adrenaline flooded his body. '*What the actual fu—*'

The other man shifted slightly. 'Don't rush me,' he interrupted, the voice a shaky baritone.

'For God's sake!' Edward's chest pounded. 'What the bloody hell do you think you are doing?'

From the visitor there was no reply, only a small movement and an almost inaudible sigh. Edward saw the overcoat bulge and wondered what he was reaching for. This bloody candle, he thought, is stopping me seeing anything. But suddenly the man's face was illuminated. He had pulled a smartphone from his overcoat and activated the torch with a couple of rapid swipes. Instead of shining it at Edward, the man was turning it on his own face.

He was heavyset, but with small hands almost hidden by the arms of his overcoat. He wore thick spectacles with owl-eyed frames; the blinking was constant. With one finger he kept pushing the glasses up his nose. The unstable smartphone light and the movement of the glasses and their shadow made it look as if the man was in a very old movie where the celluloid was edited with heavy glue. Burglars, Edward decided, did not wear expensive glasses and constantly adjust their position. In outline the intruder could have been a vagrant, with a long coat hanging off him; illuminated, he had the nervous features of a keen-to-please librarian or social worker.

'I come in peace,' he said with another shivered sigh. He looked fifty, maybe older. His beard grew from his face in patches, like mould, and there was some sweat on his forehead, but everything else Edward could see was tidy. The visitor wore a clean white shirt open at the neck. Edward was sure he saw a cufflink. He felt calmer than the intruder now – almost as if this stranger was the homeowner, and Edward the home-breaker.

'What are you doing here?'

The tall man swallowed his reply. Tried again. 'I came to see you. I know what it looks like, right? Big black guy in your hallway?'

'That's not what . . .' Edward started, resentful that he was now having to justify his panic.

'My name is Troy Barber?'

The stranger said the name as a question, not a fact. As if Edward should know who he was. He was sure he did not.

'I didn't mean to shock you, but I had to come in person and your door wasn't quite closed.'

'The frame is out of alignment. The house is in a strange position in general. Why didn't you knock?'

'I wanted to speak to you in person. Heard you on the phone. Didn't want to leave a note. Please Mr Temmis, hear me out.'

'I'd invite you in, but I've had a power cut.' Relaxing despite himself, Edward remembered the panicked promise he had made: *Live again.* 'The power goes off in the rain. Come in anyway.'

'We have that, me and Agnes. The electricians say if it's only three or four times a year, just ignore it, no harm done.'

Agnes? Edward led the visitor by candlelight to the dining room (where no one ever dined except himself). Looking back, he noticed the man's walk – lumbering, mechanical, as if he was trying to break free of gravity. Barber rolled his shoulders as he moved and sat down heavily.

With care, so the wax did not drip onto his hand, Edward pushed the candle into the only candle-holder, an elaborate tangle of swan-neck silver he had bought in an outdoor market. The flame flickered between them, brushing the dark wood of the tabletop as they sat on either side. Setting his hat, a dapper Heisenberg number, on the table between them, Troy Barber said: 'I've got in the habit of wearing it since *Breaking Bad* was on.'

'Of course!' said Edward. 'The same hat Willard White wore.'

'Walter White.'

Edward did not normally mind being corrected, but he drew the line at having his television knowledge queried by a home-invader. He looked again at the other man. He was wearing exceptionally thick spectacles. The pupils behind them really were very wide, like wells; Barber's eyeballs were a little too prominent – perhaps a misfiring thyroid? The baggy lower eyelids sagged, giving the man the crestfallen look of a bloodhound. The candlelight made his face flicker in and out of focus. In moments where the light bounced off the ceiling, Edward saw the man's head was hairless. At the top of his crown a line of deep shadow suggested an old scar that ran deep.

And then came that voice, a trembling bass as deep as the sea: 'I'm not just strolling into every house with a power cut.'

'I just assumed it was to rob me,' said Edward.

'Hey, I don't mind a little casual racism.'

'Jesus!' exclaimed Edward. 'I didn't mean—'

Troy Barber laughed for the first time. He flashed bright teeth across which a plastic dental liner was fitted. 'A joke, Mr Temmis, a joke. I'm Agnes's other half, the boss, you know. She's your boss and mine! High achiever. I'm just a flying professor.'

He paused, allowed Edward to ask the obvious question across the table in the dark. 'What sort of job is that?'

'I take classes when university lecturers are off. Used to do it by travelling, then Covid hit, now it's WFH or WTF or whatever they call it. Mostly I just Zoom my way around the country. Well, occasionally I'll be properly away. The first three weeks of December I was on the North Wales coast, which rang the changes. But I've done St Andrews from a library in Exeter. At least I can follow Agnes's brilliant career around the country. And that's why I'm here.'

'Here in Sidmouth?'

'Here in your house.' He tapped the table and leant forward, drawing Edward in, dropping his voice. 'I want to rescue her and I want to rescue you. You know about the newspaper interview?'

'A friend mentioned it, but only vaguely.' He suddenly thought of Kim. Was she still on the landline he had left dangling from the kitchen counter? Edward said: 'Excuse me one sec.' Blindly he felt his way back to the kitchen without the candle. His hand slid across the counter. He held the handset to his ear.

'Hello, Kim?'

He thought the line was open but he must be imagining a presence at the other end. He replaced the handset clumsily and made his way back towards the dining-room candle.

'The newspaper,' Troy Barber continued a moment later. He had an odd manner, constantly gulping as if he was nervous. 'The *Gazette* asked her, "How do you justify sacking a man who lost a child?" In fact it was worse – "who lost a child and saved you from a tidal wave?" *She had no answer.* It'll go crazy when they put the edition online. It cut her to the quick, Edward, I can tell you. Cut her to the bone.'

Unable to respond, Edward clumsily changed subject. 'How is Ms Chan?'

'Agnes is under pressure from London. They want her to clear out the old guard, as you know. But I stuck up for you. I said, "Why Edward, Agnes? He's not one of those . . . those slurry chuckers! Why sack him as well?" And she said you had completely lost it.'

'Charming.'

'And she said the bosses in London didn't want any Edwards on their stations anyway.'

'That sounds like discrimination,' said Edward, genuinely angry if that part of Agnes's agenda had been hidden from him.

'It's completely disgusting!' Troy Barber cried. 'So, I'm trying to help, okay, and you mustn't say I was here. Deep cover, okay?' He was twisting and untwisting his fingers. 'Do you know about the demo tomorrow?'

'What sort of demo?' The candle was burning down to the base, and Edward suddenly felt very tired. He would be on shift at the garden centre when dawn broke.

'I've been tipped off. It's all over the WhatsApp groups, I gather. There's to be a *demonstration* by your fans on the seafront at Sidmouth!'

In the dark, Edward frowned. The candle had almost burned down.

'Look,' Barber said. 'You can't fire a guy . . .' He trailed off. His words had carried a momentary flash of energy, of certainty and confidence, but now he appeared muted. The pair sat quietly like passengers at a bus stop, waiting for the next sentence to arrive. 'You cannot fire the guy who lost his son in a hit-and-run.'

Troy's sentence was like a blank firing. Edward's mind started to run.

'Secondly, and this is why I am here, she cannot fire the guy who saved her child.'

It took a moment for the penny to drop.

'She was pregnant when the wave hit?'

'She very much is,' replied Troy in the near-dark, a smile in his voice now. 'And this only came out when she was getting the once-over in hospital. So a bad day turned into a great one.' He laughed, but in a way that unsettled Edward.

'And she's well? The baby is well?'

Troy nodded. 'Right as rain. Thanks to you.'

Edward sat back, a smile on his face at last. 'I am so relieved for you.'

'It's my first. You saved my baby, mate.' Troy Barber said. 'So can I tell you what I want you to do?'

Then, without waiting for an answer, Troy Barber began to explain.

CHAPTER SIX

There were three studios inside Rock 'n' Talk Radio 92FM, and Tessa Kirkhope was at the window of the central one, 4b, which was also the largest. Daylight flooded in. The radio station occupied floors three and four in the building on Sidmouth promenade. This was the fourth and the added height kept the sea-facing rooms as bright as anything. Boiling in the summer, mind you, when the historic single-glazing turned it into a greenhouse.

It was a tricky arrangement in many ways – the hotel next door had kept the fifth floor above the radio station for guests, which meant there were strict limits on how much sound could be pumped through the studio loudspeakers on the fourth. Furthermore, the lower two storeys, plus the ground floor, were occupied by various small businesses including North Devon Small Pony Rescue. Charity staff kept trying to badge the entire building as their own operation, standing A-frame boards on the pavement showing, naturally, pictures of small ponies. In the end the smaller tenants had to agree that the radio station alone could mount a sign, so RTR was now flashing neon red against the underside of Tessa's face as she contemplated the scene on the road below.

Never in her life would she have imagined East Devon's pensioners might mobilize for a protest like this. She had lived in the county all her life, her father still working as a petrol station manager halfway between Ottery St Mary and the A30. Tessa was only twenty-six and had been scooped from a forestry magazine last year to work on the station as a researcher. She could congratulate herself that it was only five years after her graduation in media studies at Scarborough – but then again, after five years she was earning barely ten per cent more than minimum wage. As she had been contemplating this combination of triumph and injustice, the awful tragedy had befallen Edward Temmis. The station controller asked Tessa to cover his show; Edward might be off for a month at most. But now it had been nearly a year. There were rumours he had been sidelined permanently, but no announcement. Even at twenty-six, Tessa felt the show should be hers. She liked being Tessa K, going from making the tea to having it brought to her.

'Don't you just hate the audience?' a voice behind her asked.

She turned, surprised that Agnes Chan had been able to approach without making any sound. Her boss looked shrunken, as if the job had put her through a washing machine. But then, how much fun was it really to run a radio station – especially with this going on? The pink slash of dyed hair hung in Agnes's ironed-straight fringe like a wound. Tessa, instantly nervous in the presence of the person who could make or break her career, did the same as Agnes, pressing her face against the window.

It was mid-afternoon and the sun was out. Tessa contemplated how to answer the controller's question.

'Sometimes.'

'Wrong answer!' said Agnes abruptly, her breath misting the glass. 'The customer is king, even this lot. That's our royal family down there.' There were at least a hundred of them. They were holding placards and occasionally one would be flashed directly upwards at the building: BRING HIM BACK was one;

67

PLAY TEMMIS AGAIN another. One made her laugh: WHERE ARE YOU HIDING HIM, which apparently needed no question mark. Most of the protesters were women, and most of the women were over seventy. One was in a wheelchair and strapped to an oxygen cylinder, head lolling and eyes closed as if she had passed away from the excitement.

'Never in a million years did I think this would happen,' said Agnes, 'and now they're going to block the road, look.'

Tessa was conscious of the neon RTR sign throwing red light onto her face in pulses, but in the very instant she worked out that she would be visible where she stood, someone on the street was pointing.

'*Devil! Devil!*' they shouted. 'The face of the devil!'

Within seconds it became a chant, with its own distinctive melody and rhythm, like a samba, and the angry crowd was sprawling across the road as each pensioner instinctively moved closer to the building.

She recoiled, feeling sick. Agnes said: 'They're probably talking about me. A Chinese woman appears in mid-air above them and they think it's witchcraft.'

'No, it's me,' Tessa said. 'I know it's me. They hate me.' The younger woman was tall and very thin, and always got compared to Keira Knightley in a way she did not take as a compliment. She could only imagine what the listeners thought, seeing the narrow face of the carpetbagger razor-lit in vivid red. She felt tears coming.

'Oh for God's sake,' Agnes suddenly exclaimed. 'I don't believe this!'

For a second, Tessa K thought Agnes had spotted her eyes brimming, but then she saw the figure walking towards the protesters on the promenade.

Edward Temmis removed his woollen hat, feeling the static make his hair dance. He was bowled over by the warmth of the crowd around him. It was like the Facebook posts made flesh – he had never considered that caller after caller on his late-night show, all individual people with individual stories, might add up to an actual crowd, might care enough to turn up on a windy beachfront in his support. He remembered precisely the instructions of Troy Barber: speak to them, calm them, support Agnes, say you support the station, then tell them you're coming back. Make the speech of your life . . .

As he started to shush the crowd, he was conscious of a woman in a Barbour jacket to his left, with a camera. Next to her was a teenager with a notepad. Media. He waved his arms to silence the crowd.

'*Ed – ward – Temm – miss*,' was the chant around him. Older ladies were literally shoving each other to break through and touch him.

'Everyone, a word!' he shouted. Then – 'Silence!' as if he believed he could even settle the sea.

Someone called back, 'We don't want silence! We want you back!'

Edward began to speak, raising his voice as loudly as he could without it turning into a yell. 'I know the radio station wants me back and I know we'll have our show back soon – it's *our* show!' he cried suddenly, but partly out of shock because as he said the words he felt himself being lifted up. A man with a bald patch like a monk's was doubled over beside him in a green gilet and had grabbed his left knee, just as he might yank at a lamb stuck in gorse. As Edward toppled, he was caught from behind by two women – he could hear them laughing uproariously. Someone grabbed his right leg and suddenly he was aloft.

The crowd chanted, 'Our. Show. *Our. Show. Our—*'

Moved by the emotion, hearing stamping of feet on the road and now literally carried away by the crowd, Edward tried to remember any form of words that he had rehearsed. Troy had put it succinctly at his house last night. 'You saved Agnes. You saved our child. You are the hero. She has to take you back. Meet the demonstration, make a heroic speech and she will ring you the next day and give you a return date. I'll make sure of it.'

The pensioners had now moved back into the roadway. Cars were stationary all the way down the seafront, hooting and flashing their lights. Edward looked up and waved at the fourth floor, above the RTR-92 neon, but he could not see anyone at the glass.

The photographer was clicking away, the flash on now. The teenage reporter had swapped his notepad for a smartphone and was filming from ten yards back.

'*Friends!*' shouted Edward, and there was a roar of recognition. 'Please don't be cross with the radio station!' He was racking his brains, trying to remember exactly what Troy had told him he must say. 'Agnes Chan and the team are doing a fantastic job.'

Someone tried chanting, '*Put her in the bin and close the lid*', and Edward waved for them to stop.

'No, no.'

He must be the peacemaker. He was conscious of the frailty of whoever's shoulder he was sitting on, and the fact that he had limited time before the human pyramid that had borne him into the air simply collapsed. If it did, what sort of picture would that make in the paper?

So he said, 'I love Tessa K . . .!' but that only triggered more booing and a chant of '*We don't! We don't! We don't!*', accompanied by more stamping, which made the crowd sound like a marching army.

He raised his voice. 'But I'll be back! I promise I'll be back, taking your calls every single day like I used to!'

The crowd roared, and then a loud chant of '*Get him back, Get him back*' began, with some of the older protesters waving walking sticks and shopping bags, and one woman jabbing the air with a wheeled shopping carrier, which Edward assumed was empty until bags of crisps spilled out of it onto her head.

They dropped him – literally dropped him – at the doors to the radio station.

The security guard on duty made a great play of checking the crowd was dispersed before he unlocked the doors for Edward. The lopsided corridor to RTR-92's inner reception was temporary, made of white-emulsioned chipboard and bent like an elbow. Edward followed the guard down it, feeling truly elated for the first time this year. He expected some of his colleagues to come down to see him and thank him, and said as much to the security guard, who answered every remark with a chuckle and an all-knowing nod of his head. Edward took a space on one of the empty sofas and the man went back behind the reception desk.

'Geoff, isn't it?' Edward recognized the man's tattoos. He had always guessed Geoff was ex-Navy. 'You on security today?' asked Edward, searching for a conversation opener and finding the most obvious question in the world.

'On reception,' said Geoff. 'Usually boring but you brightened it up, I must say.'

Edward couldn't read his tone. 'Will you let them know I'm here?'

'"Them" as in management? Oh, don't you worry, they know. The whole building knows.'

Edward nodded. Geoff made a great show of putting his feet up and opening a fishing magazine. The place fell completely silent.

Twenty minutes later, Edward was still sitting alone on one of the tired white sofas and had looked at all the newspapers except the one he really wanted to see.

'Is there no *Gazette* yet?' he asked.

Geoff looked up slowly. 'Management removed it earlier, don't know why.'

'Possibly the interview with Agnes?'

71

'Oh, I wouldn't know about that.'

'Are they coming down at all?'

Once again, Geoff seemed reluctant to engage with the question. 'In due time and season, I imagine. Just you hang on.'

Edward stood up and sneaked back down the white panelled corridor. He peeked outside the glass doors, but there was no need to hide. The protesters had all drifted away. It was starting to drizzle. The wind had picked up, scooping water off the sea and throwing it at the occasional hardy walker. When he came back to the waiting area, Geoff had placed a heavy pair of glasses on his nose and was looking at him over the top of them.

'We had something of yours back here, let me find it.'

He ducked down, scrabbled in a drawer, closed the drawer, looked around the side of the desk. 'Wait . . . here.' He seemed to be carefully peeling a piece of paper away from the exterior of the desk. 'Ha! Someone moved it. Couldn't let visitors see it. Just struck us as funny when we saw it, that's all.'

Edward stared. 'Funny?'

'Saucy, I suppose.' He sounded a little apologetic. 'The words.'

'Let me see.' Edward was standing above Geoff, hand outstretched. The security guy chuckled, shrugged and passed Edward a brown A4 envelope. On the outside was his name, and below it the words:

in desperation from Riva

'Nothing inside.' Edward had quickly scissored his fingers between the flaps of the envelope and separated them. 'I don't see how this is saucy.'

'Well, hearing of a young lady in desperation – no, you're right,' he conceded hastily, as if embarrassed. 'Truth is, when you work the overnight reception shift, you can get things a bit out of proportion.'

'Riva from Gulverton. That's it. An occasional caller to my show.' Edward felt pleased at his recall.

'Well, do take it with you. It was in reception for a while, uncollected, then someone thought to open it up, and there was nothing inside. It just tickled us, that's all. "In Desperation." Ha ha.'

Now they were talking, Edward tried: 'Where is everyone? Where is Agnes? Why aren't they coming down?'

Geoff became serious. 'They activated the emergency security procedures. Lifts locked, et cetera, so no one goes up or down. The same thing they do for a terrorist attack.'

'Al-Qaeda doesn't have a crown bowling wing! It was just local pensioners!'

'But you must have known in advance, Mr Temmis.'

He was surprised by the sudden formality, as if this was a police interview. 'Somebody told me they were organizing it on Facebook.'

'So you did know. Oh well, good luck to you.' The security man's gaze was freighted with the unspoken comment: *You should have told us.* 'I'm afraid I was told to delay you here while the riot dispersed.'

'Oh great,' said Edward, a hollow feeling growing inside him. He had thought the event had been a triumph, and he was now fearing the opposite. 'Well, you did your job.'

'Like I say, the building's in what we call Red Lockdown, which is for an imminent attack, so the chiefs couldn't come down even if they wanted to.' He went on, lowering his voice to a hoarse whisper, 'The police may be on their way for a word. My tip – sneak out the back, Mr Temmis, while you still can. I won't rugby tackle you or anything.'

Edward left two minutes later, utterly humiliated. As he left the building, the fire bell went. He thought maybe the smoke detectors had been triggered by the smouldering carcass of his pride.

CHAPTER SEVEN

Rubbing at a smudge on the glass with his thumb, Derrick Tidy was cross. He had arrived at the station slightly delayed by a surprise lunch which had been thrown for him by his mother and stepdad. Sweet . . . but a bit annoying, as it turned out, because the delay meant all the hoo-ha at the station had died down by the time he arrived. Whoever had set the fire alarm off – it seemed to have been part of the protest, because there was no fire – had scarpered, and even the 'terror lockdown' of reception had ended, so the lifts were switched back on and there was nothing to tell his mates about in the pub on Friday.

It wasn't that he was late. The phone-in was 9 p.m. till midnight. As the dogsbody/producer, he was normally in by 4 p.m. to get things ready for Edw—oh, an easy slip after such a long time working with the big man! To get things ready for *Tessa*. Today, by the time he had arrived, parking his Škoda behind Boots and jogging through the early evening drizzle, the pensioner protest was done and dusted. Now inside the radio station, he stood in the Gents, washing his hands, contemplating his face in the mirror. A smudge had interrupted his view and he was pushing his thumb into it.

He had what a maths teacher had called 'bog-brush ginger hair', a thicket on his head that seemed to grow upwards and outwards no matter how much gel or cream he applied. The combination of gel sheen and rebellious hair meant he always looked as if he had overslept *and* been caught in the rain, and it irked him that his appearance contradicted his surname.

'Derrick Untidy' had been one of several nicknames at school, along with 'Lionel' (Lionel Messi, Messy/Tidy, etc.) and 'Match', because the combination of skinny body and flaming hair apparently made him look like a safety match that had just flared. No matter what he did to his hair, it always announced the person standing below it as being slovenly, a slob even. Not in control of his own world. Which, Derrick liked to believe, was the opposite of the truth.

His upbringing had been here in Sidmouth, God's waiting room, and his only escape from the monotony (in a house where his parents and sisters badged themselves as turbo-environmentalists and disapproved of nearly all TV) had been the radio. He had listened at every spare moment, avoiding YouTube, avoiding podcasts, never going near a PlayStation, never even acquiring a smartphone until the ridiculous age of seventeen.

Relying for entertainment on a small digital radio that could pick up stations around the world through the web, he had discovered Japanese weather and Caribbean dance. He happily travelled the world inside that radio and then came back home to the audio landscapes of BBC Radio 4 and Radio 3, and when the chance came, managed to win the coveted job at RTR-92.

'Yes, I love radio and I can make the phone-in work,' he told them cheerfully, as if he had suddenly found home after being lost. The interview panel looked at the mess on his head and they looked into his youthful face – pale, freckled, with tight lips and green eyes; not bad-looking, not yet marked by disappointment or failure. He got the job, his first.

So now he dressed for his surname, still thrilled to be making a living on the radio. He wore a tight suit from Ted Baker that pinched at his bony frame, and a white linen collarless shirt. His shoes were from the M&S Signature range, faux-leather lace-ups with a very slightly increased heel that took his height to a satisfactory five feet ten.

'Happy with it?' said a voice.

It was Cyril Weekes. One of the old guard – the Farmers, he and Tessa had nicknamed them – who, despite the thickest of Somerset accents, had somehow avoided the chop. He appeared suddenly in the bathroom mirror over Derrick's shoulder.

'With what?'

'You young ones,' said Weekes, 'I swear, you lot would swim in your mirrors if they were horizontal.'

He was, considered Derrick, a truly awful human being. There were rumours about him having been caught in a police raid on a massage parlour in Branscombe. How he had avoided getting shunted off with Vic, Brian and the other old farts, he had no clue.

'I just like to put on a suit in the morning.' He did not turn, watching his colleague's reflection.

'For the radio?' spluttered Weekes, whose face had more ruts and bulges than a cabbage. 'I've worn the same dirty cords for thirty years and no listener ever mentioned it. Mud maketh the man! Anyway, you heard about the protest?'

'Yes of course,' said Derrick.

'Your boy, Edward, to blame.'

'Really.' A statement rather than a question; Derrick did not want to be drawn. He had loved working on the Temmis Show (as everyone called it, even now) but was doing his best for Tessa K.

'Is he coming back, then, young Edward?' Weekes's use of 'boy' and 'young' to describe Edward startled Derrick, because he considered his last presenter to be middle-aged, but of course the older man now standing behind him was pushing seventy. It struck him at that moment how unfair the radio station managers had been, lumping Temmis in with the likes of Channon and Turnbull.

As if he had read the thought, Cyril Weekes said: 'I'll go back to my dairy business when they dump me. Or I'll retire and sit there reading the *Radio Times* until the prostate blows up. But as for Edward, he hasn't got anything else. He's like you, someone who does radio because he does radio. I'm not slagging him. I liked him. But the death of his son ripped the innards out of that man and I can't imagine him working again.'

'You think they'll stay with Tessa?'

Weekes was distracted by a memory. 'I saw him in Waitrose, a few weeks ago, a ghost in a long coat. Literally a spectre. And he bought that house that's falling into the sea.'

'He bought that before the tragedy, though.'

'Eh? Oh. Right. But even so. You asked about Tessa? There are worse. But you see, with Agnes and the other incompetents,' Weekes began, and instinctively Derrick braced himself for a gruesome lapse in taste, 'they don't care about the listeners one bit. If they could do it, they'd euthanize them all, shove the bodies in a laundry basket and throw them off the side of a ship like they did with Bin Laden. But that only works if they find the youngsters to replace them. And,' growled Cyril, stepping forwards towards the mirror so a downlight in the ceiling turned his hair white, 'they ain't coming.'

'I'm one.'

'One what?'

'Youngster. Under thirty, anyway.'

'Yes, but you're decidedly odd – if you don't mind me saying so,' he added, not that Derrick had a choice. 'These bosses, they just want to create a problem so they can be seen to solve it.'

To Derrick this sounded unfair. He remembered only too well the day he got a phone call from Christopher Lawson, Agnes's deputy, saying Edward's son had been in an accident and the presenter would not be in for a week at least. On the Tuesday it had broken in the newspapers that Matty Temmis was dead. That must be a year ago now.

As if reading his mind, Cyril Weekes said:

'I don't think Temmis will ever return now. He might be ready, but he can't come back after today.'

This was unusually prescient for Cyril Weekes. Ten minutes later every member of staff with a smartphone got a single WhatsApp message from the radio station, pinging all the mobiles in the building at the same instant. Some of the staff did not know the station even had the technical know-how to do such a thing; it suggested some sort of emergency. Serious-faced and wearing a ballooning red dress in the filmed clip, Agnes Chan announced from behind darkened lenses that, in the light of the extremely upsetting events today, Tessa K would be taking over RTR-92's evening talk show permanently, and Edward Temmis would not be coming back to the station.

Edward wanted to argue his case. But the station now had him over a barrel. The newspaper interview with Agnes, where the *Gazette* reporter had challenged her brutally over her treatment of him, seemed like ancient history now he had egged on a protest against his own employer.

He desperately wanted to ring Agnes and tell her: 'No, you've got this all wrong. Your husband came round and told me to do it – your partner, Troy; whoever the hell that man was. I didn't even know about the protest until he told me.'

But he never had a chance to plead his case with Agnes in the tortured days after the gathering.

The local paper carried a picture on page ten. It was not even front-page news. The image was of Edward being carried shoulder-high across the road, silhouetted against the horizon.

The headline read: ANYONE FOR TEMMIS? 40 ANGRY FANS TRY TO CARRY TRAGIC DJ BACK TO WORK. It had not helped that one of the protesters had ended up in hospital with a popped hip socket. A 'station source' was quoted as saying, 'He just won't let it go. Tessa K is finding it all so upsetting now. She was in tears yesterday. They chanted "Devil's Bride" when they saw her at the window, poor love. And the thing everyone misses in all this is that the listeners adore her. Edward's time has gone, sadly.'

Two days later, a lawyer for the company had arrived at his house from London. The young man drew a bristling sheaf of paperwork from his backpack, which had a cycle helmet clipped to the strap. Edward was told that he must sign the contract to confirm he accepted a non-disclosure agreement. He would receive a further £1,500 in exchange for having nothing more to do with the radio station. The lawyer, who popped open a tin of mango kombucha and began to vape menthol around the kitchen without even asking, said: 'Off the record, that protest really blew up on you. So think of this as a voluntary restraining order.'

Edward said, 'What if I don't sign?'

The lawyer blew menthol at the ceiling. 'We'll come for your redundancy money, because there were conditions attached when you accepted it. So please, Edward, sign.'

The cliff-top house creaked and groaned around the two men as if the building itself was angry at the unfairness, angry at the way the lawyer spoke so condescendingly to its owner, angry at the menthol. Edward wanted to say, 'Troy Barber told me to do it,' but he would sound like a schoolboy if he did. Anyway, Barber's suggestion had been sensible enough – meet the crowd, rally them, calm them, make a speech, 'Show the station the love the audience has for you.' Barber promised he would use the protest to show Agnes her mistake. 'She will have you back the following day, I promise. Just do what I say.' Edward had done exactly as he was told, and the result was the opposite of what Barber had promised. Now Troy had vanished after their only meeting.

Edward had to accept Tessa K was the new generation. Besides, she was doing well. He was forty-five, and didn't footballers only last till thirty-seven? As a radio presenter he was like the central midfielder with glass knees, already shattered.

CHAPTER EIGHT

Barbara Sinker looked at the shape in the next-door garden for a moment before she saw what it was. It looked like a scuff on the grass. But the outline was edged in fur. Wizard had clearly suffered a violent fate.

Wizard? She felt her heart start to pound as she realized that the neighbours' rabbit had died a gruesome death on her watch. The Cokers trusted her so completely that they no longer asked her to look after their pet – Barbara just did it when she noticed they were away. So this was a horrible moment. Ten yards from the hutch, she saw the ground had been dug up, as if the predator wanted to bury its meal in order to return to it.

But how to deal with the death? The Coker children were five and ten, a boy and a girl. She pictured their distress and steeled herself to fix it. The young family had been abroad barely three days. She must not ring them, because it would ruin their holiday. Was it Marbella again? Barbara had dutifully dropped lettuce leaves into Wizard's cage and changed his water twice – as always, the rabbit hid away at the back of his hutch when any visitor came close – but now she could see the predator must have got through the flap into the enclosure and dragged the poor animal out.

She asked Kim to pop over, but it was four days before she came, and when she told Kim what she had found in the Cokers' garden, her daughter's advice was forthright.

'You have to just be honest. Bury the rabbit and tell them when they get back. Is the youngest kid four?'

'Five,' said Barbara. 'But Kim, I've already solved the problem,' she said, her face brightening. 'Come and look.'

She took her daughter out through the sliding doors to the back garden. There was an icy spring breeze. She got Kim to stand on tiptoe and look over the fence.

'See?'

'What?' said Kim, looking at the brown-flecked fur of the chubby white rabbit in the hutch. 'You brought him back to life?'

'In a manner of speaking, I did. I bought another one that looked just like him.'

Kim stared at her mother. She tipped her head slightly like a bird, as if trying to shake the words her mother had just uttered into a different order to make more sense of them.

'I buried Wizard in my own garden so the fox doesn't go back to it. I've locked the hutch.'

'I bet you have.'

'He looks the same.'

Kim stared at her mother and, finally, burst out laughing. 'Sssshhhhhhh.'

'They can't hear me, Mum, they're in a different country.'

'You have to be discreet.'

Kim stared at her shoes, trainers spotted with fresh mud because she had stood in the flowerbed to see over the fence, and shook her head. 'No flies on you, Mum.'

Barbara made tea and brought out homemade biscuits, Cornish Fairings. Kim always stopped at two, but it wasn't easy. Mum made them with extra ginger, extra sugar, extra everything.

Whenever she visited, Barbara told Kim she looked thin and tried to force a third biscuit on her. 'I've made a dozen, look, and I can't eat ten.'

'Just because I stop at two doesn't mean you have to eat ten, Mum!'

'Well, you tell me what twelve minus two is, if you're so clever. You're like a rake.'

There was a silence between them.

Barbara said, 'You're judging me.'

'No, Mum, honestly. It's just that comments about my—'

'I mean about Wizard.'

A flicker, as Kim failed to recognize the rabbit's name. 'No. You've solved the problem of Wizard!'

'With my wand!' Barbara laughed, shocked at her own joke and how funny it was.

Kim sipped her tea. 'Are you hiding something? I know you were on the pensioner riot, if that's the issue.'

'Tssk.' Barbara looked genuinely upset at the phrase. 'Don't call me a pensioner—'

'—and it wasn't a riot, I know,' said Kim. 'That was just a silly comment I heard at the Falcon.' The pub in Sidford was famous for its weekly comedy night. 'It made us laugh, though.'

'Us? How is Anthony?'

'Oh, I went with a girlfriend, not Ant.' Kim did not want to elaborate. How could she describe the way his depression weighed him down, collapsing the Yorkshire giant like a Sixties' tower block? The fact that he was no longer violent towards her felt like feeble compensation.

She had only told one person about her wretched marriage. That person was Edward Temmis. She told him not with words but with actions and she knew she had used him. She knew he was insulated from her friendship circle, had never met or seen Anthony, knew none of his friends. Her customer, who happened to be Edward but might have been almost anyone, was the perfect repository for her anger and pain. She had made love to him ferociously on that one occasion, entering the empty house with him, allowing him to enter her; to sweep her clean of every resentment and regret. She had used him like a broom.

He had taken her – no, she had taken him – on the threadbare carpet of the front room in that ridiculous house. It was a hot summer afternoon and they had torn at each other's clothes. Later, as they hunted for each other's underwear, they had giggled. She had tried on his boxer shorts, stretched and baggy on her narrow hips. He had suggested trying to throw her knickers into the sea, 'an internationally recognized distress signal', and when they both laughed she was suddenly sad, knowing there was no future for this, not with her brute of a husband back at home.

As they laughed, she recognized the loneliness in his eyes and knew that he might come to love her, and do so quickly. That must not happen. The divorcé dad looking for a home who ended up in the arms (and legs) of the local estate agent – God almighty, who writes a love story like that? It would not even make a B-movie.

In the days that followed, she closed it down so completely he might have ended up thinking it was a dream. She became professional, untextable, reachable only through the assistant at work.

To her surprise, Edward bought the property. She wondered – flattering herself – whether some part of the purchase was his desire to memorialize that strange afternoon, to actually keep hold of the memory by buying the place. And then his son died. She was gone from his life completely.

'Where did you go?' her mother was asking.

'Eh?'

'Penny for your thoughts. You went a long way away just then. I was going to tell you about my boyfriend.'

'Ah! I did wonder how that was going. Where does he live? You said "local", didn't you?'

Her mother hummed and glanced away. 'That was a . . . little white lie to stop you jumping down my throat.'

'So how did you meet him?'

'His name is Henrik and he texted. We have a mutual friend and he was trying to organize a surprise birthday for her. As it turns out, when he said the friend's name, it wasn't someone I really knew too well. But we got chatting by email. He's a pilot.'

'A local pilot?'

'He's passing through Exeter next week! He spends a lot of time in Africa, which is why the emails have been sporadic lately. And he has something for me.'

'Mum, sorry, how long has this been going on?'

'Oh, probably a little while now. Maybe since late January?'

'Janu—'

'Don't you want to know what he's bringing me? I'll tell you. Another automaton for my collection, and this one is so special! He sent me photos. It's a duck.'

'He's bringing a robot duck on a plane?'

'Well, remember, pilots are trusted. But I'd heard about this duck because it has eighty moving parts inside it, and only ten of the ducks were ever made, and he thinks he might have found number eleven. It fits in his carry-on bag, he says.'

'I'm sure it does,' said Kimberley, eyes narrowing.

'Why are you so negative? Who are you to narrow your eyes at me like that?'

'Who am I? Try "your daughter", Mum.'

'But why do you think I can't be . . . active, when it's been more than twenty years since your dad went? And my painful hips, I mean, nobody sees a hip online. I can stand, I can walk, I can even shake my bottom a little if I grit my teeth. Kim, I don't feel sorry for myself, I don't get myself into trouble with things, I have friends, I don't burden you . . .'

'I know, I know,' said Kim. 'Mum, I know.'

'Next you'll be telling me it's a scam of some kind.'

Kim looked at her knees. She was married to a police officer, but she knew they got nowhere with these cases. Of course, she could not be certain it was a scam. One question would reveal the truth, but she did not know if she had the heart to ask it.

She looked at her watch. She would be two minutes late for her client if she left now.

'Don't jump down my throat if I just ask one question, Mum.'

Barbara sighed. 'I brought you here to ask about the rabbit, not to get the third degree about a duck.'

'Have you sent this man any money?'

Barbara flushed red and dropped her mug on the tray between them with such force that for a second they both stared to check the porcelain had not broken. Looking up, Kim saw real anger in her mother's face – the skin flushed all the way up to the roots of her hair, which seemed to go from grey to peroxide blonde in that instant, as if anger had taken ten years off her. Barbara stood.

'How *dare* you? As if I'm a child? As if I'm an idiot who needs looking after? Why would you *ever* insult me like this? Didn't you hear what I said? He's *giving* me something!'

Kim stood, too, slowly, so there was no returned aggression in her movement or her stance.

'I'm so sorry, Mum, I didn't mean to ask straight out like that.' Strangely, Barbara's reaction had eased her worries. The man might even be real, might even (million-to-one shot) be a good person. If her mother had been on her guard against a fraudster, what would be the problem with an email relationship? He might make her happy and he would never have the chance to take advantage.

'When are you meeting him?'

'I said! In a week, just over! Don't you listen, Kim?'

Kim looked at her watch. 'I have to pop to a client's. I didn't mean to sound a jarring note.'

Her mother shrugged stiffly and hugged her. They moved out of the house into the cold. The older woman seemed hesitant.

'My, darling, your waist is so thin.'

'Now you're judging, Mum.'

As Kim got to her car, she was conscious of her mother still standing in the middle of the garden path. She thought she heard Barbara speak, but whatever she had said was quiet enough to be masked by the car doors unlocking.

'Did you say something?'

Her mother looked down.

'Forty-three thousand pounds,' she repeated. 'That's how much I've sent him.'

Kim felt the car keys slide out of her hand and heard them drop at her feet.

*

BARBARA

Sorry to text you late at night but my daughter thinks your not real

HENRIK

What sort of crazy person is she? How does a person who's 'not real' reply to a message? I'm typing now!

. . .

See? Real. And we can be together soon.

BARBARA

😂😂😂🥹

HENRIK

Exactly. Busybody

BARBARA

😌

HENRIK

Not you her

BARBARA

Tell me about it

HENRIK

. . .

BARBARA

It's the money

HENRIK

. . .

BARBARA

She is SO upset. She was going to
shout at me for sending it to you,
I could tell, but then she saw
me crying.

HENRIK

Crying honey why? We'll be together in less than a fortnight and I for one CAN'T WAIT. Tell her Henrik loves her too and meeting her will be one of the most special moments of my life. And you will LOVE Dewey the duck.

BARBARA

. . .

HENRIK

I have your cash and will bring it in the most secure briefcase you have ever seen (as if you needed to ask!)

BARBARA

OK

HENRIK

Might even use handcuffs

BARBARA

You behave

CHAPTER NINE

Even the most gushing Facebook posts were painful to read now that Edward knew he would not go back to work. He was allowing himself a few minutes at the end of each shift to swipe through them on the refurbished smartphone he had finally got around to buying. He looked at the posts while sitting in his car in the garden centre staff car park. It was growing dark outside and the interior light was on, and the car heater too. He was determined only to look at the positive posts – he would not search out any of the vitriol directed at Agnes – but then decided he should sign out of the app for good.

Before he did, he noticed a tab that took him to Facebook Messenger and a few dozen messages sent personally to him. It had not occurred to him that people could try to reach him direct on the app, and he began to open them. The phone felt clunky and he tutted as he pressed the screen. It was more of the same – loyal listeners wishing him the best of luck, sad about his departure, angry about his treatment. There were only a few abusive ones.

> you w@nker being carried like that in the air by crumblies

It did not feel healthy to dwell on anything he saw, and even replying to the positive messages would only extend the conversations. After reading a dozen, he stopped.

He was about to sign out for the last time when he saw a name he recognized. Alongside the words 'Stevie Mason' was a picture of the young woman who had buttonholed him at the garden centre. In the profile photo she was gurning at a fisheye lens, a rose between her teeth, huge false lashes, blue eyes bright and wide. A gash of red lipstick was applied around her mouth, and in the background was a colour-saturated swimming pool.

Her message said:

> Any news of my granny please?

He typed:

> So sorry, no. Just got this.

Then, feeling he had sounded curt, he added:

> Hard for me to get near radio station for various reasons these days but okay, I will ring producer who is v loyal and helpful.

Edward was about to exit the app for the final time when a line appeared at the top of his screen:

> Stevie Mason is typing . . .

After a moment the message came back:

> Totally understood, knew it was a stretch.

> Can you remind me of Granny name?

> FFS Rebecca Mason,

He needed no help understanding 'FFS'. Edward sat in the car, looking glumly at the phone screen, regretting he had been unable even to pretend he had tried to assist the young woman. A fly had somehow got into the interior of the car and was bouncing backwards and forwards off the overhead light. He opened the car door and swished it clumsily into the cold of the car park. Flitting at the back of his brain was a tiny thing he could not make out, the blur of an idea not fully visible to his mind's eye.

He thought for some reason of a local wrestler. It had been a story in the paper. The guy's name was Denny Tajine, not in a million years a fighter's name, so the young man had asked for suggestions as to what he should call himself. The *Gazette* ran a competition and he ended up – from memory – Dent Machine, and that was that.

Why had that story come into his head at this moment?

Tajine – Machine . . .

He stared beyond the car, into the darkness of the garden centre car park.

Denny – Dent. Or was it Denting?

Denting Machine; Denny Tajine.

That was it. That was the little idea bumping against the interior light of his mind.

A person can have two names.

Edward reopened Messenger and found Stevie's 'FFS' message. In response he typed only six words.

> Did your granny live in Gulverton?

CHAPTER TEN

'We go to line one,' said Tessa K. 'Hello, Don!'

'*Hello Tessa and thank you for having me on.*'

'Don from Launceston.'

'*Just over the border.*'

'The Independent Republic of Cornwall!'

'*Born in Devon though, born in—*'

A crackle on the line threatened the call, but only for half a second.

'What would you like to say?'

'*I would like to ask you about the migrants and make a strange point, a slightly strange point but I think you'll agree with me that when I say this—*'

'Go ahead, Don! Hit me with it!'

'*Well, okay. We don't get so many on the coast of Devon. They all arrive in Kent.*'

'Because of the width of the Channel.'

'*Because of the width of the Channel being narrowest there, at Kent, Tessa, yes.*'

Silence.

'Go ahead, Don. What's your idea?'

'*It would be some method of moving them round the coast.*'

We could call it a redirection scheme. Because you see, I'm a farmer just across the Devon border—'

'Launceston—'

'—and we do, I hate to say it, we do need them. Now I know we'll have people howling about this—'

'Some, some will howl—'

'But they're not the ones who need the labour and I'll need young lads to pick my fruit in the summer and right now I'm thinking it's going to simply die and rot in the fields unless we start moving these poor people round. Also, Tessa—'

'Don, thank you. I have to cut in here because there's one more call before the news. Hello to Irene.'

In the control room, separated from his presenter by three thick panes of glass, Derrick Tidy said 'Line six' sharply to the work experience lad to his right. Trent had been at the station for two months and had apparently never seen the inside of a barber's. Or, for that matter, a razor, and he seemed to wear the same Pringle sweater every single day. But he did a solid enough job on the phones and was paid next to nothing. 'Line six, Irene in Brimstone,' he repeated as he put the fader up and flashed a green light on the presenter's desk.

'Trimstone,' Derrick said, correcting the name in Tessa's ear.

She began: 'How are you, Irene in Trimstone? We only have a minute.'

'Full of the joys. Lots to talk about.'

'Give me your top headline because we now have the news in forty seconds and you know I can't shift that, not even for you.'

'Top headline? Oh goodness. I'm eighty so I can't think quickly. Well, I've found love, how's that! Yes, at my age. I—'

There was a click and a scratch. Derrick turned angrily to the work experience lad. 'Have you done it again? Did you set it to pre-fade?'

'No, honestly, I didn't touch it.'

Tessa K was saying, 'Irene – Irene?' while looking through

the glass and holding out her hands, palms up, in an expression of 'What happened?' She turned back to the microphone.

'Hello there, Irene. Did we lose you?'

Derrick touched the talkback. 'Gone. Play trail, then news.'

The trail came on: 'Tomorrow's breakfast show features a special guest appearance from Devon pal of James Blunt . . .'

Tessa pressed on the talkback to her producer.

'Did Irene just blow up?'

Derrick flicked his eyes right to Trent, which told the story.

The trail ended: '. . . with your farming weather at ten past six, on RTR-92,' and Tessa introduced the news.

'The ten o'clock news in Devon with William Scott,' said a public school voice. Scott was in a booth downstairs.

'Sorry,' said Trent. 'I think I know what happened.'

'So long as it doesn't happen again,' Derrick said in a mock-exasperated voice, as if he was singing a song.

'How long is the news tonight?' Tessa was asking, but the direct-dial phone on Derrick's desk was ringing and he motioned for Trent to have the conversation with Tessa so he could take the call.

'Studio,' said Derrick.

'It's me, Edward.'

'Jesus!'

'No, honestly, please just hang up if I've put you in an awkward position.'

'You gave me a shock, that's all.'

'I'm still living and breathing.'

'Thank God for that. I'm in the control room – with Trent – but you must know that.'

'Trent?'

'Never mind.'

'Tessa's not there?'

'She's in her chair,' said Derrick quietly, and then whispered: '*Your* chair.'

'Okay . . . I know you've only got a couple of minutes, Derrick, and I need you to do something for me. Look something up.'

'Go ahead. Anything.' Derrick frowned.

At the other end of the line, Edward understood that Derrick would not enjoy this. Edward was *persona non grata* at the station now. He would certainly forfeit his payoff if the station discovered he had contacted his old producer. But he could trust Derrick, fundamentally a decent person, one of the best he had ever worked with.

'Derrick, one of our listeners died. Her granddaughter has asked me to look into it. I didn't think I could help until I was given an envelope with her name on. A letter came to the station marked "In Desperation from Riva".'

'What did it say?'

'Well that's the problem,' said Edward, in a tone of deep frustration. 'The letter got lost or she forgot to enclose it, I don't know. So there's only the envelope! Do you remember Riva from Gulverton? I do, but I can't remember what she called us about.'

'Riva? Odd name.'

'Her actual name is Rebecca Mason. She called us under "Riva". It used to be a common nickname if you were called Rebecca.'

'Never knew that,' said Derrick, voice lowered to a whisper. 'You want me to search the calls?'

Every caller's name and number, and a summary of their on-air comment, had been logged for the best part of a decade in a folder labelled (of course) THE_CALLS. Edward heard Derrick pat the keyboard at speed, apparently mistyping the name at first, then swearing and going at the keys again.

'This computer is so bloody slow. Now the cursor's stuck.'

Abashed at the inconvenience he was causing, Edward murmured into the phone: 'So sorry, Derrick. No panic this end.' He guessed the producers had failed to make the case for the rickety programme PC to be upgraded and attached to the network. 'A filing cabinet would be quicker,' Edward added.

'I'm letting it whirr. Smoke coming out the back,' Derrick commentated wryly. 'Well, well. Riva. Yes. Lucky for us that the name is unusual. She did call. March last year – no the year before – Riva from Gulverton, complaint about noise from farms. April – Riva again, complaint about farm traffic. I remember that one,' said Derrick, 'because she used to be a farmer herself and she was angry that they kept making trips with their loaders half-empty.'

'Anything else?'

'Last year she called three – no, four – times. All standard. Mother's Day wishes to her granddaughter, which seems like the wrong way round. Angry about the River Otter Beaver Trial. That was October. Just a couple of others, nothing much.'

'What were the others?'

'The news is ending, hang on . . . hang on, madam.'

Edward listened. So Derrick was pretending he was speaking to a woman? Was that how 'ex' this ex-presenter was? He heard: 'Trent, is the station ident ready?'

Edward's voice was guilty. 'Sorry, Derrick.'

'Was that okay? Helpful? Miss having you around, boss.'

'It was a fuck-up, the whole thing, wasn't it?'

'It's life, I guess.'

'Did you say two more?'

'What?'

'Two more times she called?'

'Oh, yes. One more than a year ago. One a bit further back. The dates are a mess. She rang about a drone club. She was very angry about people flying drones at the back of her house, and when she went to the council she said she'd had threats from them.'

'Wait, what?'

'A drone club. They must have had some fun and games in the land near her home. I'm guessing she got them shut down because she only rang once about that . . . now, wait, actually I do remember this. She was very upset, she might even have been crying. She kept saying no one cared what happened to her.'

'Good God. This is really helpful. And?'

'And?'

'Sorry, there was one other?'

'Oh, just that film competition we did. Ages ago. You choose a film and they answer three questions about it. She did well. You were reading out lines of dialogue and she got them all, I think.'

'What was the film?'

'I can't remember. Can you? Hey, I gotta go . . . bye, Mrs Sharman.'

'Mrs Sharman? Oh . . . thanks Derrick. Miss you, mate.'

'Mutual. Anytime.'

'There won't be another time, I promise.'

'There can be. Honestly. I want to help. Let me know what you need and I'm here.'

'One thing, just quickly?'

'Sure.'

'Could you look out for the letter they lost downstairs? Security thought it was a big joke. The envelope was marked "In Desperation from Riva". But when I got it, it was empty. Maybe the letter will turn up still?'

'Don't worry. If it's in the building, I'll find it.'

'Cheers, mate.'

Edward pressed the red circle on his smartphone screen to end the call. His brow was creased, the skin lined with deep furrows of puzzlement and worry. A row with a drone club? He pictured middle-aged men tramping into a field and sending humming lumps of metal airborne. Maybe photographing the land from the air, is that what they did? And they had *threatened her*, an old lady? This could be a strong lead into the mystery of Rebecca's death – but surely her family would have known if the dispute had turned into something so distressing that she would set her house ablaze? He would ask Stevie.

When he had messaged her from the garden centre car park to ask if her granny lived in Gulverton, she had replied within five seconds.

Oh my God, YES. How did you know that?

They swapped numbers and Stevie had called him instantly. He told her about the A4 envelope in reception.

'Jesus Christ on a bike, that's *it!*' Stevie cried, and immediately added: 'Forgive the blasphemy but – Granny always used big envelopes. Oh, I wish to God we had the letter.'

'If there ever was one.'

What he wanted now was to put on an old TV detective show and think. Derrick's words about Rebecca Mason's calls to the show were strangely touching. Without Edward even being very much aware of her, Riva had reached out again and again to her favourite presenter for solace and advice. And sometimes just to sound off. Farm traffic! But that was what his show was there for.

Edward thought tenderly of his late father. On school holidays in the Seventies, his dad, a maths teacher, always had a habit of taking himself off to think. He would peel away from the family and sit himself at a poolside chair or café table and then, spectacles slid halfway down his nose, he would work away at notepads which the rest of the family never saw. What was he doing with that pencil and eraser – projecting carbon levels, taking pi to another ten places? There was something of that in Edward, the desire to sit and think and work an idea through on a blank sheet of paper. He was not up for the tyranny of call-and-respond social media, and he knew now he was not one for group activities: clubs, parties and committees. He had seen the same positive trait with his darling Matty. His son had had friends but was not wildly popular. He had wanted to be an inventor. His favourite design tools were a 2B pencil and a ruler.

Edward wept quietly now, remembering his Matty's attempts at draughtsmanship on large sheets of paper. He was due at the garden centre at ten thirty tomorrow, the second shift in, so there was time to cry and time for a *Columbo*. He still used DVDs, and the squat player sat untidily on the floor below the TV on a pile of old movie magazines. He chose the episode 'Dead Weight' from the first season. But as he slid the silver disc into the DVD player, his hand stopped.

Above and below him the house was making a yawning noise unlike any he had heard before.

It was as if the building was grieving, crying for attention before its inevitable demise. Not for a second had Edward thought the house could actually go off the cliff in his lifetime – there was twenty-five yards of garden to erode first, and he reckoned that would take a quarter-century because council planners would always be over-cautious – but now, as he heard the beams yowl and gasp around him, he suddenly wondered if the whole place might just collapse in one go. It was strange – once your only child had gone, your own life counted for so much less. Even if the house had told him direct that it would be at the bottom of the cliff in sixty seconds, he still would have walked to the front door and grabbed his keys and phone on the way.

Grabbed his keys and phone.

The disc was sucked into the player. *Columbo* was starting, but the phrase would not leave him alone. The images on the television were an opening scene he knew well: a woman in a red scarf bobbing in a small boat, shots of the boardwalk in a small, gentrified harbour, close-ups of an American flag on the house, interiors of the house showing pictures of a military man with medals on the wall. But he was not really watching. *Grabbed his keys and phone.*

'Edward,' Stevie said as soon as she picked up.

'My old producer was brilliant,' he told her. 'Your granny called my programme four or five times, and one of the calls was interesting. Might need to discuss it with you.'

'What was it about?'

'She may have had enemies. I'll tell you when I know more. Short version is, I had an idea, a way of cracking this.' (On the TV the woman in the red scarf was saying, 'I'm sure I just saw a man get shot in that house,' and he was suddenly conscious he must sound like an American detective). 'It's like a puzzle. I was thinking about the fire. So – I mean – if there was an emergency here, in my home, and I'm leaving, do I just run out? No. Even a fire? If she was asleep, woken by the fire, doesn't she at least grab her phone and her keys. Didn't you say they were by her bed?'

'Yes, and she left everything. But—'

'It just says to me, you might be right. If the fire is an accident, you grab your stuff on the way out—'

'But that doesn't make any sense. If it was her, the fire . . . I mean, if Granny bloody did herself in by starting the fire, why would she jump?'

He fell silent. 'I think she hoped she would just fall asleep and drift away, overcome by the smoke. But fires are violent, fires make a noise. This one moved quickly and she was driven out of the window. Thus, no keys or phone.'

'She jumped to kill herself? But that's so awful.'

'She wanted everyone to think it was an accident, maybe because it's less hurtful for your family. By the way – I wanted to ask. You said she had a problem with her hands?'

'Rheumatoid arthritis, made her fingers all twisted.'

'And she couldn't – what, do her knitting? Use a knife and fork?'

'She could hold a fork, but she would always switch it from one hand to another because it hurt.'

'She didn't write Christmas cards?'

'Just a scribble.'

'She wouldn't have written a letter, would she?'

At the other end of the line, Stevie breathed heavily, as if understanding was coming to her in pulses. 'Anything longer than a line she dictated into her computer.'

His voice registered the excitement he suddenly felt. 'So that's where the lost letter is. That's why it was an A4 envelope, by the way. I still do that – if I print something off the computer, I reach for a big letter envelope. Doesn't make sense, but there we go. It was a printed letter.'

'The letter may have been typed on the computer, but the computer was in the house, and the house pretty much burned down.'

'At least it must be worth a look.'

Catching on to the possibilities here, Stevie said, 'If it's not melted by the fire, I could take the hard drive out. She used an old PC with a tower that sat on the floor. But we'd have to get into the house. It's unsafe. The police sealed it and then, once they'd investigated, the fire service put up a load of hoardings and warning signs.'

'Surely, your dad can get in. It's his house now.'

'Not until the will goes through. Don't ask me how long that'll be – my dad said something about probate, executors, I don't know. It has to be sold before the estate is passed on because of tax. Mind you, it's got fire and water damage throughout, so God knows who will buy it. I suppose there's insurance too, if Granny actually had any.' She sounded annoyed that she had not thought of the computer, and he suddenly wondered if this was competitive for Stevie, if it mattered to her to be first to the answers.

'In which case,' he said, 'I know exactly who can help us.'

CHAPTER ELEVEN

Edward was early. He heard the car coming from the other side of Sidmouth and knew it was Kim's. The motor roared in the cramped high street a mile away, a frustrated moan of highly tuned engine amid the stucco storefronts, and then he heard the throaty gasp and deep *zzzzummm* of heavy tyre on tarmac as the driver shifted through the gears after the tight right turn onto the promenade.

He had got here early after visiting the cemetery. There had been an unfortunate quirk of timing – this morning he and his ex-wife had come to Matty's headstone simultaneously. It had not happened before. But they stood there together in silence. Never would they have bickered in front of their son.

All she said was, 'The summer will be hard. Hot weather makes everything feel empty.'

The grave was in Topsham, south-east of Exeter, at the point where the River Exe widened as it began the last five-mile stretch before becoming sea at Exmouth. They had found a church with a graveyard above the water. Matty had loved the water.

'It's a calming view for him,' Tara said as they both stared at the stone.

Edward had wanted to respond, 'He's not here,' because he

felt the one place he could be sure his son was not resting was under this damp lump of gravedigger sod. But the two of them had argued enough for a lifetime.

The only exchange had been in the instant before they parted. 'Anything from the police?' Tara blinked against the sun, hand shading her eyes.

'No cameras and no clues,' said Edward, shaking his head. 'If only I could remember something.'

'Have they still got his bike?'

'They say it's evidence. I don't think we'll see it again.'

'How's your head?'

'The hearing won't come back, but I have this.' He touched the hearing aid.

'Oh. I don't even see it.' Then she added sadly, 'Not sure if I could bear to have his bike back.' They stood for a moment, stock-still, then parted without touching.

Now Edward heard Kim's sports car from where he stood at the top of Jacob's Ladder. His thoughts of Matty – of how he loved to be taken for a hot chocolate at the Clock Tower Café, how they would share one of those enormous pieces of banana cake – were so intense today he had to blink them away, tossing his head and closing his eyes to ensure his mind knew there was no Matty any more, not here in the café, not anywhere in the real world.

He had been watching a man kitesurfing. The man was far out at sea on his own, at least a couple of hundred yards from the deserted beach line. He had not tried the sport, but Matty had always wanted to. There was a fascination for them both, and they would often sit in the grounds of the Clock Tower and commentate inexpertly. In a rough sea, a bad kitesurfer will appear to be fighting the wind and the waves at the same time. But a good one stayed in motion by skimming the surface, using the wind against the water. Because his son was far too young to be allowed to rent a kite, they had sketched designs for the fabric.

'I will get you exactly this design when you start,' Edward had said. 'I promise it.'

How many promises like that had been broken by the hit-and-run driver who had plunged into their lives for a fraction of a second that Saturday? The person out at sea was hanging onto his kite – not quite a kite, not quite a parachute – for dear life as the wind and water worked together. Matty had not even had a chance to hang on for dear life, being dead by the time the ambulance crew searched for a pulse.

The kitesurfer must have been doing 25 mph at times, skiing over the water, skimming the surface like a thrown pebble. Once or twice the wind dropped and the fabric fell into the water. After a moment, the man would somehow guide the air back under the chute and then hang on as it billowed back to a vertical. Every five minutes or so the wind was so powerful the skier shot out of the water, pulled into the air . . . *Oh, Matty, you would have loved this so much.*

He turned to search for Kim's car. The red-roofed Porsche sat squat in a line of traffic as it crawled towards his end of the beach. He heard it revving, and had the impermissible thought: *She drives like a bloke.*

Winter left its mark on a coastal town. No one bought ice cream. Even the batter on fresh fish did not fizz as in summer. Chained up in silos by the sea wall, families of deckchairs gave off the odour of rotting canvas. Even a single day of warm English sun would bring their colours back from dead grey, but they were weeks away from revival.

It had started to drizzle when the Porsche finally slipped into a gap at the side of the road directly below the Clock Tower. Edward couldn't see it, but he heard the engine cut as he jogged down the steps. He always felt Kim's purchase of the Porsche was as much for her business as herself; the car was seen as a sign that this likeable businesswoman was doing well for her customers and her county.

Ten feet below him, the driver's door popped open. He was about to call 'Kim!', when he saw that the driver was not Kim. Edward slowed on the stairs, wondering if the man would hear him and look up. As Edward stood above the car, the top of the driver's head emerged into view first. The hair was thin and suspiciously black. At the crown was a bald patch so perfectly square that Edward thought a protractor would come up with four nineties. The car looked too small for him. The man's body, as he pulled himself clumsily past the open driver's door, was shaped like an anvil.

Wasn't this Kim's car? There was no other red Porsche in Sidmouth that he had ever seen. He had not seen any other Porsche, for that matter. So even though Edward could not see the number plate from his elevated position, he knew this was Kim's car. He froze. A gust of wind noisily opened the front of Edward's puffer jacket and with sudden horror he realized that if the car was Kim's, the driver had to be her husband.

The anvil did not look up. In thick boots – cop shoes – and carrying a holdall, he made a mess of trying to step onto the kerb and duck underneath the lowest rungs of Jacob's Ladder, nearly slipping on a wet patch as he hopped onto the walkway and then banging his head and cursing as he made his way directly below a stationary Edward.

Edward might not recognize Anthony, having never clapped eyes on him before, but there was a good chance the policeman would know the radio presenter. 'My local radio station features celebrities who are famous throughout Sidmouth,' Edward had once heard a pub comedian joke. So he did not want Anthony to see his face. He dared not even breathe in case the man looked up at him. He crossed onto the pebbled beach with a holdall in his left hand.

What on earth was he doing?

Edward suddenly worried that he might be about to take his own life. The sea was freezing cold and Anthony Cobden was walking directly towards it, fully clothed in black trousers and a black canvas jacket inflated by the wind, his big boots clacking in the pebbles. Now he was on the short line of dark red sand before the water. There was no one beyond him except a couple of fishing boats on the distant horizon and, in the distance, the kitesurfer who was still hopping up and down across the waves, totally in control of his movement on the sea. It almost looked as if Anthony had come to watch from a distance. But why?

He set the bag down on the sand and started waving. He must have waved for a full minute.

Then he left the holdall on the sand, stalked back to the Porsche, revved it and drove off with a skid.

Edward was at the top of the steps. He looked out to sea and saw the kitesurfer was wrapping up the kite and beginning to swim back to shore. Ten minutes later they stood chest-high in the water. He peered. It was not a man at all.

It was Kim.

Fighting the tide as she walked, raising her knees to reduce the resistance of the water, she quickened her step as she emerged from the sea. Pinching at folds of her wetsuit to loosen its grip on her skin, she jogged to the holdall. She unzipped the bag and shook her head. Then she looked around, and finally upwards. Edward did not want to wave, so he nodded his head. She gave him a strange look, almost a look of resentment, as if he was not supposed to have seen that mini-drama played out below him, and she wished he had not seen it because now she would have to explain it.

Then she called up, 'Twenty minutes, mate. Thirty max.'

It was a different Kim who sat opposite him in the Clock Tower Café. She had changed and tied up her hair. They had taken the corner table, although surely they had nothing to hide now.

'You arrived early,' she said. 'Didn't we say twelve?'

'Oh. Yeah. But I'm not working today. I just came when I

was ready. I got the bus down here. I had a couple of chores to do in town.'

'I like the idea of "in town", as if Sidmouth is the centre of London. What did you do – visit the Royal Opera House and get your hair done at Toni and Guy?'

'There is a Toni and Guy in Sidmouth, as it happens.' He was somewhat amazed to hear defensiveness in his voice.

'So you saw me . . . and him . . .' Kim was looking down at her cup, stirring a single sachet of brown sugar into her latte, still stirring long after it was dissolved.

'I don't know what I saw.'

'You saw my car—'

'Yes. It was definitely your car because it's the only Porsche in Sidmouth.'

'—with my husband in it.' She shook her head. 'You know, I don't want to sound self-pitying or whatever, but a depressed husband is like a heavy suitcase, padlocked, which you just have to carry everywhere.'

'And what's inside the suitcase?'

'No idea. It never opens up. Just weighs a ton. So today,' she continued, her words picking up speed as if she needed to get them out, 'he finds a holdall with a towel in it at home and decides I must have forgotten it, so he's going to drive all the way here and dump it on the sand. Then he's going to wave at me for about five minutes till I have no choice but to come out of the sea, even though this is my one escape from everything else that's going on. Then when I start trudging out of the water, he drives off anyway.' She pressed her lips together, still not meeting his eye.

It was blinding, the realization Edward had while he looked at Kim: his feelings for her were powerful, and no period of absence would break them. He focused on her compact face, framed by wet hair; the sharp angle of the cheekbones, the chin that came to a definite point, the nose, the mouth, the lips. She radiated competence and warmth. Her mouth was full. The tidy nose wiggled a little as she spoke. Her skin tanned easily, and she had caught the sun even today. Her eyes – she had a way of looking at him; the pupils wide, the irises unbroken circles of smashed emerald. Her attention was undivided. He saw himself in the black of her eyes, the delivery man in a Ring doorbell, waiting to see if someone was home for him.

'Have I got cake on my face?'

'No. Why?' he asked.

'You were staring.'

He changed the subject. 'Is Anthony still working as a policeman?'

'He's not even working as a human being. He has a new psychiatrist and new drugs, and the force has given him a month before they put him back on the streets, God help us.' She shivered. 'I sound like such a bitch.'

'He hit you. So, no, you really don't.' Edward pointed out of the window. 'I didn't know you did the para-kite thing.'

'Kitesurfing. I'll be honest. When . . . when that thing happened with you – I don't mean "that thing", I mean when you lost Matty – and stuff was going wrong for me at my end too . . . Well, I just needed something that took me away from everything. And I realized I could literally hide in the sea. I had done kitesurfing when I was at college. An old boyfriend taught me. So I took it up again.'

'I'm totally ashamed to say I was looking out to sea and made all the wrong assumptions. Thought you were a bloke.'

'My boobs aren't that small.'

'They are from a distance.'

She suddenly laughed so hard she had to choke back her tea to avoid spitting it out. 'Fair enough.'

'I was stereotyping, I guess. Person fighting the waves and wind, using a small kite, must be a bloke. That's my generation. It's a fair cop but the Milk Tray adverts were to blame.'

'Firstly, you're not that old, you lovely man. And that's not the person you are, Edward, my love.' Out of view of the two staff members at the glass cake display behind her, Kim reached out and touched his hand. 'You have a tenderness.'

He looked down at her hand on his. 'That feels quite good.'

'For me, too,' she said. 'Something about another person's skin.'

'You're married, so you have it on tap.'

'Don't make me laugh. There's nothing more lonely than a marriage where there's no . . .'

She stopped, so he completed the thought. 'Skin.'

They sat in silence.

'I didn't even need the bloody towel,' Kim said eventually. 'We have a beach hut up the way. One of the ones that got blown away and rebuilt in 2016, do you remember? All my stuff is in there. He knows that. What was he doing, trying to catch me out?'

'Could it be like a control thing?' said Edward thoughtfully. 'He wants to check you're actually doing what you said you were doing.'

'He's always saying I'm going to leave him. I'm always saying I'm not. It's his depressed brain talking. How could that happen to someone overnight?'

'What do you mean?'

'A breakdown, or whatever it is he's had, going from a thug to a lamb. His psychiatrist – when he can actually get in to see the guy, which is about once every six weeks – says ninety-nine per cent of cases are workplace stress.'

'He's seen too many lifeless bodies.'

'Charming.'

'Not yours, I didn't mean that.' Now it was Edward who laughed loudly, causing a pair of female pensioners to turn their heads. 'I think I'm disturbing my two listeners over there.'

'I'm sure your audience was bigger than that.'

He smiled.

She added, 'I bet you miss your show.'

'I do. I miss it so much.' He told her about the garden centre. He said he was enjoying the job but knew he was failing to convince her. To change the subject he asked about Barbara.

'Mum?' Kim laughed, but it was hollow. 'Now, *she's* a full-time job. You won't believe what she did. She was looking after the neighbour's rabbit and she found it dead on the lawn. Apparently a fox had savaged it and tried to bury the body. The ground was dug up. So she bought another one. She bought another one! Like they do in sitcoms! And the new one was exactly the same. But then the neighbours come back from holiday and she overhears them laughing about her. And they clearly know the new rabbit is not *their* rabbit. And she's upset so I have to go round to speak to them . . .'

She broke off, trying to suppress laughter.

'Go on,' said Edward, 'because this is brilliant.'

'They say, okay – their rabbit died before they went on holiday. They buried it. Then Mum, not knowing this, thinks she's supposed to be looking after it and reckons they've forgotten to ask. She actually puts food in the hutch without working out the rabbit is gone. Then a fox digs up the dead body. Eats half of it. Mum thinks the rabbit got killed on her watch and buys a new one. They come back, and of course they *know* exactly what she's done.'

'Oh, that's superb.'

'And the best line, when I asked Mum how she managed to feed a rabbit that was already dead and buried? "I just thought it was hiding". She actually said that. So I've given the neighbours flowers and honestly, there's nothing but sympathy for her, but she's just so . . . ashamed. Is that a thing in old age, shame?'

'Is she that old?'

'Turning seventy-one next week.'

'On the cusp.'

'She did her best and it went wrong. Exactly like the other thing I'm dealing with. Oh, now you're going to ask and I have promised not to say.'

'Don't then.'

There was a long silence, maybe thirty seconds, before Kim spoke again.

'I think I have to tell you. I have to tell someone.'

'Dead rabbit, depressed husband. This can't be any more dramatic.'

'Oh, it is. Believe me, it is.' Kim twisted her wedding ring as if working out whether she could breach a confidence. 'I'll tell you. Because I have to. And if you tell anyone, I'm going to come up to Ladram Bay and give your house one last shove over the cliff.'

'Go on.'

'She's found love. It was an online thing. I still can't work out how it started, but it seems to have been a text at first.'

'Who from?'

'A pilot.'

'Okaaaay . . .' The word was stretched with Edward's scepticism. 'A pilot.'

'Yeah, right.'

'Why are they always pilots?'

'It's so obvious, isn't it? "I love you Barb and I can't wait for us to meet" – there's a clue there – "but I need some money to sort out my passport."'

'Barb?'

'No one calls her Barb! She's already sent him two-thirds of all the spare cash she has in the world.'

'Oh, no! And you've told her it's a hoax, or—'

Kim told him, 'I have been, let's say, super-sceptical and a little cross. But she's clinging on to the idea that this wonderful man will arrive at Exeter Airport this weekend.'

'Presumably when you go to meet him and he's not there, we hear the sound of a penny dropping.'

'Oh, I won't be allowed to go. And it's not a penny that's dropped.' She closed her eyes briefly. 'It's more than forty thousand pounds.'

He stared, open-mouthed.

Kim put her head in her hands. 'How can I be cross with her? She lives alone, she assumes someone messaging online is like someone knocking at the door. In the old days you would start from a position of trust and work backwards. We do the opposite. The only reason Mum's heart isn't broken is she's still determined to believe this guy exists. A pilot in Africa with a valuable wooden duck who got stranded in Nairobi when his passport was cloned by child traffickers.'

'I'm not understanding the duck thing.'

'She collects these old, elaborate models called automata.'

'This stuff is all based in Russia, I heard. What is it called – catfishing? Romance scamming? It's apparently so common that anyone using a computer will get hit three times a week minimum.'

'How do you know that?'

'Saw it online somewhere.'

'But that's the point, isn't it? You saw it online and you believe it. She sees him online and we tell her she's been a fool.'

'Poor dear.'

'Me or her?'

'Fifty–fifty. You're the one I love, though.'

He had said it. It took Edward a second to realize. He looked down at his coffee and saw he hadn't touched it since the first mention of Barbara. Kim's cheeks flushed. He had blundered.

'Y-you can't say that,' she stammered.

'I blurted it out and I'm sorry.'

'It causes me pain.'

'Me, too. I'm sorry.' Quickly he changed the subject. 'Listen, I wanted to see you because I need your help with something. A listener who died. Her granddaughter needs to get into her house. There was a fire and it's all sealed.'

'Why does she want to get in?'

'It's all rather sad. The police, et cetera, say it was all an accident. This girl—'

'Ahem.'

'—young woman, I should say . . . she thinks her granny might have done away with herself. And she wants to know why.'

'Has she got any idea? It's a strange way to go, setting fire to your house.'

'Is it? You tip the candles over, go to bed, take a sleeping pill, the smoke comes and you never wake up. And the key thing is this – your family have no clue you made that choice, because it all looks accidental.'

'But why?'

'She was in some kind of development dispute with a drone club. I can't believe they would have tried to kill her. I just reckon the nastiness got to this poor lady, she felt embattled and lost her mind. There was a lot of odd behaviour before she died. The funny thing is that she wrote me a letter asking for help. I never got it. It'll be on her computer.'

'Won't that have melted?'

'Maybe. But I feel I should help this young woman. I like her. She's odd. Small and intense. Works in local council HR computing or something. She has that illness which makes her swear like a trooper – although, because her dad's a vicar, she then follows up with a Bible verse. Why are you laughing?'

'You should hear what you just said. It's the funniest thing I've ever heard.'

'Not the dead granny bit.'

'No,' said Kim in an indignant voice, 'obviously not that. So you want me to get you and her into the house?'

Edward nodded.

Kim explained, 'I'm guessing it's still wrapped up in the will proceedings. You need fire service permission, and you'll need to sign something waiving any claims if the building collapses around your ears. The main thing is to reach the solicitors who are executing the will.'

'Oh.' He sounded defeated. 'Shall I ask her if she knows who they are? But I don't think she will.'

'She won't. But I already do.'

'Really?'

'Edward, this is a small town and I'm the biggest independent estate agent. There is only one lawyer who does estate work when there's "dispute or damage", as they call it. If a house blows up at the moment of death, who did it technically belong to? Which is literally the situation here. So there's one expert, and if you tell me the address I'll call him for you and we'll get in.'

'Oh, you don't have to come.'

'I'm afraid I do.'

CHAPTER TWELVE

More than a mile back from the sea, Gulverton was a hamlet that still considered itself the posher part of Sidmouth. Fields to the west gave a clear line of sight to the afternoon sun. The houses were sizeable. The only newsagent stocked *Country Living* and *Your Home Furnishings*. But the tourists never stopped here, instead gunning past in estate cars with surfboards on the roof. Some Gulverton residents wanted to believe they were part of a free republic and had nothing to do with the coastal tourist spot down the road. For others, proximity to Sidmouth was the whole reason for being there. That second group were mainly the blow-ins, retirees who had worked until the Noughties and seized their pension pots before the financial crisis destroyed them. They swaggered into the only pub with the confidence of a gang of Clark Gables, immune to the quiet resentment.

If there was an old Gulverton and a new Gulverton, Rebecca 'Riva' Mason had definitely been the old part. For her, a trip into Sidmouth was like going to Manchester – she feared mugging and noise. She'd lived a quiet life but was friendly to all and sundry, and supported every local cause. Her sudden violent death had been a tragedy like no other in Gulverton. A wave of grief had swept the residents.

They were not wholly insulated from the rest of the world, because the main road roared past the western edge of the hamlet. If you missed the tiny right into Gulverton Lane on the way out of Sidmouth, you either had to make a nasty U-turn on the brow of the hill just beyond, or wait another half-mile for a safer place to double back. It was amazing how many delivery drivers took the first option. Occasionally Gulverton residents would hear the squeal of brakes and shouting on the road, and tut about how dangerous the world beyond them could be.

The last two cars to arrive in Rebecca Mason's driveway that day had made the navigational error but taken the conservative route to correct it. Climbing out of Edward's blue Toyota with him were Kim and Stevie; a minute behind them was Seamus Schwarz, the son of Mike Schwarz, the solicitor Kim had correctly guessed would have the details of Mrs Mason's will on his desk. He emerged from a battered green Mini.

The person who arrived before them had travelled from Sidmouth fire station with a clutch of yellow building site helmets that he yanked from the passenger seat of his red van with one hand using the chin-straps. Rotund and red-faced, with a Santa Claus beard, the man had arrived at least fifteen minutes early and only emerged from the van when everyone else was present. He set a large helmet on his head that said DEVON FIRE in silver letters across the dark blue.

Stretching his arms and legs, Edward regarded the front of Rebecca's home. It really was something. The building had the look of a farmhouse; the original owners might have tended the surrounding land before the main road cut off the farmer from his fields.

The large front porch jutted proud of the frontage like the chin of a champion boxer, but it was now covered by a yellow-painted chipboard hoarding and, above a series of digits painted roughly on the surface, a sign said: STRANGERS KEEP OUT. RING THIS NUMBER FOR ACES.

'Access, must be,' murmured Edward to Kim.

'Oh, I thought it was some sort of secret card-game thing,' she whispered back, 'but thank you for mansplaining.'

He looked up at the pitched roof. At first he thought it had bowed with age, but now he wondered if the fire inside the house had made the surface of the tiling sink like a cake in the rain. Certainly, some of the tiles appeared to have melted into each other. He noticed a window in the eaves that looked like part of an attic conversion, so he guessed there were three levels at least.

'Two hundred years old?' said Kim, not expecting an answer. 'Glad you brought me. I'd love to sell this. Weird mix of stone and brick, and I adore the little Romeo and Juliet balcony by the upstairs window. What we call blind building – almost as if three different sets of builders just whacked it all together, and none of them could see what the other was doing.'

'You're such an estate agent,' said Edward with affection.

He was gradually picking up clues to the disaster that had occurred inside the house. Blackened window frames and soot marks shaped like flames on the exterior said there had been a major blaze here.

The fireman was speaking. He had a way of straightening his spine every few seconds, as if he wanted to be taller, but it made his voice rasp as he did it, and sometimes the rasp turned into a smoker's cough. His introductions were elaborate and he had a list in his hand. He began with his name – 'Tick Goldsworthy, Devon Fire' – repeated several times as he offered all four a long, energetic, grippy handshake, while handing out the other yellow helmets.

'Okay, I'll be leading on safety,' he announced at last. And then, before Seamus could turn the dial in the padlock that kept the hoarding around the house secure, Tick launched into a formal briefing which he read from a piece of paper. He diverted into an explanation of his nickname that was laboured and unnecessary – as a young fireman his watch had made a loud ticking sound. Edward saw Kim's eyes roll and wondered if, despite the splendour of the house, she was regretting coming.

Briefing over, they gathered around the padlock on the hoarding that covered the porch. After a few failed attempts to set the correct combination, Seamus loudly exclaimed 'You spiteful tosser!', which would be the only words he would utter during the entire outing. Then the combination was unscrambled, Tick made another annoying joke and they filed through the gap in the chipboard.

'Heads, obviously,' said Tick. 'Another padlock here, same combination I gather.'

This lock was holding a brace against the front door. One end was clamped inside the letterbox. Seamus snapped it open first time and immediately produced the house keys.

'Well done, Seamus,' said Kim in the manner of a parent. Edward had earlier been told that Seamus was being trained up by his dad, and now he wondered if part of the apprenticeship was learning how to shout 'you spiteful tosser' at padlocks.

They gasped when they entered the interior. Tick did not need to say 'Fire damage extensive', although he did. Briefly close to Tick, Edward wondered if the odour of smoke and sweat was from the house or the man's heavy jacket. For a moment he felt his stomach turn. The hallway was roomy, like a reception space. There were wooden beams in the ceiling.

'Two hundred years ago those would have been straight. Look at the way they've settled and shifted as the house has moved,' Kim whispered to Edward.

'Thank God they didn't go up, because that might have taken the whole village,' said Tick. 'But look how black they are.'

'The wooden beams were black to start with,' Kim said more loudly. 'This was the fashion in the Fifties and Sixties. Paint it black, like the Rolling Stones. Not sure I like it but I don't think it's fire damage.'

'She's right,' said Stevie. 'They were black before the fire.'

Tick seemed not to hear. They were bunched in the space, moving forwards slowly, respectfully. The entire area – carpet, walls, ceiling – was patterned with soot and scorch marks.

Edward looked around, checking Stevie's inscrutable expression. He had a moment where he contemplated something bigger than the situation that the five of them had walked into. This was his life, he thought. This house. The outside intact but boarded up; the inside a blackened hull that no one could access without a combination. But there was hope. The house would be rebuilt. Someone would buy it and live there again. He would live his own life again. And he could live for his dead son. It would have been easy to have avoided helping Stevie, but what would be left of him if he ran from everyone?

As they moved deeper into the property, turning a corner, the space brightened. A lead-lined window that had been cracked by the heat let light in from the back garden. Tick was talking (of course) about fire damage and the way the filling in old armchairs would burn down – 'we call it deliquesce' – into a chemical so poisonous that a single sofa could have wiped out a village in Vietnam. Kim stifled a chuckle. Edward glanced back at Stevie again, and was shocked to see silent tears running down her cheeks.

Edward asked her, 'Are you okay?'

'It's bringing it all back, being here.'

'Who's crying?' asked Tick.

'No one,' said Stevie.

Now they had a choice between stairs, kitchen, and a narrow front room off to the left.

'So what would you call that first bit of the house, if you were selling it?' Edward asked Kim, hoping to distract the rest of the group from Stevie's distress.

'Reception space, dinner space, banquet area, anything,' Kim replied. 'Things always sell if you call them a "former" something.

I might go with "former stable". Leave aside the damage and you have a wonderful house here. I could sell this in a day, providing the searches don't uncover anything untoward.'

'That may be the issue,' said Edward, thinking about his suspicions over the drone club and wondering whether permission to fly drones over a neighbourhood would be a factor in the sale of a property.

Stevie's sniffles were suddenly the only noise they could hear.

'Is the young lady okay?' said Tick. 'She's so short, I can't see her.'

'I'm so sorry, Stevie,' said Kim. 'I didn't mean to come over all businesslike. This isn't a house to sell, it's your granny's grave.'

Tick said, 'I'm aware I had to escort you, but remind me of the purpose of the visit please?'

Kim got in ahead of Edward. 'Valuation for the estate.'

'And you're the estate agent, I know.'

'Yep,' said Kim. 'Seamus is the lawyer. Stevie is the family.'

'And I'm the nobody,' Edward added, to which Tick yelled, brutally, 'Well you used to be somebody!'

'Thank you for listening to the show,' said Edward and, for the first time, the whole group laughed.

Stevie put in, 'I'm fine, everyone, thank you. I know you're doing this for me and I'm bloody grateful.'

'Where is the computer?' Edward whispered into Stevie's ear.

'Round there, I think. Can I just take it?'

'I don't think so. We'd better not ask. We'll have to open the back while he's not looking and pull out the hard drive.'

'I have no tools to do that.'

'Dammit,' he said.

They were interrupted by Kim. 'This would have been a lovely place, quite large for a single lady. What's through there, Stevie? The odd-shaped room?'

'That's a space Granny used for, well, I don't know, but I told

Edward about it.' They all walked towards the narrow room on the left, dark-panelled with an unusually high ceiling, perhaps nine feet. Again the fire damage was huge. 'It's where she had her mural,' Stevie said, but her attempt to address the remark only to Edward failed.

'Oh, a mural? What was that made of, if I may ask?' Tick said. 'Some people put oil-based paint straight on the wall, and that can go up like Guy Fawkes's knapsack.'

They were all now in the peculiar room at the front and Edward saw the panelling was not dark wood – the dark was fire damage on a heavy green wallpaper, and the space had been stripped back to rafters and floorboards by the heat.

'I would need to look at the entire house to give you a final word on it, but my guess is that this is where the fire started, what we call the cockpit of the fire. Tea lights, wasn't it?' Tick asked.

Stevie gulped a sob, and Edward put his arm around her.

'Yes,' said Kim, just to avoid stressing Stevie by having to answer the question. 'Probably best we don't say more.'

'The mural was at that end,' Stevie said quietly. 'Really just sheets of paper she had printed and fitted together. A collage. I think she was just experimenting.'

There was a peculiar melted metal circle on the floor – a hoop the size of a dinner plate. Beside it was a metal pole the length of an arm, like a stalk with three smaller branches — the melted skeleton of an umbrella?

'Paper . . . God,' said Tick with feeling, 'although paper burns quick and light. You've got a chance that it dies before anything catches. Strange little room, long and thin.' He pulled himself up to his full height and, obviously enjoying the chance to deliver a lesson, said: 'Any mention of tea lights gives me enormous concern. People don't understand how dangerous they are, those little things. I once attended a blaze where a couple had placed eighteen of those tiny bastards around their bath – romantic – and left the bathroom for ten minutes. When they opened the door to go back in, a fireball came out. Oven-ready chips abolished the deep-fat chip pan fryers, which saved thousands of lives. Now we have tea lights and people just don't realize that you *must not* place them directly on *anything*, by which I mean directly without a saucer or whatever, because they'll just burn through it. The process is called double-wicking . . .'

Edward was feeling faint. The house had a suffocating sense of death and damage, and added to that was the feeling that the smell of the burned walls and furnishings had physically lodged at the back of his throat.

Tick Goldsworthy was explaining how the fire service worked after a big fire. Stevie was leaning against the wall. The soot was rubbing off on her coat. She doubled over and held her knees with both hands as if trying to stop herself being sick. 'I'm a bit overwhelmed. I don't think I can go upstairs. I don't know if I can see the room where—'

'There's no need,' said Kim quickly, glancing at Edward as if she needed the answer to a question she could not ask. 'We'll just see upstairs, I'll get a sense of it, you stay down here.'

Edward peered at Stevie: they might never get what they came for. Why had he not been more sensitive to the young woman's upset? Of course she couldn't handle a visit to the house where her grandmother had died. Of course they would not be able to simply pick up the hard drive and walk out.

Long sobs came from her now, and he wanted to put his arm around her. A fire-damaged home offered nowhere to sit, because all the furniture had turned into shapes like stiffened treacle.

'Stevie . . .' he said, almost imploring, but through her tears she waved him away.

'You go upstairs with Tick and Kim. I just need to pull myself together. This has all been a bit much.'

The others were reluctantly heading to the staircase, with Tick giving more safety instructions about not putting weight on the banister and watching out for gaps below the stair carpet.

'Honestly, Edward.'

'Really. I don't want to leave you in—'

'Bloody . . . shit, come on. Apologies but . . . really. You go upstairs. I can cope.'

As soon as Tick, Edward, Kim and Seamus had headed up the stairs towards the bedroom window that her grandmother had jumped from, Stevie moved.

She dabbed at her eyes with her sleeve. Quickly checked back into the front room where the mural had been – glanced up and down, and then stepped back and took the corner into the kitchen. The back door was locked. She felt for the key where she knew it should be, on the roof of the fridge-freezer.

'Ah.' She smiled when her fingers touched it. Now she moved at speed back through the kitchen, checking the others were still upstairs. She heard only one sentence from Tick, who was telling the other three, 'There's a reason you get a flame-spread to the upstairs without it going through the floors and ceilings . . .' and, satisfied she must have a couple of minutes more at least, she unlocked the back door.

The toolbox was by the coal bunker, where Granny had always kept it. Red with a black handle. She opened it quickly and pulled out the small set of Allen keys and a Phillips screwdriver. Then she rushed through to the room that had been first on the right as they came in.

When Tick led the other three down from the bedroom, Edward's gaze moved left and right as he searched for Stevie.

'Here!' She was in the kitchen, by the rear windows. 'Happier now.'

Entering, Tick said: 'You got the taps to work, I see.'

Stevie had raised the glass of water to her lips, and now set it down again. 'Water is fine but the glass was dusty.'

'There'll be particles everywhere,' said Tick.

Kim said: 'Are you feeling better? Only by going up there did I see what your poor grandmother must have gone through, and I'm so sorry.'

'I couldn't face it,' said Stevie. 'I think I've cried myself out.'

'So,' said Tick, 'drawing this to a close . . . Ms Cobden, have you seen all you wanted to see? Does this help with the will and valuation and whatnot?'

'Vital to be able to see it,' said Kim, 'and now Seamus can get what he needs from me.'

Kim, Stevie and Edward watched from the car as the fireman pulled out with Seamus's Mini so close behind he could almost have been being towed. Pushing the key into the ignition, Edward paused before he started the engine. He began, 'I'm sorry that all ended up being . . . I don't know, a bit of a waste of time.'

They were silent for a moment. But then he heard a rustling on the back seat and, from the corner of his eye, saw the tote bag in Stevie's lap move.

Kim, in the passenger seat, turned at the same time as Edward. 'What's that?' she asked.

Stevie did not reply.

'I think I know,' said Edward. 'It's what she came for.'

Stevie displayed less embarrassment than others might have shown. 'My tears were real at the start, steaming hell, that sodding house. Forgive my language.'

From the tote bag on her lap, she pulled a brick of stainless steel.

'You needed the computer, right? Is that it? The innards? But isn't that . . .' Kim failed to find a less brutal word, so she just said, 'Isn't that *theft*?'

'Can't be, can it, if it's part of Rebecca's estate?' asked Edward.

Stevie held the clear plastic bag by its neck. 'I knew Granny had a toolbox by the back door. Got the back off the PC and took this out. Trying to avoid marking it with my fingers. I want it to work.'

'Won't it have passwords?'

'Four zeroes! She told me it when I used her computer some-times. I just have to hope I haven't damaged it.'

There was a banging on the windscreen that made Kim and Edward nearly jump out of their skins. When the three of them turned forward, as one, Tick Goldsworthy was at the glass, looking in.

Could he see the hard drive Stevie was holding in the back seat? Edward wound the window down.

'I stopped in the road and jogged back,' said Tick, moving around to the driver's side and looking closely at them, 'because it suddenly struck me you might all like a cup of tea as I'm at the end of my shift and there's a place fifty yards down the road.'

They all said 'no' a bit too eagerly, and Tick gave them a thumbs-up as if that was the response he expected.

'You've been brilliant,' said Edward. 'Ms Cobden has seen everything she needed to for the valuation.'

'What's that?' asked Tick, pointing past Edward towards Stevie in the back seat, and Edward felt his heart miss a beat.

'It's from Japan.'

Kim and Edward turned. As if she had performed an end-of-the-pier magic trick, Stevie was now holding a huge lace fan, spread out in front of her face.

'I had a Japanese pen friend and she started my collection. She died,' said Stevie.

'In a fire?' Tick asked keenly.

'No, she was eighty.'

'Isn't it a gorgeous piece?' asked Kim, catching a glimpse of the hard drive it was hiding. 'Those dancing ladies on the lace look hand-painted.'

'The aircon doesn't work in Edward's car, so I brought a fan.'

'You do you!' boomed Tick and walked briskly off. As soon as he turned the corner of the driveway, all three of them roared with laughter.

Cross-legged on her bedroom floor, Stevie pulled the hard drive from the clear plastic bag. She had fetched a glass of milk from the downstairs fridge and, setting the hard drive down on the carpet, took a sip as she contemplated the metal object for a moment.

The hard drive had a rectangular multi-pronged socket at the back and she knew which plug would fit it. Of course, there was no guarantee the disc inside would run, but the computer she had removed it from was damaged more by smoke than by fire, and the innards were pretty well sealed. She now had a good chance of connecting her grandmother's hard drive and accessing the files. Computer problems tended to be all or nothing. Either it wouldn't work at all or she would get everything, including the letter Granny had written to Edward. The letter would explain what she was distressed by and would prove, wouldn't it, that Granny had taken her own life?

She liked Edward. A sadness about him, for sure, but since their first meeting in the garden centre she had heard the story of the hit-and-run, so she understood. Like him she had been broken once. She wanted to tell Edward to just put one foot in front of the other and keep living, but actually, his laughter in the car when she produced the fan from her bag had been the truest, deepest sound. He could laugh again! Perhaps he was on the way to a new life already. She was sure of it. He had helped her by getting them into the house. She would always be grateful. They might become friends.

As she tipped the hard drive left and right, she heard a glugging noise. She had the radio on – a talk station – was the sound from there? She could not work out why the hard drive felt as if it had life inside it, almost as if it was moving, as if something was trapped there.

Her parents were out. When she put the radio off, the house was silent. She tipped the hard drive left and right in her hands. It was moving, she was sure of it. And there was a sound, like a gulping.

Stevie held the box up to the light. She wondered if a loose fitting around the edge might allow her to see more. As she rubbed her thumb along the line of the case she felt a viscous substance. Oil? It was hot to the touch. How could the hard drive be hot? She held the unit above her face.

The light reflected off the side. She pressed her thumb into the crevice between the metal plates that were riveted together, trying to work them apart. Her thumb started to burn, an agonizing feeling. As she pulled it away, a gloop of liquid like syrup hung for a second above her face, and her eyes widened as it fell.

She put her hand to her face, wiped her eye. And then, as if a drill bit had touched her eyeball, she almost fainted with pain. She smelled burning flesh as the acid started to melt the right side of her face.

CHAPTER THIRTEEN

Edward first met Stevie's parents in the packed waiting area for A&E and, for some reason, could not stop looking at their necks.

The vicar's was narrow like a straw, wrinkled and scrawny as if a thousand sermons had shrunk it on the way through; his wife's had the width and smoothness of marble. Her body was broader than her husband's, and she kept fidgeting and pulling faces. She produced a vape at one point, then returned it quickly to her handbag. The vicar was crying, like a small animal in a trap; his wife was not.

Voice thick and growling, she told Edward they were here to find Stevie. Rushing here following a terrifying call from a paramedic, they had been told their daughter had been taken straight through to surgery. But A&E was rammed, and the pair had given up on making any progress into the depths of the hospital. They were sitting on two chairs by the window furthest from the receptionist, who had a queue of twenty to deal with.

Edward had been called by the same paramedic, who was simply ringing the last two or three dialled numbers in Stevie's phone. Edward knew nothing except that Stevie's face had been burned by acid and it was a serious emergency. He had heard the sirens down the phone.

Stevie's father stood as Edward sat.

'She's said a lot about you both,' said Edward. 'Good things.'

'We don't know much about you,' said Stevie's mum, pulling one side of her mouth down, probably meaning to sound less rude than she did.

'We recognize you from the radio, of course,' said the vicar tearfully, still standing, wringing his hands. 'On the radio you sound – shorter.' Edward had always thought it odd that he had had vicars and vicars' wives in his audience, because he reckoned his phone-in had sometimes been quite coarse, quite earthy – certainly not heavenly – and people usually rang the radio when God wasn't available.

The thought was immediately quashed by a thousand questions.

'The paramedic said her face was burned? But how? Where?'

'Moira, Theo,' the vicar said as if not hearing.

'We still don't really know,' said Moira grimly.

The noise around them rose. There must be seventy people in the space, far too many for this little Accident and Emergency department, which was bolted on to the main hospital building like an afterthought.

The reverend said, 'She was messing around with computers, which she does a lot. She works in IT – apparently, a part leaked. But leaked what? What was it, Moira?'

Moira clenched her teeth, as if she was about to drag a Jeep with a harness clamped in her mouth.

'*Gah!*' she burst out. 'We don't know. But she was fixing it and she held it up and suddenly a powerful acid fell onto her face.'

'Or alkali,' said the vicar.

'I'm so, so sorry,' said Edward. 'I can't tell you how sorry I am.'

'What brings you here? How did you know?' asked Moira.

'I met her recently and my number was in her phone, I think.' Edward did not want to tell them about the adventure in the burned-out house. Surely they would not know about that.

Shaking his small head, scratching his narrow neck, Theo said: 'Stevie was always doing computer things. We have no idea how this could have happened.'

'The acid was inside the hard drive?' Edward asked.

Theo and Moira both seemed to hesitate for a moment, looking at Edward with an expression more alert than he had thought possible. He should not have said 'hard drive'. How would he have known what it was?

Moira said, 'Edward, we don't know the wheres and hows. It must be one of those situations where the manufacturer tells you not to take the back off, and why would that stop a child?'

The word 'child' was an interesting way to describe a woman in her twenties. It was the first intimation of just how devoted this couple were to the damaged youngster who had landed on them so many years ago.

Unexpectedly, Theo said: 'We were so sorry about your son.'

And there it was, the sudden drawing back of the curtain on his grief, the whole horror exposed in blinding light – and Theo's words almost made Edward cry out in pain. For this was the hospital where he had woken on the day the accident had happened; this was the A&E unit which had handled Matty's lifeless body and taken it to a place where he, and later Tara, could spend time with their dead son. In all, they had been with Matty for more than twenty-four hours, and there was a part of him which would always be in this place.

With effort, he brought himself back to Stevie. His skin pricked – a guilty feeling he recognized from school. He had been trying to help! Why did he feel responsible? He had no idea there was some acidic substance inside computer hard drives – would there not be warnings plastered from here to kingdom come? How on earth could it have happened?

Desperate and restless, he walked to reception and, seeing the lady behind the glass still busy with a line of a dozen people, stood alongside them until a second person appeared. He stepped forward.

'Please help!'

'You have to join the queue, sir.'

'It's not for me, it's—'

'Mr Temmis,' said a soft voice behind his left shoulder. He turned. A man in a white coat who looked as if he might have been rushing had suddenly stopped, spilling some of his papers onto the floor.

'Was that me? Let me help,' said Edward. He got to his knees.

'Watch for housemaid's knee when you do that over forty,' the doctor said, but they were both kneeling on the hard linoleum and he had a twinkle in his eye.

'I hope you are well, Mr Temmis. You might not remember me; we met last March. Your son. I'll never forget that day. I wish we could have done something.'

Of course – this man had taken charge when Matty and Edward were brought in. There had been no queues on that day.

'How is your hearing?' The two were still kneeling.

'I have this now,' said Edward, turning slightly and pulling hair back from his ear. 'I will always be grateful to you,' he added, reaching out impulsively to clasp the doctor's shoulder. 'For Matty, for the respect you showed.'

The doctor nodded. Patted Edward's hand. 'And . . . any long-term issues with your head injury? You had a nasty crack. I'm Dr Lowry, in case you can't recall.'

'Headaches for six months. Nausea. Forgetting the names of doctors. Nothing really.'

The doctor smiled. 'And of course, the grief can register as physical pain. The price of love,' he said, rising and snapping the scooped-up documents into his clipboard. 'May I ask if I can help you?'

With relief, Edward pointed at Moira and Theo, whom he could see were watching him closely from the other side of the room. 'A friend of mine, a young woman, has had an acid burn. I think. I don't know all the details. Her mum and dad—'

The doctor grasped Edward's forearm with sudden vigour, stopping him mid-sentence. 'She's in my care. We should have had you through. Are you family?'

'No,' said Edward.

'Wrong answer. Did you mean to say yes?'

Understanding, Edward pointed at the other two like a referee pointing out multiple fouls on the pitch. 'Family, family. All three of us.'

'Get them to follow me. Quickly, please, Mr Temmis.'

She had had a heart attack.

The sight of her – through glass, ten feet away, because Stevie was now in the ICU – made her father burst into tears again. Moira wrapped a long arm around him. He kept saying: 'How could this happen?'

Dr Lowry peeled Edward off to one side. 'Can we talk quietly for a second? I don't want to alarm her parents. God only knows what happened here. It came pretty close to the kind of thing where we bring in the anti-terror people. But we quickly ruled out the two key concerns – was this an attack on her? Or was this her trying to attack someone else? She was on her own, right? There was apparently a build-up of acid in some part of a computer she was working on, and I gather it's her hobby—'

'Hobby? Well, she works with computers so she knows what she's doing.' Edward felt his stomach turning over, trying to absorb what he was being told, trying to understand the sight of Stevie buried under masks and tubes. 'I should tell you that I don't know her very well,' he blurted. 'The paramedics found my number in her phone. I know she's a good person. I don't understand . . .'

133

The vicar had peeled away from his wife and moved over. 'Is her heart beating? We can't see the monitor.'

'Yes. Yes it is. And it will continue to. She is induced and dosed up.' The doctor pointed into the ICU, describing what the different screens were doing. He rapped on the glass and a nurse came out.

'Her parents.'

The nurse, in her forties with a mask around her chin and a cap pressed into tight black hair, looked piercingly at them. 'I'm so sorry. Did she have an undiagnosed heart condition?'

Theo and Moira said, at exactly the same instant, 'We weren't aware of anything!' and, 'How would we ever have known that?'

'Her heart stopped because of the shock. Strong acid on the face makes not just for searing pain but also for a massive emotional shock, and that combined with the adrenaline and possibly a heart defect of some kind—'

'We weren't aware of that!' exclaimed the vicar again.

'Undiagnosed, clearly. She was in hospital when it happened, sir, and that's the main thing. She was immediately given CPR. It's beating again, and she'll live.'

'But the acid?' asked Edward.

'Hydrochloric, I'm told, which is HCl – hydrogen chloride – in water. May have been others too. Certainly it contained a formula that was extremely strong, ridiculously strong, and for some reason, so far as we can tell from the little she told us, it was in a box she was working on – a computer box, was it? – and she held the box above her head to see something and it glooped out straight onto her face.'

'Her eyes?'

'She had a glass of milk beside her and she did the right thing: threw it all over herself. As soon as she realized what had happened, she didn't touch herself either, which is vital too, but that's incredibly hard with so much burning.'

'But her *eyes!*' wailed Moira.

'Let me just say one is damaged, but I'm hopeful.'

Moira let out a sob. 'Hopeful?'

'Hopeful the other isn't.'

Again, the doctor peeled Edward away. 'It's a bizarre accident. A computer with acid in it? I've never heard or seen of it. We've kept the police away, as there's nothing they can do but pelt her with questions that she's in no fit state to answer at the moment. We have a local test for chemicals, a simple thing which every A&E has now to enable rapid action, and that's how we've identified it.'

'Can I ask where the actual box is?'

That was not Edward, but the vicar.

'We can't release it, sir, because of the danger.'

'But it was a computer part?' His voice spoke of his total confusion.

'A hard drive, I gather,' said Edward, with a cough.

'But where from?'

The doctor shrugged. 'She's said very little. A computer part. No one else involved – obviously that's the key question for us. No attack.'

'Well,' growled Moira, dabbing firmly at her eyes, pursing her lips and moving them left and right, 'that is something.'

As he was about to leave, the doctor pulled Edward towards him one final time. 'You don't have to answer this, but was it your choice to leave the radio station? My dear mum and dad listened every day but they can't bear the new person.'

'Oh, she's very good,' said Edward, automatically.

'Yes, well . . . Anyway, I'm sure it's not easy for you to be here, Mr Temmis. The ambulance just summon everyone in the mobile. They won't have known your history with the hospital.' He coughed to clear his throat. 'You must miss your son very much.'

Only the doctor who handled Matty's body could have said such a thing without it ringing hollow.

'I miss him every day,' said Edward.

*

Edward left Theo and Moira at the hospital. For them, it was about waiting now – waiting for their daughter to come round. Waiting to hear how damaged her face was, whether her eye could be repaired. Waiting for an explanation, which Edward was sure they would never get.

Now he was at home. The lights in the hallway had gone this time, flashing and dying the second he came through the front door. The house seemed to him to be at a tilt, and he had ordered a set of gyroscopic sensors from Amazon. When he had time, he would install them on the exterior walls. They would warn him if the building shifted more than three millimetres a day. The strange angles he thought he saw when he entered the hallway could have been his mind playing tricks. The house was stable; he was not.

Jesus Christ. Reflexively, he pictured the vicar. *Sorry, Theo.* Stevie's parents were older than he'd expected, pushing seventy. So they must have been forty-somethings when she entered their lives. No wonder they looked haunted.

What happened then? He powered his laptop on and googled 'acid in hard drive'. The search only came up with a piece of slam poetry headed 'Valentines Day Vengeance'. No, the acid he was looking for was the kind that burned a face. Was there (this sounded absolutely unreal, completely bonkers) some make of hard drive which was pickled in acid so the circuitry worked better? If that was the case, why did computers not have huge warnings on them? For years, people opening them up would have suffered accidents like Stevie's.

He took another tack, googling 'pour acid on circuit board'. The results were illuminating. Several websites explained how you could make a circuit board at home with cupric acid. 'Simply mix 2 parts hydrogen peroxide with 1 part hydrochloric acid and you get cupric acid which is the basis of your etchant,' said one. 'The hydrogen peroxide comes from the chemist's – yes, that's right, the stuff people use to make their hair blonde. The hydrochloric acid comes from the hardware store, usually in the brick cleaning section.' The acid would strip the copper coating from the circuit board.

Strip the coating?

That was it then. The acid had been inserted into the hard drive's circuitry not to create it, but to destroy it.

But why?

He texted Kim, desperate to offload. But the text went unanswered, and there were no blue ticks when he tried to reach her on WhatsApp. Maybe her phone was off. She would not know about Stevie.

He went to the living room and turned on a small standard lamp on a side table. It threw shadows around the room. In the half-light he looked through his DVDs: *Kojak*, *Rockford*, *Ironside*. The more obscure *Serpico* and *Wolf*. But he needed a movie. He paused in his search, pressing his hand to his chest, Stevie's body covered in bandages flashing before his eyes. Had he been responsible, by agreeing to help her get into the house? Somehow she had put herself in a grave danger which she could not see herself, and he, as a mature adult, should have been the sentinel, the gyroscopic sensor, yet he had utterly failed to spot how dangerous the movement was.

Okay. He would start with a premise. He knew from his cop shows that if you started with the wrong premise, you lost the first hour chasing ghosts, but he was sure of this single statement – someone had injected cupric acid into the computer at Rebecca Mason's house in order to destroy the hard drive. He could guess at the reasons. The obvious one was staring him in the face: Rebecca had typed the letter to him on her computer. Now there was not a trace of it left.

The generous, friendly Rebecca Mason had only one enemy that he had been told about – the drone club she had been in conflict with. He would find out exactly what and who they were. Possibly Kim would know the answer immediately.

But with the hard drive destroyed, he *had* to get the radio station to search high and low for the hard copy that Rebecca had sent him.

Edward had Amazon Prime on a free trial, and now he clicked left and right down the menu. He was looking for a movie that gave him a mystery to solve, or at least a film that took him away from this miserable situation for a couple of hours. *Jagged Edge* or *The French Connection*? No caper, thank you: he hated *Knives Out*. No Agatha Christie; the books were always better. Something older, black-and-white? In the Amazon Recommends column, he paused on 'Classic Movies You Might Like'. Underneath there was a sub-category: 'Classic Hitchcock'.

Of course, in memory of Stevie's grandmother, he would choose the third title he saw.

He clicked 'play' and the movie loaded slowly. Then the opening scene began. He had seen it many years ago. The front gates to an overgrown garden, the observer physically passing through them, and then the hypnotic female voice: 'Last night I dreamt I went to Manderley again.'

PART THREE

Two weeks later

CHAPTER FOURTEEN

How could a person be late on such an important day? Barbara should never have relied on Phyllis to get her to the airport.

The airport! A tremor of excitement went through Barbara; Henrik must already be in Amsterdam, where he had to change planes. Then her excitement turned to irritation. Where *was* Phyllis?

If Phyllis had known the truth, the irritation might have been mutual. Barbara had not been honest with her best friend about the glamorous visitor from abroad. A fortnight ago, she told Phyllis during a boozy game of cards (canasta, with Baileys Irish Cream) that the person arriving on the fifth at Exeter Airport was an old friend who, she mentioned lightly, 'I so nearly had a thing with many years ago.'

'Maybe you can have a thing now?' Phyllis had probed as she shuffled the deck of cards.

'I'm a bit long in the tooth for that, my goodness. Look at my hips.'

'You don't need hips when you're on your back in bed,' Phyllis shot back, and they both roared with Irish whiskey laughter.

'How did you meet?' Phyllis had asked, dealing the next hand.

Unable to tell the truth (online, back in January), Barbara had only replied, 'Oh, in our twenties.'

'You're lucky if he's flying over. The only male who ever flies in for me is a little woodpecker I leave nuts out for.'

Barbara said, 'I've left quite a few nuts out for mine,' because she still had the money on her mind, forty-three thousand, and she still felt guilty about the shock she had given Kim, even though she was certain she would get it all back. He had said the briefcase would be *handcuffed* to him!

Her friend's car drew up at last. Nine twenty-two, tssk. Barbara went straight out of the front door to stop Phyllis cutting the motor and getting out.

As the two women pulled off, neither saw the grey taxi that had sat waiting at the end of Barbara's road for more than an hour. Fifty yards behind Phyllis's car, the taxi tentatively started to follow.

That was the first day Edward was allowed into the burns unit at Exeter Royal Infirmary. He had been ringing daily to find out how Stevie was doing while she was in the Sidmouth ICU. He often called from the garden centre. The hospital always said the same: 'Serious but stable. Close family only.'

He would not plead; he did not have it in him to fib about who he was. Even saying he was a friend would feel dishonest. But just when Edward was on the verge of giving up, yesterday his phone had pinged with a text from Stevie's father – brisk to the point of curtness.

> Stevie moved hospitals, come to the vicarage tomorrow and we'll all go together.

When he arrived at her parents' home, it did not look as he expected. Theo was the vicar in West Hill, a pretty hamlet a little way in from the coast. Stevie had told Edward how her father looked after six churches in the surrounding area. Declining congregations meant there was no salary for seven vicars, so a single priest had to do.

Theo's volume of church responsibility (those roof appeals!) might at least be expected to fetch him an ivy-lined vicarage with a front porch bower of vines and dinner-plate dahlias. But instead the house was a 1970s horror, like a Soviet bomb shelter, light brown bricks stained with damp under PVC sills. If a building could look embarrassed about its very existence, this one did. The mould on the brickwork above the upstairs windows looked like eyebrows on a face that sagged with sadness. So this was where Stevie lived too? Like most young people these days: saving up, looking for love, living on their phones. In his mind's eye, he saw her moving under low ceilings lit in sodium orange by filament bulbs that smelled of burning dust, past bookshelves bowed with Bibles.

Opening the front door, Theo and Moira crowded in on Edward as if he was a relic in a museum case and they were tourists. Passing between them, he felt for a second like a choirboy in a church procession; the steam from their drinks incense burning. He saw the stairs to the right and was gripped by a sudden desire to dash up them and see Stevie's bedroom, where the accident had happened.

Accident? Was the hard drive still there? He would like to look at it. If there was acid in the hard drive, it was an attempt by someone to destroy it. But how would the perpetrator even have known Rebecca had written to Edward? Could there be something else on the computer?

But then if a person or persons unknown had attacked the computer, they must surely have started the fire. And that meant the fire was not set to destroy the computer.

The fire was set to destroy Rebecca Mason.

He had thought and thought about it. Turned his logic up and down, spun it around like a hissing football, seeking the puncture. Acid in the computer, fire in the house. Destroy the hard drive, murder the homeowner.

Murder? In Sidmouth? It was monstrous. It was inhuman. But it was not impossible.

The most sickening thing about it was that the perpetrator was not even being sought by the police. The fire service thought Rebecca Mason had accidentally set fire to her own home with those tea lights. Clueless Tick with his size ten boots was only too keen to blame the miniature candles that Rebecca had laid around the edge of that front room. Wait . . . had Rebecca even laid them? No. Surely the whole point was that she had not brought them into the house. Someone came to her home with acid and candles and the result was her death and the destruction of any clue to their motive.

Tick could not see the reality. The police had been unable to get their heads around it. Evil had visited Rebecca Mason that night. Edward saw it as clear as day.

'You seem preoccupied, Mr Temmis.'

That was Theo speaking. A white cat with black mottling on its face had settled by his feet. The black fur sat squarely around both eyes. 'We call our cat "Sunglasses", you can guess why,' said Theo.

'It's better than Hitler,' Edward said, but his reference (to a cat he had seen in the newspapers with a Führer-moustache) had not landed right. They both stared hard at him.

The front room they were in was dominated by a fireplace that looked like it had been attacked with a grenade. The brickwork around the fire was crumbling. The vicar, with his dog collar, sat on the edge of the large armchair, as if preparing to jump up. The chair, which squeaked every time he moved, dwarfed him. Moira was leaning over a nest table, pulling faces and sliding the table towards Edward with his mug of coffee on it.

'Oh. Yes,' Edward replied sadly, 'I must admit I am preoccupied since this happened. It's just such a lot to take in, isn't it? What a horrible . . . accident. And your mother gone too.'

'We have our faith in—' Theo began, but Moira spoke across him.

'No, no, we don't understand it at all. We didn't think computers were made of such dangerous materials. Nor should they be. They say she was holding it above her head when it dripped.'

Her husband added, 'She is terribly badly burned. One side of her face. The acid went through to the jaw. And then that cardiac arrest and having her heart repaired.'

'Jesus,' said Edward, and then corrected himself idiotically: 'Gee whizz.'

Moira fiddled with her sleeve, picking at a strand of loose purple wool. 'Open-heart surgery, poor love.'

'She was fostered, you know?' added Theo. 'So the genes . . . invisible, really. Her medical history. All we can do is pray our hearts out.'

If prayer worked, thought Edward, she wouldn't have lifted the hard drive above her face in the first place.

Moira must have agreed with Edward, because she was looking at her husband as if he was mad. They fell silent.

Edward sensed suspicion in the room. Even the cat bristled with it. He half-expected to glance at the cat and find it had removed its sunglasses to look at him more closely.

At their very first encounter, at Sidmouth A&E, he had felt their subtle suspicion. The Masons knew him from the radio, but what was he doing in their young daughter's life? He had explained as truthfully as he could without saying very much at all: Rebecca Mason had been one of his listeners and Stevie had approached him at work (he didn't say 'the garden centre'), clearly upset about her grandmother's death, to see if Edward knew what might have been troubling her. Wouldn't Riva have called her favourite radio show?

As it happened, he now explained carefully, she had indeed called. 'She wanted to talk about the row she was having with a drone club, and there was also something about local farming noise.'

'Oh,' said Moira, with a slight eye roll, 'there were always noise issues in her part of town.'

Theo added: 'She liked a row.'

Edward pressed, 'Stevie was worried about the drone club, though.' This was risky, but it might get him more information about the dispute.

'Yes,' said Moira keenly. 'They were pretty horrible to her. They even did a demo once.'

'And wasn't the name something like Mackerel?'

'No, it was *Make-Real*,' Moira told her husband stiffly. 'I looked them up after the demo. That, by the way, was about a dozen people outside her house with placards saying "let us fly", et cetera et cetera. I would categorize them as ugly but harmless.'

Edward raised his eyebrows. Moira shifted her bottom in the armchair with a twist of her hips. She set down her mug of tea on the carpet by her feet: she'd probably get up in a minute and knock that over. But then she commanded his attention in a tone as heavy as lead.

'I don't want to beat about the bush here, Mr Temmis. There is a very substantial insurance claim because the house is virtually a ruin. It's opened our eyes, this claim. The house is scorched right through. New floors, walls, ceilings, roof. New plumbing, electrics, before we can think of selling it. And of course the will is currently locked in a safe at the solicitor's. Look, you have to understand. Insurers don't pay out on suicides.'

Theo added: 'We have tried to say it to darling Stevie, but she doesn't seem to hear. If the insurer doesn't pay out, that house will stay a hideous shell, unsaleable. Worse still, we may be compelled ourselves to pay to fix it up, which we simply can't do. So it is quite important that no one "discovers" that my dear mother, our Rebecca, took her own life.'

'It certainly wasn't suicide,' Moira added.

Edward asked, 'What about murder?'

The other two stared at him for a split second, and then roared with laughter.

Kim made sure the taxi driver kept the car in front in view. Her driver was a Balkan man who had pushed his seat so far back she had to sit on the rear passenger side, her long legs folded sideways. But being in the back seat stopped her seeing the road ahead as clearly as the driver did, and once, after they had joined the A3052 and were doing sixty, she saw Phyllis and her mother in the lane beside them.

'Don't pass! Please, stay behind them!' she urged the driver. Phyllis and Barbara were directly alongside now, and she ducked below the door panel. 'Slower, please.'

In stark contrast to this mad dash for love that her mother was undertaking, Kim had left a sorry scene this morning. Anthony had seemed to be improving for a while – preparing for his return to work with phone calls during which, for a few minutes at least, he could sound professional and steady. After the call he would sink into an armchair with his head in his hands, but still, it was progress on the days when he had been unable to move from his bed. The psychiatrist had given him pills and it was possible they were starting to work. He had even burst into laughter once, three or four days ago, watching a boxing match in which, in round two, the challenger had slipped on spilt water left on the canvas in his corner and somehow pitched himself out of the ring. He had rewound the scene and called Kim in. She had spent more time watching those unusual muscles in his face create a smile which parted for a bellow of laughter than she spent on the TV screen itself.

But depression was a world of false starts, and this morning had been different again. She sensed him in bed beside her, awake since the early hours. He slept naked. His body was hairy

– the shoulders, the back, the arms – and he had always been heavy, but now the drugs were making him gain more bulk and she could feel their Superking mattress listing like a ship, her half raised above his. His sobbing meant she would not go back to sleep.

'What's wrong, Anthony?' she said at last, her face half buried in pillow.

'Depression, I guess.'

'But why?'

'Is there ever a why?'

'It came on so fast,' she said. 'Surely something caused it. If there's something going on in your life, you can tell me.'

'I feel guilty about you,' he said. 'I . . . I hit you, didn't I?'

Kim stifled a sigh. Why could he only acknowledge this now, when it all felt too little, too late? She was still choosing to stay, wasn't that enough? 'You've apologized enough, Anthony,' she said at last. 'You just need to get yourself better.'

She thought about Edward. She liked him a lot. She could not bear to feel more than that, but she loved his warmth and tenderness. He had a kind of poetry – as if he moved and spoke to a music score that only he could hear. He was the least selfish person she had ever met, and she loved that. And there was a weathered quality about him, an old-fashioned masculinity which she adored too. Their relationship would have been the perfect reason to leave Anthony, if anything had come of it. The other day, on the beach – that had been strange. Anthony waving from the shore, and then when she had walked out of the sea, Edward standing there. As if the two men were invisible to each other; as if the sum of two was one; as if each could only occupy space in which the other was absent.

While these thoughts passed through her mind, her cab had drawn up at the first bus stop inside the apron of Exeter Airport. 'No further?' suggested the taxi driver hopefully, and Kim paid him. She emerged, the terminal a ten-minute walk away.

The airport was used mainly by business types who wanted to hop to Newcastle, Cardiff, Edinburgh, Manchester without the nonsense of a train change in London. On a quiet day you could imagine no flights at all. It had a single runway and a low grey roof that looked permanently pristine. There were three bright red Royal Air Force two-seater planes, perhaps here for a display later. But the Amsterdam flight could not have touched down yet, because there was nothing else on the tarmac.

Now, Kim had to do the strangest thing – stalk her mother to keep her out of danger.

CHAPTER FIFTEEN

While Kim stood under the bus shelter at Exeter Airport, Edward was in the Masons' Hyundai heading unknowingly to the same square on the map. Exeter Royal Infirmary, conveniently located just by the city airport.

Had the couple invited him just to warn him off pursuing the suicide theory? To make sure he didn't help Stevie go in that direction?

But Stevie would not be going in any direction for a while. Edward's eyes filled with tears as he took her in for the first time since the day of the accident. All the colour in her skin had gone. Along the left side of her face there was a large stiffened bandage that sat three inches clear of her jaw line, and the exposed skin showed damage, as if it had been peppered with buckshot. Her forehead was bandaged – it had not occurred to Edward that the acid might have gone into her hairline – and the lower edge of the tape ran diagonally from her top right temple to her left ear, covering her left eye along the way. Again, the bandage over her eye sat at least two inches out from the face, thickly cushioning the delicate flesh beneath.

Stevie reached out her hand. 'Edward Tennis.'

'Temmis,' he corrected, knowing her mistake was deliberate.

'Don't make me laugh, it hurts.'

'We saw a photo. They'll rebuild you,' said Moira stoutly. The words landed awkwardly, making Stevie blink, and Edward think of *The Six Million Dollar Man*.

He was now sitting on the edge of the bed, trying to swallow a sudden lump in his throat.

Sitting up, with a pillow at her back, Stevie was swamped by a light green surgical gown that ran across her neck. It made her look more surgeon than patient. He was desperate to ask about her sight. And her heart. And the skin on her face. But he felt he should just offer comfort, so he did.

'You're an exceptional person, Stevie. You care so much.'

'I care about how this happened to me.'

'Could it just be an acc—'

'*No.*' She was suddenly firm. Her right eye blinked rapidly. Annoyance? Frustration? He had expected to find a victim, but she was a vigilante. 'Mum, Dad, can you give us a minute?'

They left.

Immediately Stevie said, 'Do you know where the hard drive went?'

'No. Surely it would have been bagged up by the fire brigade?'

'They think it was a sodding battery leak. I mean, really? A policeman came to speak to me, but he was so bloody uninterested he kept glancing out the window and commenting on the view. The bollocksing attitude of the man – excuse the bad language – was, basically, "Honey don't go looking in electronic equipment again and y'all'll be fine."' She delivered the words in a pitch-perfect Mississippi twang.

Edward's eyes drifted to the square of glass behind Stevie.

'Now you're doing it,' she said.

'I'm just wondering what that tower is, now that you mention it. Not residential, just a sort of concrete column. Not even a mile away.'

'The airport, silly. I can tell you that without even looking round.' She choked back a cough; it might have been a sob. 'I still can't believe what happened to Granny.'

'"In Desperation from Riva",' echoed Edward.

'I asked where the hard drive was and the cop – sitting where you're sitting, mister – said it would be destroyed for safety reasons as there's no criminal inquiry. I asked, "Why isn't there one?" and he was really condescending. "We can't launch the police helicopter every time there's a battery leak." He said the acid leaked inside the hard drive because of the heat from the fire.'

'I think you're right, you know.' Edward worried at his cuff. 'I did some googling and it can't have been an accident. I think it might have been the drone club.'

'What do you mean by that?' Stevie asked. She coughed, putting her free hand gingerly up to her mouth.

'Someone didn't want any trace of the letter she sent me to exist.'

'But surely they'll assume it got to you?' she said.

'Yes, I had the same thought. Well okay – then there must have been something else on the computer, but what?'

Stevie looked out of the window, not answering.

Edward continued: 'Whoever put the acid in the hard drive also set the fire—'

'—which killed Granny.'

'Yep.'

'What I don't get is why she basically locked us all – locked Dad especially – out of her life in the run-up to it all. Why would she stop him visiting? What was going on in that bloody place?'

The questions were delivered energetically, but that only seemed to drain Stevie's reserves, and she sank deeper into her pillow.

He said, 'It must be something to do with that mural.'

Stevie looked at him, her uncovered eye the brightest blue

Edward had ever seen. 'Bloody shit.' Her voice was tired now, as if she'd used up all her words. 'The mural. Shit. And the big white blousy dress and hat.'

'Yes. All of it.'

'I'm scared.'

'Scared of—'

'Scared of losing my face, my eye, my fucking hairline. Scared I'll end up looking like something out of a Stephen King novel.'

They sat in silence. Stevie seemed exhausted from talking. After a while Edward said, 'Maybe Rebecca, Riva, was depressed. Maybe she became reclusive because someone had put the frighteners on her.'

He heard the phrase played back in his head and recognized it from a dozen television shows. *Who put the frighteners on the sweetie-pie?*

'But why the mural, the big picture of the old staircase, the dress?'

A nurse arrived. 'Your mother and father want to know if they can come back in, but before they do I need to give you these – *ta-daaa!*' She struck a cheerleader pose with a narrow plastic tray of tablets, a tiny paper cup balancing precariously at one end. She was prim and tidy, with jet-black hair and fine features. 'I'm Cat,' she said, in an Irish accent. 'Stevie knows me. Hey, you okay, hun?'

'A few tears,' said Edward. 'It's the trauma. Everything.'

'It was just a moment,' Stevie said with a little resentment. It was not Edward's business to tell the nurse how she was feeling. 'I'll fucking cheer up for you, Cat, God bless you.'

'So you will,' Cat told her. 'The Celtic fringe, you and me. The worse the language, the faster the recovery. So, tablets in a second, but first a change of bed angle, then I reattach the cannula.'

'I should be so lucky,' said Stevie.

'What?' the nurse asked.

'Having a change of angle in the bed.'

'Dirty girl.' The nurse tittered. Stevie smiled with half of her face. Embarrassed, Edward looked away. Cat fussed at the cannula for a few moments, and then pressed the button to elevate the bed.

'Is she going to be okay?' asked Edward. 'The eye, I mean?'

'Data protection, she can't tell you,' said Stevie. 'Just say yes.'

Cat was serious. 'I'm not sure of the prospects. She has a tigress's fighting spirit, that's for sure. The surgeon will be able to tell you.'

'Surgeon?'

Stevie said, 'Look, I didn't want to upset you, Edward. Tomorrow they're reattaching the skin under my eye. Grafting it from my leg. Don't tell my—'

At the door, Moira and Theo said in unison: 'Don't tell us what?'

Edward could not get the image of Stevie's burned and bandaged face out of his head. Fifteen minutes later, making his way out of the hospital alone, he came up behind a familiar figure. Short, with hips wider than her shoulders, but strongly built; she wore her black hair in a clip. But it wasn't a nurse – it was a member of the public, a patient or relative, whose jeans were baggy enough to look like the kind of trouser medics wore; her jumper was health-service blue. The figure suddenly came into focus: it was Agnes Chan.

Heart pumping, he moved sharply left into a corridor that turned out to be a dead end, with a locked door barring his way marked RADIATION KEEP OUT.

What he had not anticipated was that Agnes Chan's partner was following them both.

'Oh,' said Troy, glancing by chance into Edward's hiding place, and automatically hesitating at the familiar face. They had no choice but to acknowledge each other. 'I wasn't expecting . . . a person to be here.'

A female voice, from out of Edward's view, asked: 'Who's there?'

Evidently Agnes had turned back.

'I . . . don't know,' said Troy. 'A gentleman stranded in this corridor.'

'You don't know?' said Edward sardonically, adding, too quietly for anyone but Troy to hear, 'So we haven't met, have we?'

He was surprised by the tall man's drained pallor, as if he had seen a ghost.

'I took a wrong turn,' said Edward, emerging, smiling at Agnes and gesturing at the dead-end corridor behind him.

Agnes's eyes widened. He thought she might be in a blind panic too. She attempted a casual greeting but he saw her breath was coming faster. *I saved your life, and you fired me*, Edward wanted to say out loud. When he looked back at Troy he saw the man was covered in sweat and looking as if he might throw up. His thick black spectacles were sliding down his nose; each time he pushed them back into place, they immediately started tobogganing downwards again on the wave of perspiration.

'I don't know about you, Edward,' Agnes began, 'but we're here for a check-up.' She patted her stomach. 'Nearly seven months.'

'Not doughnuts,' put in Troy. There was strained laughter and Troy pulled out a handkerchief and wiped the sweat from his forehead. The cloth came away sopping wet. He caught Edward's eye guiltily.

A young doctor with an alarming streak of yellow and red on her white coat stopped on her way past. 'Derrick enjoyed seeing you.'

Edward's ears pricked up. 'You were seeing Derrick?' His old producer, who had always fought his corner, was unwell and he didn't know? 'What happened?' he asked. 'Is he okay?'

'That he is,' said Agnes as the young doctor walked on. 'No, don't worry Edward, it's minor. He did something to his ankle so Ortho are putting it in a cast.'

'He was fixing a gutter,' said Troy.

The conversation petered out. After an awkward pause, Agnes patted her belly again.

'Well, must get on, the scan awaits.'

Nodding their goodbyes, the pair walked off. But ten seconds later, Agnes jogged back and gripped Edward's upper arm.

'Nice to see you as always, Edward. I'll make sure I give Derrick your best wishes next time he's in the office.'

No need, thought Edward. *Because I'm going to go to the ward right now to see him myself.*

CHAPTER SIXTEEN

Phyllis had something on her mind. They'd been in the airport for over an hour now, Barbara's anxiety ensuring they had arrived with a long wait for the Amsterdam flight. The passengers were coming through now in dribs and drabs, and they hadn't seen anyone who fitted the vague description Barbara had provided. But it wasn't just the waiting that was on Phyllis's mind. No, something else was nagging at her, and a good friend would always speak up.

'Something worries me a little here, you know, Barbara. I am speaking as your cards partner, your partner-in-crime on the canasta table. It occurred to me as we've been looking at all these people. Everyone is coming through for a visit, seeing their families in Devon or maybe for business. Something in Exeter or something further away, maybe a train to London. This man is coming here for you, yes? It's just a hunch, of course. But . . . if he was coming here for you, would he not have texted when the plane touched the ground?'

Phyllis could feel her friend bristling beside her, but Barbara didn't speak, nor did Phyllis take her eyes away from the emerging passengers. So far, middle-aged men, travelling alone, over six feet tall who looked like they might be able to fly a plane had been in short supply in this crowd of travellers.

'I wouldn't want to cast any doubt, dear Barbara, dear friend,' she continued into the stony silence. 'And I have the right to speak only as your driver. If this gentleman was a friend from back in the day, haven't we got *any* recent photo of him? And what's he travelling here for? Is it not odd that if he's coming through Exeter because he has some business here, he hasn't any transport? And if he *is* coming just to see you, odd that we don't really know what we are looking for?' She hesitated, then glanced at Barbara, who was clenching and unclenching her jaw. 'I'm sorry dear,' she hurried on, 'I've said too much, but I'm just airing something I worry about *as your friend*. You've said it's not romantic, but what if he was trying to – how do I say this – wheedle his way in? You have to be careful, my dear friend. As when we play cards. Hold yours close and don't play your queen until you know she'll trump mine.'

Speech over. Phyllis breathed in deeply. She had said enough. She had said too much. She had said just the right amount . . . it didn't matter. It was said, all of it. Every single part of it. She had a bad feeling about this and she needed to tell Barbara, especially if she was about to send Phyllis packing because she was cramping Barbara's style.

At that moment, Phyllis stiffened. There were at least fifty people emerging from the arrivals corridor now. Most were elderly. On the furthest side, one man, clearly alone, was dragging a Samsonite case behind him, all the while looking around as if he was hoping to see someone he knew.

'Well, I'll be. Would you look at that?' Phyllis said under her breath. Was this Henrik? It could easily be the man in the photo on Barbara's phone. And then, as if by magic, the individual – dressed in brown cords, but anyone could make a mistake – glanced in the ladies' direction, smiled, waited for a gap in what was now a steady stream of disembarked pensioners – and cut through the crowd.

'Oh my. This must be him,' said Phyllis.

She turned to Barbara, and gasped. Her friend was no longer seventy. She had lost thirty-plus years. Barbara was thirty-five. Not in her mind, but in reality. Barbara Sinker, aged seventy, was now Barbara Sinker, thirty-five. This was not Phyllis's imagination. This was an actual fact. Her pensioner friend had been replaced by a younger version of herself, the skin changed, the eyes clearer, the hair without a trace of grey.

Phyllis's mouth dropped open. Her vision tunnelled. Young Barbara's expression was imploring. Henrik was approaching. Phyllis turned back towards him, head swimming. The stranger would have to catch her when she fainted.

CHAPTER SEVENTEEN

Derrick Tidy's voice suggested he was smiling. 'I can't believe you found me here.'

'I was passing,' said Edward, sitting in the armchair in the corner of the room. 'How did you get yourself a private space? For a broken ankle?'

'Just torn ligaments I think.' The younger man laughed. 'Literally, I think they confused me with someone else. It's not that fancy. They can't even fix the light.'

He was right. The only lamp was a bedside light on the floor by the wall behind the bed. When Edward looked, he saw the plug attaching it to the socket offered only a few inches of wire. The neck of the lamp was broken. The result was that the bulb was pressed against the bright white wall, so Edward's young friend sat in silhouette against a square of hard light.

'When it's dark outside, like it is now, I feel like I'm one of those 1920s mime artists. I just communicate through hand shapes.'

Edward winced. 'There's no overhead light?' They both looked up at a grey fishbowl in the ceiling.

'Dead. They said a specialist is needed for that because it requires a ladder and moving the bed.'

Edward laughed. 'Ladder? Rules you out. What was it, guttering?'

'At my parents' house. Trying to help. Leaves had built up, I got out the ladder, trying to play the hero, rested the ladder against the French window. There must have been soap or oil on the glass or something, because as soon as I was at the top it started to topple. Anyway,' Derrick continued, moving his leg under the blanket, 'it's not broken. Ligaments pulled.'

'When did you do it?'

'Three or four days ago.'

'Well. I just had the strangest thing: I met Agnes and her husband in the corridor. That guy was sweating, my God.'

'Yeah, he's a sweaty guy. Was it hashtag awkward?'

Edward, not quite young enough to use the same slang convincingly, attempted: 'Hashtag just, hashtag a little.'

'They were visiting me, which was kind.'

'You're probably the best producer she has.' With those words, Edward felt a pang so strong that for a second he thought he might weep. He recognized the stab of loss. A desire to have that time on the station returned, to be back in the studio with Derrick alongside.

He looked carefully at Derrick, trying to see his face clearly. His former producer was like a cut-out shape in black, but the outline – the long jaw and ears, the hair that sprang from his head like flames – was still unmistakeable. Edward wondered if Matty would have grown up with Derrick's best qualities, professional discipline and personal loyalty. If he had, he was certain he would have been a proud father. Sure, the producer was an odd fellow. There were rumours of girlfriends, but nothing that lasted. The most recent had been a young woman from his church choir who looked like she was in the Amish community. But in Derrick's favour was the fact that he was organized, which was what you wanted from a producer. 'Derrick Untidy' had been the stupidest nickname. Edward would never have imagined he could make that mistake on the ladder, because he would have ensured it was roped to a wall or tended by a friend. He had never made a mistake like that in the radio studio, that was for sure.

'Is the show still fun?' Edward asked.

'Fine,' said Derrick. 'They just won't give me the numbers.'

Listening figures were everything to a producer. 'How do they hide them? I thought they were released publicly.'

'They are and they aren't,' responded Derrick. 'They've fallen ten per cent, I know that. The headline figure. But they say it's great because they're bringing in younger listeners.'

'So they've lost four pensioners and gained a teenager?' The remark was unsporting, even unkind. Edward regretted it immediately.

'Tessa is doing her best. She's never said a word against you.'

'She's great,' said Edward, now trying a bit too hard. 'Talented, young, energetic. Young.' He heard himself, heard how bitter he sounded, how his dismissal from the radio station had somehow got entangled with his feelings about Tessa K, who had done nothing wrong whatsoever.

'It was probably the Granny Riot that did it,' said Derrick quietly.

'They lifted me onto their shoulders. I never asked for that.'

'I remember hobbling around the station the day after and people asking if the pensioners had attacked *me*.'

'Ha!' Edward's laugh was empty. He had a sudden urge to add something to the mix, to see how Derrick would react.

'I'll tell you something interesting. Troy came to my house.'

'The guy with Agnes just now?'

'Yes. Very, very odd. Soon after the tsunami – sorry, *large wave* – struck the front. When he came to my house he was pretty intense, called himself an academic.'

'What did he want?'

'I think maybe he was grateful to me because I fished Agnes out of the sea. So he was trying to help. It was actually Troy who told me to go, to speak to them on the promenade, to show the radio station I was helping! He spelled it all out. I join in with the protest – as a calming presence, of course – and simultaneously he tells Agnes to take me back. He virtually promised. He sold it to me. In the event it was all a disaster.'

'Did he not get back in touch?'

'Nope. Vanished.'

'I think they thought you'd helped place the radio station under siege. They even cut the lifts.'

'As if! I ended up in reception thinking I'd get a welcome and the guy there, can't recall the name, the security guard, he was incredibly sniffy and I think he was told to keep me waiting while he got the police.'

'I think you might even be banned from the station now,' said Derrick lightly, missing Edward's flinch. 'Haven't met that Troy fellow before, and he struck me as very odd.'

He suddenly tore the cover back on his bed. Edward was confronted by a skinny white leg covered with a burr of lightest ginger, a plastic cast at the end. 'Sorry, this is getting hot. I'm out tomorrow and they've promised me crutches.'

'Who's producing while you're off?'

'Youngster called Trent.'

'There's actually someone younger than you at the station?'

'Yes, many of them,' said Derrick. 'I'm only going to take a few days. My mistake was walking on the ankle when it was injured. So, I'm going to watch old movies and not feel guilty that I'm missing the show.'

'Old movies? I saw one the other day, Hitchcock's *Rebecca*. Give it a go.'

'Never seen it, never heard of it.'

'Course you have.' Edward's mind went from the movie to the real-life person. He did not want to tell Derrick about what he thought had happened to Rebecca Mason. It was all too disturbing. 'Hey. You remember I asked you about a caller called Rebecca Mason? She was having trouble with a drone club. Did you find that letter?'

Derrick bit his lip – had he forgotten to look? But his words were surprising. 'I noted down what you said was on the envelope. "In Desperation from Riva". I put it on my desk to make sure I didn't forget. I came in early one day and I went through every office. I went to reception and then the upper floors. I hunted high and low for it. I didn't want to let you down. I'm so sorry.'

'Never mind.' Edward sat back. 'It was a long shot.'

'Ah.' The young producer looked to be in physical discomfort for a moment. While they were speaking Derrick had pulled the sheet back across his leg in stages (the limb so white, so thin, no wonder the ligaments tore). 'Why does this matter? She complained about a drone club and then . . . did you tell me on the phone that she'd died? What, you're thinking she was hit by a drone?'

'Something a bit more sinister.'

Derrick was quiet for a moment. 'Blimey. That sounds pretty heavy. Are you a private investigator now?'

'I'm trying to help someone. Her granddaughter. She's a bit of a gem, a bit troubled, and she wants some answers. The drone club is where the answers are.'

'Well, I'll leave it to you. But if you get anywhere, and it's interesting . . .'

Derrick was obviously reconsidering where the sentence was going, so Edward completed it for him.

'. . . I'll let you know and Tessa K can interview me about it.' Edward stroked his chin, thinking the movement of his fingertips in the stubble must make him look like an old man. 'On second thoughts, maybe not. Imagine if Agnes heard me back on air.'

'Might trigger another Granny Riot.'

'Too soon, Derrick, too soon.' Edward stood to leave. 'Get well, my friend. No more blocked gutters for you.'

Phyllis stared at Kim, who stared back at her, just as wide-eyed. The man who had stopped in front of them was carrying a black briefcase and could have fitted her mother's description.

Phyllis said, 'Barbara? You've—'

Kim turned to the man and then back to Phyllis. 'I followed you here. I'm Barbara's daughter. Where's my mum?'

'I thought you were her and she'd dropped thirty years or so,' said Phyllis. She turned to the man. 'Are you Henrik?'

'I am Mister Verwoerdian.' His accent was European, and because the plane had come from Amsterdam, Kim immediately guessed Dutch. The briefcase looked heavy, and it had forced his shoulders into a slight tilt. Now he placed the case on the floor and looked at them both. He had strange lips, thought Kim. When he smiled, they seemed to twist, as if they were not cooperating.

'I am from Pinpoint Materials, yes? I was told two ladies?'

Phyllis asked loudly, as if volume would help: '*Are you the pilot?*'

The look of confusion on his face was all the confirmation Kim needed. It was not him. She wondered if their expectant faces had drawn the man, who now picked up the case with a nodded apology and moved off.

Phyllis laughed, but her throat sounded constricted and she put her hand up to it. 'Oh goodness. I see what's happened. You gave me a shock.' She was babbling. 'You see, I just gave a little speech to Barbara – far too long, I think, and I was probably saying all the wrong things. I just think this is a . . . *a racket*. I think perhaps your dear mother has become someone else's racket. I'm glad you're here. I thought you were her. I honestly thought—'

Kim cut in. 'Where did she go?'

'I don't know. I turned and saw you and my first thought was that Barbara had lost a good thirty years.'

Keeping an eye on the arrivals area, where Phyllis remained dutifully with a walking stick Kim now recognized as Barbara's, Kim ran the length of the terminal. Eventually she came to a neglected-looking coffee shop at the furthest corner of the building, where a familiar figure sat hunched in a corner.

'Mum! Are you okay? I've been looking everywhere for you.'

'Kim?' Barbara hastily wiped her eyes. 'What are you doing here?'

'Are you having a bit of a cry? You caused me a little panic there.'

'Did I?'

'Are you crying? Your eyes are red.'

Barbara sniffed and looked away. 'A little.'

'I'm sorry, Mum. I don't think he was on that plane.'

'I know he wasn't. And,' Barbara fiddled with the sugar packets on the table, then looked up to meet Kim's eye, 'I think I arrived here knowing. I couldn't bear for it to be exposed in front of Phyllis. It's just been so . . . humiliating. You'll be so ashamed of me when you find out. Forty thousand. More. A fool. He made a fool of me.' Another tear slipped down her cheek, and Kim sat down next to her, pulling the chair close so she could wrap an arm around her mum's shoulders.

'No, Mum. He is a very clever criminal. You're a victim. He probably has victims all over the world.'

'He asked me for intimate pictures, Kim.' This, said with a guilty gulp.

That was the mirror, Kim realized. The portrait mirror she saw propped against the wall in her mum's lounge. Her stomach turned now she knew the answer.

'Did you send them?'

'Yes.'

'Please don't cry. You wanted his automaton. The duck or whatever it was. You got lured in because of your hobby.'

'I got lured in because I'm a lonely old maid and he told me he loved me.'

'Oh Mum.' Kim squeezed her tightly, and mentally cursed the scammer to kingdom come. 'Come on. Let's get you home.'

CHAPTER EIGHTEEN

Edward remembered Mackerel. Then he remembered it wasn't Mackerel. The drone club, Google informed him, was represented by a PR firm called MakeReal (of course!) and the operation was based at Tanner.

He was on his phone in a spare second between customers at the garden centre. He dialled the number for MakeReal, but it rang out. The drone club had a mobile on their Facebook page and he tried that, too. Using a phone was strictly forbidden if you were at the tills, whether there were customers or not. He took the risk of holding the mobile to his ear, but just as the phone was answered, Edward saw a manager running towards him and immediately hung up. *That's it*, he thought, *I'm getting the sack for the second time this year.*

The manager, Kenneth Schomes, always wore a white short-sleeved shirt, a short black tie and a big set of keys on his belt. He was tall and ungainly, and as he ran the keys bounced off his paunch and his shirt came untucked.

'Mr Temmis.' He was so out of breath he was wheezing. 'Ah, a problem at your house. The water mains people have been called in. They rang the office – some neighbour told them your old number was kaput but you were working here.'

'What do I do?' Edward asked helplessly. He gestured at the till. 'I'm at my station.'

'Go now. They need entry if they're not in already.'

He drove at speed. It turned out a public water main had burst somewhere under the ground at the back of his property, and the result was a flood of water moving past and below the house. The water had built up in the beds in the front garden, which had delayed the inevitable – a huge spill into the road, cascading downhill towards the village.

There were at least seven workmen in hi-vis orange.

'Unusual situation this,' said one, having worked out from the urgent way Edward parked the car that he was the home-owner. 'I don't need interior access, I don't think, but we'll need to go into the ground right by the extension.'

'What happened?' asked Edward, breathless. Some small part of him felt angry at Kim. The estate agent! But that was ridiculous. A burst main had nothing to do with the house's precarious position, did it? And he had chosen the cliff.

He contemplated his property. The workmen walked pur-posefully backwards and forwards along the side, splashing through deep puddles, their orange waistcoats flapping as they explained the issue. The house stood against the cloudless sky with a kind of wounded pride, like the humpback straining to stand straight. The wooden top floor – dark brown wooden slats on the exterior, weatherproofed tongue-and-groove – was more compact than the first and second storeys, narrowing the shape of the house as it rose, a kind of steepling effect. But the stress of the ground's movement over the years had also caused the lower floor to twist, so the house had the faintest look of a corkscrew. It was an unlucky building, for sure – the wrong shape and the wrong place. And now a lagoon underneath it, with God knows what consequences for the structure.

Edward caught sight of a small woman with a dog as the explanation wrapped up. Shrewish in a very literal sense, she wore a purple scarf wrapped so tightly around her head that it accentuated the long thin nose, glossy black eyes and a luminous stare. She must have approached them silently. The dog, a Chihuahua, wore a neckerchief which matched the woman's headscarf. It was tiny, as if both dog and owner had been locked in a tumble dryer and shrunk.

'I'm your neighbour, but a hundred yards away. Still the nearest house. We haven't seen you in a while.' Yet still knew enough about him to let the water company know where he worked, Edward noted.

'Today might not be the day,' said the bearded workman. 'We've got a bit of a show on here.'

'Oh, I wasn't rubbernecking,' the woman replied. 'I have to take an interest. The road is suddenly a river and I don't want it bursting through my bush.'

'I'm so sorry,' spluttered Edward. The bearded workman burst out laughing and she looked daggers at him. The second man tried to help.

'It's not the owner's fault. This is public pipework, hence the word "main". It's as much yours as his, ma'am. We can't seal it yet, I'm afraid, because we haven't got into the ground yet and we need to prop the house first.'

Propped . . .? Edward had visions of the house flooded, falling, sliding . . . propped. He quietly took himself away from the conversation, treading over the old rockery because the grass at the front was waterlogged. Standing on the stones, conscious that they were not the steadiest, he counted the men in the orange – all men, no women – and got to eleven. As he pulled his phone out of his pocket, he saw a text, already delivered:

Really would love to chat. Nothing big.
Well a little.

At another moment the message might have been intriguing, but for now Kim would have to wait. He slid the phone back into his jacket, but then it buzzed.

'Kim?'

'Julius is my name. You rang. Is this about the skylark?'

'I'm sorry,' Edward said into the mobile, 'but I don't think that was me who rang. I don't have any Juliuses in my life.'

'I've told you, the skylark went down when a bird of prey attacked it.'

'Right.' Edward was catching on, slowly. But he decided not to show his hand. 'Was this at Gulverton?'

'Of course it bloody wasn't! Not since all the trouble there. Chesterpoint. I'm telling you, a bird of prey.'

Edward said, 'Are you from Tanner Drone Club?'

Long pause. 'Julius, yes, that's me.'

'I rang earlier but I don't know about skylarks.'

The man began an explanation that Edward tuned out. The Skylark was a make of drone and it had been attacked by a hawk or an eagle, and the droners thought the bird had been trained to take it down.

'I wasn't calling about that,' Edward cut in. 'I wanted to have a chat about Gulverton.'

At the other end, the man's voice became quieter. 'What do you want to know about Gulverton?'

Tanner was rough. There was a rumour about a thousand rats living in a cesspit that was shared by all the homes. The hamlet would originally have been no more than a collection of outbuildings around a farm, now owned separately and all in different stages of disrepair. You got to Tanner by turning left at Bowd on the country road between Ottery and Sidmouth, and the smell hit you first. It was not the odour of freshly cut hay, or even the tang of muck spread across a dozen nearby fields; it was unmistakeably the stench of human excrement. Edward went to wind up the car window and found it already tightly shut. He gagged as he took the lumpy road down a steep slope towards the buildings gathered at the bottom. His car, a dark blue Toyota, started to sink into the wet earth, as if it was so ashamed to be here that it was now trying to hide itself.

Yesterday as the men from the water company had worked at his house, Edward looked up at the first blue sky for more than a fortnight; it was blue again today, but somehow the crystal sky only made the stench seem worse. At least rain had its own smell. This odour assaulted all the senses. It was deafening and blinding.

His satnav had not accepted the address, which told him the road he had followed had run out some fifty yards earlier. Boy oh boy, this felt like the 'last seen in' place you saw on *Crimewatch*, as in: 'Edward, forty-five, was last seen in . . .'

He got out of the car and looked around. The wind was cold. He drew his jacket closer. As he stood there, wondering which of the properties to knock at, he had – for no obvious reason – a thought of Kim. He had not yet managed to return yesterday's call. What if he called and she was with Anthony? In that moment, standing at the intersection of the shacks in Tanner and getting more used to the stench of the place, an unfamiliar thought came to him. Had Anthony found out about the affair – was that why he had suddenly become depressed? Had his anger at Kim's affair turned inward? But how could he have discovered it and never said a word to her?

Damn it. For once he'd call her direct. He punched 'KC' into his phone, which was how he listed her name in contacts, hiding her name from he didn't know who. The call was picked up immediately.

'Are you at work?' she asked.

'I've taken the rest of the week off.'

'I thought so. I'm here.'

'Where's here?'

'At the garden centre. I figured you won't answer my calls . . .'

'Hang on,' he sputtered. 'One single text I didn't answer.'

'I'm kidding.' He could hear her smile down the phone. 'I wasn't hunting you like a crazy person. I had to buy some flowers for my mum.'

Edward brightened. 'That's my department, normally. What did you get?'

She laughed. 'Oh, Mr Temmis, I do adore you. I really do. You're just so . . . *committed*. "That's my department"! I would've loved to see your face when I turned up in your queue.'

He was registering her word 'adore', weighing it, and wondered if it was close to love. It probably signified friendship, only. 'Tulips or muscari are so lovely, this time of year.'

'Muscari?'

'Aka grape hyacinth.'

'Yes, she needs colour at the moment for various reasons.'

'Then tulips are perfect . . .' He wasn't entirely sure what they were talking about, but it felt safe to him.

'Why aren't you here?' she asked.

'A lot happened since we went to that old house. I can't go into it all. But I'm in Tanner. There's someone here who may—'

'Tanner? What would you be doing there? That's an estate agent's nightmare.'

Edward was about to ask what she had called about the day before when a shadow passed across his face. He looked up and saw an object floating in the sky, tilting left and right as if fighting the breeze. The object whirred. Another shadow arrived on his right shoulder.

'Kim?'

'What's that buzz?'

'There's a drone . . .'

He dropped the phone from his ear. The sound got louder – the light mechanical whirr of the object above him was now joined by the same from his left, and his right, and from behind him.

As Edward looked around, drones lifted into the sky all around him.

There might be a dozen. No, surely, there were more. They came from behind the huts. They lifted in almost perfect synchronicity, some rising only fifteen feet, others travelling four times the height.

He shielded his eyes against the sun, turning, the ground loose underfoot, seeing the drones move as if to a planned position and then hover, all tilting left and right like American footballers adjusting their shoulders before scrumming down . . . The sound in the air was not just a whirr, it was a cacophony, like hornets before they strike.

He pressed the phone to his ear. 'Can you hear this?'

Whatever Kim said in reply was drowned out by the electrical purring of the drones. There was a bang in the air over his right shoulder: two had collided and one fell to the ground.

'I'm in some kind of drone . . . event – I don't know what it is,' he yelled into the handset. 'Might have to get back in the car.'

Not able to hear Kim, he shut the phone down. He was genuinely fearful that the drones might all suddenly swoop; the whirr was deafening. He reached for his car door, but just as he pulled the handle he heard loud laughter coming from the hut directly ahead of the car.

A short man wearing baggy light blue dungarees had emerged from the building with a controller in his hand. He was in his sixties, and behind him, another figure – male, enormous, round, easily six foot five, face hidden by a crash helmet – broke into a run and tore off around the back of one of the other houses.

'*Wait there!*' the man in dungarees shouted to Edward. He wore a baseball cap that looked like it had been run over by a tractor. His upper body was wide and muscled, but the hips and legs looked wasted. He wore black Wellington boots covered in mud. Edward stole a glance at his own shoes, realizing they were ruined.

'*Shaggy!*' shouted the man. It seemed to be the name given to the other, the younger one, who now lumped back into sight, running with such weight that each step sank him into the mud. Edward became conscious of the smell again, conscious that once again he had begun a conversation with Kim that had not reached a conclusion, as if theirs was a relationship of cut-off sentences.

Then, the buzzing of the drones dipped. At one moment they were surrounding Edward, hovering in tiers, poised to strike; now the motors calmed and, as one, they descended, disappearing behind the huts.

The man with the controller said, 'Fucking hell, Shaggy.'

The younger one, the giant, was running back towards the older with what looked like a broken drone.

'That should never happen. The geonet isn't even a part of it. Gen-Four are supposed to see each other.'

The younger one said, 'Search me,' the words low and indistinct, muffled by the crash helmet, the vowels seeming to catch on his tongue and disappear.

'There's a gap in the mud here,' said the older man, addressing Edward again, signalling like a traffic cop. 'Come down that way if your shoes aren't ruined already. I'm Julius Caddel and this is my daughter who everyone calls Shaggy. That's *not* to do with anything improper, it's because she has very bad hair.'

So the younger person was a woman. The revelation was Shaggy's cue to reveal herself, which she did by lifting the crash helmet off her head.

'Bad haircuts, Dad,' said Shaggy. Her face looked drawn with a crayon, the features all too big to fit the outline. Her hair was a delirious mess of thick blonde frizz.

'She has some difficulties but I wouldn't call them learning difficulties because you've never learned anything, mate, have you?'

The exchange unsettled Edward. That tone was cruel, but he could put together the pieces – Julius lived with his daughter, the daughter doting on the dad, any other family long gone, an army of drones the only area of activity beyond the home.

That, and murder.

'Did you control them all just then?' asked Edward, feeling suddenly sick as he came to the threshold of the building – he could almost say 'shack'. 'With one controller?'

'That'd be giving away a secret,' rasped Julius, a smoker's attempt at a conspiratorial whisper, and Edward, as he came closer to the man and shook his weathered hand, saw that he stood with his narrow legs unnaturally straight and seemed to be unable to pivot on his feet. The control box for the drones hung around his neck and Edward wondered how he would turn to get back into the house.

His phone beeped and he looked at it.

You okay?

'Who's that from?' asked Julius, asserting a right to know that sounded almost threatening. His lower lip was fatter than the upper one, and Edward wondered if he had smoked a pipe for years, which could do that. Now Shaggy took her father by the waist and moved him 180 degrees to face the door of their home. It was like the entrance to a garden shed, and when he shoved it, the door flew open. They walked in, Julius dwarfed by his daughter as he clanked towards an armchair. Following, Edward had the strangest thought: *I will never leave this place.*

'So you wanted me?' Julius's head was lolling back on the cushion of the armchair, sinking deep into the fabric. An antimacassar covered the head cushion, and Julius was so deep in the chair it looked as if he was wearing the lace like a bandage. 'Fire away.'

For a moment, Edward was lost for words. He wanted to come straight to the point, wanted to say, 'I did a radio show. A listener died. Quite suddenly, unexpectedly. Violently. You were the last person she had an argument with.' But he was still reeling from the strangeness of this and unsure how to take Julius's odd manner, so instead he tried: 'You're getting the weight off your legs.'

Julius's eyes had closed, but now they popped open. 'Tractor accident.' He suddenly sat forward, screwing one eye closed. 'What's this about, Mister Radio Presenter?'

Edward decided to lean forward too. Now the two of them – Julius in the armchair, Edward on the tattered sofa – were almost touching. But while Edward's knees were in front of him, Julius's shrivelled legs were splayed out straight.

Edward opened his mouth to speak, but as he did so he raised his eyes from the man's legs to the doorway, where Shaggy stood holding a plate with a piece of cake on it and, in the other hand, a rifle.

'Cake, or a bullet?' she said casually, as Edward's mouth stayed agape. She held the rifle at her side, the butt resting on a speckled rug that lay ruckled against the door frame.

The room suddenly chilled.

Julius said, 'I'm having cake, I know that.'

'I only have one piece,' said Shaggy.

'You heard her question,' barked Julius. 'She offered you cake or a bullet, and I'm having the cake.'

Edward felt a sudden bead of sweat break from the top of his neck and roll down his spine. 'I'm not sure what . . . what you mean.'

Shaggy put her hand around the neck of the rifle and, with a jerk of her wrist, expertly yanked the weapon vertically so the entire barrel jumped through her circled fingers until she snatched at the trigger guard. She now looked like a sentry at attention. The muzzle was an inch from the ceiling.

'That seems dangerous, doing that,' said Edward. 'You could blow a hole in the roof.'

'You might want to take a look at the wood up there,' said the old man, 'and ask yourself how many bang-holes she's made in it, considering she's pulled that move about a hundred times.'

'What is she about to do?' asked Edward, conscious that he was now sitting in a pool of sweat.

176

'Aim the gun at you,' answered Shaggy, to his right. And in his peripheral vision, Edward could feel the muzzle of the rifle lowered to a point less than six inches from his right temple, the young woman completely motionless behind it, save for a small left–right movement in her hips, the quiver of the rugby player about to convert.

'She's just playing,' said Julius, with his eyes closed. 'She gets a kick out of the idea.'

'Could you put the gun down, Shaggy?' Edward breathed, heart pumping.

Julius seemed almost to be falling asleep. He reclined in the chair with his eyes closed, but at the same time spread the fingers of each hand and touched the fingertips to each other.

'You've come about the drone club. That's what you said on the phone. Just say what it is, Mister Radio. *Say what it is.*'

Another giggle from Shaggy. 'Say what it is,' she repeated. The gun muzzle was now so close to Edward's forehead that he swore he could hear an echo down the barrel, like the sound from a conch picked up on the shore.

'I . . .'

'Yes?'

'I am friends with . . . *was* friends with a lady who died. Name was Rebecca Mason.' He allowed himself that small lie; she had called his show, but they had never met. 'She had a big argument with your club. What I wanted to ask was—'

Edward felt the gun push into his cheek. Was it his imagination that gave him the exact diameter of the circle of metal on his flesh? The touch gave him the exact location of the gun and – without even thinking – he moved his right arm upwards as fast as he could. His open hand hit, but did not catch, the barrel of Shaggy's rifle. The rifle jerked away from him. Shaggy screamed. Edward jumped, his right arm extended, to catch the long barrel before Shaggy could control it and train the weapon back on him. But as he jumped and caught the weapon, Shaggy tried to take control of it at her end. The shearing force – the woman turning sideways, Edward off-balance, right hand now clenched around the barrel – made Edward fall towards Julius, who screamed in pain. He ended up spread-eagled over the old man in an angled push-up position. Now the gun muzzle was beside Julius's head, pinned in place by Edward's hand, supporting his weight from falling fully onto Julius.

Edward sensed Shaggy breathing heavily behind him. He kicked out to dislodge her from the gun but she would not budge.

Julius's small eyes glittered. But for the first time there was fear in them.

'I don't want your daughter to shoot you,' said Edward, 'but unless I'm very much mistaken, you said there was either cake or a bullet, and you've had the cake.'

'Daddy,' said Shaggy from behind him. 'Daddy, what do you want me to do?'

Julius was staring at Edward, his eyes beseeching now.

'Don't shoot,' said Edward. 'Whatever you do, Shaggy, don't pull that trigger. The gun is touching your dad's head and I can't move it.'

'Daddy?'

'Let go of the gun, honey,' said Julius.

But Shaggy did not let go. She began a frantic back-and-forth movement to work Edward's grip loose, a rapid rhythm that jabbed the barrel alternately into the cushion behind her father's head and into his cheek and temple, and when Edward tried to dislodge her by sliding his foot down the gun, trying to find her hand and kick it clear, she began screaming.

'God . . . no,' said Julius.

Edward glanced left and saw a photo on the side table. The small framed picture caught his attention for a moment.

And then the gun went off.

CHAPTER NINETEEN

Kim saw the tyre tracks heading down into Tanner, and Edward's car at the foot of the slope. Seven or eight people were gathered around one of the squat houses, all dressed as if they worked on the fields. One appeared to be shouting. She pulled a face and cut the car engine.

She saw Edward in the doorway to the second house, almost tall enough to touch his head on the door jamb. She could not work out if the small group gathered around him were angry at him or just speaking loudly with each other. He looked over their shoulders and they all turned.

'Dawn of the living dead,' thought Kim, her lips forming the words soundlessly as she stepped in the mud and approached the group. But there was something in Edward's eyes that concerned her immediately.

'Shotgun went off,' said an older woman, wearing tracksuit bottoms with a tear that showed floral knickers below. 'Fucking shotgun.'

'Language, honey,' said a man beside her. 'Watch the fucks with the lady and that.' He hooted with laughter and then blew his nose loudly.

'It was a rifle not a sh-sh-shotgun,' stammered the lad with

179

the moustache. 'A Browning X-X-X-Bolt.' Kim guessed at X-Bolt. 'That's not a shotgun. A shotgun would have t-taken his head clean off,' he added.

Edward was staring at Kim. Closer now, she checked his face, his head, for blood. His eyes had a glassy look she had not seen before, and his chest was heaving.

She realized the locals were not angry at Edward. As if in a dream, he beckoned her. They fell silent as she said, 'Edward is my friend. Let me through.'

Kim walked carefully, her heels impossible, the shoes ruined, now arriving on a boardwalk that connected all the houses. They were barely more than beach huts, really, and she imagined trying to frame a prospectus: BEACH HUTS MINUS BEACH. BAD SMELL. NO VIEW. RISK OF GUNFIRE. The people around her must be the entire village, pretty much. If they were not angry at Edward, who was their target? If the gun had been fired, did someone get hit?

'Don't call the police,' was the first thing she heard when she entered the shack. She saw a gigantic woman with a bleached frizz as tangled as tree roots sitting on the floor in a doorway that led to the back rooms. But it wasn't the woman who had spoken; she seemed to be crying. An old man was standing behind the sofa with a roll of thick black tape, unsteady on his feet. He grabbed at the tape and pulled it off the spool, an action that made a sound like a dog's yelp. He turned to the window behind him and Kim saw the glass was blown out. Part of the frame was gone as well. The old man was taping up the gap. 'Shaggy,' he said, 'we'll need cardboard. An Amazon box or that old Weetabix packet please.' The woman on the floor shook her head silently.

At Kim's shoulder was Edward.

She realized he had not said a word.

'Are you okay?' she tried.

He did the strangest thing. Opened his hands and stretched the fingers, as if he was counting them.

180

'Edward? Shall I call the police?'

At the second mention of the word 'police', the room became utterly silent.

'Tell you what,' said the shrivelled old man behind the sofa, 'don't call them and I'll have a firm word with Shaggy here.'

'I don't know what's happened, but you've shocked my friend,' said Kim. She took another concerned look at Edward, who was still staring at his upturned hands, which she now saw were shaking. 'And I would say "A Word with Shaggy" is an episode of *Scooby-Doo*, not the correct response to gun crime.'

Edward was looking around him, frowning, as if he did not know where he was. He said nothing.

'The gun went off?' Kim hazarded. Edward blinked. 'The gun went off near you? The gun went off *at* you?' Kim's mouth dropped open as Edward's eyes flicked to hers. 'She shot *at* you?'

The large woman shouted '*Accident!*' from her position on the floor.

'Get the boxes, Shaggy!' her father repeated.

Someone, one of the neighbours behind them, said: 'It went off accidentally or why else would it have done that?'

Kim looked more closely at the window behind the old man's head: it had been blown out by the gun. For a second, she wanted to laugh at the fact that in this kind of house, it was the sort of thing you took five minutes to notice. Edward's silence was upsetting her now. He had plunged his hands into his jacket pocket and, shoulders hunched, was staring at the floor. Now he turned to the villagers, hovering at the entrance as if they sensed danger but were too excited to turn their backs in case they missed something. They were muttering to each other. Edward said only two words.

'Show's over.' Firmly, but without slamming it, he shut the door in their faces.

Silently, Edward picked a framed photo from the side table by the sofa. He stood staring at it, then angled it towards Kim.

Kim had never seen the person in the photo, who was photo-graphed from thirty feet above, waving into the air.

'What am I looking at?'

'That's bloody Rebecca Mason,' said Julius. 'There she is, God bless Her Irritating Highness.'

'I don't get it,' said Kim. 'Rebecca from the house fire?'

'She complained at first,' Julius said, 'but then she agreed to have us, and she was bloody delighted about it. Wanted money, the bitch. I've even got a letter.'

'This is her?'

Edward said only one word – his third since her arrival. 'Yes.'

'So this is a drone shot of Rebecca?'

Silence, while they realized Edward was not going to answer.

'That's her,' said Julius. 'She agreed to let us fly over that wretched field, which was perfect, by the way, for various rea-sons, and although she started by complaining, eventually she took money – a grand! – and got us to do that overhead photo of her in her bloody garden. If she was so angry at the Tanner Drone Club, why the hell is she smiling in the photo and hold-ing a glass of fizz? Eh?' Julius concluded triumphantly just as Shaggy reappeared at the door carrying two empty Weetabix boxes: 'You tell me that!'

'Tight bitch,' said Shaggy.

'That's *enough*,' said her father.

'For heaven's sake,' said Kim menacingly. 'Do you ever stop slating a woman who died? She did nothing wrong.'

'We found the perfect place to fly our drones and she got the whole village to block it for months on end. That's wrong in my book.' Julius paused, and for a second a look of pro-found insight and intelligence crossed his face. 'Look, okay, I can see why you came. You think we did something to her. But we didn't. A few of us – ' he gestured at the front door – 'a few of them, and me, we held a protest outside her house. But that's not the same as doing away with her.'

'Who shot her?' Shaggy asked suddenly, carrying the two empty cereal boxes close to her chest.

'It wasn't a gun,' said Kim, 'it was a fire.'

It took them another fifteen minutes to extract themselves. In her car she asked a shaking Edward, 'Are you okay?'

He was staring out of the window as she gunned the Porsche to get them as far away from Tanner as possible.

'Edward?'

'The gunshot . . .'

'It didn't hit you?'

'No,' he said, breathing deeply, filling his chest with air. 'It jolted me. It was like being shaken . . . and I remembered, Kim, I suddenly remembered the crash.'

When she dropped Edward off at his home, she offered to come in with him, but she knew he would refuse.

She was beginning to regret giving him the lift – it meant his car was still in Tanner, and therefore he was going to struggle to get around.

At least he was speaking again, although his voice and gaze were distant, as if he was sealed in Tupperware.

'I'll get a cab to Tanner and drive it back tomorrow.'

'Give it a couple of days, until you feel yourself again. Use your bicycle in the meantime.'

'I haven't used a bicycle since Matty.'

She was stung by her own thoughtless words. The pair were still sitting outside his house in her Porsche. 'Why are there cones on your driveway, may I ask, as your estate agent?'

'There was a flood.'

'The house?'

'Underneath it, alongside it. Not inside, not yet.'

'So it was the mains? A separate system? Thank God.'

'They said it was the mains.' Everything Edward said seemed to lead nowhere. Kim felt she was at a dinner party where the conversation was failing. 'Can we sit here for a while, Kim? I don't want to bring you in to—'

'Because of my atrocious behaviour last time?'

Normally that would have been the cue for a side remark by Edward – the dangerous reference to their one-off sexual encounter, Kim's instigation of it, her ongoing guilt, her constant apologies – but he passed up the chance to mock her, as if he had not even heard the comment.

'What happened in that house in Tanner?'

Edward breathed in. 'When the car hit Matty and me, it knocked me out and killed Matty. There's nothing I remembered, nothing. I had a head injury and lost half my hearing. I only know where the accident happened because the police took me back there.'

'Where was it?'

'The Amber Road out of Cubitt. A particular junction with—'

'Honestly, you don't need to say.'

'But that's what happened in their house.'

'What do you mean?'

'A flash of light, a crashing sound. The gun. When it went off, I was back there. On the road with Matty. The seconds before and . . .' He choked back tears. 'The car that killed him.'

'You're joking. You remembered it?'

'I did, I *did*, I remember. But it was so instantaneous. I saw the car swerve at me and hit Matty.'

'What car, though? Can you describe it?'

'It was there for a moment. Not a memory. Almost the experience itself. I felt it hit me, push me into the ditch, then heard the scream. But as to the car – I *saw* it – the bang, the flash of the rifle, and there it was, but I couldn't even tell you if it was white, yellow, green? It's like that old thing, "Do you dream in colour?" I saw the car but it didn't have a colour. Or it had lots of them.'

184

'Did you see the driver?'

'Yes. But . . . a teenager, I think. Lad in a baseball cap. You know, the way they wear them? Side on, like he was shielding his face from the sun. I think it was just a black cap. He hit us from behind, I know that, so I guess it was a bad overtake. Matty was in front of me. I remembered nearly all of it.'

Deep within herself, Kim felt a trace of disappointment. She wanted Edward to say he had the make of car, the colour, the registration, the exact motion it followed as it crossed the central line, whether the driver had stopped, even for a second, whether the kid was black or white or yellow or green . . . had the driver taken the cap off? Had Edward seen the face?

'I was out cold, remember,' said Edward, as if he could hear the questions she was asking herself.

'You need company tonight.'

'You're a married lady.'

She was offended. 'I wasn't suggesting . . . for God's sake, Edward, how could you . . .' But they couldn't have their first argument here, like this. So she switched tack. 'Are you certain those drone weirdos had nothing to do with Rebecca?'

Edward was thinking long and hard. She could see his brain working. He was still immersed in the shadow of that flash of memory, of Matty's death. Now, belatedly, he heard her question and forced his thoughts to change track.

'It wasn't them. I'll have to tell Stevie. Arrogant of me, thinking I could wander in and solve it.'

'But how can you be sure? They were the dodgiest bunch of people I have ever seen. Like something out of *Deliverance*, only that movie didn't smell of brake fluid.' She paused. 'And that girl, like an Action Man pumped with air.'

'I don't know what sort of Action Men you've been hanging out with.'

'My mum gave me boys' toys to resist gender stereotypes,' said Kim, staring down the road as they sat there. 'So yes, I had the mountaineer. And the mountaineer looked like Shaggy after a puncture.'

'You're crazy.' His tone, at last, was lightening.

Now it was Kim's turn to feel her mood darken. 'My poor mum. It's why I rang you. She has got herself into a hell of a mess.'

'Tell you what,' said Edward. 'The sun's going down and I have coffee. I know you're due back home but come inside with me and let's talk about it for half an hour.'

'Coffee?'

'Coffee and digestive biscuits. Half an hour.'

'How fresh are the digestives?'

'How rude! They'll be fresh if they're not underwater,' he said.

They both exited the car simultaneously, giggling despite everything. Kim let Edward move ahead to open the door. It gave her a warm glow, in that instant, how well they fitted as a couple, how they lifted each other almost effortlessly – and how the chance of the two of them ever being together as a couple was so slim it might as well have been zero.

CHAPTER TWENTY

Edward stared at Kim and asked her to repeat the number.

'Thirty-one,' she said.

'Grams of what?'

'Grams of sugar in those five biscuits.'

'How do you know that?'

'I googled it when you were in the loo. I wasn't expecting you to spring Chocolate Hobnobs on me. You said digestives.'

'I didn't expect it to be a six-biscuit conversation.'

'Five,' she corrected him. 'Three–two to you.'

He still felt that burning on his skin, which the gunshot had triggered, that stress reaction. Kim's friendship and conversation, and some of her gentle teasing, were calming him down. They had not been like this since . . . since that time last year. She would have to go soon; the realization was like an ache, a stitch from running.

'How is your husband, anyway?'

'Oh God,' she said, 'I'll need to head back. He's got medications and they have to be taken noon and night. He's improving a little, but still – I don't know what the word is. Glassy?'

'As in . . .?'

'Glassy as in you feel he's not there, just a sheet of glass two inches thick, and if he bumped into something he would just shatter.'

'You could walk through him.'

'You'd hurt yourself if you did.' She suddenly looked tearful. 'I think I went glassy earlier.'

'You got shattered earlier. Anything that takes you back to that moment on Amber Road – that would break a person.'

'And the shotgun. That was a crazy crowd. Kind of . . . raw. An argument could easily end in someone dying, and they would probably just feed the body to the pigs.'

'Good grief. Maybe that's what the smell was. People won't buy any of those shacks for a while.'

'If you could sell me this place, I reckon you could sell one of those shotgun shacks.' He smiled. 'Why do they call them that in the States?'

'Because you open the front door and see out of the back door. So a shotgun bullet would go in the front and out the back without hitting anything.' She added, 'You promise me you'll go to the police, Edward, and describe everything you remembered about the crash, every last detail? If only Anthony was working at the moment, I could get him to help sort that.'

'No. I really don't think that would be a good idea. Not in a thousand billion years. I can't imagine ever meeting him and not feeling I'd disgraced myself. And I'd give myself away.'

'It was a long time ago, Edward, our thing. And it doesn't carry. We *are* just friends, right?'

'Right.' He wanted to challenge her on that, but he could not. Was their relationship the shotgun shack, with a gap so big you pass through it without touching the sides? He remembered: *Oh, Mr Temmis, I do adore you.* 'I hope Anthony gets better,' said Edward after a moment, 'and I'm really sorry to hear about your mum.'

Kim had laid out the facts of Barbara's story, the episode at the airport and the aftermath. She managed not to cry. Some vicious bastard – probably in a country far away, say Russia or Nigeria or Uzbekistan, probably in a boiler-room operation where people sat at long desks searching for British pensioners to con – had successfully scammed her mum for nearly £45,000. You could call it catfishing, because it was romance they were offering. The promise of the antique-duck automaton to add to Barbara's collection of precious models was a brilliant stroke, well-researched and perfectly designed (like the interior of the fictional duck) to win her mother's trust. With Kim's help, Barbara had quantified the loss and reached the final and exact figure of £44,353, which was the bulk of Barbara's life savings, if you didn't count the house, which was in itself a problem because there was still a mortgage. It did not include lost future interest on the swindled money. Nor did it include emotional injury, and a greater loss – of pride.

'This bastard made her feel attractive, actually made her feel loved by a man, and I don't know if she'll trust anyone again,' Kim said in an exhausted voice. 'And the mirror.'

'Mirror?'

'I told you! The portrait mirror propped on the floor. You may well ask what she was photographing with that.'

'God, no.'

'But why can't an old person be sexual? Not my mum, obviously but . . .' Kim trailed off tearfully. 'She might have to sell the house. When Mum and Dad divorced she got the house on the basis that she got the debt too. It's not a big mortgage, but unless she goes back to work, she'll have no way of paying it off.'

Edward looked at her. They were sitting across the kitchen table from each other, with only accusing specks of Hobnob left on the single plate of biscuits he had produced. He licked his finger and pushed it into the plate to pick up the crumbs.

'Disgusting,' she said, and he could not tell if she was referring to foreign con artists or his own lack of manners.

The flood had not shown up inside the house and for once Kim did not apologize for selling this jinxed property to him. Edward wondered if she had run out of unnecessary apologies. He peered at her with interest, and the deepest feeling of friendship washed over him.

'What can I do for Barbara? Is she Barbara Cobden?'

'Barbara Sinker.'

'So that's your maiden name?'

'How quaint you are. Yes, my virginal spinster maiden name. Kimberley Sinker. It's like a fantasy cruise-ship name – um, no, you're right, it's really not.'

'Please go immediately to your cabins on HMS *Kimberley Sinker*. I don't think so.'

'Edward, you're sounding back to your normal self. A little.'

'I wonder if that's happened to other people – a shock suddenly triggers a memory you didn't know you had?' Edward was conscious he had left a wire dangling. 'But on the other thing, what can I do for your mother?'

'Nothing, Edward. Okay, it's why I rang. I wanted to open my heart a little. Not easy to do that with a depressed husband, so I rang you, but now I just feel I'm using you again.'

'You're not using me. You're using my biscuits.'

She ignored him. 'Plus, you have other priorities. You have to go to the police and tell them what you saw before you forget it again. It's a serious crime like murder, what happened! Write it down, please! And then I guess one of us should talk to Stevie.'

'Oh.' That side of it had not occurred to Edward. He felt he had done his best for Stevie, and dreaded her expecting more. 'I'll do it. I'll say that whatever befell her grandmother, it wasn't murder by drone club.'

'And they didn't drive her to suicide?'

'Not if she's clinking champagne glasses with them.'

'The Tanner people were ghastly though—'

'But imagine a murder plot hatched by Tin Man and Action

190

Girl. They'd probably shoot each other in the car on the way there.'

'So what happened to Rebecca?'

Edward stared into Kim's eyes. They were purest green now, as if they had changed with the level of her concentration, and he saw how smooth the skin on her face was; he longed to lean over and cup her cheek.

'We did our best to find out and we didn't,' he said with a sigh. 'Not suicide, not murder, just an accident. A sad accident caused by a combination of dozens of bits of paper stuck to the wall and thirty tea lights. Which will thrill Stevie's parents, because they're stressing about invalid insurance. But come on, I must be able to help your mum somehow. She was always such a supportive listener.'

'Oh, she still is. She loves you, *As-In-Wimbledon*.'

'She mentioned her collection of automatons on the radio once, didn't she?'

'Of course she did. And she would have said auto-*mata* by the way, naughty boy. But they are so hard to describe. "Wooden miniatures that do something special when you turn a tiny handle, crafted before anyone had invented batteries, with tiny cogs". I know I'm not selling it.'

'You must have been excited about them when you were a kid.'

'Yes, I think I probably was.'

Edward thought for a second, as if willing something to the front of his head. Then he said, 'At least I can ring my old producer and get him to do your mother's story, the con artist, as an item on the show. His name is Derrick Tidy. He's still very loyal.'

'I don't know if she'll want the world to see her folly.'

'She could do first name only. We don't have to say the word "Sinker" at all. Might help others,' he pushed, ever the journalist.

Kim lifted her eyebrows, weighing up a choice she did not want to make. At that moment, her phone vibrated on the table. It was face down; not once had she looked at the display since they had sat down together. He was saddened by the thought that she might be called away.

'Business?'

She stared at the screen. The light made her face clown-white against the dimmer yellow of the kitchen lamps. 'Definitely not pleasure. Poor Anthony,' she said. 'He says he's staying with his mother tonight after having a panic attack at hers.'

'Where's his mother?'

'Why do you ask?'

'I was sort of hoping you might say Brazil.'

'My, my, Mister Temmis! Would this be the first time you've flirted with a lady?' She put on a Southern-states accent to say it. Kim picked up a copy of the council recycling schedule, which happened to be on the table beside her, and fanned her face comically. 'Look at me blushing, sir. No, she's Exmoor, nearest town Minehead.'

'I didn't mean anything by my comment.'

'Believe me, I know.' Was that the slightest regret he detected in her voice?

They were heading to the front door a minute later. She turned back. 'I know it's crazy for me to say this, but I love this house. The shape of it, a bit Bates Motel, and the spectacular view . . .'

'I love it too.'

'Just don't become the view. If you hear it going—'

'They don't just fall off the edge,' said Edward, suddenly so amused he wanted to burst out laughing. 'Is that why you're running to get out of here?'

'It hadn't crossed my mind!'

She returned his grin with the warmest smile. For a moment their eyes met and there was nothing that needed to be said.

There was a lightness in her step. He loved this about her – the sense that she controlled her world with force and good humour, in a way that he felt he never could. She made things happen; he had things happen to him. She was a queen, and he was a fool.

But this, he realized, made no sense. Her businesslike approach to life had run aground in the angry mess of marriage to Anthony. Did he love her because he saw how much more she could be without her husband?

'I bet it did cross your mind, though,' said Edward, with a wry smile. 'Crash, and the two of us plunging two hundred feet down to Ladram Bay with the local paper printing our photos under the headline MYSTERY OF LOVE RIDDLE DUO. I saw you fiddling with your car keys so I know you were panicking.'

She laughed freely, eyes shining, looking back into the house as he opened the front door for her. 'I'm always the estate agent, I know. But I do honestly like the stairs.'

And in that moment, as he turned back towards the hallway, it came to Edward in a rush.

'The stairs,' he said blankly.

'What is it?' Kim asked.

'Wait, wait,' he said, 'I have to think.' He put an arm out to find the wall and leant his weight on it. 'Look, look.'

'At what?'

'The stairs – think about Rebecca. She was into movies, wasn't she?'

'I don't know.'

'She was, she was. Because when I asked Derrick to tell me what she'd called the show about, one thing was . . . oh, God, this can't be.'

'Ed, tell me!'

'And on the floor,' he said, 'the metal circle on the floor . . .'

'What circle on what floor?'

He put his hand on his forehead, as if he was about to collapse, but it was really just to control the sudden lurch from logic to realization that was happening all across his brain.

'I know what happened. I know why she died. I must go to Stevie.'

'Let me come.'

'No, Kim.'

'Mate, you don't have a car. Either you come with me and you tell me what's going on, or you can damn well walk twenty miles.'

CHAPTER TWENTY-ONE

Going via Tanner to pick up his car added fifty minutes. It was dark. The ramshackle hamlet was quiet, thank God. He ran down the hill with his keys, holding his breath against the stink, dreading Julius or Shaggy or any of the other villagers appearing. When he started the engine, lights went on in the shacks around him. Luckily the tyres gained traction and he was off before anyone emerged, reversing up the hill, headlights dipped.

On the road they both did three-point turns and he led the way. They had just missed visiting hours at the hospital. Thankfully the senior nurse behind the desk, an older lady with long eyelashes and cheeks as red as supermarket apples, looked at him knowingly. 'You must know Turnip.'

'Ah, yes,' he said. Turnip was the nickname for Brian Channon, one of the RTR Farmers. 'Gone now from the radio, of course.'

'You and him! You were my absolute favourites.' He wondered how that was possible, but took the compliment. She had a deep Devon accent, trim hips and a curvy chest. Her eyelashes literally fluttered at him. She sighed. 'Oh well. Times change. They got rid of the wood, brought in the plastic.'

'Out with the old,' said Kim, and Edward wanted to shout:

195

It wasn't my age, those bastards were twenty years older; it was because I lost it when my son died.

'Stevie – our patient – she mentions you often. Go through, but hush-hush. I'm going to say you crept past me while I was on the loo.'

Stevie had been under the surgeon's knife. As she had fore-warned, skin had been moved from an area just above and behind her left knee to below the burned eye. What would her eye look like? He wanted to see it now, to reassure himself. But it was still covered.

'They restored the lid and they say the op went as well as it could have,' Stevie announced in a tired voice, 'but I don't fancy looking in the mirror for a while. Hello, Kimberley. It was very kind of you to get me into Granny's house. I don't think my parents even found out, thank you sweet Jesus for that particular fucking mercy, and I apologize for my language.'

'Sssshhh, Stevie, with your awful cursing,' said a soft nurse's voice from the corridor.

'You don't need to apologize,' whispered Kim. 'You just need to get your friend Edward here to tell us what on earth he thinks he's worked out, because I couldn't get a word out of him before now.'

Edward pulled the curtain around Stevie's bed. He couldn't see many patients elsewhere in the ward; perhaps some of the beds might be kept empty because of staffing issues. It was past 8 p.m., and occasionally the footsteps of a nurse or porter would cross the room. But now it was deathly quiet, the lighting low. Edward sat on the edge of Stevie's bed and, with Kim to his right on a squat plastic chair, spoke in a level voice to the younger woman.

'When they told me what Riva had called the show about, I missed the significance of it. I focused on the Tanner Drone Club, the problems she'd had with them. But that wasn't the most important thing Derrick Tidy told me. He's my ex-producer and he's been brilliant with all of this. He said she'd called to take part in a film quiz but he couldn't remember the film.'

'Okay . . .' said Stevie doubtfully.

'Leave that for a second. You described a mural, right?'

'In her house?'

'Yes, in that strange narrow room at the front. The first thing to go up when the fire started. All that paper. And the dress as well! That beautiful dress. What colour was it again?'

'White.'

Kim was looking puzzled. 'Nobody mentioned a dress.'

Edward pulled his mobile phone from his jacket and swiped to find an image. 'I just looked this up and screenshotted it. Listen. "The white dress should be easy to copy. Those puffed sleeves, the flounce, and the little bodice".' He was reading from his phone.

Stevie asked, 'What are you quoting?'

'It's a line from a famous film. The film your lovely grandmother knew so much about that she won a contest on my show with it as the subject. Hitchcock's *Rebecca*.'

'How do you know this?' asked Kim.

'My old producer, Derrick, mentioned the quiz but neither of us understood it was such an important part of this. Rebecca breezed through all the movie questions. He didn't remember which film. Nor did I. So I went back through the social media. We had a hashtag for the contest, and sure enough, on the night Riva played – calling herself Riva, of course – there were a handful of tweets. One said, "Big up this Riva lady for the *Rebecca* knowledge!", which gave it to me. But that still meant nothing, and I almost forgot about it. But the mural your granny stuck to her wall, all that paper, the dress and so on – when it was described to me I didn't understand it, didn't see the relevance. Of course, when we got to the house it was all ashes. It was only tonight that I got it. Kim was at my house and she pointed out—'

'The staircase,' Kim put in, sounding puzzled.

Stevie propped herself up on her elbows. 'Go on.'

Edward touched his phone and swiped the screen. 'Was this the picture your dad saw? Did he show it to you?'

'Yes and yes,' said Stevie quietly. 'That's the *exact* picture.'

'That's a screenshot from the movie, which she must have somehow printed off across multiple sheets of paper to recreate as a full-wall mural.' Edward stood and began to pace on the small area of available floor. 'So what do we have? A mural of the staircase. I watched *Rebecca* a few weeks back. Her name was in my mind; there was nothing more to it. It has a famous opening line – 'Last night I dreamt I went to Manderley again.' In the dress scene, Rebecca appears at the top of a big staircase wearing a white dress. She thinks her husband will like it, but then she finds out she's been tricked by the housekeeper into wearing an outfit favoured by his late wife.

'So our Rebecca – your Rebecca, Stevie, your granny – loves the film. We have the dress, and we have the backdrop. And we just need to ask why?'

'Some kind of fantasy?'

'For sure. And why not? She lives alone and she wants to dress her home like a film set, dress herself like a film star, and appear at the top of the famous Manderley staircase because it's a movie she loves. And there wouldn't be anything alarming about that, but for the rusted metal circle I saw on the floor.'

He sat back on Stevie's bed. The ward was so quiet he could almost believe the other patients were listening.

'A metal circle. Charred rather than rusted. Did you see that, Stevie?'

'I don't know,' said Stevie. 'Possibly. I had my mind on getting the computer, so I was distracted.'

'Kim?'

'Nope.'

He continued, 'It was on the floor in that narrow front room. Like a hoop. And next to it was what I thought was the remains of an umbrella. A metal pole with three smaller branches. It wasn't an umbrella.'

'Go on,' said Kim.

'I couldn't work it out. Then, we were leaving my place earlier, Kim and I, after we'd had a torrid time with the drone people—'

Here he was about to add an explanation, but then having breathed in to start it, waved away the intention, as much a hand signal to himself as to Stevie. There was no point in talking about Tanner now.

'Yeah, well, anyway, Kim turned around, didn't you, and said something about the staircase?'

'I guess so.'

'And it was like a spark across my brain, a shock of realization. The mural, the dress, the movie. That metal circle was what was left of a ring light. The light you buy to do online socials. The metal pole with the branches was not an umbrella. It was a tripod. She was lighting herself for someone else! She was performing, your dear grandma. But I think she was being taken advantage of.'

'Like my mum?' Kim's voice was quiet, hoarse, and Stevie turned to her, puzzled.

Edward asked, 'What did you say?'

'Like what happened to my mum.'

'What happened to your mum?' asked Stevie.

Edward stood up suddenly. 'Of course,' he said. 'My God.'

CHAPTER TWENTY-TWO

The senior nurse popped her head around the curtain ten minutes later. 'Probably time . . .'

'Yes, yes, of course,' said Kim, about to stand, but Stevie waved the nurse back. 'Just another five, Janette? Please?'

The older woman smiled. 'Well. As you are our best patient . . .' She clacked away again.

Stevie touched the bandage as if checking it was still there. Edward looked intently at her as she spoke. 'So what you're saying, Mr Temmis, as I understand it, is that someone wicked fixed on my lovely granny. Made contact with her, exploited her – shit, I so want to bloody swear about this but I mustn't – fucking hell. They exploited her love of that movie, and God knows how they knew about it . . . and then, then what?'

'I hate to say it,' Edward began, 'but I think it may be the same scam Kimberley's mum suffered. This is a . . . what, a former Soviet republic thing? Or Albanian, or Caribbean, or what?'

'Racist,' said Stevie.

'Come on. It's where a bunch of people sit in a room somewhere far away and they just pound the phones and they make connections and—'

'And my mum loses over forty grand,' Kimberley put in. 'And your granny—'

'I don't know if Granny did lose money, though?' asked Stevie. 'Was she scammed?'

'Would your mum and dad know if she was?' Edward asked. 'Old people have savings in all sorts of places. For all we know, she posted him cash from her mattress.'

'Do you think it was a love scam? Did she have her heart broken?'

The question hung in the air, because Kimberley was blowing her nose, and Edward stood up again and paced the few steps of space within Stevie's cubicle. 'Wait. We're missing something here. The fire was not an accident. We know that because of the acid. We have to assume the person who destroyed the computer also killed your granny. I'm sorry, Stevie, to put it so bluntly . . .'

Stevie stared intensely.

'And they did it deliberately, because she knew something, and there was something on the computer that identified them.'

Silence as they all took it in.

'Accounts?' suggested Kim. She pushed the tissue back into her handbag. Edward saw how red her eyes were; she had been crying. 'I'm sorry,' Kim added.

Stevie murmured, 'It's me that should be upset.'

'But my mother,' said Kimberley. 'It's just so wrong, and so sad.'

'We can get to this,' said Edward. 'We can get to it just by looking at the facts. Barbara and the duck. Riva – Rebecca – and the movie scene. Someone makes a bond with these women, but with Rebecca something happened to make them realize she was going to expose them. Oh, damn, damn,' he whispered, exasperated, sitting down and then standing again. 'It must be the letter. The letter must be the reason she was killed. She had worked out what was going on.'

'It is somehow fitting,' Kim began, 'that one woman is conned with a glamorous vision from classic Hollywood cinema, and my poor mum gets done with a wooden duck.'

Stevie spat out her laughter as if it was a mouthful of something that tasted rotten. Then she groaned. 'You mustn't make me laugh, either of you.'

'Sorry,' said Kim, the hint of a smile lightening her face a little.

'But you said before, Edward, the killer is going to assume you got the letter,' Stevie continued. 'So why would they go to all that trouble?'

'Okay.' This logical block kept pushing him back to square one. 'So there was something else on the computer. Must have been.'

'Money transfers, maybe?' suggested Kim.

'Evidence of the payments. Could be. But we have that with Barbara and it doesn't identify anyone. They have burner bank accounts.'

Stevie said something Edward did not hear. 'Let me turn this up.' He touched the hearing aid.

'I just said we're not making progress,' said Stevie, 'and you have to go.'

'But we are making progress. Whoever scammed Rebecca and Barbara is a killer,' said Edward, 'and they're local.'

'But we still have to go,' said Kim. 'We're wearing Stevie out.'

'Wait – local?' Stevie asked abruptly.

Sighing, as if this had already been explained, Edward said: 'You can't set fire to someone's house from Lagos. You can't put acid in a computer from Tel Aviv or . . . or whatever the capital of Albania is.'

'Tirana,' said Kim. 'And I'll tell you something else. They'll have other victims too. I have an idea.'

Kim's idea had to wait. Booted out of the hospital, they were about to get into their separate cars when Kim made Edward promise he'd speak to Devon Police in the morning about his memory of the day Matty died. There was precious little new to go on, but he knew they would not be impressed if he had remembered something, anything about the driver who hit them both and then did not feed it into their inquiry.

If there still was an inquiry.

He rang them first thing, but when they asked him to come to the station in Exeter, he realized he could not plead for yet another day off from the garden centre. He needed the income and he needed, as pathetic as it sounded, to build up some sort of recent employment history to avoid looking like a washed-up DJ whose life had fallen to pieces. So he must catch the attention of Kenneth Schomes. It was mid-April, and when Edward tracked him down by the front entrance, new customers pushing past with empty trolleys gathered from the car park, Schomes was wheezing. His chest lifted the sweat-blotched white shirt he always wore. The keychain on his belt hung heavy, as if it was causing his exhaustion.

'Packing,' he said. 'Packing cactus.'

Spring was here, with a dry breeze and bright sunshine. Regardless of the difficulties he might have with any other employer if he threw this job in, there was a part of Edward Temmis that would be reluctant to leave the garden centre before spring had fully sprung. When you lose a child you lose everything; status never bothers you again. And no job outside a paint factory offered the engorgement of colour a place like this gave in spring. Even the customers seemed to come into bloom, arriving with happy smiles and bright jackets instead of hats and gloves.

Schomes and Edward sat in a small office behind the information desk, where a large floral swing-seat had sat unsold for

203

three years. Edward could not read the man, with whom he had spent very little time.

'I need to ask—' Edward began carefully, but he was interrupted.

'You need to ask for another day off.' Kenneth Schomes looked halfway between amused and frustrated, like a driver stranded at a junction because he could not choose left or right. 'You've had a fair number.'

'To be quite honest, I have,' said Edward.

'Well,' Schomes began to huff, and Edward noticed a line of moustache so thin it had been invisible until this point; was that the old Hollywood look, the Clark Gable? 'You *are* a celebrity, I suppose.'

'I was. Not now.'

'My mother keeps asking to meet you,' said Schomes, and Edward could not take his eye off the moustache. Was it Gable or Errol Flynn who wore one – the pencil, wasn't it? Like a single line drawn in 2HB? That 'tache was in fashion almost a century ago! 'As far as Mother's concerned, you're still there on the radio every day,' Schomes continued. 'That's how devoted she is.'

'I'm honoured.'

'The dementia has been difficult for us all.' The sentence ended with a gasp, and Schomes suddenly sneezed loudly enough to rattle the window behind him. 'We have hay-fever season coming now. Do you suffer it, Mr Temmis?'

'Do call me Edward. No. Never have done, fingers crossed.'

'It can knock out half the workers on a bad day. We had to close the canteen once and throw all the freshly baked away. And I can hardly tell our people to come in when we've got more pollen here than the Soviet army.' The comparison was so impenetrable that for a second Edward forgot why he was in the room. 'So we don't want to lose you, Edward . . .'

'Right . . .'

'No, we don't, and I have to tell you, happily, that last month you were voted Star Employee for March.'

Edward was in no doubt that a sensitive newspaper piece in the *Exeter Express* about the first anniversary of the tragedy, and the stalled police inquiry, had been passed around the garden centre. He'd found a copy of the double-page article, separated from the rest of the paper, on a tray in the canteen. Star Employee for March (when he had barely worked twelve days) was like an embrace from his colleagues, all of whom he liked.

'That's good. Thank you.'

'So what can I do for you, Mr . . . Edward?'

'I might need . . .' He was about to ask for a day off, but then an alternative struck him. 'Maybe just a room next week for a couple of hours, for a private meeting?'

To his surprise, Schomes laughed. 'Like a bad astrologer, I didn't see that coming! That's a modest request. Do I ask why?'

'The police want to see me.' Edward added quickly, 'In relation to the death of my son.'

To his great surprise, Schomes leant forward slowly at the desk and began to cry. The tears emerged as he bent his body at the waist, as if the movement of his midriff was squeezing water from his eyes. The tears became sighs. The sighs, deep sobs, which caused his chest to heave again.

This meeting was not going how Edward had imagined it would. He had taken Schomes for a jobsworth, a man who resented any status Edward might have brought with him. But it seemed that in the small world of the portly manager of a Devon garden centre with a 1920s moustache and keys jangling from his slacks, Edward had the status of David Beckham. And the death of his son had affected more people than he could ever have imagined.

The name of the police officer was Jordan Callintree. He was younger than the last one, who was younger than the one before. If this investigation took any longer, they would be sending someone's baby.

He and Edward sat in a room near the tools section. The door to it was hidden, only accessible if you moved an artificial tree, which was like a big-armed wooden coat stand. From it hung a range of mid-sized saws and electric cutters with the word SKEFFERS on them in orange. Moving the display created jeopardy: would a saw fall? Edward was impressed that the police officer mucked in. It took three of them to shift the stand. A minute later, the cop sat down opposite him and opened his file.

'I see you are still carrying an injury?'

'Oh, no. Well, occasionally my hip hurts a bit,' said Edward. 'Since the crash. My walk is uneven. But it's settled down, mostly.'

'Anything else?'

'I lost the hearing in this ear.' He showed the hearing aid.

'Well, we . . . have not made progress,' the policeman said after a moment spent shuffling his papers. His voice was higher than Edward expected and there was an intelligence in his eyes that surprised the older man. They were the same height and had made the room feel small when they entered together.

'We have not made progress,' Callintree repeated, 'and that pisses me off.'

Jordan Callintree was not wearing his police uniform, and he had made a great show of asking Edward to inspect his warrant card. 'By all means ring the number here if you want to check me out. I didn't wear the work suit because I find it makes intimate conversations like this more difficult. I am sorry for your loss.'

Those six words had been spoken to Edward so many times in the last year that he almost wished people could just use an acronym (IASFYL, pronounced *Ice-file?*) to save time. He resented any expression of concern that was less than six inches deep. But, for obvious reasons, people's sympathy tended to be shallower than his grief. Rather than be angry at them, he turned his resentment on himself. It was complicated.

Somehow Jordan had said the six words with a level of sincerity he had not heard in a long time. Schomes had cried; Calltree showed he cared. Surely there was a chance of catching the man who had mowed down his son?

'It's unusual,' said the police officer, 'to have a case where no one witnesses the miscreant.'

'I prefer the term "murderer", but yes.'

'I don't know if you'll get "murder" from a jury, Mr Temmis. It sounds like terrible driving, and then the despicable driver's crime – he hits, he runs. There'll be a big jail sentence if . . . well, we aren't there yet. I would guess he asks for manslaughter and we say, "You can have it if you plead guilty", so no trial. But for me the mystery is this. Normally someone would report a damaged front bumper. Or blood on a driver's door. But this person covered his tracks. Or hers.'

'His,' stressed Edward Temmis. 'That's why I called. I had a shock the other day – ' he would certainly not be getting into the gunplay in Tanner – 'and it gave me, I guess you could say, a flashback.'

'Mind if I record?' The police officer had his mobile in his hand.

Edward nodded then shut his eyes. 'You know, in a dream, you can't see colours? And then everyone starts saying, "I dream in black and white." With this it's almost the opposite.'

'Go on,' said the policeman.

'Well, that's just it.' Edward opened his eyes for a second. The cop was slight and skinny at the waist. Clean-shaven with no jaw; when he opened his mouth his chin dropped away. But his face shone with a cat's curiosity. Edward shut his eyes tighter.

'The car . . . either I see no colours, just greys, or I see loads of colours. A regular car. So I don't have a memory for you.'

'Do you at least have a shape for me?' the policeman prompted. 'You said "regular".'

'I'm no Jeremy Clarkson, but I can have a go at guessing a model,' said Edward. 'Ford Focus? I don't know. It could be anything. Name a model and I'd probably say yes, that one.'

There was silence, during which Edward, still with his eyes squeezed shut, wondered if he was disappointing the officer. He opened his eyes to see the constable standing over him and wondered how he had moved so silently.

'The driver?' said PC Callintree. 'Anything on the driver?'

Edward looked down at the man's iPhone, still recording, the screen lit. 'My partner . . .' What a slip that was. 'I mean, my *friend*, a lady called Kim, says this is the bit you'll want to know. He was wearing a baseball cap.'

'Back to front?'

'No. Sideways. It had some sort of pattern on it. Like I say, young, maybe a teenager.'

'Boy racer, sounds like. Remember the pattern?'

'No, sorry. Dark blue hat, white stitching maybe, or a crest?'

Callintree pushed his fingers together until they interlocked, then twiddled his thumbs. Edward had not seen anyone do that for years.

'Could you see the face?'

'Like I say, definitely a young man.'

'Ethnicity?'

Remarkable, in all the conversations with Kimberley, and in all the interior dialogue he had had with himself, this question had never been asked.

'White.'

'Really? You're sure?'

'It's Devon.'

'That's not my question. I'm not asking you to guess, Mr Temmis. I'm asking you what you know.'

'Young white male in baseball cap.' He nodded with more confidence than he felt. 'Do you think you're going to find him?'

'Things come out. His mum sees a blood spatter on a J-Cloth or he makes a drunken slip on a night out. People give themselves away.' Callintree must have noticed that Edward did not look convinced. 'And in terms of the accident – you were knocked off your bike and badly hurt. I've been to the spot. I've seen it. You went into a bush, your poor son Matty hit the tree. I hate to come back to this, as I'm sure there's never a day when you don't think of it, Edward – your son was killed by the driver, no question. But we are struggling to work out if he came from the front or the rear. The skid marks don't help us, which is very unusual.'

'Why not?'

'When a driver slams on the brakes, that's when the wheels lock and you get a superb imprint of the tyres on the ground, what forensics call "a melt", that can last for weeks. Here we have no melt. So we can't even tell what direction this man was coming from. Did he hit you head-on? I mean, from the front?'

This had just come to Edward! He had had no memory of the actual trajectory of the car, only the explosive pain of the impact and the noise of the vehicle as it stopped, reversed, and then left them. Wait . . . reversed . . .

'He came from the rear.'

'You're sure?'

'He came from the rear, hit us, reversed. After reversing, he drives on.'

'Did he get out of the car?'

'No. When he hit my bike, it flipped me off. He pulled the car back. I heard that. I saw stars. But I saw him. Saw the cap, saw the lad, saw the car. So he came from behind, headed off in the same direction. I must have passed out a second later. I don't remember seeing Matty at all during this.' He sighed deeply.

'But no tyre marks. Such an odd manoeuvre, almost as if the

car was aimed at your son, but that's ridiculous. It sounds like he wasn't speeding and, if he didn't skid, he didn't brake. So he was, what, three times over the limit? Or could it be an electric car, very nimble, anti-locking on all four wheels? Not an SUV, though, no chance of the ground being unmarked. And what colour was it?'

Edward ground his teeth. Hadn't he remembered enough for a single meeting? That said, this was the first police officer to give the impression he might actually keep the investigation alive. He had been to the spot where it happened . . .! Even that phrase sounded corner-turning. Edward wanted him to feel encouraged by his efforts to remember.

'If I think about the colour of the car, it's so confused. It could be black, white, green, yellow . . .'

'Red?'

'I don't think it was red.'

'Blue?'

'It could have been blue.' This drew a grimace from Callintree, who moved to his phone, sat down again, and swished his finger across the screen expertly. 'I'll get this written up.'

'Does it help?'

The young police officer stared at the screen.

'Hugely.'

Edward could not tell if he meant it or not.

CHAPTER TWENTY-THREE

That evening, he found a WhatsApp message from Kim that had been sitting unopened all day.

> Righto, my idea – see what you think of this – is to get your old radio show to do a shout-out for people who've been romance-scammed. Don't do it under your name, people will get too interested. Just a small on-air announcement by Tessa.

He read it at home. The weather was warm, summer was coming, and with the later sunset he was able – for the first time this year – to put on an overcoat and sit at the end of the garden, near the line where the land fell away. The sea whispered from below.

Why was he trying to chase down the person who killed Rebecca, if indeed that person even existed? He tried to answer his own question. Because there was no 'if'. Because he was damn sure Barbara had been targeted by the same team. Team? Person? He sipped at a mug of tea. He had bought sun-sensitive glasses, and they were darkening as if at the height of summer, but too much – so now this was like one of the old movies, where the night scenes were all filmed in the day with the camera exposure down. The sun was still up, but he was sitting in the night. How apt.

Old movies . . . Hitchcock. The thought took him back to *Rebecca*, the movie. In the film he had only recently seen, the naive new wife of Maxim de Winter is conned by the malicious Mrs Danvers into dressing exactly like Rebecca, the late wife. Her ensuing appearance at the top of a staircase in a flowing white dress was, he now understood, one of the great moments in Hollywood. Rebecca Mason knew the film and loved it, probably drawn to it initially because of the shared name. Her predator knew that and exploited it. What animal gets a woman to re-enact a movie scene to win her trust, to burrow into her life? Stevie's grandmother had made it too obvious, with a DIY mural and her £7,000 dress and ring light, and when she banned her son and family from the house, Edward was guessing, it put too much heat on the killer, who did away with her.

It didn't sound right, though. A murder as disgusting as hers must surely have been justified by a more direct threat to the perpetrator. His insides turned at the thought that the old lady had written to him, and the bloody radio station had lost the letter. The security guards treated the empty envelope as a joke! Surely the letter had the answer? What if the letter *had actually identified* the scam artist? But the killer could not know she had written, much less that the letter had been lost. Killing her did not unsend the letter.

Again he went through it: Barbara scammed, Rebecca scammed, Rebecca killed and the computer destroyed. That was it in ten words. All that work, all that thinking he had done, the life-changing injury to young Stevie . . . it all amounted to an insoluble puzzle. Barbara scammed, Rebecca scammed, Rebecca killed. A six-word mystery.

Irene.

The name 'Irene' just came to him.

Where had that come from? Why had an Irene lodged in his consciousness and jumped out, just now, like popped toast? Who was Irene?

Edward fished for his phone, thinking he needed a WhatsApp group with Kim and Stevie where he could ask the question. He lifted his darkened glasses to see the screen. The light made it difficult – the sun was low now, flashing on the sea below. It would be gone in an hour, but at this moment it had command of the horizon. Each passing minute brought a new shade of pink, of orange and blue, to the thin line of cloud where sea and sky met.

His lock screen was Matty, and he paused and looked at his son. It was a summer holiday photo. Matty's hair was wet from swimming. It stuck up, brown-blond, and there was his toothy grin. His shoulders were draped with a towel and he had his trunks on. He was probably aged five or so in the photo. Tara and Edward had been parting, but Matty must have been oblivious. Certainly if he felt sad about the split, he managed to hide it. He could make sunlight with that happy face.

There was no one but Matty, even though Matty was no more. His son had loved the adventure, the madness, of this house. The idea that it might fall. He had kicked three footballs over the edge in the last two months of his life. 'Not your fault, mate,' Edward had said. 'That last shot was deflected off me so I'll take that.'

He could see the two of them now, father and son, silhouetted against the same golden light. The darkest hour and all that. It had worked in reverse for them: dawn had come first, then darkness. Edward regretted the failure of his marriage, but that had been five years earlier. As Matty approached his teenage years, their weeks together had been joyous – for Edward, at least. No, he was sure that went for Matty too. Edward would be looking forward to the next Saturday from the moment Matty left. Twice a month he would pick Matty up from Tara's in Exeter for their week together (sometimes bumping into her accountant husband or other children and always feeling like the ragged-trousered gate-crasher). Together they would drive along the sea. Matty had been just about to hit the bolshy years, perhaps. But for now the young lad would talk and talk. Marvel movies, Manchester City, heavy metal . . . oh, yes, he was into his music, getting it from his dad. Everything from AC/DC to Al Green. They would shuffle the songs in the car. 'You Shook Me All Night Long' followed by 'Let's Stay Together'.

Edward's head lolled back, and the tears ran down his face. The soft breeze picked up, not cold, more like a caress in the glow of golden light. He angled his head further back as he cried, so the thin lines of wet flowed into his ears and he felt submerged in his grief. As his eyes closed, he saw himself and Matty in the car, tearing down the cliff path at Teignmouth. They were laughing. The car suddenly had no roof, and above them cartoon lightning forked in the sky. Thunder rolled. But there were no clouds, only that golden, colour-saturated sunlight. The car roared on the cliff path. All they did was laugh. He and his son. Louder and louder laughter, and the roar of the engine above the music now deafening. A bucketful of water hit them like a bad effect in a theatre, water thrown by a stage hand to create the effect of rain. They both looked up – rain from a clear blue sky? Still they laughed. Still the car's engine roared as they took the corners.

And then the impact. The two cyclists had been on the left side, but not close enough to the edge of the road. The corner was blind here and both had been hit by Edward's car. He was breathing like a hundred-year-old, his chest heaving . . . Matty was screaming.

They stopped a hundred yards down the road. 'We must go back, Dad,' said his son, crying and trembling as they stepped out of the car.

They walked the hundred yards back to the scene. The bodies were crumpled with their bikes, a tangle of spokes and broken limbs. There was groaning and a pool of blood on the road that widened as they stood there. Edward looked left to the horizon and felt the sun on them, not kind now, not glowing gold, but white and harsh like a police searchlight. Slowly, they came closer to the two victims. Edward stepped ahead of his son to shield him from the horror. He felt his son's hand on his shoulder. Behind him, Matty was saying, 'It's you and me, Daddy. You and me on the ground.'

Edward's focus tightened, his gaze like a camera. He saw the faces. His, and his son's. On his shoulder, the hand tightened.

He opened his eyes. Now he was back, back on his chair at the end of the garden where he had fallen asleep.

The shock of the dream had brought him out in a sweat. His dark glasses, he noticed, had fallen to the ground.

But the hand on his shoulder was real.

Tara spoke. 'Did I wake you?'

He faced the sea. She was the only one he could say this to. 'I was dreaming about Matty.' Behind him his ex-wife let out a sigh that seemed to come from somewhere deep within her soul.

He reached across his chest and placed his left hand on hers, turning his head an inch to catch a glimpse of the dark, delicate skin. She squeezed his shoulder.

'I woke you,' she said. 'I came to find you, no one answered the door, and then I saw you here.'

'I dreamt . . .' he started, but he knew he must not say. 'We were in a car, the roof was down, it started to rain buckets, we were laughing.'

'A happy dream.'

'Yes.' He stood and turned. Normally Tara wore bright gemstones and gold necklaces – which not only looked perfect against her skin but also, in Edward's view, projected the subliminal message: *I married well the second time.* She wore the kind of jewellery a local radio presenter could not afford, much less the assistant in a garden centre.

But today she was not wearing any of it. Usually she wore large false eyelashes; they were gone too. There was no make-up, none of the usual eye shadow. He thought she looked prettier without it, then chided himself for always being The Bloke – scoring every woman on looks, even a woman he hadn't slept with for six years, long after the sex had stopped.

'I come in peace,' she said. 'I had to see you. I didn't mean to wake you.'

'I didn't mean to sleep,' he said, and remembered that he had been about to WhatsApp Stevie and Kim, though he could not for the life of him recall why.

They both turned. The sun was halfway set now. 'It's beautiful here, and I can see why you bought it, but is it safe to stand this far down the garden?'

He pointed back at the house. 'The garden is fifty yards. It used to be a hundred. It took a century to halve in size. The rest won't go for at least half an hour. If we hear a rumble, we can move.'

'It's his birthday. That's why I had to see you.'

Edward sighed. 'Every day is his birthday. Every day is the day he died. Nothing ever hurts less than yesterday; nothing will ever hurt more than tomorrow.'

'Maybe we should try to celebrate the time we had?' she said. 'Rather than how soon he left?'

'Yes,' said Edward. 'Weren't we so lucky to have him?'

Tara started to cry and he took her in his arms. 'I just had to see you,' she said. 'No one suffers it like me and you.'

'We love you, Matty,' Edward said into her shoulder.

And then another voice, from near the house.

'Am I interrupting?'

They broke apart as Tara whispered, 'Kind of.'

A well-dressed young man with hair like a burning bush was standing by the corner of the house. The red hair sat over a white face. The man was tall, young, and might have looked athletic were it not for an ungainliness in the way he walked. He wore thick-soled trainers, white with black laces. The shoes looked new. His tread was heavy on the gravel path at the side of the house, and he limped. He was carrying a bunch of flowers.

'Derrick,' said Edward.

'Your producer?' Tara whispered.

'He was, yes. Lovely guy. All good.'

Derrick approached. 'It's chilly out here. Have you got waterworks trouble?'

'I beg your pardon.' Edward's indignation was affected.

Tara giggled, a sound he loved. 'He means the digging at the front, the barriers and whatnot.'

'Oh yes, the public main,' said Edward. 'It exploded underground or something. They had to access it via my front garden. You did well to get down the side – Derrick, this is Tara.'

Derrick would have known of Tara's existence by implication, because Edward had always talked proudly of their son to his producer.

'I won't stay,' said Derrick, 'but I was very conscious that this was Matty's birthday.' He held out the flowers.

'How kind,' said Tara. 'Thank you, Derrick.'

'And this is why I love my producer, and most of why I miss my job. Who else would be so kind? How is the ankle?'

'Coming along nicely,' said Derrick.

Weeping again, Tara said: 'Well, Ed, take the flowers.'

'You call him "Ed",' Derrick observed awkwardly. He added gravely, 'It was a big thing in my life when it happened, Matty's death.' The young producer's suit was natty, but in his discomfort he had shoved his free hand deep into the jacket pocket, pulling the shoulders into such a lopsided angle that Edward thought the material might rip. 'It was the biggest tragedy that can befall a man.'

Tara dabbed at her eyes.

'A man, a woman, a mum, a dad,' Derrick elaborated quickly,

217

determined not to miss anyone out. It was strange, thought Edward, that Tara had been melted by a stranger's kindness. He was used to seeing her more steely; perhaps because, after a marriage ended, most of what was left was business.

They were an odd threesome, there on the cliff top. Derrick, Tara and Edward. Both men towered over Tara. The last of the sun was exaggerating their shadows to such an extent that the dark lines licked at the back wall of the house thirty yards away.

'Nice to see your place, Edward,' said Derrick.

'Of course, you've never been here.'

'It's stunning.'

'So long as it doesn't fall off the edge,' said Tara.

'That's how you get a bargain,' said Edward seriously, and to his surprise the other two burst out laughing.

At the same instant, Tara and Derrick both said: 'I should go.'

'Derrick, can you stay for a minute or two? Just got something I need to ask you.'

'So long as it's not about how you run Tessa K over,' Derrick said. But the joke landed terribly badly, and Edward got caught in a sudden, sharp memory of his dream – he and Matty in a convertible knocking down *each other*, finding their *own* tangled bodies, riders killed by their *own* car. So what did the dream mean, discovering your own body, and you the killer? And then he remembered how he woke with Tara's hand on his shoulder, the hand he was now shaking.

It was the way they said goodbye normally. They both needed the formality. He escorted her to the front of the house, she climbed into her car, and was gone.

'Very nice lady,' said Derrick when Edward returned.

There was, thought Edward, something about Derrick that was surprisingly clumsy. The joke about Tessa K, and now the observation on Tara, which was the last thing an ex-husband needed to hear. Still, Edward reminded himself, the lad was not even twenty-seven and still learning. 'How did you get to my house, mate?'

'Bus and taxi.'

'I was without my car recently,' said Edward. 'I couldn't get anywhere.'

'Did it break down?'

'I parked it somewhere.' Edward paused. He might as well say. 'If you must know, in Tanner. Someone had to take me back to get it.'

'Why on earth were you in Tanner? You're lucky if you got the hubcaps back. And the place stinks. You know there's a farm with seven thousand pigs further down the valley?'

'I wondered what the aroma was.'

They went inside. There were French windows into the lounge and Edward retrieved the key from underneath a plant pot.

'I wanted to ask you something, Derrick, and as you're here . . . It's a bit – on the QT. I need something announced on the show. It might help me get a story.'

'A story? About what?'

'Well, put it like this, if I got a big story, would you cover it?'

Derrick thought about it for long enough to offend Edward. 'What, have Tessa K interview you? That might be a bit strange.' He was inspecting his nails. 'What's the story, anyway?'

'I can't really say. It's to do with . . . do you call it catfishing?'

Derrick paused. 'Romance scams.'

'Exactly. Could you announce something on the show for . . .' But Edward did not finish the sentence because he sensed Derrick was uncomfortable with the idea. 'No, it's okay, I won't pressure you, don't you worry.'

'Agnes would need to okay it.'

'You'd have to ask her?'

Derrick paused. This was excruciating, and Edward wished he had never gone down the road of trying to use leverage with the young producer. He was suddenly conscious of his selfishness. The lad had only come to deliver flowers and sympathies.

They sat in silence for a moment, and then Derrick continued. 'Look, I know it's painful being shut out. But bring me the story when you have it and I'll definitely see if we can do something. That's my promise.'

'It's more than kind,' said Edward, 'and I guarantee I'll never, ever take advantage of your love and concern.'

'Tell me if you need anything doing, okay?' said Derrick as he exited the front door.

Edward said, without thinking, 'Irene.'

'Eh?'

'Does that name mean anything?'

'Not especially. I'm sure we have lots of Irenes who call us.'

'I must have heard one of them on the air, and remembered it for some reason,' said Edward, puzzling at the way his mind was working.

After Derrick had gone, Edward was still deep in thought. He went slowly to the end of his garden, past a line of markers in the grass — just wooden tent pegs he had found, with a sign painted on a small square of hardboard as a warning: no further. Under the sunless sky he went on, like a blind man feeling for the road's edge through the soles of his shoes. He took just a few steps towards the edge until he could feel the soil becoming softer and less reliable. The evening gloom stopped him seeing more. He heard the water breaking on the rocks below.

He stood until a moment of vertigo swept over him, a dizziness and nausea that brought him to his knees. Barbara . . . Rebecca . . . *who was Irene?* Like the conman's victims, Edward was trapped by the scam. Every answer brought more questions. There was no escape.

If he threw himself over, he could be with Matty. The sea begged him. *One more step to be with your son. A small step for a man . . .* Just like Riva's death, it would be written off as an accident. The rocks below cried out: *Come. Be free. Take your boy in your arms again.*

He stayed there, on his knees, for a very long time.

CHAPTER TWENTY-FOUR

Kimberley had not told Edward the truth about Anthony. He was not staying with his mother; that had been a lie. Her husband had been sectioned in the secure wing of Decla, the biggest psychiatric unit in the county. Anthony Cobden had been found passed out under the last row of seats in Screen 4 of the Radway Cinema, dressed only in a pair of underpants. He had somehow got in during a break between showings. No one could find his other clothes. Anthony would have been tasered had the arresting officer not recognized his boss.

Everyone called the unit Decla. Officially it was DCLA, short for Devon County Lunatic Asylum. The controversial initials were kept only because a posse of influential private funders insisted. And it was a fair argument. The institution's past was interesting, educational, and not a little horrific. Lobotomies had been performed here in the 1940s, and then electric shock therapy with only a gag for the patient. In a neglected side room, viewable on request, there was still a small exhibition of straightjackets, mouth-clamps and other restraints.

The place was modern now. When she arrived, Kim found the floor clean and the staff receptive. She sat down with a youthful man who might have been a nurse or a doctor or a senior consultant – she missed his introduction, and was left constantly looking for clues. He wore denim jeans and a surgeon's blue tunic, a strange combination.

'Your husband is in danger of self-harm.' The doctor wore a Covid mask, even though the pandemic was long over, and above the brown eyes she saw only a large forehead and shaved crown. The accent was Irish. She imagined him studying in Dublin, emerging from lectures caught in the rain, drenched and handsome. 'This happens, Mrs Cobden. There are two thoughts I would like you to have. First, his pain will go one day and he will be better, if we can protect him physically during the worst, which is our job here at Dec . . . at the unit.' He seemed to find the mask unnecessary at this point, pinched the green fabric and delicately repositioned it under his chin.

The nose was chiselled, the mouth at rest in a half-smile. He tipped his head left as if appraising her and she, noticing a wedding ring, guessed at a new wife, younger than him, with a pert blonde bob and a child on the way. 'Sorry. Masks are a habit.'

'I'm sure,' she said. 'You want me to wear one?'

'No, no! I use one only because of the sheer weight of numbers in my working day. And because, whisper it gently, you don't get as many colds. I was saying – about your husband: first, he will get better, and second, this can happen to people at any stage in life. The broken brain and the broken leg are both real.'

'But . . . is there a cause?'

'Do you know,' he said, 'the biggest single misapprehension we find among relatives, and even our patients, is that a change in brain chemistry must have "a cause". Many people fall into severe depression for no obvious reason – perhaps there was a subtle build-up of workplace stress over many years – but once a person's brain chemistry is changed they, or their loved ones, dive deeper and deeper for "the cause". People end up on a psychologist's couch for years searching for this mystery "cause", when actually the unhappiness is due to brain chemistry.

Serotonin is the current model, but we don't really know. A change in our brain chemistry can lead us to regret a thing we haven't thought about for years. Sometimes a patient will find one particular event in their childhood and . . .'

Kimberley was distracted. A message had popped up on her phone's lock screen:

> We are going to have to appeal for our victims by advertising in local paper I think . . . long story

It came from Edward. She saw she was now in a WhatsApp group with Edward and Stevie, and wrenched her focus back to the doctor.

'I see you're busy, it's no problem,' he said without irritation.

At that moment, as the phone found a better connection, Kim saw a dozen work messages arrive about houses her colleagues were buying or selling.

And one from Stevie, an immediate reply to Edward:

> Say what now?

'Gawd,' Kim said, turning off the screen. 'I run an estate agency and there are days when everyone wants me to look at something. It's "Should we tell them about the wobbly Velux?" and "There's a dead animal in the conservatory we can't identify", as if I must have the solution.'

'I'm looking to move,' he said brightly.

She managed enthusiasm, although troubled by the idea that Anthony might know she had arrived in the unit and be expecting her by now. 'Okay. Just tell me what I can do for you.'

'I wouldn't dream of burdening you at this moment, with my work gear on. I just need a flat with a view. Me and my husband. Three bedrooms. But we'll do it another time.'

So much for the 'new wife with pert blonde bob and child on the way'. Kim had her phone open again and clicked to create a new note. 'Give me your email address and I'll be in touch.'

'Seriously? Would you?'

'Of course! It's my job. I'll need to ask a few boring questions first. Location, price range.'

'Happy to answer all those. My name is Dr Michael Tilson, one L, one S.'

She typed the name and the email address: michaelzzztilson@gmail.com. 'You know,' Kim began, back in her WhatsApp messages now but not feeling so guilty about it, 'I just got an interesting message from a friend. You're a psychiatrist, right, Dr Tilson?'

'Michael. Consultant psychologist.' His eyes moved fractionally, as if sliding to professional mode.

'The friend wants to write a public appeal and I wouldn't know where to start.'

'An appeal for what?'

She bit the bullet. 'A newspaper ad. Oh, it's so complicated. Someone fleeced two older women with a romance scam. One of the victims was my own mother!' she exclaimed. 'The friend wants to find out if anyone else has been affected. If there's another victim – maybe two, three of them? But if there is, I think there'll be a chance no one else in their life will know and they are going to be hugely hurt and embarrassed. And the way this thing has worked . . .' She leant forward. 'If you've time?'

'I sure do.'

'The scammers seem to find one thing the person is completely and utterly passionate about, and they create an intense connection through it. So, this is very different from cold calling, phishing, whatever. With most online scams, they cast the line a thousand times hoping for a single bite. In these cases the scammer is like a sniper. The victim really does feel loved by them. It's so personal. And they fall for it because they *want* it. And then they send money. Thousands.'

'Jeez. Your mum did?'

'I got in just before she hit forty-five thousand.'

'God, no. How are they finding their victims?'

Kim thought about it. 'I wish I knew that.' She went on, 'And the strange thing is, Mum still can't bear to think someone used her own personal passion to lock in to her, and I think if I left her to it, they'd be back in touch and she'd give even more.'

'Christ. What was the passion?'

'You'll laugh. She collects these little Victorian models called automata which work with—'

'I know what they are. Beautiful little things. I went to an exhibition once. All miniature handles and cogs.' He took the mask off his ear and then placed it on the desk. His neck was hairy, and thick tufts of black hair went all the way down into his blue top, even sprouting from a gap between the buttons. He was an attractive man. Strong and sensitive, with sinews moving in his forearms like piano wires as he drummed his fingers soundlessly on the desk. 'How can I help?'

'I don't know how to word the newspaper ad to get the best response – could you help me? I don't want them to read it as "Call this number if you've been an idiot." They need encouraging.'

He took a cheap biro from the desk and bit the cap off. With the piece of plastic still between his teeth, he tore a piece of paper from a notepad and started to write. 'The key is that they mustn't feel ashamed,' he said, his pen pausing. He crossed out a word, added another. 'Shame is the worst thing. Shame is what created this unit, shame is what brings me my patients.'

He pressed his finger into the paper and spun it, then slid it to Kim.

A Lady Who Loves Revenge? If you're over 60 and a stranger took advantage, meet me on Thursday to plan what we do next.

'Oh. That's not what I expected.'

'You don't like it? Wait.' He gestured for the paper. 'I need to use the word "online", don't I?'

A Lady Who Loves Revenge? If you're over 60 and a stranger took advantage online, meet me on Thursday to plan what we do next. Carry something yellow.

'Yellow?'

'Otherwise, how will you know them?' His face darkened and he stood. 'Now it gets harder. I'll take you to see your husband, if I may. This won't be easy. Are you ready?'

CHAPTER TWENTY-FIVE

Renaming the Secret Squirrel had been controversial. The pub had been the Grand Old Duke of York since the 1880s, named after the nursery rhyme sung about a prince no one remembered. Then the modern holder of the title had been caught in an American sex scandal and the council in Ottery St Mary consulted on a rare measure to force the name change on the pub owners.

The councillors got the publicity they craved, including national headlines (LATEST SHAME FOR ANDREW: EVEN DEVON BOOZER TURNS ITS BACK). The Grand Old Duke became the Secret Squirrel, the pub-sign portrait of the moustachioed Prince Frederick – the entirely innocent duke of the nursery rhyme – exiled to landfill. It was swapped with a painting of a small blob of red fur with narrowed eyes and buck teeth and a large acorn. Of course, the change angered some of the older residents. Then it all settled down and the pub owners were grateful for the attention. The tax on draught beer was killing them anyway, which is why, this weekday evening at 6 p.m., the middle-aged man who arrived in a leather jacket was only the third customer.

'Sit anywhere, love.' The landlady was precise in her

movements, setting down the pint of Ottery Angel so not a drop was spilt. In the empty pub, the sound of a full glass hitting the varnished surface of the counter was like the clang of a church bell. The beer was thick and warm, and Edward felt his mouth watering.

'I'm expecting . . .' he began, and rephrased. 'Well, I don't really know who I'm expecting.'

The landlady gestured around the empty space. 'Anyone you bring will be very welcome in these hard times.' The décor was busy, with every spare inch of wall covered by framed prints from antique books. In the corner there was a tatty flag draped between two of the wall lights, and below it, almost hidden under the cloth, two women with craggy faces and identical floral jackets were talking to each other.

'Oh, I feel I recognize you, love,' added the landlady, but Edward would not be tempted to blow his half-hearted disguise: a high shirt collar and an old pair of thick-framed glasses.

'I'll go over here,' he said, pointing to the other side of the pub. He wanted this to be private. He would keep out of the way of the other customers. The newspaper ad had given the pub name and time and said the contacts should wear or bring something yellow. That was all. He wasn't sure he liked Kimberley's wording, but she had pulled rank by saying a psychologist had advised her. Fair enough. He looked at his watch. He was early; Kim was due at eight because she was viewing a property on the other side of Exmoor.

As he supped his beer, the two women on the other side of the bar caught sight of him, stared, said something to each other and stood up. He saw now that they were twins.

'Are . . . are you . . . the radio . . .?'

They were what his father would have called handsome. Strong, tough women in their sixties who probably owned a smallholding somewhere. He imagined them farming together and the animals being unable to tell them apart. That said, there was a difference between the two – the woman standing straight opposite him had hair dyed mouse-brown. She was the one who had spoken. Her twin sister had let her hair go to grey. It was the almost perfect control test of dye versus grey. The effect was peculiar – his eyes should be telling him the mouse-brown-haired woman looked younger, but somehow her sister looked better for her grey.

He was about to find out why.

'The radio!' said the grey one.

'Wimbledon!'

'What are you doing here, Edward?' said Grey.

This was tricky. He could not say what his mission was. He needed to protect the identities of anyone who came to meet him.

'A bit of research,' he said.

'Oh!' said Mouse-Brown, whose voice was hoarse, her breathing a little quick, almost a wheeze. 'Another radio show? We miss you.'

'Did you both listen?'

'Absolutely,' they chorused. 'We are Angela and Olive, and it's lovely to meet you.'

This was a little awkward, he thought. They had spotted him and now, if anyone arrived in the still-empty pub, the twins might well feel they were part of the conversation.

But then Olive, with the grey hair, plumped herself on the stool at her table. 'Can I tell you something?'

'Go on.'

'Olive, no,' said Angela from above them, wheezing as she breathed.

'I must, Angie.' She turned to Edward and dropped her voice. 'We are here for a secret meeting and we've been told to wear yellow.'

Edward, mid-sip, choked on his pint, the warm beer going up his nose. Coughing and hacking, he placed the pint down and pushed the other stool towards the mouse-brown Angela, beckoning her by rolling all his fingers towards her. 'Well, then,' he said, when he could speak at last. 'We must talk.'

With a little hesitation, Angela sat.

Edward whispered. 'The message was from me. I didn't see your yellow.'

Olive pointed at the multi-coloured flowers on their jackets. 'There and there and there and there.'

He bought them drinks. They sat on the red-cushioned couch that ran along the wall, and Edward took a stool so he could face them.

'Can you tell me what happened? Was it a scam?'

The women were suspicious at first but, as Olive said, 'We trust you, Mr Temmis, because we both listened religiously.'

'I'm grateful.'

'So we feel we know you as . . . a man. We couldn't believe your show ended but we know about your son, of course.'

He looked down at the beer mat, tracing with his thumb the outline of the otter on the card. His vision tunnelled. The beer mat swelled unevenly as if seen in fisheye, and his heart raced. Any mention of Matty did that.

'Which of you was scammed?' He looked up when he felt able to control his voice.

'Me,' Angela's voice rasped.

'No. Both of us,' put in Olive.

These two women, one grey, one mouse-brown, both in their sixties, spoke like heartbroken teenagers. Olive had had a text message asking for Angela's phone number. She had thought nothing of it; the person had been in the twins' year at school in the Seventies, or so he said.

'You see, I was diagnosed with lung cancer fifteen years ago and it was touch and go,' Angela said. 'I lost a lung and a bit of my voice box.'

'Wait,' said Edward. 'I think I remember you calling about this. You rang my radio show one night, didn't you?'

'Not me. Olive did. Olive rang about me, and you were very kind.'

Olive joined in. 'I talked about her lung cancer and how they were treating it. The twins thing came up. I suppose it was interesting, why one of us got it and the other didn't.'

'I think I can remember the call. Wasn't there a mention of smoking?'

'Well, that's the thing,' said Angela, and now the thinness of her voice and the way she sometimes struggled for air made sense to Edward. 'Olive smoked and I didn't. I got the cancer. So that was mad.'

'And then someone got in touch with you?'

'After the cancer was treated, successfully thank God, although a lot of knife-work was involved . . . Yes,' said Angela. 'Lawrence Mahoney was his name. Very kind-sounding indeed. Working in the Loire Valley and apparently very wealthy. He wouldn't have heard the radio show out there. He said he had seen a post on Facebook, or maybe Friends Reunited—'

'It doesn't matter,' said Olive impatiently. 'The point is that he had identical twin girls and one of them had fallen ill with lung cancer.'

'Exactly the same story!' said Angela. 'These poor girls were sixteen. And he had so many questions. He sent me photos of them, his daughters—'

'Who probably didn't exist,' Olive added quietly, and Edward nodded slowly, still looking at the beer mat.

'But we spent so long talking about it, and the conversation ranged, about the treatment and of course about the healthy twin—'

Olive added, 'Which is where I came in.'

'So then he organized a conversation for us with the healthy twin, because he said she was so stressed that her sister was going to die and she was going to die too—'

'He had a French accent he'd been there so long, so he pronounced it "*Lor-ronz*".'

The story was coming out faster and faster now. The conversation with the healthy twin had been on speakerphone; the exchanges with Lawrence Mahoney had mainly been text, and sometimes a Voice Note on Snapchat, which he seemed to want ('because the message disappears,' Edward said sadly, like a commentator explaining action on the pitch), and at no point had he asked for anything other than advice and comfort from Angela and Olive.

'But then it got romantic,' said Angela. 'I saw you looking at my hair. It's a wig, okay, but I think I'm still a handsome woman. He fell in love with me.'

'Angie!' said her sister. 'You are presenting fiction as fact.'

'It was fact at the time.'

'Of course it was, Angela,' said Edward. He realized now that it was her cancer that had added the extra years, with the resulting baffling effect that Angela, mouse-brown, looked older than Olive, grey.

'I don't smoke any more,' said Olive, as if they were competing. 'I knew they were getting close.'

'He proposed to me.'

In the silence that fell after this remark, Edward became conscious of the pub customers behind him.

'He said he loved me and if his twins got through this it would be down to me and my encouragement and we should spend the rest of our lives together. We were messaging each other a hundred times a day by the time . . .'

She trailed off. They had now been talking for forty-five minutes. Pub customers had gradually filled up the lounge behind Edward, who had moved his stool closer to the table to shield the sisters – this was such a terrible story. The scam artist used Angela's cancer as the way in; seemed to have involved Olive as well, as counsellor to his 'healthy daughter'; and now, he knew,

Angela would mention the money. But her next two words were not what Edward expected.

'She died.'

'Who?'

'The poor girl,' said Angela, 'his poor daughter.' She began to sob, and Olive reached out and took her hand. 'You can see how real this was for Angie. She talks about these people as if they actually existed.'

'Died in the night, so he said. He was with her.'

'As you say, Angie, it was true at the time,' Edward insisted.

'It was so true,' sighed Angie, and in that sigh Edward thought he heard all the things the poor woman had lost.

'The money was almost separate,' said Olive. 'Like, an afterthought. If it was a scam—'

'It was a scam, Olive,' Angela sniffed.

'The clever thing was that for the whole of the first year Lawrence never mentioned money once. But after his daughter died, he fell into a depression and couldn't work – listen to me, I'm talking like it's all true as well now.'

'It was true *at the time*,' Angela repeated.

Edward kept wanting to ask: 'How much?' He had been so engrossed in this story of illness, love, crime and death that he had closed out the sound of pub customers behind him, not even turning around to look for any individual who might be here to meet him.

'There was a twist,' said Olive. 'I told you I was involved too. The funeral for his daughter was held during the pandemic and so we couldn't travel. But his depression, his *alleged* depression after the death of his *alleged* daughter, deepened. His business went—'

'His alleged business,' Angela insisted, and both women were in and out of the story, one minute treating it as fact, the next fantasy. It was clear in this moment how the lives of the sisters were interlocked: what happened to one happened to the other.

'He opened up a separate line to me,' said Olive. 'He needed money to pay his creditors so he could leave France and marry Angela. My sister knew about that. But his surviving daughter had become anorexic through all the stress and he needed to get her expensive treatment. He didn't want Angie to know because he felt it would upset her too much. He said he wanted me to be like a godmother to his daughter. He sent me photos.' Her lip wobbled. 'I wasn't having the romance, but I've always wanted a child in my life.'

How much? Edward was increasingly desperate to ask. How much have you wanted one and how much did you lose? Because it was almost the same question.

'He split us off,' said Angela. 'He told me the wedding plans must be secret from Olive and he told Olive that Valerie's illness must be kept from me.'

'Valerie, his daughter?'

'Pronounced the French way,' said Olive.

'Of course.' Edward was beginning to think that Olive was tougher and more angry about what had happened. Angie was still clinging to a thread of hope that the story might yet be true, and the fantasy wedding would happen.

'Neither of us wanted to be single, childless. We live together because we are all each other has.'

'Can I ask how much you gave this man?' he interjected gently, keen to bring them back on track.

Angie looked anxiously at Olive.

'I don't want you to think we are rich if we say the number out loud.'

'Say it quietly,' Olive said. 'There are people in the pub now – oh.'

Both the women looked up at a figure who, appearing behind Edward, had laid a hand on his shoulder. He smelled Kimberley's perfume before he turned.

'Have you seen this?' she said, but he was so desperate to

get an answer from Olive and Angie that he barely heard the question.

He laid his hand on hers, where it had paused on his shoulder.

The older women saw the movement – her hand, his shoulder, his hand – and, with their flinty, experienced gazes, their eyes, which had seen so much, must have understood something even Edward and Kim did not see. The moment passed. 'Sit down for a sec, Kimberley, because Olive and Angela here were about to tell me something.'

She remained standing. 'No, but look! Behind you!'

Hiding his annoyance, Edward gripped the sides of his stool and, taking the weight of it, manoeuvred it around.

Kimberley stood aside.

The pub was full – there might have been a hundred people standing talking to each other. The hubbub had risen slowly behind Edward, and he had been so engrossed with the sisters he had not noticed. Now, as he turned, the crowd began to fall silent. They knew his face. They were in their sixties, seventies, even eighties. Some of the ones looking at him nudged the nearest person to stop them talking.

Then he saw a man and a woman at the front, shrunken and shrew-faced, both carrying tins of custard and holding them out to him.

Behind them was a tall, narrow woman in a dark blue cap who wore a daffodil brooch on a navy jacket. A man near her had a yellow scarf that said WOLVES. He was starting to speak, but Edward could not hear what he was saying over the ringing in his ears. He glanced back to see Olive and Angie, noting again the flash of floral yellow on their jackets – how had he missed that when he first saw them? – and the way their faces seemed to shine as they, too, understood what this crowd was here for.

In outstretched hands there were two more tins of custard, a banana, a bright yellow coat, a yellow skirt (far too thin for an evening in May), a gang of yellow blouses, and a woman pointing at her watchstrap, which looked orange to him, but still he understood. A figure at the back, hidden by the crowd, was waving a lemon overhead. And still the man at the front was speaking.

'My wife,' he said, sound coming back in with a sudden whoosh. 'She didn't like the football but I've come for her. They took everything. She died of shame.'

Edward's jaw hung open. He had expected half a dozen people at the most. If just the two sisters had come it would have been remarkable. But this was shattering.

Kimberley's hand stayed on his shoulder, and he felt it move with her sobs. He had never seen her cry like this. She still had her coat on. He wanted to stand, to embrace this extraordinary group of hurting older people – this community no one would ever care about, whose pain would be thought of as ridiculous, the blame for whose financial losses would be placed on them. His legs felt so weak he was pinned on the stool.

'Everyone is here for you,' Kimberley said, sniffing. 'I came five minutes ago and I took a good look. Everyone has yellow. Every single person you can see.'

He turned to Olive and Angela.

'Do you want to say, before this gets mad?'

The pub was now completely silent. Whatever the sisters said would be heard by the whole room.

Angie could have whispered the answer, but she said it out loud. 'One hundred and twenty-six thousand pounds.'

'To rescue his business and get his daughter treated,' Olive told the room.

The crowd made a strange noise – not a gasp of surprise, more a groan of recognition.

In the silence that followed, a female voice off to the right said a single word. 'Bastard.' The voice sounded familiar to Edward. It did not match with any of the older faces he could see. He saw

237

someone had come in through the pub door, because the top half of the frame was visible, and when it banged, the people to his right glanced towards it and then parted.

Through the middle of the crowd stepped Stevie. There was a frisson in the gathering, as if this was a key moment in the evening. Stevie wore a black eye patch and a wide-brimmed black hat from which hung a single cork. Perhaps there was a fancy-dress box at the vicarage? She tottered on heels and stretched her neck to give herself the height she lacked. The effect was of a young woman who had come to the wrong party. Despite being the shortest and youngest person in the room, her appearance commanded the audience completely.

'Room for one pirate?' she asked. 'I wasn't invited, but I'm bloody well here.' Now she stepped into the centre of the room, standing with her back to Edward as if this was her show. He felt – and was ashamed to admit it to himself – a smidgeon of upset that Stevie had moved centre-stage.

'We thought . . .' began Edward, but Kimberley's hand squeezed his shoulder to stop him.

'My grandmother, who we called Granny Riva, was a victim of this sick bastard fiend too,' announced Stevie, the Glasgow accent dominating the words as she paced left and right in front of the crowd like the MC at an open mic night. Edward prayed she did not add '. . . *and she was murdered*,' which would surely cause panic in the room.

'We don't know anything about him except that he strikes locally. So he's not a fucking Russian.'

'Language, Stevie,' said Edward. He caught a glimpse of Stevie's parents – what, wait, why were they here? They had come ahead of their daughter. It made no sense.

'Pardon my language. I have a condition, unguarded speech, and my face was attacked, and stress makes everything worse.'

'He or she,' said a voice from the crowd.

Edward stood. 'Say again?'

Next to him, Kim said quietly, 'I know that voice.'

'You said *"he's* not a Russian"', but it could be he or she.' The words came from the back of the room. The speaker was hidden, sitting at a table along the far wall.

Edward found the strength to stand behind Stevie. 'This young lady has become a good friend,' he announced. 'She is determined to find the person behind these scams, but she's suffered for it as you can see.'

Stevie turned back and shot him a glance, as if banning him from saying more about how her injuries had happened, perhaps because her parents were here.

The pub landlady appeared next to Edward. 'Do you mind telling me what the hell is going on here, and by the way, are you aware that they've set up a tab with your name on it?'

Edward blanched. Kimberley, for the first time that night, let out a slightly choked but raucous laugh. 'I'd be amazed if that wasn't done by my mum at the back. Hello Mum!' she called to the person who had said it could be he or she. The crowd were beginning to talk amongst themselves, so any response from Barbara was drowned out. 'She won't have expected me to be here,' said Kim as she filed through the customers towards her mother.

'I mean,' the pub landlady continued, somewhere between telling Edward off and thanking him, 'I haven't had this much custom of a weekday since pre-Covid. I'm loving it, honey. But I'm running low on Campari and I really do need to check you can pay. Or will the young lady who's in charge do it?'

'I can pay,' said Edward quickly, 'because this is all down to me. But I just need one favour.'

CHAPTER TWENTY-SIX

The pub landlady obliged. She closed the lounge bar for a 'private party', so customers who were not here to see Edward Temmis had to use the other entrance to the saloon. She locked the door between lounge and saloon – 'I'm breaking the law here, but the local PC's mum is in your crowd' – and that gave Edward and Kimberley the chance to take stock while Stevie took note of everyone who had come. 'Confidential, confidential', she kept saying when she was given a name. But very few needed persuading. It was as if stories they had kept in the dark were suddenly flooded with light, and once they began talking about what had happened, they could not stop.

Edward and Kim resolved that each individual or couple should be interviewed somewhere private. The landlady, having apparently now decided she was grateful to be hosting Ottery St Mary's biggest event so far this year – probably the first flash mob in Devon's history – allowed the use of her dilapidated office, a room appropriately decorated in daffodil yellow. There was a desk, an old-style single sodium light bulb that hung from the ceiling, and a dozen files spilling papers onto the floor. The carpet had been so crushed over the years it was a sticky matted lino.

Kim, hovering by the office door and never quite leaving the room, said: 'I just asked my mum what was that thing she shouted about the scammer being "a man *or* woman"? She said we shouldn't rule things out. But I think it would be easier for her if there was no man behind it. Less pride at stake, strangely. A woman – she would see that as pure crime. But it's a good point.'

'It really is,' said Edward. 'Man, woman, pair, could be a whole football team – we just don't know.'

'She still wants to be in the queue. I think it's empowering for all of them to tell their stories.' Kim laughed. 'I said I couldn't believe our little advert in the paper reached so many people, and she replied, "You think you lot invented social media? We have our networks, believe me." I thought she'd given up the crown green bowling social club subscription.'

Stevie and Edward laughed quietly. 'And what are my parents doing here, for God's sake?' asked Stevie, swivelling her one exposed eye. 'They're not victims.'

'Are you sure of that?' asked Kim.

'No,' she said after a moment. 'So – either they are secret victims, or they're just here to keep an eye on me. My dad is acting so oddly. They ask about my every movement. They knew I was heading down here to see you. Since I got out of hospital, they've been bloody treating me like I'm fucking twelve, and please excuse my French.'

'You're looking better,' said Edward.

'I'm looking ridiculous,' said Stevie.

'Your language has certainly improved,' said Kim. She wrapped her arm around the younger woman. The three of them discussed what to do with the crowd. They worked out the pub would need to stay open beyond midnight to get details from everyone who had come. There were ninety-seven visitors who had as many as sixty individual stories to tell. Some had come as couples. One story came from a family of six. But most were alone, and the vast majority of those who were alone were widowed women. Kim organized who was going into the landlady's office next. In the room, next to Edward, Stevie took notes on her phone, which made him nervous. 'Please back that up every few minutes, Stevie. If we lose it I couldn't bear it.' Stevie rolled her eye.

They got into a rhythm as each new visitor arrived in the cramped office. Stevie would guarantee never to share their information without permission. She would take the person's full name and address – email at least but postal would help too. She noted down when the scammer first made contact and how; what cover story was used to lure them in; how much money was lost. They would follow up, they promised, for any missing details. Tonight had to be just the headlines, because they had never expected so many to come.

Again and again the question came up: *How did a criminal find out so much about these old people before they had even made contact with them?*

Edward promised that if he ever contacted the victims again, it would be up to the individual or couple whether they even wanted the conversation.

'If your money is found, we will be in touch, of course. If we get any information, we will be in touch.'

They asked each victim if they could remember a codeword. Sticking with the yellow theme, which Edward still felt blind-sided by, they made it 'lemon'. So if Edward, Kim or Stevie got in touch with a victim, they would leave their number and say the word 'lemon'. The victim could decide whether they wanted to be back in touch or just leave it.

Time ticked on. Nine, ten, eleven o'clock. The landlady came through to say she had had a request for Espresso Martinis – 'how many?' 'Eight' '*Eight?*' – and needed to know if they were covered by the tab because she charged £10 each. Then the bar ran out of crisps. At eleven thirty, the landlady came through to the office again.

'I trust you completely. I don't know what's going on here but it's the best-behaved queue I've ever seen, and I can tell these people need their appointment, so here are the keys.' She added, 'Your wife is paying the tab.'

'My . . .?' That must be Kim. Of course.

A few of the visitors had drunk too much and were frustratingly incoherent when it came to recalling what had happened to them; one woman could not even remember why she had come to the pub, but Stevie whispered, 'Not wine. Dementia,' which was heart-wrenchingly sad.

In fact, it was all sad.

The stories had a common theme. Contact was made by text or Facebook. There was an expression of interest in a shared passion – one woman had been involved with the refurbishment of Bideford Railway Station, closed since the Sixties, and the scammer had clearly been researching different kinds of paint he could interest her in.

He had told her, 'Blood and custard was the colour combination in the Fifties and Sixties, I believe.'

Exchanging messages, she found the scammer polite and well-informed. The online seductions always fitted the same pattern – long conversations about a shared passion, slowly giving way to talk of love (which some of the victims had hidden from their husbands), and then, lastly, the sudden request for money.

The Bideford Rail paint scam was a matter of two thousand pounds only, which was to release a huge order of enamel held at a warehouse after a 'technical error made my bank go totally offline', the scammer had said. Edward knew he needed to resist the question, *How could you fall for that?* When the victim gave their bank details, there was then a secondary attack on her account that drew another £2,000 before being detected by the bank's fraud team. There was never any paint.

'I feel I've heard this story, or part of it,' said Edward as Stevie clicked away at the smartphone note.

'Yes I suppose you have,' said the victim, who looked as if she had once been wealthy but was now – he could see – unable to afford good dental work and kept covering her mouth out of apparent embarrassment. 'We all love your show, Mr Temmis. Well, we did. And I called you. I told you all about the lovely railway project on your programme. I'm so glad you have a memory of it. At that stage he hadn't been in touch, so it was all good.'

She had lost four thousand pounds. Edward assumed the likeable, hurting twins, whom he called 'Mouse-Brown and Grey' now he had forgotten their names, would be the biggest losers with £126,000 missing. It would explain why they were so keen that they arrived first, he thought. But as Stevie put the total sums defrauded into her phone, others came close. A woman in Appledore had paid £90,000 for a lifting operation to rescue the submerged fishing boat her husband had died on. A vicar's wife in Narrow Holman with a cleft palate had been persuaded that £180,000 would reverse the disfigurement of every single child in Malawi with the same condition.

When Kimberley walked into the office, saying, 'That's it. All done,' Edward turned to Stevie.

'So that was weird. Seeing your parents tonight.'

'I know,' she said. 'I don't really have an answer as to why they were here.'

'They didn't come to see us though. I thought you'd invited them?'

'Eh? Considering I wasn't invited myself—'

'Girls, girls,' Kimberley said, standing over them, hands on hips, like a teacher trying to stop a squabble.

'It's a mystery,' said Edward, almost to himself. 'And your father said to me, "The truth can be dangerous". And he said it in a really offhand way. So what did he mean by that?'

Kim looked suddenly alert. 'The truth can be dangerous?'

'It sounded like a warning. It sounded dark,' said Edward.

He looked at Stevie, who appeared exhausted now and said, without conviction, 'Maybe it's better for the insurance if they can prove it was murder.'

'God knows,' said Kim.

'God's about the only person the scammer hasn't tried it on with,' Stevie said.

He wanted to ask Stevie about her treatment, and when exactly her hospital stay had ended, but Kimberley broke in before he could speak. 'Where are we with it all, then?'

'Where we are is that it's after one in the morning, and the lovely landlady gave us her keys, so we can lock the doors and drink all her Chardonnay,' said Stevie. 'Except I can't, because I'm on antibiotics.'

'Where we are,' said Edward, 'is that we have sixty-something stories. This scammer was phenomenally busy.'

'If he's local he must be the biggest bloody employer in Devon,' Stevie groused.

Upset by these words, and tired, Edward frowned at her. 'Can you be a little more respectful? I'm here because you brought me into this. I was about to speak to them and you marched in and took over. These people have suffered. These old women have been shafted.'

'And my grandmother was murdered.'

Edward fell silent.

Kimberley said, 'Right, well if we've sorted that little duel out, I suggest you total the sum that's been conned – add them all together – and we go to the police with it.'

Edward frowned again. He was not happy taking it to the police because he thought – although he did not want to say it out loud – they would mess it up.

Stevie grunted. 'I'll total the amount in a second. But remember, there's only one murder and that's my granny. The police have all the details. They've been to the house and they've decided she lit thirty tea lights and was burned to death by her own stupidity. So how does it help to give them another sixty-odd cases?'

Kimberley, towering over them, said: 'So it's down to the three of us? How can *we* investigate them? Where do we even start?'

'I guess,' said Edward thoughtfully, still not sure which side of the argument he was on, 'we have the advantage in that we're connected. Kim, through your mother. Stevie, your grandmother. And me through my show. Did you see how many of them listened?'

'That's the demographic,' said Stevie, who was apparently determined to annoy Edward with every single utterance. 'Very old people.'

'True,' said Edward, equally determined to stay patient with her. 'But some of them gave everything they had. Some were poor. There were a couple of younger women, too. What about the lady who sent the scammer her rings to be cleaned and reset?'

Stevie flipped at her phone screen, trying to call up the details. 'Can't find the name. She told you about it on the radio, she said.'

'She didn't tell me she'd lost them. She told me she had not even two tuppenny pieces to rub together, she lived in a farm rental with her baby, single mum with no job, and she said the *Antiques Roadshow* was coming to Honiton and it might buy her rings, which were worth at least a thousand quid each, and they were the last thing she had to sell, her mother's jewellery. And the reason I remember her from – what? Two years ago? – is that I had to explain the *Antiques Roadshow* don't actually buy things.'

Kim said: 'Wait. That's the second time the same name has come up.'

'What name?' asked Stevie.

'My mum was talking about the *Antiques Roadshow* too.'

Edward said, 'Well, we can't rule anyone out.'

'Whenever I see her on TV, Fiona Bruce looks like she's quite busy,' Stevie said seriously. 'Could she be running this on the side?'

Suddenly Kim and Edward were roaring with laughter as Stevie, always literal, was trying to work out what she had said. When Edward breathed in, he found his cheeks wet with fresh tears. He was still thinking about the lady scammed out of her mother's jewellery.

'That scam on the single mum in the farm rental,' he said, 'is so despicable. She had nothing except the jewellery. She called me and said so. The scammer got in touch and promised to get the rings buffed up and reset.'

'Oh. My God.' Kimberley did not so much sit as she said the words, hand over her mouth, but dropped into the chair on the far side of the table, rocking back on the legs. 'Oh. My. God.'

'What?' said the other two simultaneously.

'If what I think is true . . .'

'Wha-what?'

Stevie and Edward leant forwards.

Kim spoke slowly, spreading her right hand across the table and running her left forefinger along the protruding bones in the back of her hand, as if sending trains down railway lines. 'Can I just do a little experiment for a second, before I tell you what I'm thinking. Stevie, how many names are there in your list?'

Stevie looked at her phone for ages.

'Including your mother, including my grandmother, sixty-two.'

'Give me one at random, Stevie. Give me an unusual one.'

Not needing to be told twice, Stevie spent a moment scrolling on her phone. 'Irene McDonald. Aged seventy. Lives in The Close, Trimstone. Widow. Lost £16,700. She was restoring the habitat of the wild beavers near the River Otter. Just as an amateur. The scammer—'

'Wait,' said Kim. 'Before we get on to what the scammer did to her, Ed, tell me if you remember her call.'

'Her call?'

'To your radio show.'

Irene! Finally he had the reference. The name had been echoing in his mind but he had not been able to work out why. Now he remembered.

'Funny you should mention that one. On the evening I called Derrick for help finding the missing letter, he was producing Tessa, and I heard Irene introduced. It was quick,' said Edward. 'Tessa K said there was one more call before the news, and said, "Hello, Irene". She was from Trimstone, wasn't she? And I had heard the caller say, say what exactly . . .'

He trailed off as he thought, then it came to him.

'She said, "Oh goodness. I'm eighty so I can't think quickly. Well, I've found love! Yes, at my age." And then Trent messed up and the call ended. I didn't hear much, just the thing about finding love.' He blinked at them. 'Do you think that was important?'

'Yes, but was that the first time she'd called the show? Think, Edward.'

He cudgelled his brains. 'I don't know,' he said eventually. 'She could have called Tessa K since I left the show. She did have that familiar tone the callers get once they've spoken to you a few times.'

'Okay, but Edward,' said Kim, 'did you see what I did there? I *know* she called the show.'

'Was there something about wild beavers?' Stevie read from her phone. 'The scammer said he could build a jetty for the beavers. He just needed money for parts and labour, and to get it delivered from Croatia.'

'I don't know about that.'

'That would have been an earlier call,' said Kim, with a certainty that astonished Edward.

'How could you know that?'

The room fell silent. Stevie looked up from her phone. 'Oh God. I see now.'

248

'What do you see?' asked Edward. 'Both of you are talking in riddles.'

'Every single one of these victims—' Stevie began.

'—*called your show, Edward.*' Kim jabbed her finger into the list. 'Every single one.'

'They called *before* they were scammed,' said Stevie.

'It's even more twisted than that,' Kim said, and she slumped into the chair on the other side of the desk. 'Heaven help me. I run a business, employ ten people, and I couldn't see this when it was staring me in the face?'

'Couldn't see *what*, please!' Edward was begging now.

Stevie offered her open palm, as if showing Kim through a door. 'You say.'

'It's not just that they called before they were scammed, Edward. They were scammed *because* they called.'

CHAPTER TWENTY-SEVEN

She had shouted, but there was saltwater in his ears and the words were carried away by the wind and the crashing of the waves.

Edward was struggling. Every single kitesurfer he had seen in the sea at Sidmouth had been surfing, jumping, landing – no matter how foul the weather they managed to produce a full ballet of movement with never the slightest hint that the sea might sweep them off the stage. Sometimes they joined the spray twenty feet above the surface of the water, lifted as their kites flew towards the cloud. But he had not even taken off once. He was not at one with the sea; he was not even at one with himself. He had jumped, maybe a couple of feet, and fallen into the water every time. Edward was frustrated and angry, and, knowing he was out of earshot, cursed loudly.

Within a second, Kim was beside him. 'I'm sorry,' she shouted. 'I thought it would be your thing. You said you were teaching . . .'

He looked up at her as the wind took the rest of her sentence. 'My God,' he said, 'your body. You look like Halle Berry as Catwoman. I hope I'm allowed to say that. You're . . . ripped.'

'I can't hear you!' she shouted back.

'That's a bit of luck!' he shouted.

If she heard, she was pretending not to. He got closer and raised his voice. 'Embarrassingly, I told Matty I would teach him, but I didn't tell him I needed to learn first.'

She laughed, throwing back her hair. They were in the same spot where he had seen her out at sea that day, beyond the groynes, the great grey piles of rock that posed the greatest danger to anyone carried by the wind. That time he had seen her, initially not recognizing her, they were still at the start of working out what had happened to Barbara Sinker and Rebecca Mason – they didn't yet know that they were two connected cases, or that he had a criminal in his audience. That day, her husband had suddenly appeared in the red Porsche and Edward had hidden himself like a coward.

A coward? He was starting to think he might be one. He had never confronted Anthony Cobden over the blows and bad treatment Kimberley had taken; he had had to be dragged into investigating the scammer, even though his programme had brought the victims and the criminal together. And now he was scared of the sea.

Kimberley jumped off her board. They were both in wetsuits but it was still cold.

'Will people talk if they see us?' Edward asked, again hearing the interior voice: *Coward.*

'No one in Sidmouth can focus this far out to sea.'

'I thought you were an estate agent, not an optician.'

The water rose, bearing them both upwards for a second. She asked loudly, 'Do you mind being seen with me?'

'I mind falling off my board twenty-five times and being seen *by* you.'

'That's a little different,' she said.

'How is Anthony?' The change of subject was so clumsy, the wind did him a favour by snatching the question away.

She got him to stay on the board, using the kite for stability.

She showed how the kite should move from left to right – 'never to a point in front of you, because you just get dragged into the sea' – and the best way was to imagine 12 o'clock above your head and move the kite as if you were taking it half an hour back from 12.15.

'Eleven forty-five?' he said, knowing the one chance he had of being a good pupil was understanding what he was failing to do.

'Be positive with your steering, Edward, be aggressive. Use the kite like a handle you're pulling on, don't just wait for it. The wind is there when you want it. Have some balls.'

Infuriated by his ineptitude, he lashed into the wind. And a miracle happened. A gust took him – a jump higher than anything he had seen her do. He was fired into the air as if by a cannon. Arcing upwards and across and then – the bigger miracle – descending like a bag of sand but landing stable on the water for a second, wobbling on the surface of the water and then regaining control.

'My oh my oh my,' shouted Kim as he stretched his arms in a spoof Olympic-winner pose and promptly fell back into the water. She pulled off a jump half a second after he landed that was not nearly as dramatic. As she landed ten yards from him, he climbed back onto his board.

'*Have some balls!*' he shouted. '*You can do this!*'

She called back, 'Are you cross with me? Good!' It was raining.

'I'm thrilled!' he shouted. 'But that was pure fluke!'

It was an early summer day, but it had quickly got as cold as a winter night as they drifted further out to sea. The black cloud above them seemed not to be affecting the seafront, where streaks of bright sunlight clawed at the beach area like a cat trying to paw at the solitary sun-worshippers.

'We're quite a way out,' he said, the wind lulling enough for her to hear him at a normal volume.

'He is mad.'

'What?'

'To answer your question earlier, about Anthony. I hadn't

wanted to say.' She brushed hairs away from her eyes. 'He is in the asylum.'

'Decla?' Everyone knew it. The sea had pulled them together now, and she reached out and held his board, locking them together.

'The very same. Trauma, apparently.'

They bobbed up and down in the water.

'But what trauma?'

'Who knows?' she said. 'Maybe there's a general heading of "Police Trauma". The psychologist said he treated someone who had a breakdown after stepping on his boss's bonsai tree at a private party. The man was off work for two years. Everything affects everyone differently. I've been to see him every day,' she added. The wind had fallen as they spoke, and the surface of the sea was calm for a moment.

'Do you want me to come?' Edward asked.

'To Decla? Are you kidding? He doesn't even know you exist.'

'I thought that might be an advantage.'

'I said "Have some balls", but I didn't mean that many. No, Edward, you can't visit my husband in hospital.'

'Two out of ten,' said Kim brutally, once they were in the café above Jacob's Ladder.

'I thought you liked this place.'

'That's my score for your kite-work today.'

'Oh.' He managed a wry smile. 'I guess I tried to blag it.' He looked at her, knowing, more consciously than ever, how much he loved her, but fighting the conclusion because it would only cause him sadness. He suddenly wished that he had kissed her out at sea, just pecked her cheek in that moment where she had reached for the cabling around him and pulled their boards together. He could have kissed her wet face and tasted the salt.

'Ten,' he said.

'Ten what?'

'You're ten.'

'A ten? Like the old movie?'

'What movie?'

'The one where someone scores somebody a ten, literally some *body*, because he sees her in a bikini.'

'And then he crashes his kite board,' Edward added.

'And then scores someone a ten because he thinks she's ripped.'

'I didn't think you could hear me.' He felt his cheeks warming.

'I don't hear inappropriate compliments. I couldn't hear you shouting, *I love you*. There's a filter under Advanced Settings.' She reached over to him tenderly and put her hand on his. 'You're forgiven. And I like you just as much. Now, tell me why you're not working on a Friday?'

'No!' he was jolted. 'Friday? That can't be. Oh God. I'm due in at three.'

She turned and he followed her gaze to the large clock above the counter. Three thirty.

He picked up his mobile but saw the text before he could dial.

'It seems they got there before me.'

He showed her the screen.

Sorry Mr Temis. You've done your last shift. Come in & collect your stuff and return yr uniform thank you. BW Pippa Middelton

'Uniform?' asked Kim.

'Just camouflage, night goggles, a bearskin. No, I'm joking. Uniform is a basic blue shirt and black trousers so the mud doesn't show. No silly hat, I promise. I don't even know who this woman is.'

Kim was crestfallen. 'Do you want to work as an estate agent?'
He was silent, brooding.

'Honey, it's not a crisis,' said Kim. 'We'll get through it.'

'There is no "we", though, is there?'

'No,' she said sadly. 'I suppose there isn't.'

'I should have kissed you out there. I wanted to.'

'Don't.'

He wished he had not said it. She took a sip of her coffee
and looked around. The other customers were all retirees. There
were three women at a table laid for four who looked as if they
had been swimming.

Edward leant over to Kim and lowered his voice: 'Do you
think they were a group of four and one got lost at sea? But they
were set on having their coffees anyway.' They both sniggered.

'A hardy generation,' Kim said, solemnly.

The radio on a shelf above the fresh cakes was playing RTR-
92, currently on Madonna's 'Like a Virgin'.

'They're upgrading their playlist,' said Edward. 'I don't even
know who does the mid-afternoon show now.'

'I do,' said Kim, surprising him. 'It's a woman with a surname she says is spelt "Tarte with an 'e'".'

'Honor Tarte. Of course. She came over from Plymouth. But
how do you know that? I didn't know you listened at all.'

Kim leant forward and pushed her palms into the side of her
face, inadvertently narrowing her features as she dropped her
voice.

'When we met them all in the pub on Monday, we worked
out they were all connected through your show.'

'*You* worked it out, Kim.'

'Whatever. So the first thought is that the scammer is in the
audience. He listens every night—'

'Right, obviously, and then he tracks them down—'

'Obviously!'

'So? What am I missing? I mean, I know I'm an unemployed

male with a house falling off a cliff, but I'm not completely off the pace.'

'Think about how the victims were contacted.'

'Social media?'

'Mostly, no.'

'They were texted, I guess. Isn't that it? That's how Rebecca was contacted, that's how Barbara—'

'Stevie has copied me her list.' Kim waved away his concern. 'Don't worry, it's locked, and it will never be shared with anyone other than you, me and her and, if necessary, the cops. I went through it.'

He stabbed at the carrot cake with his fork, desperate to reach the conclusion before she did.

'Let me guess.'

'Please do.'

'They were texted, most of them? Right? That's the key thing. I can't believe I missed that, but then what does it mean?'

'Think.'

He ate the cake slowly, chewing it absent-mindedly.

'Wait,' he began.

'Go on . . .'

'If they were texted,' he said slowly, 'the scammer isn't in the audience. They're inside the radio station.'

'Bang on, Ed. You don't get mobile phone numbers that easily. So whoever is doing it is using that studio computer of yours to get the numbers. In answer to your question, yes, I know who "Honor Tarte-with-an-E" is because I'm creating a little tree here.' She slid what looked like a diagram out of her purse and pushed it towards him across the table. 'I'm trying to work out who goes into that building every day, and who's been there long enough – this rules out Honor, by the way – to have done a million-pound crime under everyone's noses.'

He looked out of the window, hardly able to believe his ears. 'Wind that back. How much?'

'That was the easiest part, totalling the column Stevie had marked "Sum Stolen". It's a shade over one million pounds. Speak of the devil, here she is.'

Stevie walked in, breathless. This time she was not wearing a cowboy hat but a baseball cap and, uncharitable though this was, the thought crossed Edward's mind that she was dressing flamboyantly and wearing the eye patch for the attention. Why did he feel like this? He was being unfair. Stevie was covering the top of her head because the hairline had gone; the black eye patch might be temporary, but she needed it. She was wearing a tutu of some sort, a skirt that fanned out in layers of pleated taffeta. Bare knees. Doc Martens and red socks. No acid would make this girl hide herself.

All the other customers in the café looked up and stopped talking. Kim stared at Edward as if to gauge his reaction to her arrival. He let his eyebrow move – more a flicker than a movement – which was the subtlest indication that he had not been expecting their mutual friend. Once again, he was unsettled by Stevie.

She went to the counter to order.

Kim said, 'I saw that movement of your eyebrow. The "what's going on here, then?" look.'

'Maybe I was enjoying it being just us two. Selfish, I know.'

'Maybe,' said Kim, 'you're the journalist who thinks this story is *his* scoop.'

'But it's not.'

'Stevie and I wanted to speak to you together.'

That rang an alarm bell. Kim's tone had changed. As she said the words, she sat back in her chair and folded her arms.

When Stevie came back from the counter, carrying a tin of Sprite on a metal tray, they spoke aimlessly. Stevie had also totalled the 'sum stolen' column, and spelled out the figure exactly: 'One million and ninety-two thousand, four hundred and forty-three pounds, but I'm sure that might be ten per cent out either way. Some people could not be sure exactly what they'd lost; for example the person who sent the scammer her father's medals.'

'I remember that lady,' said Kim. 'A George Cross?'

'Victoria,' Edward murmured. 'We'll have to just say a million.'

'The thing I can't work out is this,' Stevie began. 'He creams a million quid off all these desperate old people, and he's doing great business, and then he actually murders one of them. Why? What did my granny do? Why would he take that chance, really? He could have just ghosted her.'

Edward looked at the two women. Kim's hair was still wet. He wanted to talk more about Anthony, about their feelings for each other, even though they would never spell them out directly. He could not allow himself to think they might one day be together, and for now, seeing the waves of dark hair tumbling over her athletic shoulders, he knew that he must never say the truth of his feelings – he loved her desperately.

He was jolted back to the conversation by Kim saying to Stevie: 'You might as well go ahead. Edward, you may not like this.'

'What?' asked Edward. 'You're worrying me.'

'Stevie wanted to say it.' Kim sat back and nibbled the nail on her little finger.

Stevie said, 'Kim and I have talked and talked. You see, those numbers can only have come from the radio station and more particularly from your show. And we just think it all adds up to the same conclusion, and we wanted to tell you what we think.'

'Conclusion may be the wrong word,' said Kim.

'Go on,' said Edward, who could not imagine what might be coming. Absent-mindedly, he slid the edge of his fork around the plate to catch the last pieces of carrot cake.

'We think we know who did this,' said Stevie. 'The person behind all of it.'

'Well, tell me.'

'We think it was you.'

CHAPTER TWENTY-EIGHT

Barbara Sinker's hips were hurting again. She had been to the doctor this morning and an unfamiliar young locum had explained anti-inflammatories to her as if she had never heard of them. When he said 'NS-AIDS,' Barbara spelt out the full name.

'Non-steroidal anti-inflammatories.'

He gulped. 'You've had them before, I guess.'

Overcome by pain and frustration as she left the surgery, she threw the box into the first waste bin on her way home. The journey would have to be done on rubber-tipped sticks and a bus.

Two hours later, she found Kimberley sitting on her front doorstep, crestfallen.

At the end of the garden path, Barbara threw out her arms, accidentally casting aside one of her sticks as if acting out a biblical miracle.

'What! No welcome?'

'Welcome, Mum. But it's your home.'

'In that case,' said Barbara, chirpier now her daughter was here, 'welcome, Kimberley. Where's your door key?'

No answer. The grimace on her daughter's face did not shift.

Gingerly, Barbara picked up the walking stick she had dropped and clicked up the garden path. There was no other sound. Standing above her daughter now, and conscious of the sweat gluing her blouse to her chest and shoulder blades, Barbara saw a look in her daughter's eyes like that of an injured animal.

'What is it, dear? Is it Anthony?'

'It's not . . .' Kimberley paused. 'Well, it's not *not* Anthony.'

'Not not what? You silly thing.' Barbara unlocked the door. As they went into the hall she said, almost inaudibly: 'So is it Edward?'

Seeing Kim flinch, Barbara felt like the amateur darts player who had suddenly thrown three treble twenties. When they sat down in the lounge together, she watched Kim's eyes flicker around the room. The pensioner had left one of her automata on the table – a tiny piece in wood, intricate and fragile, showing a woman at a sewing machine – and for a moment her daughter let her gaze rest on that.

'Mum, I can see you want to give me the third degree, but you summoned me to help with your laptop.'

Barbara thought she might be allowed just one comment on her daughter's personal life . . .

'Your father is, in many ways, a kind and lovely man. I remember watching from a window when he built you that tree house.' Barbara turned in her chair and gestured vaguely towards the garden and the field beyond. There was a copse at the end of the garden and the tree was still there. 'Your dad was good with his hands.' Barbara resisted any suggestion that this could be taken on more than one level, which she knew would appal her daughter. 'He loved you, and in his own way, he loved me. But he was better with his hands than his heart. I remember watching him, with that magnifier of his, using a microfile to make little figures out of raw nuts. But he never made anything out of me.'

'What do you mean?'

260

'Roy just wasn't there. Emotionally. He never attended to me. Such precision with his hands, but that's where it stopped. I would have loved him to turn that magnifying glass on me, but no. I was more alone as a married woman than I am now.' She added, 'We're friends these days, of course.'

'This isn't very twenty-first century, Mum, is it? Marrying a man and expecting them to turn you into something. You're not a walnut.'

'It was nutmegs and he called it micro-sculpture. Besides, we were very much twentieth century. He's the one who got me into the automata. Actually, he made that one.' She pointed at the little figure with the sewing machine, but she could tell Kimberley was losing patience. She could say only one more thing before the conversation closed.

'My darling Kimberley, if you're alone with Anthony, as alone as I was with your dad, then you can move on. It's a rule – you can't build your happiness on someone else's sadness. If you want to be with Wimbledon—'

Kim almost spat her tea out when Barbara used Edward Temmis's nickname. For the first time since she had arrived, Barbara saw her daughter's features soften.

'We've fallen out. He doesn't speak to me any more.'

'Oh darling!'

'Something . . .' She looked away, worried at a nail, which Barbara hadn't seen her do since she was a child. 'Something was said, something that hurt him badly. It appeared to come from . . . me. I can't say any more.'

So the moment for intimacies was gone, as if a heavy curtain had dropped between them. Barbara picked up the cup and saucer she always used for her tea – Kimberley would only ever take hers in a mug – and the room seemed to fill with the sound of the china clinking, and her swallowing.

Kimberley spoke next. 'You said you needed help with the laptop?'

Barbara struggled to remember. 'Oh. It's a programme called WhatsApp which I've resisted, but apparently I do need to be on it. I just can't get it to work on my computer.'

'It'll only work on your phone, that one. It needs a mobile phone number. I'll have to take a look. But Mum, given what happened with that person who scammed you – can I ask why you would be wanting to open yourself up any more online?'

Barbara wanted to be cross at this mollycoddling, but Kimberley had given her leeway to speak on the subject of marriage to Anthony, so she did not show her indignation. 'Some of the ladies I met in the Squirrel are on it. They have a victims' group.'

'Oh.'

'It's called LADIES WHO LYNCH, but there are men as well. We don't believe in all that "survivor" nonsense. We're victims and we want revenge. And I felt so much solace that night, I wanted to join it.'

'I wondered why you were in such a positive mood. There's nothing like a good lynching.'

Ten minutes later, Kimberley had downloaded the app on Barbara's mobile. She asked casually, 'Do you remember calling Edward's show, Mum, about your little models? You did, didn't you?'

'We call them *automata*, and yes, since I called him a lot, once a fortnight probably, of course I would have mentioned the collection. Why?'

Kim did not answer. 'Can I use your phone for a minute?'

'Did you forget yours?'

'I want to call someone from yours. Long story.'

Barbara watched, puzzled. Her daughter took her own phone out of her jacket pocket and scrolled for a moment. Then she tapped the screen on Barbara's as if typing a number.

'Excuse me,' said Kimberley, stepping out into the hall. 'Private call.'

At which point Barbara understood exactly what her daughter was doing.

Edward assumed it was Kim calling again when he heard the phone go. He had declined all her other calls. But now he picked the phone off the kitchen table and saw the number was a new one. The screen said unknown caller.

'Hello?' said Edward. So old-fashioned, he thought, picking up a phone and answering a call like this. He looked out of the back of the house towards the crumbling far edge of the garden and the blank blue sea beyond it.

He was still unable to believe what had happened in the Clock Tower Café. Every morning in the three days since, he had woken with a physical pain in his stomach. A void in his head that swiftly gave way to a migraine. He felt as if he had been in a pub fight and someone had slammed a chair leg into him – yes, *punctured*, that was how he felt.

He wanted to believe it was Stevie's Tourette's that had spoken, her uncontrollable frankness, and that there would be a sudden, alarmed protest from Kimberley and a tumble of *Oh goodness me Stevie you didn't mean to say that I'm sure.* But Kim had simply looked from Stevie to him and back again. Far from correcting their young friend, she had let the words settle like green gas on a World War One battlefield. Heavier than air, they reached his lungs and choked him.

Far, far too late, Kim had tried to soften the blow. 'I think we've overstated things a little, haven't we, Stevie?'

But Stevie had made it worse, loosing a blizzard of words at him. He had access and opportunity, and if all the contacts had come from his show then wasn't he the obvious person to have done it, and isn't it likely a divorcé DJ with a new house might be in financial difficulties, and who else knew Stevie was going to try to open the computer and could put acid inside it to hurt her and why else would he have taken such an interest in Riva Mason's case and how do we even know Riva wrote to him, or was the letter she wrote the reason she was killed, because he got it and opened it and saw she was on to him?

'Stevie—'

At last Kim had grabbed the young woman's arm to stop her. Stevie had said, 'It's what we both think.'

'No, Stevie, no. We *suspected* something. You can say that. Not that it's what we *think*, because that's unfair on Edward.'

'*Suspected?*' cried Edward. 'You too?'

He slashed his arm right instinctively, and a cup flew at the wall. He left the table clumsily to pick up the pieces. Every other customer was staring now. The woman behind the counter knew he was a regular, but 'even regulars can't behave like this, sir,' she told him angrily.

He unleashed a flood of angry apologies to the staff as he scrabbled for the shards of porcelain.

He was so upset he did not even want to defend himself. He could have said he was only involved in this mess because of Kimberley's mum and Stevie's gran. That although the computer that held all the contacts for his show was not linked to the network, it had a piece of card stuck to it bearing the words 'USER NAME studio4, PASSWORD SaveTheWhale' so the terminal could effectively be accessed by anyone in the building, including cleaners and builders. He could have said to Kim, 'Do you really believe I'm the kind of person who does a hit job on sixty old people, when my whole show was about giving them a bit of fun and company in their old age?'

He said none of that. Any protest would only sound suspicious and make *him* angrier. Standing, he froze with the broken pieces of cup in his hand, blood rushing between his ears, hearing (as if in the distance) an argument that had broken out in front of him between Kimberley and Stevie. He saw the staff and other customers watching. And then, without a further word, he made a little bow to his two companions and left.

Now he waited for the person at the other end of the phone line. There was a crackle and a muffled voice spoke for half a second.

'Who's that?'

'Sorry, Edward. Bad line. Can I call you back?'

'Hang on, Derrick,' said Edward, recognizing the voice and moving through the misaligned French windows into the garden. 'I only get a signal when I'm on the edge of this cliff.'

'That sounds like the title of someone's autobiography. You be careful there, remember I've seen the drop,' added Derrick. Not for the first time, Edward appreciated the caring tone of his former colleague.

'Did you say something about a funeral?' Edward asked.

'The memorial for Walter Breames.'

'Oh!' Suddenly Edward was interested. 'How did I not know this?'

'The local Legion wanted to put feelers out before anyone talked about it publicly, because they didn't want a damp squib. But they came back to me on Friday saying they think there might be three hundred there. And they're a bit worried.'

Walter Breames had been one of five hundred black aircrew who served in the RAF during World War Two. Most were from the Caribbean. Nearly all were now dead, if they had not died during the war itself.

A caller to Edward's show – a local bricklayer – had mentioned the presence of a 'very distinguished veteran' in a care home in Topsham more than two years ago now. At this point, Breames had been in the early stages of dementia. The call had got quite a response from other listeners, including a Devon historian called Malcolm Prissy. He regularly rang the radio show with snippets of Devon County history, and was always boring to the point where, once or twice, Edward had to shut the fader on him and blame a technical fault. On this occasion it was different.

Prissy called an hour after the first mention of Walter Breames and explained why people like him were important.

'The USA had separate black units. In the RAF everyone worked together, all races. The colour bar went on day one of the war. And here's the thing. White airmen knew if they were shot down they would be captured and imprisoned. Their black colleagues knew they would be shot on sight. So yes, they were fighting in support of this country, but also fighting because a victorious Hitler would have enslaved the Caribbean.'

Two weeks later, the thoughtful bricklayer was back on the line. 'Some sad news about Mr Breames. I went to visit my mother yesterday and discovered Walter had had a massive heart attack last week and that was it.' He added, 'Not a single visitor for the last two years, so sad.'

They rang Malcolm Prissy for an on-the-spot eulogy.

'From what I've gleaned in the last fortnight, I think that Officer Breames was actually *not* from the Caribbean. This makes it more interesting. Sierra Leone was a British colony and he came from there. God rest his ancient soul and God bless the internet for making this search possible. Now Edward,' he continued, addressing the radio host, 'I think Officer Breames was probably with the Halifax Bombers flying out of Yorkshire. He might have been a navigator. That's what I think is most likely. Bear in mind he'd be using compasses and set squares in the belly of the plane, while it was actually in the air! I can't be sure, but I'm close to being sure. If I was an antiques collector, I would say this particular relic was worth an astonishing amount and I feel ruined, *ruined*, that he died without a pot to piss in.'

Trust Malcolm Prissy to ruin it. The reference to Walter Breames as if he was a cracked antique, and the coarse language, triggered an avalanche of complaints – 'disrespectful' was the politest word used – and Twitter lit up. For an hour, late that evening, Edward's name trended across the UK for the first time, along with #CancelPrissy.

By the morning the row had faded, but the life of Walter Breames started to get attention. The *Daily Telegraph* ran an article. That night Edward spoke about him again, telling the story. Malcolm Prissy managed a safer tribute, having now discovered that Breames successfully navigated twenty-two missions over Germany. On the twenty-third he was shot down and forced to parachute onto farmland with no cover available except a line of haystacks. He hid deep in the third one. German soldiers raked the first and second haystack with their machine guns. Breames heard the weapon magazines being changed as they prepared to shoot into the third haystack, and emerged from his hiding place with his hands up. The Germans were so shocked to see a black airman that they did not fire. Walter Breames spent the rest of the war – another twenty months – in Stalag Luft 1 before being liberated by the Russians. After the war he had been a captain on one of the *Windrush* boats, taught maths in a secondary school in Exeter – where he was known for flamboyant suits and shirts – and served as an independent councillor until retirement thirty years ago. He had never married.

The loneliness of Walter Breames's final years had really got to Edward, and he talked about it on his programme several days running. 'Someone must know him, someone must love him,' he had said. The cremation had to take place within a week of the death and a photographer from the local paper got down to the event, expecting a handful of attendees.

But there was not a single person present other than the care home manager and a bored vicar, and the photographer wrote a piece about how he had set down his camera in order to become the only attendee. 'I wept tears of sadness' was the standout line, accompanied by a picture of rows of empty chairs and a wicker coffin, underneath the headline: A HERO BIDS THE WORLD GOODBYE, BUT I WAS THE ONLY ONE WHO HEARD HIM.

The reason the Devon branch of the British Legion were 'a bit worried' about the memorial for Walter Breames, which had taken the best part of eighteen months to organize, with so many people having a loud opinion about how his legacy should be marked, was obvious as soon as Edward began his long climb to the church. The Legion thought Navigator Breames should be remembered somewhere that befitted war service in the sky, and so they had reached out to the highest church in the southwest of England, St Michael de Rupe in Brentor. The problem was that the highest church was also one of the smallest. St Michael de Rupe, whose foundations were laid in the twelfth century by a local landowner, stood at the top of Brent Tor and was visible for miles around.

Had the British Legion checked the diocese website, they would have found the warning: 'The church sits 40 in its box pews. With more chairs we can accommodate 60. Nevertheless it is a magical place to be married. We have a 4x4 which can be used for the ascent but this requires booking.'

Ascent? That also should have rung alarm bells. Three hundred people wanted to mark the life of Walter Breames. It was the first day of June. The sun was bright but there was a chill in the air. Edward wore the right footwear for the climb; many did not. Some of the congregation for this special service were deep into old age, sons and daughters helping them up the Tor. One old man wore a greatcoat that might have been a father's from the First World War; a tanned thirty-something ran in silk jogging shorts, bouncing from rock to rock like a fawn. The jogger stopped with the greatcoated pensioner and helped him for a while.

Edward saw a mop of red hair as he reached the top.

'This is insane,' said Derrick, who was manifestly unfit; he'd dropped onto a smooth lump of granite with only a hundred yards still to walk. 'Are we going to miss the service?'

'The word went down the hill a minute ago that they'll wait for every last person,' said Edward, also out of breath. 'I'm so glad you told me about this, Derrick. Puts everything in perspective. Lord God above.' He looked up at the church, and now thought it the perfect place for Walter Breames's last good-bye, the building perched on the crag at the top of the Tor like the first tooth in a baby's mouth. The lone, high church; the solo aviator flying his last journey.

Derrick rose from his temporary seat. 'How come you're fitter than me?'

'I'm not. I just walked more slowly. I knew they wouldn't start on time.'

'It's the radio guy in me,' said Derrick. 'Two p.m. means two bang on, so I rush for the deadline. I'm a bit Kate Bushed now.'

'At least your ankle's back in working order.' Edward felt a tug on his arm. A breathless woman in middle age had run up behind him.

'Hello! I'm Amanda Schomes,' she said brightly.

Derrick paused, evidently unsure whether to stay with Edward or not. The church was almost within touching distance now. They were in the middle of a group of others. One or two had recognized Edward. Someone shook his hand. Brushing away a sweaty line of hair from her forehead, Amanda Schomes added, 'Kenneth didn't want me to catch you up, but I did.'

Edward searched the filing cabinet of his mind, found nothing on Amanda Schomes, but when he put 'Kenneth' and 'Schomes' together, he immediately had a picture in his mind's eye of his old boss at the garden centre.

'It's very upsetting,' she said. 'Kenneth was away and his boss fired you.'

Edward shot Derrick an embarrassed glance.

'Pippa Middelton, nothing to do with *the* Middletons, who are spelled differently apart from anything else, took on some of Ken's duties and something cropped up with you and that was it. And Ken loved you, so he's broken-hearted.'

'That's very kind.'

Derrick said quietly, 'Shall I find us seats?'

'Oh, I don't think there'll be seats! We shall have to hang by a bell rope or something,' Amanda said, the voice surprisingly posh, her cheeks flushing. Edward considered how agile she must be, to have chased him up the hill and managed this conversation without ever breaking off to catch her breath.

'I'm Amanda.' Now she was introducing herself to Derrick, stopping the younger man from leaving.

'Is Kenneth still back there? He honestly doesn't have to worry about me.'

'Oh but he *does*. And I'll tell you for why. My mother – ' here the woman lowered her voice – 'was one of your crowd at the Secret Squirrel.'

Edward was still so angry with Kim and Stevie that he could not bear to think about that evening without feeling inflamed at the false accusation. He had wanted to move on from the feeling that he was responsible to the victims of the scam, but he now knew he would not be allowed to.

'Sorry Derrick, this will all sound a bit mysterious, but maybe you should know about it.'

'Quite so,' said Amanda briskly. 'Everyone should know about it, I think.'

Edward could see this woman had no filter at all, and he would have to be explicit. 'I am not sure we should speak openly, only because a lot of the victims are so mortified that they don't want other people knowing.'

'What were they victims of?' asked Derrick, a perfectly innocent question, but Edward could feel the conversation tumbling, like a bullet from a misaligned gun muzzle, towards the computer in his radio studio. And he did not want it to do that right now because he would understandably face a never-ending list of questions from Derrick.

'A terrible confidence trickster,' said Amanda, at which point Kenneth Schomes appeared and saved the situation. They all braced themselves against a gust of wind, so strong it made them all burst out laughing and broke the tension.

'You don't have to apologize to Edward,' said Amanda. 'I have done so already.'

'We'll sort it out,' wheezed Kenneth. 'I'll have a word with—'

'No need,' said Edward, mortified now by having Derrick hear this conversation about how he could not even hold down a job at a garden centre.

'Shall we go in?' Derrick asked. 'I think half the people still on that hill are going to be standing outside the church for the service.'

They were an odd group: Derrick, Edward, Amanda Schomes and Kenneth.

As they waited for the service to begin, and new arrivals took spaces on the apron of grass and rock around the church, breathing deeply in the thin, high air, Amanda hissed at Edward: 'My mum actually called the scammer.'

'Did she get through?'

'A couple of times. But he just hung up at the other end straightaway.'

Derrick whispered into Edward's ear, 'I'm trying not to ask questions, but you're really going to have to fill me in on what this is all about. It's just too interesting.'

Edward had the length of the service at St Michael de Rupe to

271

stay schtum. It bought him time. It would not be right to speak, even in hushed tones, during the remembrance for Walter. The church staff managed to find spare hymnbooks and passed them around the crowd; each was shared by four or five people. At some point the outdoor loudspeaker they had run a cable into fizzed and blew. The vicar's voice now had a faint, ethereal quality, as if she was speaking from a summit somewhere across the moor. There was a light shower, lasting no more than a minute, and then wind chased the guilty cloud away.

During the service Edward said only three words to Derrick. 'This is special.'

Edward's phone vibrated and the screen showed a message:

YOU MUST CALL ME.

'Looks urgent,' whispered Derrick, unable to miss the all-caps message.

It was from Stevie. Without speaking, Edward powered the phone down so it could not call for his attention again.

As the service went on it became less and less audible. Edward begged himself to use this brief pause to think. His first instinct was that Amanda Schomes had messed things up for him. Just as he had begun to want out of the whole situation with the scam, mainly because of the terrible way Stevie and Kim had behaved at the Clock Tower, Derrick was now being drawn into the story. And, if he was going to solve this thing, Derrick was the ally he needed. Someone at the radio station was accessing the contacts for his show, and undoubtedly they were getting in from the programme computer. Whoever it was had got away with a million pounds. If he was *persona non grata*, as Derrick had said, he'd need a mole on the inside to help . . .

They did not leave the Tor quickly. 'Two hundred and eighty-two!' one of the organizers had cried after the service. 'Your doing, Edward!' The use of his name alerted a dozen people to his presence, and soon he was being gently mobbed.

He felt all the more responsible for making sure the whole crowd descended the Tor safely, and Derrick seemed happy to hang back to lend a hand. It meant that they both stayed behind, the unspoken subject hanging between them. Derrick said, 'I sometimes forget how popular you still are with this—'

'Age group?'

'"Valuable demographic", I was about to say.'

'Gorgeous people, I love them,' said Edward, who had been touched and patted by the hands of almost everyone who passed. 'But Walter's memorial isn't my gig, Derrick. You made it happen.'

'The Legion made it happen. They got three hundred pensioners up a mountain to shelter in a building made for fifty.'

'Look at them, though.' The summit was clear of worshippers now, and the two men watched from above as the long line of people snaked back down the hill, a handful stopping, presumably to wait for the next shuttle in the vicar's Land Rover. 'Makes you proud of what we can do.'

'We bloody miss you so much,' said Derrick. 'Boss, it's not the same without—'

'Don't let's be slating Tessa. Not right or good.'

'But she isn't.'

'Isn't what?'

'Isn't you.'

'I was broken.' He squinted out across the valley laid out below them, feeling the beat of his heart, feeling the pang of sadness in his stomach. 'I had to go. I couldn't recover from Matty quickly enough and I still haven't.'

A large bird squawked above them and a shadow passed. They both turned at that moment to look at the sun, shielding their eyes.

Derrick said, 'Tell me what's going on.'

'Let's sit. I'll be as quick as I can.'

'You don't have to be. Take your time. Tell me everything.'

The sun warmed Edward's back as he looked out over Dartmoor. They were sitting on cragged rock above the path, where there was a sheer drop of around thirty feet. Both men had removed their jackets to cushion the surface and were dangling their legs over the edge.

'I should have asked you for help earlier, or at least told you about it. But it got out of control. A part of me didn't want to engage. I didn't know where to start.'

'What?' asked Derrick, alarmed. 'You're worrying me. Is a scandal?'

'Yes, it's a scandal.'

'And does it involve me?'

'It involves – no, it doesn't involve you directly. But it involves the radio show we made together, and the computer in that studio.'

'Humble Reggie?'

Edward had forgotten the computer had a name, christened after the engineer who would regularly have to come down the road on his bicycle and get it working again when it froze. The first time he called round, Reggie from IT Assurance, 180 The Promenade, Sidmouth, had told them, 'Gents, in my humble view, and I stress it is just my humble view, you will need to invest in a new computer before too long. We are not talking decades – in my humble view.'

The phrase 'we are not talking decades' presumably meant 'sometime next month', but they couldn't prise the money out of Agnes for a new PC when, as she correctly said, 'It isn't on the network. It's just an electronic filing cabinet. Clear out the clutter from the hard drive, blow the dust out with one of those doobries and it should work fine.'

Humble Reggie the IT guy had his nickname shifted to the computer. Edward had forgotten all this because he had never once logged in to get a number – as he saw it, that was the job of his production team.

'I don't think I ever logged into that . . . box,' said Edward. 'It seems an exaggeration to call it a computer. But where does it come into this?'

'I'm going to tell you, but I need you to promise me that you won't take any action as a result of what I say. I need to decide really carefully what to do, and that may be nothing. And secondly, Derrick, I don't want you to lose your idealism as a result of what I'm about to say. You do a perfect job. You're a perfect producer. You're young and you have it all ahead of you. Above all, you are *kind*. So I don't want you giving up because you're disgusted by what's happened.'

Carefully, he wove his way through the story. Something told him not to go near the death of Rebecca Mason because the murder, if it was a murder, was so appalling. Besides, there was too much guesswork involved to feel he could burden Derrick with the details. He dreaded to think how the younger man would react if he were told his programme database was implicated in the killing of a listener, so he simply said she had died tragically after writing a letter to him – how suspicious that sounded – and that the letter had gone missing and Stevie had come to Edward for help. Rebecca 'Riva' Mason loved Hitchcock, and Barbara Sinker collected automata – 'every victim was accessed through their love of something'. He talked about the dozens of victims who took over the Secret Squirrel.

'Every one of them a listener. One of ours, Derrick!'

Edward spoke as he leant forwards, over the edge, staring down at the rocks below. It allowed him to focus.

Eventually he fell silent. There was no noise apart from the squawking of birds, and, in the distance, a tractor chattering its complaint about being fired up so late in the day.

'You know everything,' the voice behind him said.

Edward turned. Derrick was standing above him, blocking the sun.

'Jesus Christ,' said the producer, 'I'm shaking.' He kicked his legs as if there were ants in his trousers. He was almost dancing with anxiety. 'You're sure it's our computer?'

'Yes. Every single person was on the show. Every single person told their story to me. Every single person was contacted.'

'Good grief. So what next?'

'So, I was thinking – what if I got into the radio station and worked a nightshift, and I just tally up all the contacts and when they rang us? Because what I need is the date they rang the show. Then I can match it with the date the scammer contacted them. If any victim was scammed *before* they rang our show, the whole theory blows up.'

'And it couldn't be a listener? Surely it could just be a listener?'

'How would a listener get their mobile numbers? And for all those people, more than sixty? Impossible.'

'But we all use the same name and password, which is written on Humble Reggie, right there above the screen, on a piece of torn cereal packet as I remember. Frosties. It's still there! I see it every day. Anyone can log in and everyone leaves the same trace.'

Edward thought for a moment.

'Okay. So someone is accessing the system when you're not there. Either after the show – at midnight, say – or before you get in. I'm going to assume you haven't seen anyone doing that?'

'I've seen loads of people in the production area. It's not private!'

'But on that computer? Regularly?'

Derrick thought about it. 'There was someone. I only saw him a couple of times, though.'

'Who? Tell me!'

'God, Edward. I feel I'm completely stitching someone up here. If I say the name—'

'Say it!'

Now Edward was standing too. On the roof of the church, a line of crows formed the audience to this tense exchange, the sun throwing their stark shadows across the tiles. Edward noticed for the first time a set of brand-new solar panels and thought how out of place they looked.

'Bloody say it, Derrick!'

'The person who is married to Agnes. Or her boyfriend. I can't remember the name. Whatever. Tall black guy. He was in there. Twice. At around four p.m., when I come in.'

Edward's gasp was so violent he felt his lungs blow up like party balloons. 'That – bastard! Of course! I knew it, I knew it! Troy Barber. I spoke about him to Kim. My friend Kim. I said he was dodgy. Goddamn,' Edward shouted, not even half-bothered that anyone still in the tiny church would hear the blasphemy. 'Shit, Derrick! I knew it! I knew it! That fucking bastard. That's why he stitched me up.'

'Wait, wait—'

'Why should I wait? He's stolen those numbers, he hacked that bloody useless computer and he chased them all, chased them all, all those poor old dears; and then when I nearly got wind of it, when I got a letter from Rebecca Mason which presumably said exactly what was going on, he kills her and—'

'I didn't know about any of this until today.' Derrick's voice shook and he looked even more panicky, as if he had suddenly started a chip-pan blaze and could not find the fire blanket.

Edward immediately felt sorry for his former producer. He could see his temper reflected in the young man's fear. Of course it was Barber. Barber had privileged status at the station, being the controller's partner, and he could float around the place like a ghost. 'Maybe I *will* call the police in.'

'Wait. What did you just say?'

'I guess I should call the police?'

'Before that.'

'Barber?'

'Before Barber. You said *he killed her*. That's what you said. Killed who?'

Edward stared down the Tor, looking at the way the large shadow had begun to creep over the lowest slopes, spreading itself like a stain.

'I think we should head down,' he said quietly.

CHAPTER TWENTY-NINE

That night, Edward stared at the ceiling, hearing the old house creak and yawn around him. The yawns were almost human sounds – he swore he heard the house cough sometimes, or even burp like an old man in the corner seat at a pub, nursing a third Guinness.

Tonight the building's yawning started him off. Edward yawned back at it, then yawned again and again, lying on his back, sending deep-lung air into the room like smoke rings. Call, answer, call and answer. He had taken to wearing his hearing aid in bed, against the specialist's advice – 'Place them on your bedside table and if possible slide open the battery drawer to avoid unnecessary power consumption' – because if the house fell, he believed it would shout a warning. He wanted at least the chance of hearing it and waking.

He could not sleep. He should have been more sparing with what he had told Derrick, because he did not want the jumpy young man to take matters into his own hands. What if he told Agnes about their conversation?

His right leg kicked out in bed, a sign of his frustration. Why, why had he spilled details on the fate of Rebecca Mason? Far from wanting to solve the crime, Derrick might even become reluctant to help; why would he want his contacts computer tied to the killing of the old woman?

Two deaths. Matty on a road. Rebecca in a fire. Edward was desperate to see through this, to see a future where he could live without grief pressing in on him at every turn. Kim . . . he so wanted Kim. He knew he wanted her in his life. But in the very instant he discovered that single glowing coal in his frozen heart, she had thrown iced water over it. What in God's name were they thinking, Kim and Stevie, to suddenly declare him under suspicion? How on earth could he have done any of those scams, let alone all of them? Apart from anything else, when the scammer was operating, he was mourning his son. The fact that they had missed that fact – or, worse still, chosen to ignore it – made him thrash out again in bed. Okay, the accusation had been Stevie's. But Kimberley had let it go to air. She was the quality control inspector who waved the car with three wheels through the assembly line.

The house yawed. That was the word – somewhere between a creak and a yawn, like the sound of a huge load placed on a beam, the movement an aircraft makes when the atmospherics cause it to swing like a bead on a pendant. He tried to shut his eyes. The scene at the top of Brent Tor played out on the inside of his eyelids.

Now he was wide awake again. The letter . . . the letter from Rebecca Mason must be the key. She wrote to him and she died. She was killed because she wrote to him. The letter had not been lost inside the radio station at all.

It had been intercepted.

The security staff in reception had left the letter out where anyone could see it. Troy Barber had picked it up without them realizing; easy as pie. Barber had quietly taken the letter from the envelope and left the envelope. Then he had killed Riva.

Edward had asked, early on, 'How would the killer know Rebecca wrote to me? If they did know, why would they think killing her would cancel the letter?' The killer knew she had written because they *physically saw* the letter arrive in the radio station.

Ironic really. When a few ancient listeners turned up for a gentle protest outside the building, the staff on security had virtually declared a terrorist incident and locked the building down; but when a fraudster and soon-to-be killer intercepted a letter right under their noses, they did not even blink.

Edward must have fallen asleep, because the bedside phone woke him with a start.

The name on the display said Tara and he snatched at it, immediately fearing terrible news.

But the voice at the end was calm. 'I know it's one in the morning,' said his ex-wife, 'but I was thinking about you and I couldn't sleep.'

He was out of bed himself now, naked and stepping towards the bay window. Through a crack in the curtains, he saw the moon sparkling on the sea.

'I'm sorry,' he said, triggering strange laughter from her.

'You don't have to be sorry that I can't sleep!'

'I'm sorry for everything.'

'For fuck's sake, Ed.'

'I couldn't sleep either. I just got off.'

She sighed at the other end, long and deep. 'It's always Matty,' she said. 'I have one second in the day, a wonderful second, when I wake, where he is still with us. And then the world tells me he's not.' She pressed on, as if she feared this was sounding like an accusation. 'I blamed you a bit, you know?' She coughed, but it could have been a sob. 'More than a bit. That was so wrong. I have another family. You just have you.'

'Me's enough.'

'You and that madhouse you bought,' she laughed. 'Still, if you lose your son, you're allowed to be mad.'

'How long can we be mad?' he asked.

'For ever, I think.' She breathed, so deeply he thought he

could smell her toothpaste down the phone line. 'I need to say this. If I blamed you, I was wrong to. If I held it, my anger, I was wrong to. You were a great father.'

He wanted to say, 'Not on that last day,' but he knew she did not want to hear that.

'You know I blamed you, right?' she said.

'It was natural. I was with him when—'

'You shouldn't. I shouldn't. We had our beautiful son and we lost him. We loved him and we lost him. I can't bear to think of you on your own, Edward, piling blame on to yourself, and then thinking of me blaming you too. You need to look after yourself. You're a lovely man.'

He tried not to cry. 'The police want to see me again,' he said, hearing his voice as if it was someone else's, trying to stay factual. 'The last cop who was on the case – can't recall the name, but he was super-smart. Name had "Tree" in it.'

'Tree. I just can't go near that side of things or I'd be banging on their door every day. Babe, you tell me if there's progress, but that's not why I'm calling.'

'Why are you calling, love?' They never called each other 'babe' and 'love', not any more, but right now it felt like the most natural thing.

'I'm calling because I had a dream that you took your own life – my love. And it was a very real dream, and I came straight downstairs because I wanted to say, you and I, we'll get through this, and we need to be here for each other.'

'I'm here for you.'

'Ditto.'

'I didn't take my life, and I shan't. I still have things I want to live for.'

'That's my boy.'

The phrase felt wrong – she might have used it of Matty once. To cover the silence, he said: 'I might have found someone. Someone I like.'

'She's a lucky one.'

He went to bed happy, and the house was silent.

The next day, he returned to the garden centre. As requested, he arrived at eleven and went straight to the office of Kenneth Schomes, feeling a strange moment of déjà vu as he sat down – like celluloid spinning backwards off its spool, he saw their last encounter flash by in a second. He had been asking for permission to see the policeman. Schomes had cried.

Schomes shook his head. 'I couldn't believe that bloody Pippa Middelton gave you your marching orders.'

'I thought I'd been sacked by a member of the royal family.'

Kenneth's laugh was an accidental explosion of snot and tears. From a desk drawer he pulled out a handkerchief that looked as if it had been used to oil a bicycle chain. Like the trick mime artists do, he wiped his face and, when he pulled the cloth away, he was wearing a different, mutinous expression.

'Pippa Middelton behaves like she's in the bloody . . .' He thought better of it. 'No, I mustn't. Look, Edward. You're in the hardest time of your life, I see that.' For a second he looked as if he might cry again. 'Your son. The radio job – oh,' he went on, 'and don't tell me it's been your ambition to work in a garden centre because I won't believe it.'

One day, if he ever got back on the radio, that would be the title of his autobiography. *Don't Tell Me It's Been Your Ambition to Work in a Garden Centre Because I Won't Believe It* by Edward Temmis. It would be bought by pensioners across Devon.

Then again, it might not be a happy read. It would have to document the hateful robbery of sixty of his own listeners.

Sixty? More than that, probably, but he had heard sixty stories in the pub. What if there were another sixty, another hundred, hurting too much to come forward?

The thought chilled him, and he was missing what Kenneth

was saying. He caught the rear end of an apology 'for my wife's behaviour on the hill', which was followed up with, 'She will always be grateful, that's the thing, and she's a runner.'

'A runner?'

'Hence she ran after you.'

'I did think she was fit.'

'Oh, she's fit all right,' said Kenneth proudly, at which point the bundle of keys on his belt were dislodged from his waistline.

'She said her mother was at the pub.'

'Yes! Amanda's mother,' Kenneth said. Again his face changed – the glee of recognition, the misery of the connection. Edward noticed the pencil-thin moustache. 'It was her pride more than her wallet that got hurt.'

'I have a memory that she only lost a pound because she sent a specimen amount first. She's still there on our spreadsheet – our very secret, locked, offline spreadsheet,' he added quickly.

'Yep, that pound,' Kenneth said sadly, as if the whole family missed it. 'But you see, it underplays what happened to her! The crim was like a snake, wheedling its way in! He-she-it, whoever they damn well were, pretended to be an older man who went to the football with her father. Exeter City, of course, the Grecians. When she was a little girl. And her dad topped himself way back when she was eighteen and at college, so it's all emotional. And he-she-it-they, whoever the scum are, had all the match programmes from that time, including pictures of her and her dad, because she'd been a mascot once – she called your show about it, by coincidence, I don't know if you remember – but he needed to release them with a payment of . . .'

The words became a blur. Yet again, the pattern. The connection through his show, the vicious attempt to befriend, to romance, to rob.

At the end Kenneth said, 'We both, from the bottom of our hearts, want to thank you for bringing the victims together. Amanda's mother won't go to the police over a one-pound payment.

But it means so much that you are trying to follow up and wrap, as it were, your arms around this hurting crowd. So we want you back. We thought today we'd have you welcoming the customers, and directing them, if that suits? We'd love you at the front. I'll take care of Princess Middelton.'

Edward did as he was told. He did not resent it. He gladly welcomed customers who came into the main display area through the sliding glass doors. He spent two hours at the doors and must have greeted more than a hundred customers.

One face he saw rang a different bell.

'Jordan Callintree,' said the policeman. 'Don't worry, not here to see you, buying a birdbath for my lovely wife.'

'We don't have any that size,' said Edward, a 1920s music hall joke that – amazingly – made the police officer laugh out loud.

'Just a quiet word, Mr Temmis. Might have some news for you soon. I wish you could rack your brains about that car. We have a paint fragment.'

'I tried,' said Edward, panic swelling, breath quickening. Please, he thought, nothing about Matty now!

Seeing how flustered Edward had become, the officer backed off. 'I have tried to keep everything from you. I went back to the spot and we cordoned it off for a week. You might have heard about the queues and the rerouting. We picked up every bloody speck with forensic tape. The first lot didn't investigate properly. We have leads now. And by the way, there's no birdbath. You have a good day, sir. Keep racking that brain if you can. Every little helps. I didn't mean to upset you.'

Officer Callintree turned and headed back to the car park. It struck Edward that he had never seen the officer in a police uniform, and, as he greeted each new customer, he followed the thought through . . . what if he wasn't a police officer? The scammer had created dozens of fictional characters to rob his listeners. Stevie and Kim had thought for a second that he,

Edward, was at the heart of it. Troy Barber posed as a university lecturer but was a fraudster and probably a killer. Rebecca had two names. Kim had mentioned Fiona Bruce. Even Stevie's father was acting oddly. Was anyone who they said they were?

He remembered Callintree's warrant card from their last conversation and put his fears aside. Another thought struck him: if Walter Breames had watched his own memorial, might Matty be looking down on his dad? He was conscious of his phone buzzing with texts in his pocket and finally, on a loo break, he looked.

> Hey, it's Kim. Did everything to reach you – even calling from Mum's phone so you wouldn't know it was me. Anyway, Stevie has found something 😲 and we should meet. No way in 10000000000000 years did I ever mean to say you were to blame. I let her say it. She's an odd girl. My fault. Don't leave me hanging

He replied:

> Let's meet tonight. I'm sorry. Bring her too. I know who did it. I know everything. Spice Route

CHAPTER THIRTY

Spice Route was an Indian restaurant in Budleigh Salterton about ten years past its peak. Any money the owners had invested in the last decade seemed to have gone into making the car park look presentable – the flower border was better than the food – and parked cars were surrounded by half a dozen varieties of orchid that spilled over the rockery above the tarmac.

Kim brought Stevie in the Porsche. She was momentarily concerned when she saw Edward was already waiting for them as she drew up – but no, she and Stevie were punctual and Edward was early. The two women had spoken in the car – whatever had happened between Stevie and Edward, whether it was a personality clash or something more serious, they needed to pour oil on troubled waters now. Still, Kim's nerves jangled as she pulled on the handbrake, took the keys from the ignition and looked over at her passenger.

The acid had left its mark on Stevie and she wore no hat today to disguise it. The young woman's hairline was scarred, and the scarring, from one side of the forehead to the other, was more visible than anywhere else on her body. The skin even showed individual indents where drops of acid had landed. Stevie's thick, crinkled hair, a shade of blonde that was almost strawberry, had retreated from the damaged skin, stray hairs leaning back like terrified onlookers at the scene of a fire.

'I might have to wear a wig,' said Stevie, seeing Kim looking, because the compact car forced them together. 'Do you think I should wear a wig?'

'You have nothing to hide,' said Kim. 'You are a very beautiful and very strong young woman.'

'My arse,' said Stevie.

'You can swear on both our arses,' Kim rejoined. 'I mean it.' But now she was looking at the glasses Stevie wore. The eye patch had gone, but these were spectacles with one clear frame and one shaded. Her top lip was also swollen on the right like a boxer's. In short, she looked damaged.

'I've come off Instagram,' said Stevie. 'Not sharing pictures no more.'

Kim nodded thoughtfully. 'Can I ask: what happened between you and Edward? It seemed like there was a build-up where you started to annoy each other.'

Stevie said, 'Lord, I don't know. I think he feels I dragged him into it.'

'I've got my own theory. I think this is the first thing he's cared about since Matty. And you know how painful it is when your body is numb and feeling comes back?'

'Maybe he just wants to be in charge.'

'He's honestly not that kind of man,' said Kim. 'But look. If he's difficult, if he's grumpy sometimes, you have to understand his loss. I'm going to be rude and say that what happened to your granny was terrible, absolutely awful. But imagine having a child, and being divorced, and then you go cycling with your kid and he's killed. And you never find out how it happened. He does well to get out of bed in the mornings. And we shouldn't have said what we said about – you know.'

They sat for a moment, frozen in their thoughts. Then

Edward ducked to look at them through the windshield, half-smiled and slowly started to walk towards them.

Kim said, 'I know he hurt you. But he was offended and you should just give him a polite apology.'

'You fucking love him is what you do,' said Stevie, a small smile on the edge of her lips.

Kim resented the way her passenger had pushed her way to a truth she was in no position to acknowledge. She went for the dead-bat answer: 'My husband is very, very ill and I have to tend to him.'

'I'm sorry,' said Stevie, for once not choosing the wrong words.

'And that's exactly what you're going to tell Edward, okay?'

Edward was close to the car now but looked reluctant to come nearer. He had his hands in his pockets like a shamefaced schoolboy.

Stevie pushed the passenger door open like a rugby fly half, with a bolshy movement of her elbow.

'Your girlfriend says I have to apologize to you,' she announced, which made Kim furious, but when she looked past Stevie to Edward there was no indignation.

The door on the Porsche fell closed, and because the interior was almost soundproof, what happened next was like a silent movie. Kim saw Edward throw back his head and laugh. He reached out his arms and took Stevie in them. Quite to Kim's surprise, Stevie reached around Edward's waist and held him tightly. She could almost have been his daughter, so close was their embrace.

Exiting and locking the car, Kim approached.

'I couldn't get you on the phone. Even when I dialled from my mother's number.'

Stevie said, 'Edward, you had every right to be angry with us. We were out of line.'

Kim wanted to say that it was *Stevie* who had accused

Edward, and *Stevie* who had come up with a litany of reasons why he might have committed murder and fraud all over Devon, so where this 'we' came from, she had no idea.

Luckily it was Edward who spoke now. He took all the blame on himself. 'Hey, it was a wretched time. You have to eliminate suspects. I lost it and broke one of the cups at the Clock Tower.'

'It was a saucer,' said Stevie.

'Stevie.' Kim felt she was constantly having to rein her in.

'No need to tick her off!' Edward laughed. 'Stevie, *you* are the hero of all this. You have been so badly hurt and yet here you are, wanting this bastard caught. And I'm now going to tell you something that'll blow your minds. I know who it is. One hundred per cent, I know.'

They stood outside and Kim watched as Edward told Stevie what he had discovered. She found herself staring at the side of his face as he spoke, marvelling at the line of the jaw, the strength and precision in that bass broadcaster's voice, gravelled like a driveway. The first time he had met Troy Barber was bizarre, he told Stevie – 'the man virtually invaded my house.'

Kim remembered being on the phone to Edward, exactly as he described it. 'Edward, I hung on for a good ten minutes, worrying, while you found out who was making the noises. You never came back to the phone. I just had to assume you hadn't been murdered by a burglar or something.'

'Are you coming in, folks?' An Indian waiter was at the door. 'Can I look for your booking?'

'Just give us a minute,' said Kim. 'Did we book?'

Edward politely gestured to the waiter that they would be just one minute more. 'It was surreal, the visit by Barber. I trusted him. I was desperate to get back to the radio station. He told me to meet those pensioners on their protest and Agnes would cave in to the pressure. It had the opposite effect. In fact,' he said, expressing the thought as it came to him, 'I wonder if he whispered into her ear: "You must never have him back now. He's making you look a fool." Do you know, I bloody well bet he did. I completely fell into his trap.'

'Why are we sure he is the perpetrator?' asked Stevie.

'He was seen. He was using the contacts computer for my show. Derrick saw him—'

'Tell Stevie who Derrick is,' Kim prompted.

'My producer. I've tried to spare him some of the horror of this thing, getting his help but not telling him everything. He's young and a bit naive. He is producing Tessa K now, of course. Hey – you sent me a message, I've just remembered. I got it when I was at a memorial service with Derrick and I couldn't reply—'

'You couldn't reply because you were in a humongous sulk.'

'Yes, that's it, I couldn't reply because I was in a humongous sulk.'

Kim eyed Edward carefully, checking that the tone was light. She did not want any more swordplay between them or someone would get hurt. The conversation stalled for a second until Kim said, 'Tell him, Stevie.'

Again, the waiter appeared. 'Is the name Tennis? As in Wimbledon?'

They all laughed. 'Close enough,' said Edward. 'We just need another few seconds – go on.'

Stevie continued, 'It was staring me in the face! Me and my idiot brain. Granny had Google.'

Kim and Edward waited for more.

'A Google account. She was on Gmail. Yeah? Dad set it up. So she must have had a cloud setting. You know, Google Drive and all that. And knowing her and Dad, I was betting she was on the default setting, where you get a bit of free storage and it backs up your hard drive until you hit the limit.'

'So there is a cloud somewhere with all her files on,' Kim explained.

'And the letter!' exclaimed Edward. 'The bloody letter, which started all this. It may not matter now.' Kim shot him a puzzled glance, and he added, 'Because we know about Barber.'

'But the letter might show us why he killed Riva.'

'True . . . so you're in? The account?'

'No.' Kim and Stevie responded simultaneously.

'Password issues,' said Stevie. 'I was sure my dad would know it but – I don't know what's up with him at the moment. He was kind of weird when I asked him. He's been very odd lately about it all. He won't even take a guess.'

'How many times can you try it before you get locked out?' Edward asked.

'I think three. Dad says he reckons Granny changed it anyway.'

Edward sighed. 'Like I say, it may not matter. Let's get the Tennis table and I'll tell you what I'm going to do.'

As they moved into the restaurant, Kim had a text. The name came up as Dr Tilson.

Need you to come tomorrow please. Any time after 9.

She was used to bad news about Anthony – at least, the absence of any good news whatsoever – but there was something about the text that took her into new territory. She was continually fearful of a message saying Anthony had taken his own life. But that horrific prospect could not be the meaning here, because who would write, 'Your husband hanged himself. Call back in office hours'? She wanted to reply with questions, knowing that the likeable, hairy-chested doctor was well-disposed to her; she was already trying to find him the apartment he wanted. But allowing an Anthony-emergency to disrupt this reunion of their trio seemed like yet another drag on her life by a husband who had brought her only small amounts of love and happiness, and much more in the way of violence and misery.

The other two were talking, speculating about passwords for

292

Rebecca Mason's cloud – 'Hitchcock?' 'Danvers?' – but the sound was smudged as it arrived, like conversation heard through a wall. Did she still love Anthony? Love him even with the trace of remembered love? The half-life of love. She had felt love once, when she thought of him as a big, beautiful, huggy Yorkshire bear, before she knew him. Before the bear snarled. Before the hug broke ribs. Before the ridicule and the bullying, the cutting comments about estate agents, the snarky remarks about her skinny bum and her tits, 'not exactly on the Kardashian voluptuosity scale'. Before the violence.

Was she still with him because, when she was a little girl, her mother used to tell her tales of Florence Nightingale and Mother Teresa, heroines who never left the sick to pursue their own happiness, who stayed at bedsides, not even popping out for a fag break?

Edward Temmis had been her fag break. When they had visited that half-ruin of a house, she already knew which room they would make love in and on which patch of carpet. She allowed herself the smallest smile at the memory. He would have thought – men! – that the initiative was all his. When he seized her by the waist and pressed her to him, and she felt his erection, he would have thought the move had come as a revelation to her. His was the impulse, hers had been the plan.

But it had gone too far. She had made love with Edward Temmis on the old carpet, and then the broken sofa, with an abandon she had never felt in her life before, unwittingly spreading her heart open for him more than she ever had for Anthony.

Far from making her feel guilty for betraying her husband, it had made her feel less guilty for staying. But something . . . ah, this was the only part of the memory she found difficult.

She had been around the rest of the house with him as an estate agent, not a lover, and when he smiled knowingly at her at the end of the visit, on the driveway, she had coughed uncomfortably and looked at her shoes. His face had shown confusion and then understanding – that was it, there was no more. Maybe Edward had even asked himself if she had done this before; maybe he had started to think they had gone to this ruin of a building for this purpose alone, for her purpose. She had taken him to the cliff edge of her life and gently thrown him off.

In the days that followed the event, she understood her own heart better. Edward had been the single betrayal during fifteen years of marriage. This was before Anthony's breakdown, and Edward was the instrument of revenge on Anthony for his cruelty. But her pop-up lover turned out to be more than a mere tool. Edward had bought the house that she had only shown him out of mischief. She wondered if his purchase was some strange signal to her – she had brought him to a joke of a property and performed a ridiculous seduction, and he had taken both seriously.

Then, just as she was beginning to fear, or hope, that Edward might be more of a presence in her life than she had expected, Matty had been killed. Like a camera lens crash-pulled from space, everything was reduced to a pinprick on the surface of a distant earth.

'You okay?' Edward asked her, bringing her back to the room with a jolt.

'Um, just a little caught up in husband matters.'

'Is he still ill?' asked Stevie bluntly, and then, without waiting for an answer: 'And can you decide what you want to order, Kim, because the bloke over there is staring hopefully at me and I don't think it's because he fancies women with half their hair and only one eye.'

'Stevie!' they both said.

'One eye, half a nose, a hairline like an Irish footballer. Come on, let's decide what we want.'

Kim looked at Stevie compassionately. There was no gloss she could add. Her face was very badly damaged. She noticed that the almost-orange tan, obviously applied from a bottle, had now faded to a pasty white. Edward had lost his son and his job. Kim was only being asked to care for a sick husband, and yet she begrudged it. She would call Dr Tilson tomorrow at nine.

*

Edward could see that Kim was distracted by the message on her phone. She ordered very little, as if she had lost the appetite for food and conversation. To his surprise, Stevie more than made up for Kim's reserve. She explained that she was on a combination of painkillers and immune-boosting drugs, 'and something else with a "z" in the name,' and the side-effect was a reduced appetite and talking a lot.

Edward joked, 'How will we know when they kick in?' which made Kim laugh but jolted Stevie.

'Are you saying I eat too much?'

He turned beetroot red and apologized; she laughed at how 'oversensitive' he was.

Kim said, 'Tell me about it,' and suddenly they were a trio of sleuths again, locked in, the odd triangle, tucking into the food and being sociable.

Before them were a korma, a madras, chicken tikka masala, naan, rice, onion bhaji, poppadoms, and something that looked to have chickpeas swimming in it. 'What do we think of the food?' Kim asked, drowning the spices in lager.

'The car park was nice,' said Edward.

After a while he decided it was time to tell them what he was thinking.

'If we don't get the Google passcode for your granny's account, Stevie,' he said, halving and quartering a poppadom with satisfying snaps, 'we have to do what Troy did. We have to get what's on that studio computer. I've been thinking a lot about it. The computer gives you the names of the callers who rang me, the date, the subject. I go in. I pull them off. We marry that up with our list – why are you laughing?'

'Pull them off,' repeated Stevie.

He was about to be cross with her again, then glanced at Kim, who was smirking too.

'I don't know what else that phrase means, but yes, I will *extract* them. I'll save them. Then we check them against the Secret Squirrel list. And I guarantee it will match. I guarantee every scam will turn out to have happened soon after the caller's contact details got put into the computer. And then we have . . . a case.'

'How do we prove it was Troy?'

He turned to Kim. 'Yup. Good point. There's a shared login, so that won't do it. But I figured it out. I reckon he was listening to the show – for which I'm obviously grateful, every little helps – and then he went into the building every time he needed the details of a caller. Which would be at least once a week. So what we'll do is get the CCTV from security. Derrick will do it. Again, we need the timings off Humble Reggie to prove it.'

The women both looked quizzical.

'That's our nickname for the computer.'

Kim said, 'What if he didn't use the front entrance?'

'Hey, let's stay positive! The CCTV is in the corridors too and it goes back years. So let's say Barber went in on the first of November and we have CCTV of that. We then just need to show there was a login that night while he was in the building. We match the visit to the login, the login to the contact, the contact to the crime.'

Kim was looking at him piercingly. He could not read her expression. It was lodged in some difficult place between friendship and love. It was caring, almost maternal; not possessive, more inquisitive: the look of the museum visitor who peers into the glass case. As he looked at her, her lips parted, and he found it the most sensual thing.

The madras was finished, but the korma was being offered around by Stevie. 'Fucking mild this, apologies again for my—'

'Just one question,' Kim broke in. 'Who are you getting to do all this, getting the names off the computer?'

The three fell silent.

'You're looking at him,' said Edward.

'That waiter?' Stevie's question might even have been serious.

'You?' asked Kim.

'Me. I'm doing it.'

'You? But are you even allowed into the station now?' asked Stevie.

'Derrick will let me in.'

'Security won't stop you?'

'There's a . . . back way for passholders.'

'Why can't he just get all the stuff off the computer for you?'

'I can't ask him. It's too much. It'll take hours and he won't know what he's looking for. And I'd have to pass everything from the Secret Squirrel to him, and then he's going to get a sense of the scale of it and he'll totally panic. I don't want to get him fired. He's been brilliant for us. I want to keep him in the dark as much as I can. If he gets too alarmed, Derrick might go to Agnes and she could tell Troy.'

'How do you get the CCTV footage?' Stevie asked, scooping up the last piece of chicken korma and then folding and dipping her naan into the bright yellow sauce.

'Once we have the dates, and it's a more manageable task, I'm going to ask Derrick for that as well.'

'So he's almost on our team.'

'Well,' Edward said, 'the Beatles *were* four.'

'The Beatles weren't investigators,' said Stevie, taking the analogy far too seriously. 'This group feels like my tribe, you know? Big sad deaf-aid guy, Porsche queen and Acid face.'

Kim and Edward both spluttered with shock. Kim asked, 'When are you doing this, Edward? I want to come with you. At least sit outside.'

'I'm doing it tonight.'

The restaurant seemed to fall silent. The two women put their cutlery down and looked at each other.

'Derrick is letting me in tonight.'

297

CHAPTER THIRTY-ONE

The door clicked. It was ten past midnight, an hour after Tessa K's show had finished, and here was Derrick, face in shadow, exactly as arranged at the back door to the studios.

The door was open only a few inches, as if a chain was stopping it moving further.

'Cameras?' asked Edward.

'There's no camera out here because of privacy, etc. You'd see everyone going down the street.'

'I'm sweating like Prince Andrew,' said Edward.

'I'm worried because there's a fire notice here,' said Derrick through the crack. 'It might be connected to the alarm. That's what it says.'

Edward stared at the narrow line of face wedged in the gap between door and frame, the pale skin and the burning bush of red hair. 'I thought those warnings were always made up. What does it say exactly?'

With a squeak that might have woken the dead, Derrick pulled the door closed. He reappeared a moment later. 'It says this door is alarmed.'

Edward sighed. 'Let's do it.'

Derrick pulled, Edward pushed, and the door opened.

There was an explosion of noise – the wail of the fire alarm, echoing all the way down the concrete stairs, so deafening that both men instinctively covered their ears – but then it stopped.

'Was that it?'

Derrick responded, 'Maybe it's just a sign that the door was opened. We should get out of this staircase or you'll get me sacked.'

They ran lightly up the stairs, Edward conscious that their footsteps would echo. The stairs were hard concrete, no carpeting, all painted white – no one ever used them.

'There's a camera on the next level,' said Derrick, stopping suddenly. 'They'll want to see who set off the alarm, so I'll walk past on my own. They'll think it was a fag break or that I took a shortcut.'

'How do I get past?'

'You crawl.'

'What?'

'I shifted the camera up an inch earlier. You might be able to see it there. See? So it's mainly pointing at the next flight. We can't go up to the third without doing something to swerve the cameras. As I go past it, it'll film me from the waist up. No sound either: for reasons of confidentiality, they disabled the microphones. So when I approach, you stay low, keep left of it against the wall, duck under it, and dive through the door before it closes.'

Edward scuttled behind Derrick. He peeled left, and, exactly as the young producer had told him to, went on his hands and knees underneath the CCTV camera. Then through the door to the radio station corridor.

'Basically we now have to hope there's no one around.'

'I can't thank you enough.'

'I would take the baseball cap off, Edward. It just makes you look suspicious. Go and sit at the computer, close the door, and if a security guard comes in just say, "Good evening".'

'They'll ring the bloody police!'

'But what else can you do? Lock the door and they'll know there's something iffy going on.' They were on the fourth now. Derrick reached for the door to the production area.

The room was dark. Edward remembered thousands of programmes done here. The studio was on the other side of two panes of thick glass to mute conversations in the production suite. The fluorescent lights flickered on. 'These lights always were shit,' said Edward.

'The computer hasn't improved either.'

And there it was. The username and password stuck on the front of the display on a fragment of Frosties packing, a screen-saver – flying Windows – which Edward had not seen for years.

'It's such an idiocy, not replacing this dinosaur,' said Edward. 'What if it goes down with all the contacts on it?'

'Putting contacts on networks creates problems with the law these days, so having them stuck on a standalone piece of junk helps us with our GDPR compliance apparently.'

'Um, okay. I thought you could just ignore all that stuff.'

'Not really, Edward.' Derrick shot him a quirky expression, as if the last thirty seconds had perfectly described the difference between presenter and producer.

'You can back it up, there's a USB port at the back. I'm assuming you've brought a drive?'

'A fob like this?' said Edward, producing from his jacket two finger-sized devices with a USB plug at one end. 'I even brought a spare.'

'How many names are you looking for?'

Edward looked embarrassed. 'There are about sixty victims.'

Derrick's jaw dropped. 'What? I'm hoping I misheard and you said "six".'

'Sixty-two at least.'

'That's shocking. And upsetting.'

'Look, they all gave me permission.' It was not a deliberate lie, but what Edward meant was 'they all allowed me to have their details when we drew up our list at the pub', so it was close enough.

'Remind me why you need what's in here if you already have it?'

'We're going to pin this on Troy Barber. I'm going to show it was him. I need the two lists to line up, and then we're there.'

'And then – what, the cops?'

'I want Troy bloody-snake-in-the-grass-Barber to admit what he's done. I can't take it to the police first, a lot of the ladies won't allow it. I'll take him to the police instead. Or,' Edward added, thoughtfully, the idea just occurring to him, 'maybe I'll just take him to his victims.'

'Hmm, the controller's squeeze goes to jail. I'm so glad I'm not part of any of this wildness,' said Derrick. 'But remember – you promised you wouldn't get me the sack.'

'Before you go, let me log in.'

The piece of card stuck to the computer monitor said studio4, PASSWORD: SaveTheWhale.

'Upper case S-T-W, no spaces, okay,' murmured Edward, typing one-fingered. Derrick made him feel older than his years. They watched the PC begin to hum its approval at what he had typed. 'I can't thank you enough.'

'I'm doing it because you're the boss, that's all. You got me started in this wonderful business. Once I leave this room, I'm denying everything,' the young producer concluded.

'Understood.'

Derrick peered closely at Edward, gave what looked like a shrug, then turned and left without another word. He seemed uncomfortable, thought Edward. He would be able to leave the building through reception without needing any excuse for being late tonight. But Edward had no idea at this moment how he was going to get out himself. Stevie had checked the memory stick he was using, yet he did not trust it. What if the tiny fob ran out of space; what if it was corrupted? He would use the technology he trusted – he would take photographs of the screen on his mobile.

There were three fluorescent strips in the ceiling, each giving out a different kind of dirty light. The one in the centre flickered slightly, and he remembered that flicker – a subtle zap, an infrequent dip-and-glow, as if a moth were caught inside the tube and travelling up and down searching for escape, avoiding electrocution. When his job had been to sit on the other side of the glass, he never considered his producer and researcher might be troubled by the infrequent pulsing of an overhead light, but he knew now it was going to give him a migraine.

He looked up. Beyond the computer was the broadcast studio itself, shrouded in darkness, its last show done for the night. *Tessa K . . .*

He set the memory stick down next to the keyboard and began to type in the search box for the first name on his list.

The Porsche, being red, was not easy to hide. Kim had suggested Stevie ask her parents if she could borrow their nondescript black VW Polo, but Stevie said her father would definitely ask what it was for and point out that, with sight in only one eye, his daughter had all kinds of form-filling to do before she could drive again. Which would just be a hurtful conversation for Stevie. So here they were, on the promenade, in the Porsche, slung low behind a windowless white van that hid them just enough.

To see the radio station entrance, Kim and Stevie had both taken seats on the left. Kim in the front passenger seat, Stevie in the back.

'There goes Derrick now,' said Stevie.

'You see pretty well still, don't you?'

'It's that mountain of red hair, piled on top of his head. The profile. Couldn't miss it.'

Kim said, 'So he's let Ed in the back?'

'Shouldn't we message Edward to tell him we're here?'

'Then he might ask why,' said Kim, 'and we'd have to say it's because he hasn't thought this through.'

'You don't think he can get out.'

'That's exactly what he hasn't thought through. We're here to help him get out. See the guy in reception? If he hasn't fallen asleep, one of us is going to have to do a striptease.'

'To distract him? Start practising now,' said Stevie, 'because I'm out. A naked me would only be exciting to a burns specialist.'

'Not fully naked,' said Kim, staring at the building. 'Do you know what? There on the fourth floor – I think that's where he's working. That light flickering. There.'

'I guess so.' Stevie thought for a moment and yawned. 'How's your husband?'

Kim suddenly felt short of breath. 'I have to ring his psychologist tomorrow morning. Something is going on. He won't tell me. I texted to ask, "Has he tried to take his own life?" He said no, but I must come for an informal meeting as soon as possible and he can only speak privately. What does that even mean? So in answer to your question, I don't know and I'm in suspense. TMI, sorry.'

'Maybe he's tried to give all his money away to the doctor. I've heard that's happened before.'

'He doesn't have any money. He's a policeman on sick leave. He only has his pension. And he can't give my money away. I've locked it down.'

'I wasn't being totally serious.'

'Then please don't be.'

'Don't be what?'

'Not totally serious.'

'Okay.'

They watched as an hour passed, slowly. And nothing happened.

*

In the production room, Edward had left the door ajar as he tapped at the computer. A speaker on a coffee table in the corridor played the live output of the radio station. From midnight till five, the word 'live' was misleading – RTR-92 ran a tape supplied by a local audio production company that included gaps with a high-frequency pulse that automatically triggered the station's adverts.

But the sound of the speaker in the corridor would stop Edward hearing anyone approaching. He'd taken a chance, quietly slid out through the door and pulled the cable from the back of the device. Back at the desk, he was struggling with the format of the computer files. His first dozen searches had pulled up nothing. He was about to ring Derrick to ask how to use the search bar, because the computer must have had five hundred listener profiles on it, when he struck gold.

In the Secret Squirrel he remembered a woman in her seventies called Fay Farringdon, partly because the alliteration stuck in his mind, and when he remarked that the initials 'FF' would look good in a signature, Faye had replied, 'It wasn't good at school, where I was nicknamed "Fast Forward", and then, when my sister arrived, they called her "Rewind", which caused her complete confusion, as you can imagine.'

Faye's story had been particularly upsetting. She had called his show to talk about funding an orphanage in Romania.

'I know that sort of thing is out of fashion now, but I had seen a documentary and I wanted to help, so I rang.'

She had visited an orphanage for herself. That had been in Timişoara, in the west of the country. After talking about it on Edward's show, she had been contacted by (she thought) the head of the orphanage that was featured in the TV programme she had seen. This was like a miracle for her. He approached her by text initially, which caught her with her guard down, because the man (she could not remember the name) said his friends in Timișoara had passed on her details, 'as a good person.' He followed up with multiple emails about the children in his care. One had to be chained during the day because of a brain condition similar to epilepsy (it had a very long name). It needed forty thousand pounds to get him an operation in the UK, but what he really needed was a decent home . . .

The money went. The boy never existed. The number rang out. The police were not interested – Faye had been one of very few who went to Devon Police to report the scam. She was told the scammer 'operated, almost certainly, within a different criminal jurisdiction.' Abroad. She had at least got a small crowd gathered around at Ottery St Mary Police Station when she burst into tears. She left with a pamphlet on *Victim Support: Your Rights*, and the gentle apology from the station sergeant: 'We only have one police car, you see. We can't chase criminals in Romania with that.'

Faye Farringdon. He remembered the name, and he had the details given to him in the Secret Squirrel. First contact from scammer: *9 October*. Means of contact: *Text*.

He tried typing Faye_Farringdon with an underscore instead of a space. The name came up in glowing green text on the Excel spreadsheet.

Call: 30 September. Mobile number: 07700 900464. Subject: Wants to support Romanian orphans after seeing TV doc.

Edward swallowed. That was not coincidence. He checked his list. Sure enough, ten days after Faye's call to his show, she was texted by the scammer, who can only have used this very computer to find her mobile number.

He was about to grab his phone to photograph the computer screen when something stopped him. There were footsteps in the corridor, getting closer.

Kim peered at the person who had walked past the radio station twice. The tall man had rounded the corner at the end of the high street and walked straight past the RTR-92 frontage, and she had given it so little thought she did not even mention it to Stevie. She glanced back and found the younger woman asleep, her single-shade glasses abandoned in her lap. Distracted, Kim looked at Stevie's injured eye. The acid scars fanned out from the eyelid like the painted rays of an Aztec sun; she thought of that Bowie character with a zigzag painted down one side of his face. Well, if anyone could channel Bowie's spirit, it surely was Stevie.

When she turned back to the radio station, the man was gone. Kim mumbled to herself, 'Now Edward, you special man, let me find your number quickly.' Anthony was in no position to check over her phone as he used to, but old habits died hard. Edward's number was stored under 'R' in her contacts, without his name attached. The pseudonym was Radio One.

As her hand hovered over the number, caught in her uncertainty, she glanced up at the street.

'Stevie,' she hissed. 'Stevie, wake up. Look.'

On the back seat Stevie was breathing heavily – almost a snore. Kim could not raise her voice, could not turn. She did not want to lose sight of the man outside the radio station. And she did not want to attract his attention, even from a hundred yards away. She dropped the phone in the footwell of the car, a loud clank that made Stevie snort awake in the back seat.

'Whassup?' she slurred, dozily.

'There's a man,' whispered Kim, even though he surely couldn't hear her. 'There, can you see? He's walked past twice now.'

There was a tap on her shoulder. Stevie passed her a bright blue cylinder, no more than six inches long, which Kim now saw was the kind of toy telescope you find in a Christmas cracker.

'What am I supposed to do with this?'

'Pull it from both ends.'

'It's a toy!'

'It might work a little. I brought it just in case. Mini telescope, five pounds from a car-boot sale.'

Kim brought it to her left eye. Unless her mind was playing tricks, this was undoubtedly the same man who had appeared twice before.

'I'm looking at this big guy who keeps reappearing. Can you see him, Stevie?'

'Sure. Tall, black, Heisenberg hat.'

'Heisenberg?' Kim queried. She would have called it a pork-pie hat. In the scope, which gave her a surprisingly clear close-up from a hundred yards, the man moved slowly, with a lumbering walk, rolling his shoulders like a prop forward. If he was a vagrant he was well-dressed for one. And – she lowered the scope a smidge – he had delicate hands. Even at this range she could see they were not large like a goalkeeper's, which the rest of his body suggested, but small like a pianist's.

'Traveller looking for a hotel?' suggested Stevie.

Maybe. He wore a light tartan-patterned coat which looked too heavy for summer.

'This is now his third pass of the building.'

He was now clearly trying to see the interior of the entrance without attracting the attention of anyone inside. He was briefly bathed in the white light of the main reception area and, as the light caught his face, it seemed etched with nerves. Now she saw nervousness spread across the whole body and wondered why that had not been the first thing she'd noticed.

'Sweaty bugger,' said Kim, pushing the parts of the scope back together.

'Nervous?' Stevie asked.

'About something, definitely.'

She tried to see into the reception area. There appeared to be no one at the desk. Perhaps the tall visitor was also attempting to work out if the ground floor really was deserted because, in a movement so swift he could have been a Wild West gunslinger, he simultaneously produced a pass, swiped it on the card reader by the door and slid through before it had even fully opened.

Kim felt horror suddenly engulf her. 'He's gone in, Stevie! He's gone straight in! I think it must be Troy!' She reached for the phone in the footwell, but her desperate fingers could not find it.

Edward sat with his smartphone poised. On the PC screen were the details of Faye Farringdon's call, and he was desperate to take a picture. But he could swear he had heard a sound outside the room. The smartphone sometimes made a shutter sound when he took a picture, and he did not want to draw attention if there was someone in the corridor.

He put his forefingers behind his left ear and deftly turned up the hearing aid. Too much, and it would howl. Not enough, and he might miss that soft footstep on the carpet. But as he moved the tiny volume control, he was almost deafened by music. Someone in the corridor had plugged the loudspeaker back in.

As silently as he could, he rolled back the wheeled office chair he was on and, rising, moving sideways, pulled open the big soundproofed door to the studio. At least this monster never creaked – the hinges were oiled weekly, because during a live show producers often needed to move silently in and out. There were, in fact, two heavy doors. The first opened outwards, the second needed a push. For a long five seconds, he watched the first gradually fall back and close.

The light in the production room did not leak much into the studio itself. The thick layers of glass which separated the two rooms were about the width of a large landscape paint-ing and seemed to block light as much as sound. The windows were uncurtained, but it was night outside. The result was that Edward stood in the sparse studio area shrouded in darkness. As he waited, he pushed himself into the wall. Pressing into his waist and shoulders were the sound-absorbing black foam cones which were used to deaden the acoustic, and he felt them make way for him. He imagined the wall carrying his imprint for days, like tape marking the outline of a body on the floor of a crime scene.

The door in the next room moved an inch, and then opened fully. From the darkness, Edward saw the head of one of the security guards, topped by his cap of office, a peaked blue hat of the sort American cops sported in movies. Had someone bought the security guards' hats from Amazon? The night staff were not the same receptionists the radio station used in the day, and were under instructions to roam the building widely from hour to hour.

The security guard looked around the lit production room but ignored completely the studio space where Edward was standing. It was pin-drop quiet where Edward was, and, although he had not planned it this way, his blue jeans, dark, unpatterned shirt and navy jacket would be helping him disappear against the foam wall. He watched, conscious of the way the acoustically deadened room made even his own breaths die as soon as they emerged from his mouth. He was not worried about being heard; he was worried about being seen.

The guard looked uninterested, and then his attention was drawn to the desk with the PC on. At first Edward thought he was looking at the screen – the computer faced away from the on-air studio, and if the screensaver had not come on it would still be showing Faye Farringdon's details – but the man was leaning towards a spot to the right of the keyboard.

He picked up Edward's mobile from the desk and answered it.

Stevie said, 'What's going on?'

Kim hushed her with a frantic wave of her hand. Then, as the phone was answered, she said: 'Edward?'

There was breathing but no voice. She quickly checked her mobile screen by pulling the device away from her face. Yes, she had dialled the right number. The words 'Radio One' were lit up.

'Edward?' she said again.

'He doesn't work here any more.'

'Oh.' She was about to say, 'But this is his phone!' when she realized that would be a schoolgirl error.

'I must have dialled the wrong number,' she said.

'No, no, I don't think so. This is his studio. The radio station got rid of . . . I mean to say, he left a few months ago.'

'Sorry to bother you.'

Kim hung up and checked the line was dead before speaking. 'What the hell was that?'

'What?' asked Stevie in the back seat.

'Someone answered his phone in there. He's gone AWOL and meanwhile Troy Barber has just walked into the building.'

'You're joking.'

'Yes! That must be who we saw! Really tall black guy, small hands, thick owlish specs – who else in Sidmouth looks like that?'

'We need to warn Edward!'

'Exactly! But I can't ring his phone again. Think, think – what do we do?'

CHAPTER THIRTY-TWO

In the darkness of the on-air studio, pressed against the black foam insulators, Edward held his breath and watched. The security guard was speaking into his phone but nothing was audible. The conversation was short. When it ended, the man peered at the handset. He turned it up and down, staring at the back and pressing the screen. It must have locked and was obviously giving nothing up. The lockscreen showed a photo of Matty. It could have been anyone's son.

Edward murmured to himself, 'Put it back down. Put it back down.' But the security guard pocketed the phone and left the production room.

He should not have been angry – he was the intruder – but Edward felt blind fury and frustration. Faye Farringdon was the only contact he had found so far, he hadn't even managed to take a photo of the computer screen, and now his camera was gone. He would have to use the memory stick to pull the details from the PC.

Back at his seat next to the mixing desk, he pulled the computer towards him. His fingers probed the back of the screen, but he accidentally dislodged the power cable and it went black.

'For fuck's sake!' he shouted, as quietly as he could. Now

he got down on his haunches at the side of the computer. He had to hope the security guard did not come back, because this looked seriously suspicious now – he, the semi-famous ex-presenter, hiding behind a desk examining the ports on the back of a computer console.

He plugged in the power cable and found the correct socket for the memory stick. Then he stood and moved back around the desk to turn the computer on.

There was a movement through the glass, in the darkened studio space where he had been standing not five minutes earlier. Edward's stomach turned. Was there someone in the shadows? He reached for the door handle, but was overcome by a sudden stab of fear. Instead of pulling on the handle he turned the locking mechanism.

Edward stood, chest heaving. Suddenly a figure lunged out of the darkness to grab the door on the other side. The person pulled the first studio door open but when he pushed the second it would not give way. A muffled bump indicated that he put his shoulder to it, but still it did not give. He stepped back, was lit momentarily in the boundary of light from the fluorescents above Edward's head, and then Troy Barber shrank back into the shadows.

Edward's instinct had served him well. Troy could only get to him by this door, or by exiting the studio through the only other door, which led to the corridor, which must have been the way he had got in while Edward worked on the computer. He could go fifteen feet down the corridor and get into the room Edward was in. So Edward locked that door as well. If the security guard heard any of this and came back, so be it.

Edward stood in the illuminated production area, staring into the blackness of the studio.

Then he turned left, to the bank of lights on the wall, and threw the top switches on.

Lit from above, not with ineffective fluorescent strips but

with the crematorium-white glare of the LED downlighting the station had thought would be a good way of saving money, Troy Barber appeared for a second to be floating in the air. His face wore a maddened, unhinged expression. It seemed to fold in and out of anger, frustration and misery. Barber began shouting, yelling his head off, but the insulation prevented even a squeak from moving through the wall that separated them.

Edward stared. It was as if a silent horror movie was playing out on a screen before his eyes. He could do nothing but watch, and try to think quickly – was Barber about to come for him? The other man tried the door between them again, grappling with it as if with a wild animal. Then Barber stepped back and focused on Edward, his eyes aflame, the pupils red. He breathed deeply, his chest rising and falling.

Edward moved two steps right, never taking his eyes off Troy Barber. He had a means of communication. On the desk, alongside a panel of faders, was a plastic green button marked 'Talkback'.

'Troy, what the hell is up?'

The other man seemed shocked to hear the voice from next door.

He said something.

Edward pressed the talkback button. 'Wait.' He looked closely at the panel and found another button, blue this time, marked 'Return'. He pushed it to open the ambient microphone in the studio. Now he could hear the other man at last.

'Stop it. *Stop* it. Don't do it, I'm warning you.'

Edward pressed the talkback button again. 'Don't do what?'

Troy Barber began raging. Edward was late hitting the return button, but he did not need to ask what he had missed.

'—you *fucking* will kill us, kill us, kill me, *fuck off* with your enquiries you bastard, you don't know what you're doing, you don't know what you're dealing with, just *get lost* and *get your arse* out of here tonight you absolute arsehole of—'

313

Edward released the button. He had a fleeting moment of gratification. He had correctly identified the scammer and so inflamed Troy Barber that he had been forced to rush into the radio station to try to stop what he was doing.

'You'll have to kill me to stop me,' Edward said on talkback. 'And do you really want to do that? I'm pretty sure you'll have been picked up on half a dozen cameras on the way up here.' He added, 'You tell me what you want to do. Because I'm going to get to the bottom of this. And I'm locked in here, so you can't touch me.'

Troy Barber stood for a full thirty seconds, shaking with anger. He must have worked out that he could not leave the studio through the far door and get into the control room via the corridor, because he had seen Edward lock himself in. But he seemed now to stretch far beyond his six-foot-six frame as he hunched over, fumbling within his coat for something. He suddenly straightened, lunging upwards, chest heaving, cheeks blowing in and out. He looked like a man trying to inflate a weather balloon.

And he had a knife.

The knife was at least eight inches long, wickedly sharp, jagged on one side, and caught the downlights every time it moved in his hand.

'Troy, come on . . .' Edward tried weakly, his knees near buckling.

He saw Troy screaming in reply, but this time did not press the return button to hear the words.

'Troy, I need to know why you scammed all those old people.'

The other man stopped. He stood there shaking, the bright white light above him making him look like a ghost, whitening his hair and the upper half of his face.

He had drawn the knife from the interior pocket of his long, tartan topcoat, and Edward focused on one particular detail – the blade had caught the material on the way out, and Barber had simply slashed at the coat to free it. So now the right side of the mac had a rip in it, separating like a Seventies lapel. Troy took the knife and pointed it directly at Edward. The tip vibrated with his anger.

Edward hit the return button.

The other man said, 'You will kill me.'

It was a strange use of words. Before Edward could respond, Troy Barber changed his grip on the knife, so now he held it like a candle. Again the blade flashed in the light. And he drove it into his left shoulder.

'God, Jesus, no, Troy – don't do this . . .'

Blood spurted from the gash as he pulled the knife out.

'Stop, Troy, stop!'

'*You did this!*' shouted Troy Barber. 'Your hand is on this!'

Now he plunged the knife into his thigh. His trousers – lime green – were immediately soaked in blood.

He switched hands and moved the knife to his left hand, stabbing himself in the ribs. The blow was not forceful, as if his own instinct for survival was now slowing him down. But still he stabbed again and again, and then—

As Edward watched, the far studio door burst open in a flash of movement. Derrick Tidy appeared behind Troy Barber's left shoulder, moving with the pounce of a cat, and for the first fraction of a second Barber did not detect his presence, so his about-turn with the knife was incomplete. Derrick caught him off-balance, grabbing Barber's mac by the rear collar and pulling him backwards. Both men fell in a tangle of arms and legs. Barber smashed his head on the studio table on his way to the floor, a stunning blow. Derrick, also on the floor but now astride Barber, kicked a leg across the other man's body, pinning him or moving the knife away, it was hard to see which. Edward stood on tiptoe, trying to work out if Troy Barber had knocked himself out. Then Derrick had his hand around Barber's wrist and was shaking his arm to work the knife loose, and shouting—

Edward pressed the return button to hear. 'Get security now, Edward! Now!'

His fears of being discovered in the building long gone, Edward plunged towards the production room door. He almost tore his shoulder wrenching at it – of course he had locked it – and then, as he twisted the lock on the door and opened it in a single moment, he glanced back and saw Troy Barber enveloped in a scissor grip by Derrick Tidy's legs. He could not see the knife. He saw Derrick shouting, but heard nothing.

He ran down the stairs to reception. As he plunged through the double doors that led to the main building, he felt as though the air had blown out of his lungs.

'What—?'

The security guard, sitting at his post behind the main desk, saw him and suddenly jolted upright. Simultaneously both he and Edward noticed Kim and Stevie on the street outside, hands raised as though about to bang on the glass.

Kim called through the glass, 'We rang Derrick because we saw Troy go in.'

The security guard was standing now. 'Mr Temmis! Well, well – I think I might accidentally have picked up your phone – now let me see.' He started opening drawers to find it, evidently not having worked out that Edward was, technically and in every other way, an intruder.

'Please,' Edward said breathlessly, 'there's a man with a knife upstairs – the tall guy with the glasses who came in earlier, he's fighting with Derrick, my producer – you need to get help . . .'

At that moment the foolishness of what he had done struck Edward. Seeing Troy Barber restrained, he had rushed downstairs to security. He needed to return to the studio now to help Derrick.

'Get these women to call the police, they're friends of mine . . .'

It was all the security guard needed to hear. He clicked the opening device on the door and Kim and Stevie crowded through it, almost falling over each other. 'Derrick came straightaway—'

'He's up there now! Barber has a knife! Call the police, Kim!' shouted Edward, heading back towards the doors. Stevie was already dialling. He added, 'Stay down here, both of you,' although there was no sign of the two women moving for the stairs.

'The lift's too slow – I'm Douglas,' said the security guard as they took the stairs together. He was large but strong and Edward saw the muscles in his legs as he bounded two, three steps at a time up the staircase. 'Knife, you say?'

'Yes but he was stabbing himself.'

'What?' Douglas paused on the stairs, almost causing Edward to crash into him. 'Maybe we should leave him to it.'

'Derrick Tidy restrained him,' said Edward, furious at being delayed for a cheap joke. He overtook the security guard, emerged at the purple shagpile of the fourth, and came to the door of the on-air studio. There was a thick glass porthole in it and he looked through.

'My God,' he said.

'What?' shouted the security guard at his elbow, but Edward answered only by pushing the studio door open.

In reception, Kim and Stevie waited for the police. They had got through straightaway on 999 and described the emergency – a man with a knife had broken into the radio station and might have hurt someone, they didn't know. Yes, they were in reception. Two people had gone up to see what was happening. The security guard and someone else. No, they would not put themselves in danger.

But the next movement in reception was not the police. The door behind the security guard's desk opened and he emerged with a shattered-looking Derrick Tidy draped over his shoulder. Derrick looked as though he might be crying – he was rubbing his face, rubbing his red hair, then holding a hand over his eyes and squeezing as if trying to wring out a recent memory. He straightened up when he realized he was in reception, and Kim stared at him, but he turned his gaze away. What had he been through? His hand, she saw, had been slashed.

'We need the police up there,' said the guard. 'It's about as serious as it could be.'

Kim gazed distractedly at the guard. Long legs, shoulders that were set-square-straight, almost as if he had left the coat hanger in his jacket. His peaked cap looked almost comical, a completely unnecessary addition to the uniform in a coastal town in Devon. Until tonight. What did 'as serious as it could be' mean?

'Where's Edward?' Stevie asked.

'I left him with the intruder. I mean, fuck's sake, the guy had a pass, he had a staff pass, which is how he got in, but I have no idea why he went up there with a knife.'

'Is Edward hurt?'

'I believe he is dead.'

Stevie gasped.

Kim's legs buckled. 'Noooooo, Jesus no, nooo . . .' Her voice choked into a strangled groan, a pure animal noise of grief.

'Mr Troy Barber,' the guard added. 'That was the name on his pass. Dead.'

Kim was suddenly silent, listening keenly. So not Edward?

The guard faced Derrick. 'How does the man have a pass? Does he work for the radio station? I mean, I see he must have got in when I was away from my desk, but you still can't do that without a pass.'

Kim was not wondering about the pass. She was wondering how Barber had gone into the radio station with a knife and ended up dying himself.

As though reading her mind, Derrick said, 'Edward will tell you. Troy arrived and started stabbing himself in front of

Edward. I don't know why. I tried to disarm him but he wouldn't stop.' He began crying, hand in front of his eyes, shoulders shaking. 'He plunged the knife into his own neck.' Derrick opened his jacket a few inches and there, across his shirt, was a long line of blood. 'It was like a fountain, I couldn't stop it.'

'Bloody hell,' the guard said. 'If I had seen that, first thing I would have assumed was you'd taken a hell of a slashing there.'

'My hand did. Across the back. I tried to grab the knife.'

Hearing Stevie crying behind her, Kim asked: 'Is he really . . .?'

Before she could clarify, before Derrick or Douglas could say whether there was any breath left in Troy Barber's body, the wail of two police sirens cut through the night. The cars arrived in the street so keenly they jumped as they stopped, like dogs remembering their chains. The vehicles blocked the promenade in a V-shape. Four police officers jumped out and ran towards the building.

They couldn't get in at first. The guard rushed behind the desk for his keys, or for the switch that activated the revolving doors. The officers banged on the glass. And then the banging stopped.

Kim turned to see what they were staring at. Edward had appeared through the door furthest from reception and was standing, staring at the police cars. His face was covered in blood, and his jacket had the sheen of the same red wetness.

For a second there was complete silence. The police stared at Edward. He stared – strangely – at the two cars to his left, the blue lights animating him like a cartoon figure. The guard and Derrick stood stock-still, Derrick holding his bloodied hand.

And then there was pandemonium.

CHAPTER THIRTY-THREE

Stevie, Kim and Edward took the table in the corner of Sid-mouth Costa, hidden behind a pillar where no one would see them. They had said three o'clock, though neither of the women expected Edward to be clear of the police by then. But he had given a preliminary statement and that, for now, was enough.

Kim put a friendly hand on his knee as he spoke. It was funny – to her it felt like the most natural thing in the world, to be here for him.

He was saying, 'There was an officer there who I know, who is dealing with Matty's death. I think he felt sorry for me. I was open. I said I had been let into the radio station because I wanted to get some of the old contacts off the computer. That's not a crime. They had bigger fish to fry.'

'Do they know what Troy Barber had been doing with the contacts?' Kim asked, 'With the old people?'

'They suddenly got very, very interested when I told them. I guess if they can pin it on him now he's dead, they get to say they solved sixty crimes in a day.'

'Great for their stats,' said Stevie. She was wearing her medical glasses: one clear frame, one shaded to hide and protect the burned eye.

'And we get the money back?'

'I have no idea,' replied Edward. 'Strange . . .' He shivered. 'Agh, I'm still processing. At the end of the evening, I was out of it.'

'You were.'

'It was the police cars. I had a sudden memory of losing Matty. I went back into that space.'

'Derrick is a bit of a hero, isn't he?' said Stevie. 'Disarming him?'

'Tackling a bloke with a knife? I wouldn't,' said Kim.

'Not just "a bloke" either,' put in Edward. 'A crazy guy. He was unhinged. Luckily he hit his head on the table on his way down and stunned himself, or he would have had the strength of a whole rugby team.'

'Why would Troy do it? Okay, he ran the scam, he got a million quid, I understand that . . .' Kim wrinkled her nose. 'But coming there to attack you and attacking himself? Guilt?'

Stevie nodded. 'Yes. That's it. He came there to kill himself and he wanted you to watch. What did he shout?'

'I think it was "You will kill me." That must be about exposure, right?' Edward said. 'He went mad when he knew the doors were locked and he couldn't stop me. Or maybe he was just a total fruit loop throughout. He was, like I say, unhinged. Batshit crazy. Mad as a box of – snakes, frogs? End of story.'

Kim said, 'And then he stabs himself in the neck in front of that poor lad, Derrick, who didn't even know him.' She saw her mobile buzzing. 'Oh, Mum, of course.'

'Derrick?' Edward repeated. 'No, I don't think they did know each other.'

Barbara Sinker spoke as soon as Kim touched the phone screen. She put it on speaker, low volume, and the three of them listened.

'I've just got the paper, oh my God!' Barbara exclaimed. 'Listen to this headline – KNIFEMAN RAMPAGE AT RADIO STATION –

and it says he killed himself after someone tried to tackle him? It's four pages of the paper!'

'Yes, we're looking at it now,' said Kim, a kind of truth.

'Who's "we"?'

'Me and a friend.'

'Two friends,' put in Stevie.

Her mother always managed to say the wrong thing, and Kim now sensed one of Barbara's foot-in-mouth moments coming and wished she had not shared the call.

'How is Anthony?'

And there it was. 'I have to go in for a meeting tomorrow about him. It was going to be today but I had to move it.'

Edward nodded at Kim, as if he understood. She pulled her hand away from his knee; it could not be there when her husband was the subject.

Down the line Barbara asked, 'Darling, a meeting about what?'

Kim chose the easy lie. 'Something to do with billing. The money for hospital extras. Just bureaucracy.'

'Oh dear. I wish I could help, but . . .'

A gasp came from the phone, the sting of a painful memory. Gathered around the phone, Kim, Stevie and Edward exchanged significant glances. *But all my money was stolen by Troy Barber*. Barbara did not know that yet, but she would.

When the call ended, Kim said: 'We need to try to get the money back. Barber must have it.'

Stevie, who had been quiet, was suddenly colouring, as if angry. 'Wait. Have you forgotten something, you two?'

Edward understood. 'I think we have.'

Kim frowned. 'Go on.'

Edward said, 'Rebecca.'

'Yes. My granny was murdered by that man. We are sure of that, now, aren't we? Lured into those silly games with the movie set, lured into buying that dress, the ring light, tripod, doubtless replaying the scene on video or a live call – hey, are there tapes of that? – then made to love him and burned to death, that mural the fire-starter, and then my scarring – his acid. *His fucking shitty acid everyone.*'

'He's gone now, love,' said Kim, but she kicked herself for sounding so trite, because it just made Stevie angrier.

'Sorry for my language but you can get your mum's money back. My granny's gone for good. As is my face.'

'The man was pure evil,' said Edward. 'He must have known that, or why would he take his own life? Stab himself in the neck?'

'Was he dead when you went back up?' asked Kim.

'Derrick had tackled him and got him on the floor with his legs around him. But Troy must have got the knife back and used it on himself.' He added, 'I wonder how Agnes is. I think I should try to find out.'

'Agnes?' asked Stevie.

'Troy's wife. Edward rescued her from drowning and she fired him,' Kim put in succinctly.

'Thank you, Kim.' He addressed Stevie. 'Troy is – was – her partner, spouse, whatever and . . . oh shit.'

'What?' both women asked.

'The father of her baby.'

'She's expecting?' asked Kim, and Edward nodded.

Stevie said, 'Shall we meet up again tonight? You'll have to excuse my flashes of anger. I just can't believe the viciousness of it. It will take me a sodding long time to calm meseln.'

Her Glasgow accent was more pronounced when she was tired or upset, and right now she was both. Perhaps they all felt cheated of a necessary revenge?

'He was vicious with himself in the end,' said Kim, 'so maybe he was equally disgusted.'

'He cheated justice,' said Edward. 'He cheated us all.'

'I know we both have embarrassing parents,' said Stevie to

Kim, 'because I saw your face when your mum called just then and started on about your husband.' She glanced meaningfully at Kim and Edward. 'Hey, look, you can't hide anything from me, you two – I know you're potty for each other – but anyway, I still think my parents are more embarrassing.'

She was fiddling with her phone, as if there was nothing more to say. Kim prompted, 'Go on.'

'Oh, I'm trying to find the wretched thing here. Email from Dad. He finally gave me Granny's password. He was being weird about it.'

'Bit late,' said Kim.

'My thoughts exactly.'

'At least you can find the letter that started all this,' said Edward. 'I think we know what happened now, right? She writes to me, Troy finds the letter, destroys it and kills her.'

Kim was listening. Something didn't sound right, yet she couldn't put her finger on it. It was all too neat. But there was no doubting that Troy Barber was at the centre of it – why else would he have been spotted tapping away at the contacts computer, night after night, with no reason at all to be there?

Kenneth Schomes was aghast to see Edward.

'You look like you're still getting over that horror! I never expected you in today. Amanda has cooked you a goulash. She has a Hungarian mother.'

The sentences flowed together perfectly but made no sense to Edward.

'I won't put you on reception today because you'll have too many well-wishers. Everyone has read or heard about the shocking events. I think the stockroom to hide you away. Or just take the evening off? Honestly.'

'I need to work,' said Edward. 'Thank you for being so gracious and – ' he remembered Amanda – 'please thank your wife for the goulash.'

They were not used to seeing him in the stockroom, a cavernous space in the basement. The stock manager, a young woman called Bianca with a narrow chin and large earrings, came up to him.

'I've told the staff to give you privacy. We have some potted plants – Peperomia, grape ivy, Montera Swiss cheese – which need labelling and checking for transit damage.' She pointed. 'If they're okay, maybe take a selection upstairs in the lift? Three or four? Use the trolley and remember your safety lifting, because we don't want you hurting yourself after everything you've been through.'

Again, he could barely make sense of the words. As if he was in a dream. He must have lifted a lot of plants and he must have had a white coffee and a sticky bun at some point, because when the shift ended, his back and arms ached, and there was a raisin stuck to a milk stain on his trousers. He went home in a daze and sat in the almost-dark, the house creaking around him as if offering comfort and an embrace. He opened the French windows at the far end of the kitchen and let in the sound of the sea. The swell on the water sounded more pent-up than usual, restless as if a storm was coming. He felt the same.

When things were like this, when the world seemed to be a north magnet and he south, and every single place, every person, repelled him, he needed to take time alone, or scream his feelings to the world. He had gone to the school football match on that wintry day and shouted as a way of venting his distress, pushing the reality of Matty's death away. It had been selfish of him, to let others see and hear his pain, especially the kids; he had not been thinking straight back then, and he would not go to a school football match again. Shouting for his late son needed to be done in private now.

He went to the end of the garden – as far as he could in the dark without losing his footing – and screamed his son's name at the sea. Louder and louder he screamed, yelling into the summer night until his chest heaved with sobs and his voice was choked by heavy tears.

He needed to live with it. He would learn patience with that dark star in the middle of his heart. He was living for Matty now.

He turned back to the house, his sanctuary, more precarious even than he was. He could hide here for as long as it delayed its inevitable collapse into the sea.

He must check on poor Derrick. God knows how this most unmasculine and sensitive of young men had managed to hurl himself at Troy. He was holding his phone, wondering if he should call Derrick now (or would he still be in the hospital? There was that hand injury, and a swollen eye) when the screen lit up. The brightness was set to high and now, with the evening gathering and the sun gone, it nearly blinded him.

The display said one word: Agnes.

'Hello?'

He heard sniffing at the other end.

'I need to talk to you.'

Edward said slowly, 'I am just so sorry. I saw a lot of it. I don't know what got into him, but he's the father of your—'

'Stop,' Agnes cut in. 'You'll make me cry. Whatever happened last night . . . I just need to tell you something.'

'Me?'

'You.' The line broke up for a second with a series of clicks. 'Because I'm standing here wondering why you were in my radio station last night, and knowing it must be the same reason he took his life. And if we both say what we know, I think we'll have both parts of the jigsaw. And I need the full picture, Edward.'

So that was it. The final errand – to explain to the woman who loved Troy Barber that he was a killer and a fraud. But what could she know that he did not?

'Did you say standing?'

'I'm outside your house.'

CHAPTER THIRTY-FOUR

She looked like a ghost. Just as Troy Barber had done, when Edward had switched on the studio downlights and the cold white glare had greyed him, taken every shade of colour from his body. With Agnes there was still the bodily presence – she was in a baggy dress, as always – but she seemed to have shrunk as a person. They stood in the garden. She wanted to speak, obviously she did, but she let him say the first sentence.

'It was a horrible scene.'

She bit her lip.

'It is that.' She added, 'Did you see him . . .?'

He waited.

She tried again. 'Did you see him take his last breath?'

'I'm actually not sure, Agnes. I came back upstairs and he had . . . I hate to say this, Agnes, so explicitly, but he had taken the knife to his neck, I think while trying to stab Derrick Tidy, who had a hold on him.'

'No!' she exclaimed, although she must already have known this. 'Poor Derrick. So young, just starting out. Loyal and keen. I wish I could tell him how sorry I am.'

'Is Derrick okay?' asked Edward. 'I haven't been able to find out today.'

'He's in the hospital.'

'For the second time.'

'Mmm?' Agnes did not recognize the reference at first. 'Oh yes, the poor boy with his ankle. Troy and I visited him.'

'I bumped into you there, too.'

'Okay. Yes.' She was agreeing vaguely, agreeing without remembering. Too distracted, too broken to recall much more than her own name and that her partner had taken his own life.

Edward said, 'I don't want to describe the scene with Troy. The wound was fatal. By the time I got back upstairs he wasn't breathing. I did try.' Now he had a shocking memory – him pounding Troy's chest while an exhausted Derrick Tidy panted in the corner of the room, bent double.

The knife had still been in Troy Barber's outstretched hand. As he pumped his chest Edward had wondered about the hand suddenly moving and driving the knife into him. He watched the fingers, looking for any impulse. But Troy was lifeless.

'Anyway,' he continued, trying his best, flailing around for a sentence that would sound wise and was not a platitude. 'Anyway, we have the sea to remind us that in the end life does go on.'

'Not his, though,' said Agnes. 'Not his.'

He looked at her more closely in the dark and realized that the voluminous dress she wore was a maternity fit. Edward wanted to say something about Troy's life going on through their child, but he could not think of any form of words that could be a comfort. *A fraudster and a murderer, but at least you're carrying his baby.*

'I owe you an apology,' Agnes said suddenly.

'For what?'

'He had been against you.'

'Oh?'

'He must have been very troubled, Edward. He poisoned me against you. It started with the football game, when you cheered for Matty and upset all your boy's old friends. So what? You were grieving. But Troy showed me it on social media and told me to sack you. Said you were a liability. Then I was thinking I'd made a mistake when I did it. You pulled me out of the sea, which was like an omen – I dump you, and you save me, all in the same moment.' She sniffed, rubbed a hand across her eyes. 'But I still didn't see I was wrong. You're a good person, but Troy made me act like a bad one. He said no, hold firm, don't let Edward back. He said you were a narcissist, said, "He'll do anything for attention", and then what made it worse for you—'

'I know what you're about to say. The Granny Riot.' It was funny, the way their shorthand for the gathering of furious listeners outside the radio station now had permanence.

'Yup. He told me you must never be allowed back.'

Edward laughed without smiling, without humour. A hollow laugh. So Troy Barber needed him out of the way, in case his scam was spotted. It made sense. Edward knew his audience. He would have detected the agony they were going through. Were he still at RTR, he could have sniffed out the illicit use of the studio computer. A story or complaint would have reached him – it almost did, if only Troy had not intercepted the Riva letter – and he would have solved the mystery from inside, in half the time.

'I felt my authority was on the line,' Agnes added, and Edward felt a sudden flash of frustration with her. He lost control for a second; he had to say it. 'You know – he came here! To my home!' His voice rang with outrage. 'He told me about the . . . the protest. The day before. I didn't even know about it! He said it was coming and I should join them, and he would make sure you had no choice, you'd have to take me back, and he would make sure you did.'

She was shaking her head. Then she whispered, 'What a snake. He told me the opposite.' After a moment she murmured, 'What I don't understand is why? Why the fuck? Really, *why?*' The last word was shouted.

It struck Edward in that moment that she might know nothing about Troy's scam. 'I don't know if you are aware of . . . the other stuff.'

She breathed deeply. There was no light in the garden now. He put on the weak exterior lamp, pressing a button on the back wall of the house, and gestured at a garden chair, but she waved it away. He was about to speak, but she started herself, unprompted. 'I want to say this without it sounding like I'm accusing you. You went into the radio station last night, Edward, because you knew something was going on, something very wrong, something that involved Troy? And Troy came in to stop you? Am I right?'

He sighed. 'That's about the long and short of it.'

'And there's a part of me that wants to know what the hell he was up to, and a part of me that never wants to hear his name again. Why would he come in to stop you, and kill himself instead?' She added, without explanation: 'Maybe I already know the answer.'

The wind picked up. The feeling was like a hand stroking Edward's face, and he thought of Kim and her mysterious appointment tomorrow morning at the hospital. Agnes and Troy, Kim and Anthony. Two buoyant women with men like dropped anchors. He must not be unfair to Agnes. Troy had manipulated her, too.

'I found out a whole lot today,' she said. Having no question from Edward, Agnes offered an answer anyway. 'He was in a lot of trouble. Real torment.' Another pause. 'I mean, I knew. I'd found a prescription for Xanax. He'd never suffered anxiety before. Stress, but not anxiety.'

Edward wanted to say sarcastically, 'Fraud and murder can make a person anxious, so I've heard,' but he had to hold on to his anger or she would become defensive. He desperately wanted to hear everything she had to say. Agnes was a victim too.

'I found out today why he was so jumpy.'

Edward tipped his head, reaching for the control on the back of his hearing aid.

'This afternoon,' she said. 'His death – a therapist felt she was able to get in touch. I had no clue.'

'Go on.'

'It's disgusting.'

'Does it relate to pensioners?'

Agnes looked so shocked it took Edward aback. 'Pensioners? No, the opposite.'

She tangled and untangled her fingers, in and out, up and around, a knitting motion.

'He was having – without my knowledge – some therapy. He was in a bad, bad way. The therapist used to go to our church. She was all over the place.'

'All over the place?'

'She had been in a quandary. He had confessed something to her and she felt I should know it now he was dead.'

'Right.'

'She was, frankly, a pretty useless therapist, an amateur really. Just a qualification through the post and a good heart. Basically she was out of her depth. I nearly blew her off, she was so jumpy.'

Edward let his anger show. 'I would say those sixty pensioners, and Rebecca Mason, might say there was a confession worth hearing.'

Like a pedestrian about to cross a road who sees a car leap into view at speed, Agnes took Edward's words like a shock to the body.

'You'll have to repeat that for me to understand it,' she said. She was finally moving towards the rickety wooden chair he had offered. They took seats opposite each other, almost invisible in the gloom.

'Do you want to explain that?' Agnes said. 'The sixty pensioners thing?'

'Let's leave it for now. I don't want to give you more to worry about. You carry on about the therapist. I want to hear this.' Edward was surprised at the command he heard in his voice, the firmness. 'Therapist first.'

He heard her voice without seeing her speak. He closed his eyes so as not to miss a word.

'The therapist,' she repeated. 'Troy came to this woman with his nerves in shreds. I mentioned the Xanax, yes? He had something very bad happen to him online. You know he teaches university courses on Zoom when there's an absent lecturer? They call him a Flying Professor, ridiculous title. He was approached on his email by a young woman asking for help with medieval literature or something. She was local, or said she was, and apparently she was on a course where he had stood in. How would he check that? Her photo was a bit, um – saucy, shall we say? He told me about it, joked about whether it was appropriate for a student. That's the start and end of what I knew until today.'

'What did the therapist tell you?'

'It all got sexual. They went offline, off the university intranet. They were on Snapchat I think, perhaps because the messages disappear—'

'He thought he was safe.'

'Yes, Edward, exactly. He thought he was safe. Don't ask me how it happened but he wanted pictures and she sent them. And he sent some to her.'

'God.'

'What an idiot. A married man an idiot, who would have thought it?'

'Was it breaking the law?'

'Not the law, so he thought, but his contract. He isn't – wasn't – allowed to have relationships with his students. There were more than a hundred photos. But it got far, far worse. She wanted to meet in the city. He drove twenty miles to Exeter. When he turned up, he was ambushed.'

'No.'

'It turned out the girl he was in touch with was fourteen. So he actually had a hundred illegal pictures on his computer, and when he arrived to meet this "university student" in an underground car park – I mean, any normal person would run a mile, right? – he suddenly got caught in a really bright spotlight, and they were filming.'

'Who is "they"?'

'I don't think he ever saw them. He was in shock. The whole incident gave him PTSD. He saw the outline of a person, that was all. That was when he changed, I can see now, in hindsight. He was sweating day and night after that. Maybe there never was a girl. The people with the camera and the light were shouting, *"You've been caught by the Paedo Vigilantes!"*. That was the phrase he told the therapist they used again and again, with a man shouting, "You knew she was fourteen because she told you! She told you!" And he, I gather from the therapist, he claims she didn't say, but who knows if somewhere in all those messages she had given her birth year or something, right? And so he must have this filth on his laptop, the pictures—'

'But I never heard this story. Did the group not expose him or put it on YouTube or—'

'No. His nerves must have shredded waiting for it to happen. It never did.'

'He paid them off,' said Edward suddenly, with certainty.

'No! He was as poor as a church mouse.'

'I can guarantee that he wasn't,' said Edward. 'When you do the probate and all the technical stuff around his assets, you'll find a million pounds somewhere. Or at least – you'll find he paid a million to his blackmailers. That's it! That's what happened!'

'No way!' she cried out. 'How . . . why?'

'It's such a long story, and it's so painful. I can't tell you now. I found out when a young woman called Stevie Mason came and saw me. I'll tell you at some point. But for now, just find that account. Because it will be important to a lot of people.'

'I'm scared of what you're not telling me.'

It was astonishing that Agnes knew nothing of the massive scam her husband had run. He watched the moon pass behind a cloud, as if even distant planets were finding the conversation unbearable.

'Edward, do you think he came to the radio station to kill you because of what you had found out?'

'Yes, I think so. But I locked him in the studio, and it was like he was caged, hurting himself to get free. Let's move indoors. It's getting really cold out here.' Edward was shivering. He stood, towering over Agnes, and gave her his hand.

Before she stood up, he said: 'What he did was wicked. I have to warn you. Truly, truly wicked.' He thought of Rebecca Mason, flying from her upstairs window in a burning negligee.

The chair creaked as she left it. In a sliver of moonlight he saw that the expression on her face had changed. She did not want to cry. The tearfulness had been replaced by determination and it had happened in an instant.

'I want you back on the radio station,' she said suddenly. 'I'm going to move Tessa K to breakfast and I want you to go back to your old show with Derrick when he's better.'

Agnes Chan left. Edward was so tired he sank into an armchair and fell into the deepest sleep without even locking the French windows. He was woken by the early rays of the sun, shimmering across the sea. He looked out at the garden – a ritual he realized had started unconsciously, measuring the number of metres of grass he had left and checking none had disappeared in the night.

He made coffee and remembered Kim, going into the hospital for her important meeting about her husband this morning. He texted her:

> Hope nothing untoward about today's meet with the doc, hope it all works out okay, love from me x

Then he completed the trio in his mind – as if there was no couple without Stevie. How had she described them? Stevie had used some memorable phrase. 'The big guy, the house lady and the burned crisp.' He thought again of the damage to that young girl's face, the sightless eye, and was once again revolted by the thought that Troy Barber had worked that trick with the acid. Did his blackmailers keep pressing him for cash? Is that why he kept the scam going? Is that why he got desperate and tried – successfully – to stop Edward from being allowed back to the radio station? Holy mother of God, what a mess.

Edward wanted to be happy that he was getting his old show back, with Derrick at the wheel. The move would give Tessa K a much-deserved leg-up as well. But for now he just felt exhausted. He was due in at the garden centre today. He would have to work until the radio station reopened his job.

As he showered, he closed his eyes and an image came to him of the car that had hit him and Matty on their bikes.

He could picture it now.

He opened his eyes and it was gone.

The colours . . .

He was so close to remembering but equally it might never come. He would speak to Jordan Callintree today and get an update. Doubtless the Devon police were still crawling over the radio station looking for clues to Troy Barber's motivation. Edward would have to decide, with Kim and Stevie, whether to tell them about the crimes the man had committed. If any of the money was left, it should go to the victims.

In the shower, he heard his mobile phone ring. It was on the other side of the bathroom and he tripped on a towel as he tried to get to it. He answered the phone, but all he heard was howling. It was so loud he thought for a second it was a fault on the line. But there was no fault. It was Kim. The howling turned to crying – not weeping, but sobbing that became a primal yell.

'Kim? Kim? Are you hurt?'

He checked the phone display. The call was from her.

'Kim – speak to me!'

'The car!' she shouted down the line.

In his mind's eye, a vision of Matty in front of him on his bike appeared. But it was as if he was seeing it filmed on a drone. Father and son were on the Amber Road out of Cubitt when . . .

'Kim? Kim!'

Now, he heard only breathing down the line. He heard the vehicle coming from behind him and Matty; Jordan Callintree asking, 'What colour was it?' and Edward replying, 'I don't know. Many colours.' A car of many colours?

Did it come to him before she said it?

Many colours because it had been a police car.

'Anthony hit you in his car. Anthony did it deliberately.' Kim spoke slowly with a space between each word as if she couldn't bear him to miss a syllable.

'It was deliberate. He'd found out about us. I think it was my mum, a chance comment about how she'd seen us out that day. Do you remember? Zizzi in Exeter. Me and you. And she mentioned it to Anthony. And he – being the control freak he is, *was* – he put everything into finding out. He knew. And because he knew, he meant to kill you. He drove his car at you but I don't think he saw Matty. He hit you from behind. Matty hit the tree.' She sounded as though she was bargaining with herself. 'No, he can't have. You got out of the way somehow. The car hit Matty. Which explains what's happened to him in the year since the accident. He can't live with himself because he killed your child.'

PART FOUR

Three months later

CHAPTER THIRTY-FIVE

'Line four,' said Edward into the microphone. 'Line four is Rebecca.'

As always, the name gave him a spark of memory. He sat in the studio, the red light above his head, with Derrick through the soundproofed glass to his right. The researcher Trent had gone, replaced by Debbie; Debbie had lasted only a month before deciding she wanted to train as a nail-bar therapist. The new researcher was a nineteen-year-old called Astral who identified as they/them and wanted no further questions on the matter – which was fine with Edward, who had gone beyond minding about details like the gender of his production assistant. He wanted no conflict in his life any more of any sort. He had needed more strength, these past three months, than he could ever have imagined he had in himself.

Rebecca on line four was not *that* Rebecca, of course, although the name would always take him back to the months of chaos that had followed Stevie's first approach to him in the garden centre. The ends were tied up now, as far as they could be; he was seeing Agnes later in the hope that she could tell him they had found at least some of the stolen money. If they did not, it was up to individual victims whether they wanted to go to the police. This was no longer an investigation for the trio of Stevie, Kim and him. The perpetrator, Troy, was dead. There would be no more scamming of the audience, no more murder.

He had gritted his teeth and returned to his show, feeling a duty to come back, feeling that he must not let the death of Matty destroy any more of his own future. He would honour his son by living. He would honour him by going back on the air, and enjoying it.

He could not bear to think about Anthony Cobden. The man's nervous breakdown had been caused by the killing of his child. How could that killing be described as an accident when he had deliberately swerved the patrol car at Edward? Jordan Callintree had updated him soon after Decla had – as it was legally obliged to – passed on the details to the police.

'I'm not sure he'll be in a state to stand trial,' explained Callintree, when he called to debrief. 'Although my view is this needs to be done properly and publicly so there's no question of him getting away with it.'

'Hmm.' Edward baulked at that. 'I'd rather – I really would rather there isn't a lot of speculation about what might have motivated him.'

'I think I know what you're referring to, sir.'

'My relationship with his wife.'

The police officer was silent.

'Does that have to be part of this?'

'Above my pay grade,' said Callintree. 'If there was a trial, and he pleaded not guilty, I would guess so. But you really can't fight a case if you've confessed, as he has. And right now he's apparently – I stress "apparently" – unfit to enter any kind of plea at all.'

'How did his confession come about?'

'In therapy. He had to have ECT, electro-convulsive treatment. He got it into his head that he would never recover because of this "block". They say there's elements of bipolar with him, so possibly he has massive ups and big downs. Whatever. Seems he had to tell someone. He was medicated, so that's disinhibiting. But you can't confess a crime in secret to a psychiatrist. The code has changed. These days they have to report it up the ladder. The shrink told Cobden's wife first, as a courtesy, which to be frank I felt was a cheek. She could have destroyed evidence.'

'Poor Kim. Why did no one find the damage to the car?'

'You'll be shocked at this. Well, no,' the police officer corrected himself, 'maybe you won't be shocked at all. In Devon and Cornwall police, we don't go around asking if this or that patrol car has been involved in a crime. They all get a little battered. And we tend to assume, wrongly in this case, that police solve crimes rather than committing them. He took advantage of that rather basic flaw. He'd wrapped the bumper in a tarpaulin before he hit you. And he put a bash in it deliberately the following day, with a very obvious prang in the station car park.'

'The attack was pre-planned?'

'Oh yes. He had it in for you. He has confessed every scintilla. The tarpaulin, how he chose the route, put an AirTag on your bike in the weeks prior, which is a serious offence in itself, and how he disguised the use of the car at the station. There wasn't much damage to the vehicle, by the way – your child was killed by the impact of his body being thrown against a tree. I'm sorry,' he paused. 'I didn't mean to say it as brusquely as that.'

Edward exhaled slowly. 'It's okay.'

'The reason there was no "melt" – do you remember I gave you a very dull speech about tyre markings when a vehicle suddenly stops? – is because he never applied the brakes. This monster really meant it.'

'He meant to hurt me like he hurt my son.' Edward blinked, rolled his shoulders as if getting used to a new weight on his back that he would always have to carry. 'I wish he had got it the right way round.'

'He's a violent man,' said Jordan Callintree, 'according to his wife.'

'I wonder why I remembered the car being driven by a lad in a baseball cap.'

'I thought about that. You know, it's funny how the mind works. You see baseball cap, you think teenager. Your mind saw the cap and you worked back from it. The cap had a pattern on it, you said. I guarantee that was police issue down here, the blue-and-white check. He did not intend you to have any memory of the crash. He did not intend you to leave the scene alive.'

'Sometimes I wish I hadn't.'

The police officer left a respectful silence, as if taking this in.

'If it was me,' he continued, 'given the malice involved, given the planning, I would have a full prosecution and the jail sentence to suit.'

Edward was silent.

'I promise you, Mr Temmis – the second he is fit, the second he walks out of Decla, we'll be on to him like flies on a turd.'

Edward did not know what to say, because he did not really know what to think. A part of him dreaded the publicity from a conviction and sentencing.

'Mr Temmis, are you in touch with his wife any more, can I ask?'

'You're joking.'

The 'Rebecca' on the line now was a Rebecca Wilson – again it triggered him: Wilson/Mason sounded close – and she wanted to talk about seagulls and the way holidaymakers did not understand they were pests.

'They will swoop and blind,' she said.

'Has anyone been blinded in Sidmouth?' he asked.

'Very nearly,' said the caller.

He looked over at Derrick, who had thrown back his head and evidently exploded with laughter, inaudible through the glass.

('Did they go to the "Very Nearly Hospital"?' Derek cheekily asked through the headphones.)

They had moved his studio from the one invaded that night by Troy. Humble Reggie had somehow been upgraded, so the programme's contacts database was no longer running on battered Windows 95, but within a brand-new Apple iMac with the latest software. 'Proud Reggie', Derrick called it. Edward thought of it as a parting gift from Agnes.

She had had to go. There was no future for her in Devon with so much turbulence in the wake of the violent death of her partner. Publicly, the story of his massive fraud had not been told. Occasionally rumours reached Edward. That Agnes's partner had been embezzling money or stealing equipment from the radio station. That he had been part of a betting syndicate that was working in cahoots with the Saturday afternoon sports programme. That he had been meeting prostitutes in the building at night. That he was a psychopath responsible for three unexplained stabbings in the Exeter area. Only Edward knew that the truth was more incredible than even the wildest rumours.

'Ten calls in that hour,' said Derrick, bustling into the studio with a coffee for Edward. The news was on now. 'I think we can get twelve in, boss, but I'm in your hands.'

'I loved Kenneth Trent-Towers,' said Edward into the talkback microphone.

'Towers-Trent,' Astral corrected from the other room.

Derrick stood next to him in the studio. 'Poor guy. A collection of Hoovers and his wife says either they go or I do, and he's asked her for time to think it over!'

The producer lowered his voice. 'Are you okay,' he began, suddenly serious, 'if there's a news item about Anthony Cobden and your son tomorrow? I have had a tipoff that he may be about to face a court.'

'What, with a guilty plea?'

'Either guilty or they'll say unfit.'

So far as Edward knew, no one was aware of how his relationship with Kim had caused her husband to take revenge. And he did not want them to know.

'Do we have a motive for it?' asked Edward grimly. 'I mean, any reason?'

Derrick chose his words so carefully, the older man wondered if he knew something. 'There won't be evidence heard if there's no defence. And if he's confessed, there's no defence. I don't see how the court would go into any background.'

'There's an officer who's helped me. I'll ring him first thing tomorrow.'

'Did you tell me you were seeing Agnes tomorrow?'

'Shit!' exclaimed Edward. 'Early doors.'

'Are you still working at the garden centre?'

'Once a week for a few hours. I like them down there. They were there for me when . . .' He breathed in with a shudder. 'And what would I have done without you, Derrick? I'd be toast. What you've been through—'

'A cut to my hand, a slash to my ear, nothing much.'

'But you saw a man die.'

'So did you,' Derrick said, quietly. 'We both went through that together.'

'I wouldn't want to again.'

'Let's not talk about it,' said Derrick, clapping his hands together and straightening up. 'I can't even bear to think about Rebecca Mason.' He brightened. 'Hey, at the weekend, what about I ask the Mariners' for the back room? I'm turning twenty-seven, the age all the great rock stars die.'

'You are so bloody young!' Edward exclaimed, faking a punch to his stomach that Derrick overreacted to, the unruly bush of ginger hair on his head moving in slight delay. It was remarkable, he thought, how a sensitive, utterly unphysical young man like Derrick could step up in a single moment and show such astonishing bravery. For tackling Troy Barber while unarmed, Derrick Tidy had received a police commendation.

Edward asked, 'Are you bringing anyone special?'

'Mary.' That was his elusive girlfriend. 'I know there's not much space. They've got a snooker table in there now. Might even ask the Farmers.'

In the last three months, taking advantage of her own imminent exit back to a job in London, Agnes had got rid of the last members of the old guard, Wendy Goodenough, Cyril Weekes and 'Lord' Keith Wenn. The rest, now outsiders, had piped down, unable to compete with the horrific news of Troy Barber's onslaught. The younger station staff – Derrick's generation, all in their twenties – now felt able to refer openly to the outgoing bunch as 'the Farmers'. The bloody surgery on the old guard was complete and Agnes had left, with the official explanation that she was an expectant mum and would want time with her newborn.

'Do you have a lady friend to bring?' Derrick asked. 'I always think our lovely listeners hope you're with someone. They often ask me before they get put through on the air.'

'Do they? What do you tell them?'

'They feel for you because of Matty. They ask how you are, and then they sigh and say something like, "I do hope he finds someone to be with soon".'

'I don't think I'd tell them if I did,' said Edward.

'So I take it you don't? I'm your producer, I'm allowed to ask! I was just thinking about the party.'

'I'll be there, don't worry,' said Edward, avoiding the question.

Agnes becoming a mother somehow seemed to have reset her emotionally. Her life was centred on her son, Wilbur. She had brought him to the seafront, where the three of them gravitated towards the same bench where Edward had chosen to meet her all those months ago.

'I thought you'd worry about a wave.'

She shrugged, her eyes invisible behind the darkened glasses. 'That seems like it happened before the dawn of time.' To his surprise, she began breastfeeding her child. It was a warm day in mid-September. He tried not to look at her as she reached inside her blouse.

'You seem calm.'

'Giving birth does that,' she said. 'You have no other priority in the world but getting this little scrap home safe.'

'Wilbur is a lovely name.'

'You'll laugh. His second name is Muyang. After my dad. It means "bathe in the sun".'

'He'll be a bit shocked by Sidmouth then.'

'Bathe in the rain.' She laughed at her joke, but ironically, that was when her pain showed most. It was as if the laughter got trapped on its way out of her – stifled by an invisible cloak of sadness she was wearing. Perhaps motherhood had released Agnes from worries about her career. Certainly she no longer had to think about the hostility of the Farmers. But the shadow of that awful night at RTR-92 would hang over her life for a long, long time. There was no point pretending otherwise.

Come to think of it, he would do exactly that. Pretend otherwise. 'I'm loving my job and I want to thank you for giving it back to me.'

'I'm delighted. How is Derrick doing?'

'Keen as mustard, as always. He turns twenty-seven at the weekend. He joined us as a boy!'

'I spent quite a lot of time doing what you asked me to,' Agnes said, pulling down her spectacles an inch and fixing him suddenly with a beady stare, at once intensely intelligent and . . . what? Angry? Indignant? It shocked him, and he looked away, his gaze dipping accidentally to the baby's mouth on her nipple. She went on, 'I did it. I got others to do it. And . . . nothing.'

'You found nothing?' He was incredulous.

'I think it was a wild-goose chase, Edward,' she said. Again, there was the slightest suggestion of anger. She minded being asked to do something as pointless as looking for a million pounds in her husband's empty accounts.

'He never had any money. He borrowed mine. He was paying the mortgage on a flat in London and that was suspended for six months, so I've had to sell it. Why would he default on a mortgage if he had all that cash swilling around?'

'I don't know.'

'You're going to tell me he paid it to the people who stitched him up with the young student?'

'Yes. Yes, I believe so. He did the scam to pay off his blackmailers.'

'I got a forensic accountant in. When someone dies, if you are the beneficiary – and thank God I am – you have quite amazing powers of access and discovery. But there was nothing to discover. There is no account anywhere in the world with his name and National Insurance number attached, nor his address, nor any address we've ever used.'

'An assumed name?'

'Maybe that's it. In which case we will never find it. But they went through his computers too. All the web browser history, looking for a bank login that he might have been using. All the apps on his phone. And his laptop. If he had a secret account, I don't think he was ever looking at what was in it, ever paying out of it – it just doesn't seem credible.' She added, 'It cost me a lot,' as if she was about to ask Edward to pay.

He shook his head disconsolately. 'I don't want it to end like this. The last time we were on this bench, you fired me. I guess it's lucky I don't work for you as an investigator.'

She chuckled. 'It's okay. Just allow me to vent. I'm angry with Troy and he's not here. All I care about right now is this little one. But you had me worried – did you say *a million?* Sadly, I think Troy just . . .' Her eyes welled with tears; the emotion of her loss was never far away. 'He was under so much pressure he exploded. He took his own life because of the shame at what he did with that teenage student, who wasn't even real, because don't those "paedophile hunters" create fake profiles anyway?'

To Edward it didn't sound right, but he had no other explanation.

'I want to thank you for meeting me.'

'We're down for the week,' Agnes said. 'I'm travelling with my sister. She's been such a help.'

'Do I get to meet her?'

'She's off for a long walk along the Jurassic Coast, I'm afraid.'

'And left you holding the baby.'

'That she did.'

'I'm sorry I sent you on the goose chase with the money.'

'Those geese ran pretty fast.'

Edward stood, and had a thought as he got to his feet. 'I saw you and Troy in the hospital. You were there to visit Derrick. Do you remember? He had a broken ankle, I think. And I remember Troy was sweating so badly. He looked terrible. I think he must have been in the middle of it then.'

'I'm sure he was. Goodbye, Edward.'

Still breastfeeding, and unable to stand, Agnes raised her right arm to shake Edward's hand.

He walked off past the amusement arcade. Something drew him back and he stopped at the open frontage, under a moulded plastic lightbox with the words SIDMOUTH IS THE BEST FUN EVER! with plastic outlines of fish and mermaids. The machines in here were the old ones, the classics from the Sixties and Seventies, and Matty had loved to play on them. He went to the penny falls and watched the coins piled up on the edge, all edging closer but never falling. Then he changed a pound coin for fifty two-pence pieces and started to play himself.

After forty coins, he had got nowhere at all, until, with fewer than ten tuppences left, he managed to start an avalanche that won him at least sixty pence for his stake of eighty.

He rummaged in the metal tray for his winnings and then, as his hand closed on a fistful of coins, he found he could not withdraw it. He smiled. Wasn't there an old proverb or an Aesop's Fable about that? The monkey who was trapped with his hand in a box because he refused to let go of the nuts?

And then suddenly, as he opened his palm and let some of the coins go, every individual thing fell into place in his mind, every event took its rightful position, as if a single thought had rolled at last into its intended place, and every other thought and fact had followed. He gasped and dropped the rest of the coins as if they were burning hot.

He knew what had happened.

Finally, he understood everything.

CHAPTER THIRTY-SIX

Barbara no longer mentioned Kim's weight loss. 'Darling, you're so thin,' had been the refrain for years. Even when Kim was not getting thinner. Now she genuinely was, shedding half a stone since the divorce proceedings had begun, her mother seemed not to notice.

'I don't like to saddle you with my worries, Kimberley, because I know you have enough of your own.'

This was a first. So far as Kim was aware, her mother liked nothing better than to saddle other people with her worries. 'Mum,' said Kim tenderly, 'saddle me.'

'I know you don't want to talk about Anthony.'

Kim managed a hollow laugh. 'That's not your worry, it's mine.'

'Yours is mine, darling, but okay.'

Kim was amazed her mother did not push harder. She guessed Barbara would have encouraged her to hold firm and get out of the marriage. Had she known what Anthony had done in the police car that day, she might have dragged her daughter out.

'Mum, you have to take my word that it's for the best.'

'He wasn't getting better from that dreadful breakdown or whatever it was.'

'It was nothing to do with his illness. I was in it for the long-term.'

'And then something happened.'

'And then something happened,' Kim repeated.

'And things changed.'

'And things – what is this, Mum, *Crackerjack*? You can't just say stuff and get me to repeat it. That's not how conversations work.'

She dreaded a 'not guilty' plea and the details coming out publicly. It was the kind of story that could go around the world, appearing on news programmes from California to Canberra. An English detective discovers his wife's liaison with another man, uses an AirTag to track the man's weekend travel habits, aims a police car at him on a country road but kills his child instead. No witnesses. Disguises a mark on the vehicle by 'accidentally' hitting the bumper against the concrete wall of the police station car park the following day (what had Edward remembered? *A car of many colours?*). Scuppers the investigation by continually assigning extra duties to junior officers on the case. As a consequence falls into a major depression with psychosis which renders him unfit to plead for a considerable time.

Or maybe for ever. Kim would not complain if it never came near a court. For her the best outcome would be a guilty plea and a mitigating statement from his lawyer which made no mention of her fling with Edward Temmis.

She had noticed her hands had begun shaking at odd moments, and then more and more often. She could not bear the idea that her betrayal of Anthony had turned his inner violence on to Edward and Matty. Why did she not think that might happen? Did she not consider she was pulling Edward, a virtual stranger, into the orbit of Anthony's evil? Without that single afternoon of her taking selfish carnal pleasure in the cliff-top house, an eleven-year-old would not be dead. She would trade every future caress the world had in store for her to undo that passionate moment in the past. But nothing could be undone. She was undone. She was to blame. She had lost her appetite for everything now – for work, for food, money, laughter, the Porsche, even for the sea. Perhaps she could be lost at sea herself. Perhaps that was what she deserved. An hour on the kitesurf, and she could be gone.

Except that would kill her mother. And she wondered what it would do to Edward. He had every right to hate her. They had not spoken since Anthony's story had come out. She wanted so much to console Edward, but now she felt she was the source of all his pain.

'. . . and I just wondered whether you could advise?' Barbara concluded.

Kim shook her head, as though to clear it. 'I'm sorry, Mum, I only caught the end of that.'

'Kim! You drifted.'

'It happens quite a lot these days.'

'I hate to raise it.'

'Raise anything, Mum.' Kim looked down to where Barbara was pleating and re-pleating the napkin she held in her hands. 'To be honest, I'd rather you were raising than probing.'

'I was saying – I'm going to need an operation on my hips and I'm going to have to pay because it'll be more than two years waiting on the NHS. And added to that, you'll know there's a mortgage on this house still because of the divorce, because I took the equity. It's all getting very tight, and I don't want to go to your father.' She started to weep. Kim immediately shuffled around to her armchair, dropping to her haunches and doing her best to put her arm around her mother. It was too much: Anthony, Troy . . . *the evil that men do.*

Barbara leant towards her daughter, allowing herself to be folded into the embrace. 'I understood,' she sniffed, 'there might be a chance of finding the money that was stolen . . .?'

'I don't know, Mum, I don't know.'

'Can you not get in touch with Edward?'

Kim knew this was coming. She could not tell her mother why it was out of the question to ring Edward for the time being. She could not say, 'My husband killed his son. I don't even want to inflict the sound of my voice on him.'

Barbara's tears were flowing now. She said, 'I could last perhaps six more months, but nearly forty-five thousand pounds, love – I just don't know where I'll get it. I'm not asking you for it. I want to know if they got it back off that . . . man.'

Kim asked, 'If Troy had had a million pounds in his mattress, wouldn't we know?'

'Can't we find out?'

Kim thought. She groaned as she stood up from what had been an uncomfortable position. 'I'm just making Old Lady Noises,' she said. 'I'm not groaning at you.'

'You should hear my noises.' Barbara patted her nose and eyes with a lace handkerchief she had produced from the sleeve of her jumper.

'I suppose,' said Kim, 'there is one thing I *could* do . . .'

She actually did two things. She looked online for the resale value on her Porsche. It might be fifty thousand less than she paid for it three years ago, but it was as good as new, which would help. She would get forty-five, assuming it survived an inspection by the dealer, who would huff and puff over every imperfection.

Before she set the sale in motion, she rang Stevie.

After Troy Barber's death, the two had texted and emailed a little, but never met. They were not consciously avoiding each other – Kim had a divorce to settle and all her mother's travails to deal with. Stevie was presumably just exhausted by the whole thing. Where could it go now? The perpetrator was dead. Unless they found the money. That really would be a development.

'Where are you?' said Kim.

'Back in the office after seven tons of sickie leave. Back to my HR computer stuff. I had forgotten how many helpdesk calls are "I've forgotten my password". At least there's no acid in anyone's hard drive.'

'How is your . . . face?'

'Ach, it hurts like shite. They said it would. Scarring. The good sort of pain.'

'Your eye?'

'Sometimes it itches so much I just want it out. But they say any light I get is good for the brain.'

'I'm so sorry, Stevie. Maybe we should meet?'

Stevie said, 'Like – be mates? I think we should be. But you didn't call.'

'I've had a nightmare, to be honest,' said Kim.

They met during Stevie's lunch break in Toot's, the coffee shop by the lifeboat station in Sidmouth. It was a glorious, cloudless day.

'I heard a funny story about this place,' said Stevie, pointing at the signage. 'There was a local guy who had made a boat out of his bathtub, with an oar and a bedsheet, and always left it chained up in that cove over there. He kept setting off "for Scotland" with his dog! A thousand miles! But every time he went, the tub would get about half a mile and sink, and he'd have to be rescued. So one night the lifeboatmen just broke up the bathtub with a set of sledgehammers. He never set sail again.'

'Saved his life, I should think,' said Kim.

Stevie no longer wore an eye patch. Her wounded eye, the left, looked as if it had oil on the surface, and the eyelid was lumpy with scar tissue. The side of her face with the worst burns looked as if it bore the vestiges of bad acne, although the slightly darker grooves and dents were lines rather than spots. The tip of her nose was marked.

'How is it looking?' asked Stevie, following her gaze.

'It just makes me so angry. But also, if I'm honest, Stevie, so admiring of you. You're hard as nails.'

'My mum and dad have been on the warpath. It's interesting to see a vicar lose his temper. They've been all through Rebecca's accounts, and they finally accessed her Google Drive. She paid the scammer more than twenty thousand pounds before she ran out of money.'

'Oh God.'

'Twenty-one thousand. Three cheques for seven thousand. It's still not clear what exactly she thought she was paying for. She had some emails about saving a Hitchcock archive, but there were no replies from her. She might have responded by ringing. She was never a big emailer. Any phone number on an email, she calls it. Never types the reply.'

'Bless her. A Hitchcock archive sounds like the kind of thing.'

'Wasn't your mum forty?'

'Forty? Oh, I see. Yes. She and I were just talking about it this morning. Just under forty-five thousand.'

'More than twice as bad.'

'Twenty-one thousand, nearly forty-five thousand. Except it doesn't work like that, does it? Depends how much you had to start with. Depends how humiliated you've been. As it happens, it wiped Mum out. It made her feel small. But your granny lost her life.' She stirred her tea, feeling the weight of so many individual losses.

'My parents are in denial about it. My dad's been so weird, I can't even . . .'

Kim said, 'My mother wants me to find out if they've recovered the money. It's kind of why I wanted to meet. She wants me to get in touch with Edward to ask him, and I can't.' Stevie knew nothing of Anthony's attack with the police car. She added, 'Please don't ask me why.'

'Once Troy Barber was dead, it was case closed for old Eddie.'

'Why do you say that?' Kim asked, a little too sharply.

'He hasn't responded when I've texted. So I guess he thinks, case closed.'

Surely, the reality of it all was far more complicated. When the truth about the killing of Matty emerged, Edward would not have given the scam at the radio station another thought.

Stevie shrugged. 'But I can ask him. I'll ask him for both of us.'

'Are you sure?' Kim paused, and a thought occurred to her. 'That letter your granny sent – did you ever get into her email server to find it?'

'We got the password to her Google Drive. Do you remember I mentioned that? I'm sure I told Edward. But my dad went in first. He changed the password. So I couldn't access the Drive.'

'Because we were desperate to see that letter, weren't we?'

'Dad was really weird about me accessing all the stuff on her cloud, so he wouldn't give me the new password. I gave up asking. I figured, once we knew about Troy, there was nothing more to find out.' She paused, evidently hearing Kim's dissatisfaction in her lack of a reply. 'Okay, okay. I'll ask Edward for us both.'

Kim had the sudden sensation of her heart physically tearing – as if the blood had gulped into the wrong ventricle and the organ had burst in her chest, splitting in two. She placed her hand on her sternum, as though to hold it all in.

Stevie frowned. 'Are you okay?'

'Anxiety,' said Kim.

'It's fucking understandable,' said Stevie.

More and more, Stevie hated living at home. She knew how much her mum and dad had put themselves out for her since the accident. Apart from anything else, her mother's lavish generosities would never let her forget. Cocoa last thing at night, served with a rattle of mug and saucer, and never mind about knocking; tea and toast at first light. Someone had to massage the silicone gel into the burn scars.

Stevie was grateful. Grateful to be in a loving home, grateful to be back at work after so many weeks off. But 'grateful' sounded close to 'grating', and that is what her mother did with her. Dad was a closed book, but Mum was intrusive.

Irritated beyond reason, she felt that her need for her parents' care had allowed them to make her a child again. If only she could afford to buy a place to live, but no one in their twenties could these days. Maybe she would meet someone and they could do it together. Not likely at the moment. She couldn't face Tinder or any of the other apps she had tried in the past, partly because there was no angle that would not show her damaged eye and expanse of hairless forehead, and partly because everyone within two miles seemed to be a farmer.

She wondered about her dad. Had he even noticed her suffering? He lived for his flock, for the parish in West Hill and half a dozen others. After the death of his mother, he had fallen into a stubborn kind of grief, refusing point-blank to be alerted by Stevie's concern that something wasn't right. Thank God he had not found out when she accessed her grandmother's home without his permission.

But his manner had become secretive, and when he discovered the password for Rebecca's Google Drive he had told Stevie – 'COUNTRYSIDE, all capitals' – but then immediately prevented her from accessing it by changing it.

'There's nothing for you in there, is there?' he had asked. Was he trying to force her to admit what she was searching for?

She would speak to Edward about the money, but first she went to her dad. He was in his study, working on a sermon, dwarfed by the office chair, wearing a tight, small suit. The house might have been a block of cement without a single memorable feature, but the garden beyond the study window was immaculate. She looked past her father at the dahlias and hydrangeas and the freshly mown lawn lit up in the sun. Stevie had a momentary flash of her grandmother's fatal descent into her own back garden, lit up by fire. She put the terrible image out of her mind.

'Dad, can I ask you something?'

He kept his back to her, making the sense of intrusion all too obvious. 'You may.'

'Why wouldn't you let me have the password for Granny's drive?'

Without hesitation, but still staring at the sheet of paper he was making notes on, he said: 'Why wouldn't you tell me why you wanted it?'

She sighed. 'I knew you were upset when I said what happened to Granny might not have been an accident.'

'Why do you think I might have been upset by that?'

Although he still had his back to her, she saw that his pen had stopped moving on the paper.

'Insurance,' she said, and kicked herself immediately for her honesty. Would she ever learn?

He turned, and she thought he was about to explode with anger. 'Really?'

'Yes, really. You told me you thought it couldn't be suicide. I thought because of the insurance, you wanted it to be not her fault, an accident.'

She felt movement at her feet and looked down to see the cat, Sunglasses, entering the room, as if this was going to be a conversation worth hearing. Her father, wearing his dog collar and sitting like a child emperor in the high-sided office chair, stared at her, red in the face.

'And you took it upon yourself to investigate, Stevie.'

'No, Dad, I—'

'Don't *lie!* Don't *lie* in the *house of the Lord!*' Theo suddenly shouted. She had never seen him this angry. He recognized it himself and breathed deeply, his hand across his stomach as if he was physically in pain. 'I know what you did. It gave me an ulcer.'

'What did I do?' Stevie asked, all innocence, but knowing she might have to drop the pretence.

'Let me tell you something. You'll not have noticed this, because you don't pay much attention to anyone but yourself, young lady, but I belong to a tennis club which plays on the court at Tipton St John every Saturday.'

Stevie stifled the urge to roll her eyes. 'I know *that*.'

'Well, okay, so you have noticed. We are a motley crew. Different ages, different abilities. One of the worst players is a gentleman called Timothy Goldsworthy. Do you know him?'

'No.'

'Never met him? Short, rotund, loud voice?'

'No.'

'He says he took you round Granny's house after the police closed it off. He might have introduced himself as Tick.'

'Oh. From Devon Fire.'

'That's right. Care to explain? Why you got access to a house that even I wasn't allowed into at the time?'

'To be honest—'

'Well, that would be nice,' her father cut in, his thin neck tightening like a cable under tension. 'If you could be honest.'

'I thought something bad had happened to Granny, and no one seemed to care.'

His face changed. 'We cared. Your mother and myself. I . . . cared.'

'You wouldn't listen when I said something was up and I wanted to go and see for myself.' He had not yet added two and two – not yet inferred that the hard drive containing the acid must have been removed from his mother's home.

'And then you had your own terrible accident and, heavens above, that almost killed your mother.'

'I know, I know.'

'And then . . . then you come to me and you want access to Granny's cloud files. Do you understand why I might have been reluctant? After your secrecy and your lying?'

'Yes, Dad.'

His tone had softened. She thought that some of his anger might just be an outlet for his grief, so she decided to try complete openness.

'You know about the scam now, because Granny lost twenty thousand pounds. You know about the whole thing because you heard about the meeting in the Secret Squirrel and you came, to my surprise, without even asking me. I didn't feel you would help me, Dad. I thought you would try to stop me, just as you're trying to stop me now. But the reason I wanted the password – I should have told you this, Dad – is because she wrote a letter to Edward Temmis.'

He blinked. 'That peculiar radio presenter?'

'Well, he isn't peculiar actually,' she said, surprising herself at how defensive of Edward she suddenly felt, 'but he may bear the scars of having his son lose his life on the road eighteen months ago.'

'Ah, of course. I should be more respectful of that. He came here, you know?'

Stevie waited for the explanation. A voice came from behind her.

'Yes. Came and sat in the living room. We thought he was a very rum chap, possibly with intentions towards you.' Her mother's frame filled the poky corridor. She was wearing an apron and rubbing her hands, which had flour on them, and her fingers were so pudgy it looked as though she was kneading eight breadsticks.

'Mum, Dad, I went *to him*. He didn't know me. I told him what I told you. That I was worried about Granny. *He* helped me.' Stevie's unspoken extra sentence hung in the air, an accusation. He helped; you didn't.

Perhaps that was not fair on her parents. What evidence did they have of foul play, other than Rebecca's strange behaviour before her death, and the sheer unlikelihood of her setting fire to her house with tea lights? Stevie had not told them about the letter Rebecca Mason had hand-delivered to the radio station, which she must now do.

'Before Granny died, she wrote a letter to Edward asking for help. At least – I think it said that, because the words on the envelope were something like, "In Desperation from Riva". You'll recall she loved Mr Temmis's radio show. She always called herself Riva when she rang.'

'I think I know this,' said Moira. 'A lot of her friends used that name for her, since school.'

'She was "Riva from Gulverton" when she called Edward's show,' said Stevie. She did not look at her mother, but addressed her next remark to her father. 'All I ever wanted to do was find that letter. Edward says he never got it.'

'He might be lying,' Moira put in.

'Believe it or not,' said Stevie, 'I did consider that. But if he was, why would he be helping me? He didn't even know who she was.'

'He might be lying about that, too,' said Theo.

Stevie ignored him. 'It went missing in the radio station, so it seems pretty certain that Troy Barber, the fellow who went mad in there, intercepted it. But I always felt that if I got the letter, I would know what happened. But the hard drive was in the fire – ' *best move on quickly,* she told herself – 'and none of us thought of Google Drive. Then when we found the password, you locked it.'

'Your father was angry,' said Moira.

'And if you're going to be Hercule Poirot, you need to tell us,' Theo added.

'I don't know who you're talking about.'

'Good God,' said Moira.

'A famous private detective,' Theo said, chuckling, which
– although it was at Stevie's expense – emptied the room of
tension. 'I was hopping mad when that balloon of a man,
that firefighting Santa, Tick, when he said you'd been round
the house. I couldn't believe my ears! Without telling me,
Stevie!'

'After all we've—'

Theo broke across Moira, still concealed in the small corridor to Stevie's right. 'No, Moira! We swore we would never use
that phrase in this house, and we never will.'

It was as if the mouse had roared. Moira, always the bigger
and louder voice in the marriage, apologized meekly.

'Do what you want with this and know that I trust you,' said
the vicar. He turned back to his chair and tore a strip of paper
from the bottom of the page he was working on, then wrote
something on it.

'Capital W, capital H, no spaces,' he said.

Stevie stared at the paper. The password was WestHillparish.
'I could have guessed that,' she said.

'But you didn't,' said her mum fiercely, and her father winked
and turned back to his sermon.

The call to Edward was short. Half an hour after the tense conversation with her parents, Stevie rang him.

'Hey!' his voice was warm. 'I was thinking about you.'

'Oh, bloody hell,' she said. 'What in the name of hell's worst
dogs did I do now?'

'How are you, firstly? Back at work yet?'

'Sadly yes. Same old drudgery. Council IT is not the sexiest.
Had a guy yesterday in the bin rotas, he was looking at porn,
and when they fired him, he said, "That's not fair, everyone's
looking at porn." Now they want me to find out if he's right.
That's a full week's work. Twat.'

362

'I am going to a birthday party on Saturday. Why don't you be my plus one?'

'You're not for real.'

'It's at the Mariner's. My producer. The one who saw me through the whole thing, me being sacked, being reinstated.'

'How old is he?'

'No idea. No, wait – he said twenty-seven.'

'Too old for me.'

'It would be a great chance to catch up.'

'I never get invited to parties.'

'Well there we are.'

'Can I bring Kim?' The question had come to her so easily that Stevie did not pause before she allowed it out of her mouth. *Damn my bloody thoughtlessness, putting him on the spot like this.*

Was there the slightest delay in Edward's response? After a fraction of a second, he came back enthusiastically. 'You know what? That's a great idea. I would love her to be there.'

Stevie was desperate to ask questions, to find out why Kim and Edward had apparently stopped speaking, but she must stay on her assigned mission. So she put on an almost professional voice to ask.

'I have a question. About the money that was stolen. Granny Rebecca lost twenty thousand, and, to be honest, that's quite a hit for my mum and dad because they don't have much, although they'll have the proceeds of the house sale, but that burned down . . .' She pulled herself up. She was drifting. 'Kim and I both want to know if they recovered the money.'

'No,' said Edward stiffly. 'I'm so sorry. I met with Agnes. Troy had nothing anywhere. I would love to tell you they are going to find it, but I can't.'

His answer was strangely stiff, almost as if she'd asked the wrong question.

'Do you know something you're not telling me?' she asked, after a pause.

Edward breathed heavily. 'Why do you say that?'

Stevie asked, 'Well, do you?'

Finally the reply came.

'Stevie, I know everything.'

CHAPTER THIRTY-SEVEN

The Mariner's Net was split-level. You walked in and immediately were at the bar. Order your drink, turn around to face the tall sash windows, and there was the sea, winking at you from the other side of the promenade. Pass the bar, and you came to a short set of stairs that led down to the second level of the pub.

When Edward arrived, there was already a crowd, and they were trying to bounce the full-size snooker table out of the centre of the downstairs room.

'They should have bloody moved this for you's, Der,' a voice boomed. 'Don't bounce it! Slide it!'

Edward immediately recognized the voice as Vic Turnbull's. So the old guard were here? He never thought Derrick Tidy would actually go ahead and invite them. Although Derrick was the sort who fitted in anywhere. Edward wished he had the same quality.

He looked around. It was eight thirty. Unbeknownst to those present, Edward had been in a pub around the corner for an hour. Derrick had asked him to make a short speech, and he had spent an inordinate amount of time working out what to say about his producer. But he was there mainly to make sure he caught Kim and Stevie so they could all arrive together. Perhaps they had got in ahead of him. He had not seen them.

As he stood at the top of the flight of five steps, wondering where in the room the Mariner's snooker table would end up (it had no wheels, and sliding it was making grooves in the dark wood floor, but for some reason the pub manager was watching and cheering as the men in the room shuffled and bounced it sideways), Edward felt a tap on his shoulder. He turned and looked down at Stevie, for once not shocked by her injuries. She had taken trouble to cover them. Then he looked up at Kim, almost the same height as him in her heels.

She looked dazzling. Her hair was lighter than he remembered, almost blonde now, and the lipstick on her lips was freshly applied. She wore a steampunk braid jacket with a high collar, and leather trousers. He could not think of anything to say other than, 'You look beautiful – both of you.'

But now he noticed their expressions. Both serious. Behind him there was chanting and cheering as the snooker table was finally shoved into position. He glanced back and saw that one of RTR-92's security guards was trapped between the table and the wall, and Wendy Goodenough had shouted, 'That's Darwinism right there!' – and it was strange, turning from the hilarity in the room below to the two sober faces behind him.

'Are you both okay? You look like you've seen ghosts,' he said.

Kim spoke. 'Before we go down there, can Stevie show you something?'

Edward looked at Stevie and saw her begin to draw an envelope from her bag.

Agnes Chan's arrival was modestly done, and drew no eyes except Edward's. She came down the short set of steps to the lower level, her spectacles flashing light and dark as if in alarm at what she was getting into. He looked at his watch. Nine thirty. He had a bottle of champagne someone had thrust into his hands to open for Derrick. He saw the birthday boy move to greet Agnes, and once again marvelled at the way his surname was so appropriate for his dress sense – his frame was gloved by another tight-fitting suit, and he wore a quiet tie and high-collared shirt – but his hair was like a bush two foxes had been fighting in. What was that film, *Eraserhead*? He only knew the poster. The man with vertical hair.

Stevie and Kim were in different parts of the room. It was interesting to Edward that nearly everyone here was from the radio station, as if radio was the heart and soul of Derrick's life. At one point he had met a couple of younger people and, not recognizing them, asked how they knew the producer. 'We all worked on hospital radio with Derrick,' was the answer. He talked to Tessa K briefly, and they realized how much they had in common. Her radio heroes – Ken Bruce, Steve Wright, Kenny Everett – were his too.

He moved through the crowd to welcome Agnes, who was stuck a little at the foot of the stairs. But as he reached her, she still seemed to be mid-conversation with Derrick. She looked at Edward over Derrick's shoulder, who turned.

'Edward! This is quite a crowd. I'm just sorry we're all squashed against the snooker table.' He turned back to Agnes. 'He's going to speak, which is what he does best.'

Edward could barely hear, and as he turned his hearing aid up, he heard a zap and a buzz that suggested the battery was going. Curse it, he thought. Why now?

He looked back at the room. Derrick was holding his arm. Agnes had come around to greet him as well, but her words were lost. He turned his good ear towards her and she took it as a sign that he expected a kiss, so she stood on tiptoes and pecked him on the cheek. He shifted his gaze and saw Kim, staring at him, in conversation with the small, wiry Keith Wenn, who looked like a child beside her. She was evidently desperate to escape. She mouthed '*Now*' at him, and he nodded.

Brian Channon, on the far side of the snooker table, at a nod from Derrick, called the room to order by banging a fork on his beer glass. Clink, clink, clink, smash – the glass broke. Channon laughed, everyone applauded, and the room was silent.

Derrick said, 'I'm so glad you're all here! Many happy returns to me!'

Cheering, more enthusiastic applause. Was this the first time the station staff, even those recently ejected, had got together since the Troy Barber horror? If so, it explained the warmth in that clapping – this was partly a celebration of Derrick's heroism. Perhaps that made it easier for the presenters ditched by Agnes to attend and not feel like confronting her. The station itself had gone through a bigger trauma than any individual.

'I'm so pleased that everyone made it.' Derrick name-checked a few of his friends in the crowd, and said his parents were late but would be coming soon. He raised his glass. 'To RTR-92. Because it's the radio station that's brought us together. It's had a hard time lately, but it survived. And it's still at the centre of so many lives. We were overdue a party, I reckon,' added Derrick. 'Edward, over to you.'

Edward caught Kim's eye. She pursed her lips into a narrow O, as if considering something. He looked for Stevie in the crowd and could not find her. Maybe she had hidden herself along the back wall, for once not wanting to be the centre of attention.

'Hello! It's good to be back!' said Edward, and there was a cheer. 'All of us are here because we love the radio station—'

'Not me,' interrupted Brian Channon. 'Bloody hate the place.' There was some laughter, but also some shushing.

'I feel like the Father of the House,' said Edward, 'as I'm

about the oldest person left. Don't worry Agnes, not having a go at you!'

'You're next,' said Vic Turnbull grumpily, but this time the response to him was all hostile, with even Wendy Goodenough saying, 'For God's sake, Vic, be quiet. You and Brian are behaving like the Kray twins.'

Shocked laughter, glasses clinking. 'I feel I ought to say, with everyone here, that the radio station has been through the most awful time,' Edward continued, 'and I'm so glad we're almost out of it. If you're wondering what I'm talking about, there's a lady in this room who could tell you. Where are you, Stevie?'

After a short pause, Stevie raised her hand at the back. 'Here.'

'Stand up!' shouted Brian Channon, a joke about her height.

Edward was suddenly unsmiling, his voice more insistent. 'Stevie revealed a plot. More than a plot. A serious crime. Happening at RTR. A major, major crime, right under all our noses! To scam our audience.'

The electrifying silence was so complete at this moment that Edward instinctively reached for his hearing aid to turn it up. When he did, it buzzed and zapped again. He moved the dial to off. The silence was real.

'I repeat – a heist on our own audience. They used the contacts computer in my studio to harvest dozens of phone numbers. My listeners, many elderly, were secretly approached and conned. The sum stolen from them was about a million pounds in total.'

A pin-drop would have been deafening at this point.

Edward repeated, 'Just over a million pounds.'

He looked at Derrick, who was rising on the balls of his feet like a policeman and wore an expression suggesting he felt his birthday party was being hijacked; but he was not going to complain, because the drama of this moment was worth it.

'And obviously, Troy Barber . . . I'm sorry Agnes, I didn't realize you were coming, and I don't want to make this uncomfortable for you . . . Troy was the perpetrator. Dead Troy. He was seen using the computer, when he had no business being there. And when I went into the radio station one night to properly log what was in the contacts computer and work out when and how it was accessed, he attacked me with a knife.'

Edward looked at the floor. 'Or perhaps I should say that he attacked himself. I was in the control room, and I managed to lock him in the studio. He killed himself. Thrashed at himself with that knife. I saw it happen. It was truly horrifying, a serrated blade. A bloody gash in—'

A young woman at the front squealed.

'I'm sorry,' said Edward, 'you don't need details.'

'Oh but we do!' laughed Cyril Weekes, who was clearly drunk already and was immediately shushed.

'Derrick knows what it was like, don't you? Derrick was there. Our hero,' added Edward, making the younger man glow.

Edward stared at the faces around the room. Around forty people were crammed around the snooker table, and he now realized the drinkers in the pub upstairs were starting to listen too. In front of him, the previous research assistants Debbie and Trent were poised with drinks six inches from their lips, as if the glasses had frozen in mid-flight to their mouths.

'Strap in,' said Edward, and now he spoke quickly. 'Since Troy's death, I've discovered he was being blackmailed. He'd had some inappropriate sexual contact with – he thought – a student. The girl was underage. He went to meet her and was ambushed by a group called "Paedo Vigilantes". But there was no girl, underage or otherwise.'

A cough from Brian Channon, loud enough to be a gunshot. 'How do you know all this?'

Edward was reluctant to get into the details of the therapist, so he pointed at Agnes. 'You can check this with Troy's partner. She found out after he died.'

'Fair enough,' said Channon. 'I always like to get receipts.'

'Ssshh, Brian,' said Cyril Weekes, who was not laughing now.

'Troy got pounced on by the Vigilantes. They shone a bright light at him. But that was it. No police follow-up, no YouTube exposé. Why?'

No one said a word.

'Because in exchange for their silence, Troy could perform a service. And the first service was to get me sacked.'

A rumble in the room. Edward tried to turn his hearing aid back on. He could not read whatever emotion was being expressed. He said, 'You have permission to laugh. The famous "Granny Riot". Troy told me to join it, I did, then he told his partner to sack me – and she did.' Agnes was nodding. He coughed. 'Shall I carry on, or shall we party some more?'

There was no sound in the room. They were riveted to the spot. Even the drinkers on the upper floor wanted to find out where this was going.

'I couldn't work out why Troy had got me fired,' Edward continued. 'And I started wondering, who was using him to get at me? And what else were they using Troy Barber for? I'll come back to this.'

He caught the eye of Agnes, who looked as if she might plead for him to stop, but at the same time she needed more. He pulled out his handkerchief and wiped his forehead. It was boiling hot in here. The bar staff had stopped serving.

'Stevie, who you'll remember from the start of my remarks, her grandmother, Rebecca, was murdered. Her home was set on fire because she had not only been defrauded but most importantly, *she had identified* the fraudster. Until today, I wasn't sure how Rebecca Mason had done it. The person had led her a right dance, getting her to dress up as someone out of a Hitchcock movie—'

For the first time, there was a challenge from the audience. Vic Turnbull snorted derisively. 'He got her to dress up? More fool her.'

Stevie erupted in fury from about six feet to his right. 'She was old, and she trusted someone, because they had her fucking number out of your system and they knew all about her! Give her a break, you rhubarb-crumble-faced twat! She got bloody burned alive!'

The room fell into shocked silence.

Edward continued, 'The fire was in December, and my immediate thought was Troy. But then I had the faintest memory – Troy was out of the area then. By pure chance, he had told me he was in North Wales. So I checked. On the night of the fire itself, he was at a dinner in Bangor, and I know that because I've been through his Facebook posts. So the fire can't have been set by Troy. And this made me absolutely certain that Rebecca Mason was killed by whoever stitched up Troy with the girl photos.'

The weather forecaster, Ashley Courtney, had her hand up.

'Why are you telling us this? You sound like you know what happened but you're not sure if you should tell us.'

Edward said: 'I'm telling you because it affects each and every one of us.'

He had lost his thread. He was about to say, 'Where was I?' but he thought the attention span of the room was at its limit and might snap. He gold-fished, looking for the start of the next sentence – but the next words came from a most surprising quarter.

'This happened to my sister!' began Lord Keith Wenn, red-faced and with a drink in each hand. 'If you're saying that my sister is one of the victims of this horrible rat, whoever it was, she lost eight thousand pounds!' He said the words with a vicious, almost triumphant slur, and a mist of spittle accompanied them from his mouth. 'So I want to listen.'

Edward had his place now, and spoke quickly. 'Imagine elderly Rebecca Mason jumping from her bedroom window in her nightclothes. Her house was on fire. She was burning when she jumped. Rebecca was conned out of more than twenty thousand pounds. There were sixty-two of these scams – sixty-three, if Lord Wenn's sister is included. Derrick, are you sure you don't mind if I carry on?'

Derrick shifted, rocking back and forth on the balls of his feet. 'Shall we leave it there? It's a great story, but maybe one for the police?'

'I'm happy to stop there,' said Edward, but it prompted tumult in the room. Derrick waved play on, but there was a furrow pulling his eyebrows together.

'Sixty-three frauds and a murder.' The prompt came from Kim.

'Thank you, Kim. But actually, two murders.' Edward pointed to the back. 'Stevie, whose grandmother, Rebecca Mason, died in the fire, Stevie had some very bad injuries earlier this year and I went to see her in hospital. Strangely, when I was there, I saw Agnes with Troy. They had just been to see Derrick. You'd hurt your ankle three days earlier, yes?'

'Yup.'

'And you were in a private room.'

'Clerical error,' said Derrick, prompting laughter.

'I don't think so. I think you paid for that. You see, when I left the hospital, I had the strangest memory. You'd done your ankle fixing a gutter three days earlier, you said. But then you told me you'd been hobbling around on it for ages. That was the phrase, *for ages*. "I remember hobbling around the station the day after the pensioner riot", you said. But the Granny Riot was weeks earlier. And the doctor told me you needed to be in hospital because you'd "tried to struggle through" on it.'

Derrick shrugged. 'What does it matter?'

'I commented on Troy Barber that day too. Said he acted

nervously, and you said, "Yeah, he's a sweaty guy," which made it sound like you knew him. But a minute later you were asking me who he was, as if you had no clue.'

The room fell silent.

Edward asked Derrick: 'Who told me Troy Barber had been on that contacts computer at odd hours?'

The producer's eyes narrowed. He did not answer. He started that rocking motion again, rolling his weight on and off the balls of his feet.

'Only one person told me,' said Edward, addressing everyone. 'And you believe your producer, right? And the thing is: the timing of your ankle injury matters. Because I think *you* were in Rebecca Mason's house when it caught fire. And I think *you* hurt your ankle jumping, as she did, from the upstairs window.'

CHAPTER THIRTY-EIGHT

The first loud laugh came from Brian Channon, then all of the Farmers joined in, and soon the rest of the room was laughing.

'Brilliant! Love it!' they shouted, as if this was part of some elaborate charade that Derrick and Edward had organized for their entertainment.

Edward looked at Derrick. He saw the tension in the young man's body, the readiness to run. But he could also see that Brian's remark had opened the room to the possibility that this was a party stunt put on to entertain the crowd. If he played up to that, Edward could force Derrick to let the story run.

'I'm glad you're enjoying this!' said Edward, as pockets of conversation followed the laughter. 'Hold on a minute now, quieten down please.' Edward waved one arm, trying to keep their attention just a little longer. 'I'll just add a key fact, if I may. Stevie's dad had been so worried about Rebecca before she died that he had broken into the house himself. He became trapped and had to climb out of a window. I think Derrick got trapped too. I think Rebecca went to bed, Derrick broke in and created a fire from thirty tea lights to make it look like an accident, but then found he couldn't escape. So he had to follow the fire upstairs. He ran upstairs, and there she was, standing in the open window, not wanting to jump. He shoved her to her death. He followed and did his ankle in.' Edward added: 'Bet you've never had a party piece like this before! It's going well, Derrick!' Once again, the producer was rooted to the spot, apparently thinking his only option was to encourage the thought that this was all for show.

Someone at the bar on the floor above, a man ordering a Guinness, was being shushed.

'One more thing – if you'll just let me get to the end – relates to the hospital visit. Troy Barber was a nervous wreck after he had seen you, but why? I saw him in the corridor and he looked like he was about to pass out. But the two of you had never met, supposedly. So I'm going to take a guess.' He was having to raise his voice above the murmurs of a crowd trying to work out what they were watching.

Wendy Goodenough shouted, 'He has an allergy to ginger!'

More laughter. But something odd was happening in the room. Although the older generation had decided this was all a joke, a silly piece of theatre put on to enliven the evening, most of the faces Edward saw in front of him were becoming serious again. They began shushing the others.

There was silence again.

'You're not far off with that, Wendy,' said Edward. 'You see, my producer has famously untidy hair, which sticks up like he's had an electric shock – it's distinct, and unmissable. When Troy Barber was ambushed by the so-called "Paedo Vigilantes" in that car park, Troy couldn't see who filmed him. There was a "really bright light" on him. But the thing about a bright light is that you see the outline of the person behind the light. And I'm going to take a guess it was the person standing next to me right now. Because Troy saw that outline again. At the hospital, when he visited Derrick sitting up in bed, the lights in the room were faulty and all he could see was his silhouette. And it shook Troy to his core.'

Derrick murmured, 'Just total guesswork.'

Something had changed in the room. The people who thought this was play-acting realized it was not, because Derrick had begun to shift uneasily on his feet.

Wendy Goodenough said loudly, 'What is this all about? It's quite tendentious, really. Sort of guesses.'

'I thought we were at a party,' said, of all people, the young Astral.

'Astral,' said Edward, 'you've reminded me – in defence of Gen Z, which is you, Trent and the other younger staff, I'd like to point out that when a caller, Irene from Trimstone, got cut off, it wasn't Trent's fault. Derrick did it because she had just started talking about having found love in old age. He did not want that on the air, and – Derrick – you absolutely did not want me to hear that, did you?'

From the back, Agnes spoke. 'You said there were two murders. Who was the second one?'

Again, silence. Perhaps people felt genuine sympathy for Agnes Chan.

Edward said, 'The second victim was Troy.'

At that moment, Derrick emitted a wail like a wounded animal. He turned left and right, but no sooner had he tensed his body to run than Keith Wenn lunged at him. The smaller man wrapped himself around the producer, toppling him back into a wall.

'My sister!' shouted Wenn. His wine glasses smashed on the floor. He had flown into Derrick, and tackled him crossways, so the younger man was smothered by his body and toppled back against the wall. 'My bloody sister! How dare you?!' Derrick was now off-balance and pinned by Wenn, who gradually pulled him from the wall by his wrists, and stood with Derrick in a vice-like grip. 'Meat handcuffs till the police arrive.'

Edward stared at the two men as he spoke, speeding up

now, desperate to get to the end. 'Troy Barber was sent into the station to stop me. Derrick here suddenly burst in on him. Why? Because it was all getting too hot, and this was the perfect way to dispose of the one individual who must have known everything.'

He looked at Agnes significantly.

'Who was tackled by Derrick and then, we're told, while restrained on the floor, stabbed himself in the neck.'

'He'd already been stabbing himself before I arrived, you fool,' said Derrick from behind Keith Wenn.

'He had, yes. He might have attacked me – as you wanted him to – but when I locked him in the studio he knew the game was up. Self-harm as a form of self-hate. That's what I saw. You turned him into a bug-eyed madman. Your foot had been on his neck for weeks – metaphorically. The knife was real. But I don't believe his hand was on the weapon when it plunged into his neck, because a second before I left that room, he had knocked himself out. The person who killed Troy was you, Derrick.'

Brian Channon called, 'Jesus Christ, this has been worth the entry fee!'

'Do I get to speak?' said Derrick, trying to get free from Keith Wenn, who yanked his wrists every time he moved.

'Let him go, Keith,' said Wendy Goodenough.

'Could I just blow my nose, Keith?' asked Derrick. Wenn released a wrist. Derrick pulled a handkerchief from his suit pocket.

'Two murders and a million-pound fraud,' Edward concluded. 'I think I've said all I have to.'

'It doesn't add up to much, though, does it?' asked Derrick, snuffling in the handkerchief behind Keith Wenn's shoulder, addressing the room with what seemed phenomenal composure. And alarmingly, about half the people in the crowd shrugged in agreement. 'It doesn't add up to a string of beans,' Derrick continued. 'I got slashed by Troy Barber, remember?'

'You were slashed on the back of the hand, where there'd never be serious damage, and through the ear. The earlobe to be precise, one of the bloodiest parts of the body. It was almost as if you did it yourself.'

'Well, I didn't,' Derrick told Edward, 'but I understand if you've been cross with me for producing Tessa K, who you were rude about every single time I saw you during the time you were off air.'

Edward stared at the floor and shook his head, blood rising to his cheeks.

'You know,' said Derrick Tidy, 'I'm only twenty-seven but I've done my defamation training. I don't think your little speech was libel because no one printed or broadcast it. But I reckon it's the best example of a slander that any of us will ever see. Racketeering and murder? Really, Edward? Really? I know that since your son died you have struggled. But I was there for you. I visited you, I called you, I even prayed for you every bloody Sunday. I never thought you would come back at me like this.'

Edward felt his heart sinking. Suddenly he felt unsure of himself. He had presented what he thought were facts, yet he had been so deeply immersed in the events he had described that he wondered if all he had offered were, as Wendy Goodenough said, 'sort of guesses'.

But as he looked up, he saw a piece of paper being waved at the back of the room.

Stevie.

'Hang on,' said Edward, 'maybe we can allow Stevie to have a word. Her granny's violent death surely grants her that. Let's hear Stevie speak.'

At the back of the room, against the wall, Stevie was aware of all eyes turning to her. Some of the older people in the room, instead of turning their heads, shuffled their feet so they turned to her with their bodies. She wondered what they made of this short girl with the damaged face.

She waited for everyone to stop moving, then lifted the envelope in her hand, allowing her audience to get over the shock of seeing her face for the first time.

'A letter was delivered to the radio station in an envelope marked "In Desperation from Riva". The letter was intercepted as soon as it arrived, and the envelope left empty in reception. The only reason I have the letter is because it was saved to Granny's Google Drive. Rebecca was crying out for help from her favourite radio presenter before she . . .'

Stevie paused. If she said 'before she was murdered', she risked sounding like she was following Edward's guesses with more of her own. The case he had built made sense only to him, to her and to Kim. There was not even enough solid grounds for Derrick to be arrested, as it stood, let alone for a court to find him guilty of anything. Not without more.

But she was holding *more*.

'Before she died violently,' she said. 'In a fire, in her home, started by a bunch of tea candles left on a wooden floor which she, by the way, would never ever have used, ever, let alone left unattended like that.'

More guesses.

She needed the letter.

They all needed it.

She pulled the page of A4 from the envelope, handed the nearest person the envelope – Agnes Chan, who had moved closer to her – and stretched the paper out as if it was a proclamation.

'Can I read the letter to you?'

Everyone tensed. Brian Channon simply said, 'Go.'

She read. '"Dear Edward, you are my favourite radio presenter and I write to you in desperation. My name is Rebecca Mason but I've always used my school nickname "Riva" when

I've called your show. Recently I have been a bit silly and got into what I think you'd call an *online relationship*."'

Stevie looked up. 'Those last two words are underlined. My granny writes, "I rang your show about cinema and I did a film quiz and you asked me about my love of the film *Rebecca* by Alfred Hitchcock. Anyway a man got in touch with me. This and that went on. It all became quite passionate in an online sort of way and I suppose I enjoyed it, more fool me. At some point he asked for money (long story about a Hitchcock archive needed saving) and I paid more than twenty thousand pounds and then, *of course*" – another underlining – "he was gone with the wind, to use another film title. More fool me, I suppose you'd say. But anyway there were one or two times he rang me and spoke to me and I thought he might be local."'

Stevie paused. She sensed the room becoming restless. As if this was going to be yet more speculation, yet more – what was Wendy Goodenough's word – *tendentiousness?*

She pulled at the A4 in her hand to spread the last paragraph of the letter clearly, but her good eye was streaming and her rapid blinking was sending a line of tears down her cheek. She tried to staunch the flow by placing the palm of her hand into her seeing eye, and as she did so, with her vision occluded completely, she felt the paper taken from her.

Alarmed, she blinked.

Agnes had it.

Stevie reached for the eye drops in her handbag and listened to Agnes's voice beside her.

'The last paragraph I can read for you, Stevie,' she said. 'Rebecca writes, "I'm sure the conman was using a throwaway phone but by the miracles of technology my phone stored his number. And because I was sore about what had happened I rang the number sometimes, but nothing. Once or twice it said

'Out of Service' or it just gave me an unobtainable tone. But it was therapy when I got cross about losing my money and being made to look a fool. When I got cross I would call the number and even though it never got answered, I would scream and shout a bit into my phone. Silly I know.

'"One day I was feeling particularly upset and so I called the phone when I was in the big Waitrose in Stowford Rise and the strangest thing happened.

'"I heard a phone ring in the next aisle. I listened and a man said hello down the phone, but he was also speaking in the very next aisle. Well of course, I didn't want him to know I was standing so close to him so I started whispering. I needed to keep him on the line for at least a few more seconds so I could see him, so I said the one thing I was sure would do it. I said, 'I've got your money.' As I said it, I moved along the cereal aisle, past the batteries and sewing needles, and then I turned the corner so I could reach him. He said 'What?' down the line and I saw a man ahead of me on the phone and I *knew* this was him. Don't tell me where I got the courage from but I walked up to him and, still on the phone, but now staring him in the face, I said 'You sick bastard.'"'

There was a gasp in the room. Stevie was staring at the floor. Agnes read on.

'"He put the phone away like he'd been stung by a bee, dropped his shopping and ran off. All I can say about this man is that he was quite tall and wore bright trainers and very tight blue trousers. And he had lots of messy red hair, very red, standing straight up on his head. Edward, I wanted you to know this in case you could put this message out on your show to find the con-man. In desperation, Riva (Rebecca) Mason from Gulverton."'

Agnes folded the letter and cleared her throat. Stevie's eye was no longer irritated. Everything was in high-definition and she could even see specks of dust in the air. She looked at Agnes. Her mouth was open.

From the front of the room was a scream. 'Lord' Keith Wenn had stepped back suddenly from Derrick Tidy, and was grabbing around his back. A penknife was sticking out of his left shoulder.

'From his pocket, fuck him!' shouted Wenn.

Stevie moved forwards to grab Derrick Tidy, but he had already gone.

CHAPTER THIRTY-NINE

There was immediate chaos. Three of the older presenters jumped after Derrick a split-second after he peeled away from the gathering, but they collided and fell over two of the low tables. A woman called Kay Tawney, who was on secretarial support and barely spent two weeks a year at RTR-92, and who everyone assumed was as quiet as a church mouse, picked up a snooker cue but was disarmed by Christopher Lawson, the stand-in station controller, just as she brought her arm back to launch it like a javelin at the disappearing figure. Derrick did not go out of the bar at the front. He darted left into a separate saloon room (full of stored furniture, with a young couple in a corner locked in a passionate embrace, shocked by the shouting and running around them), then charged down a narrow corridor to the Gents. There he locked himself in a toilet cubicle.

Agnes and Edward got to the loos first. Then Agnes turned: 'Everyone stay back. Let Edward talk to him.' She pushed the group at the door back and yanked it shut behind her.

Edward heard the hubbub quieten outside the door. He pressed his heel against it.

'I can't keep them out for long, Derrick, so for the love of

God, for Troy, for all your victims, we need a full accounting. You can't run away. Was that your penknife?'

From the lavatory cubicle he heard a snort.

'You don't fucking get it, do you?'

'Get what?' asked Edward, wanting to keep him talking at least.

'They can spare it.'

'Who?'

'All those old bastards. Money to burn.'

A pulse jumped in Edward's temple. 'Not Rebecca Mason, Derrick! Not Barbara Sinker – she barely has two cents to rub together!'

'Mason lived in a million-pound house!' he shouted from inside the cubicle. 'We're still living with our mums and dads.'

'Who's we? Did you have an accomplice?'

The response to this was a roar of jagged laughter from the other side of the door. 'Yeah, about ten million of us. We've been robbed. They took everything. I was getting a little of it back.'

'Most of your victims were poor!' Edward's hands shook. 'What about Troy, and Riva – Rebecca – they *died*, Derrick! And you just stabbed Lord Wenn in front of forty people!'

'He's not even a lord!'

Derrick was shouting so loudly through the lavatory door that his voice echoed in the washroom for a full second.

At that moment the entrance behind Edward gave way, the main door banged against the wall, and two policemen appeared. They almost blocked each other in the doorway.

'Let's get him out,' they shouted, and Edward moved aside as they approached the cubicle. 'Sir – you in there – either open the door or stand back. We'll break the door down in three seconds. Three, two, one—'

The nearest officer, a tall woman, crashed into the cubicle

door and it gave way easily. Above the cistern, an open window flapped. The cubicle was empty.

When he was caught, four days later, Derrick Tidy had shaved off his hair and had somehow got to Exmoor, where wild campers reported a man begging threateningly for food.

The papers had been full of the search, even the nationals. 'Thought to be living rough on Exmoor' and 'distinctive mop of red hair' would always sell a story. His arrest was the first real involvement of the police, who brought Edward, Stevie and Kim in to understand better what they were dealing with.

Edward was reluctant to share the names in Stevie's log. He did so on condition that the victims of Derrick Tidy – those who had come forward at the Secret Squirrel – would be contacted individually, and not in a way that alerted other family members. For this assurance he sought out Jordan Callintree, who had now been promoted to detective inspector.

They sat in the police canteen.

'I'll take personal charge of this case, Edward. You can trust me,' said DI Callintree.

'I know I can trust you. I just don't want someone to make an error, ring a victim's house, the husband sees it, asks the wife what it's all about.'

'Each and every person will be contacted discreetly. You said the password was "Lemon"?'

'Yes. Where's Tidy now?'

'In F wing of Exeter Prison, where he can be properly assessed.'

'Assessed? For what?'

'Every kind of malignant personality disorder which might give his lawyers the chance to argue he didn't know what he was doing. Meanwhile, no bail. That was rather handy, him trying to escape via Exmoor. We argued he's a flight risk. He might be inside for a year, you know. This is a fiendishly complicated case and we have half an incident room to look at it. I don't know if we'll get him for the murder.'

'Murders.'

'We won't get him for Troy Barber, Edward. I know your view on that. I just can't see how he gets convicted when the poor man invaded the radio station with a knife in the first place, not to mention you saw him stab himself with your own eyes.' He paused. 'Speaking of which, we've had some analysis back on the Barber laptop. So yes, a folder with saucy pictures, but no idea who they are of and no proof the person in the snaps was under-age. I won't go into more details, but it's possible they were Photo-shopped images done by Tidy himself. They served a purpose.'

'Troy was an idiot.'

'If you're right, he let himself be played.'

'Quite.'

'To convict Derrick Tidy, we have to find the money and we need his computers to give us connections with your list of victims. Rebecca Mason – well, we'll see.'

'I'm sure he did his ankle when he killed her. He didn't get treatment at the time because it would have aroused suspicion. It wasn't broken. I didn't see him in that period, remember, because I wasn't at the station. So I'm guessing he takes painkill-ers, walks on it, gradually makes it worse, finally surrenders and goes into the hospital. The fire started downstairs, he couldn't get out where he got in, so he had to jump. And the letter, Callin-tree, the letter. It puzzled me for a long time – how did the perpe-trator even know the letter had been sent? How did they know it had not been received? The only answer could be that they inter-cepted it at RTR-92. When Derrick saw that letter, Rebecca had to die. But the ankle brought Agnes to the hospital with Troy—'

'Who must have had the shock of his life.'

'I wonder whether that meeting in the hospital sealed Troy's fate. After that, Derrick knew Troy could identify him. I shouldn't have called Troy an idiot. I feel so sorry for him.'

'I feel sorry for those pensioners,' grunted Callintree.

'Derrick had some weird inter-generational warfare thing – "I'm living with my mum and dad, so I've got a right to rob pensioners." Totally bizarre.'

'Are there a lot of fruitloops in your industry?'

'Ha!' Edward laughed, before asking tentatively: 'And the other matter?'

'Not good news, I'm afraid.'

The table was booked in the Clock Tower Café for six people at 2 p.m. Edward had ordered the scones – a peace offering to bring all parties together. He and Kim knew they had to be careful with what they said, but they wanted to begin on a good note.

'As bad as this has been,' he started, 'as terrible as it has been, we've all met each other through it, and we should now toast each other with Devon tea.'

He looked around the table as Kim, Barbara, Stevie and Stevie's parents all raised their teacups, tapping them hesitantly against one another's.

Theo, wearing his dog collar, stood unnecessarily. 'I'm aware I didn't behave well. I tried to stop my wonderful daughter—'

'Whom we love so much,' put in Moira in her husky baritone, shifting her weight in her chair, staring at the table.

'—from putting herself in danger or, as the gospels might say, upsetting the applecart.'

'There were literally no applecarts in the Bible, Dad,' said Stevie.

'I dodged and swerved and I reckon – in the eyes of Mr Radio here – I probably looked very suspicious. But I just wanted to protect my daughter.' He turned to look directly at Stevie, and his eyes were suddenly flooded with tears. 'In that, I failed.'

'I'm *fine*, Dad, God!' said Stevie. 'I'm not making a speech because I'll just . . . make sweary sounds. But I get the odd bit of light in the bad eye. And the scarring, you know, it is what it is. You don't need a face to work in IT.'

'Oh, darling Stevie,' said Kim.

'Well,' said Barbara, 'I would call this *sleuthing*. Like Theo here – pleased to meet you, by the way – I am aware I also got in the way. My fantasy man was exactly that. Lesson learned. But today the police called and said they hope they may have some of the money so I can buy at least one new hip.'

'True,' said Edward. 'They've got his accounts. But forensic work on money takes a long time.'

'Fifty pence on the pound?' asked Moira. 'That's what I heard.'

'I'm glad we have some sort of ending,' said Edward. 'And especially glad we have all become friends.'

'Plus,' said Moira, straightening her back and immediately towering over her husband in the seat beside her, 'we have you back on the radio. And this time, I've actually started listening.'

They laughed. In the hour that followed, they talked and swapped stories. Kim asked about the vicarage and when it was last sold, and Edward told her to stop behaving like she was at work. Barbara and Moira seemed to get on. Stevie left first, to get back to her job at the council. Quickly the others left too, until it was only Kim and Edward.

'Do we have room for cake?'

'Ah, that might cause me trouble in the sea,' said Kim. She had her kitesurfing kit with her but agreed they could share a slice of carrot cake.

'I'll be at the shore, watching out,' Edward said.

'Oh, with your rubber ring, ready to throw?' she teased.

'There was so much we couldn't say just then,' he said quietly. 'The others don't need to know about us.'

'Ha! You're kidding yourself. Stevie knows and my mum guessed.'

She had told Barbara about Anthony's attack on Edward, and it had been the hardest conversation. It had shattered her mother. 'Anthony will be in hospital for the foreseeable future, and possibly face no charges at all,' she said. 'I need to know he'll never put on a police uniform again. You know what they told me? "We think that unlikely." The chief superintendent!'

'They don't want to prosecute,' said Edward. 'Well, Jordan Callintree, the super-keen young officer does. He really is red-hot. But the police force as a whole don't want it, and can I assume we don't either?'

Kim answered at a tangent. 'You know, a long time ago, when I was dealing with such a sick husband, and not knowing why . . . it crossed my mind. It was just there at the back of my mind, a thought I couldn't even acknowledge to myself. "Had Anthony found out about us?" I just left it there at the back of my mind. I thought he might have found out and been enraged, but it didn't make sense that he would find out and have a nervous breakdown.'

'You were right the first time. He found out and was enraged. Then—'

'Don't say it, darling.'

'So do you want him in court?'

'I want what you want,' said Kim, leaning in.

'I want you,' said Edward, leaning in too.

His phone went.

'It's the neighbours,' he told her, putting his hand over the mouthpiece. 'They say my house has fallen into the sea.'

Her jaw dropped and her face went white.

'I'm kidding,' he said. 'The water people say the pipe repairs are done and they're moving all their stuff. They need access. You want to come? I don't have my show till later.'

'I was going to kitesurf.'

'Come in your professional capacity as my estate agent.'

'You know what happened last time I did that,' she said.

He leant towards her with a smile, and as her face inclined towards his, he murmured, 'Maybe it will happen again.'

Acknowledgements

I would like to thank, above all, the fabulous Martha Ashby at HarperCollins. She had lunch with me and gave me the idea. I went away and wrote the book; she went away and had two children. My book hit her desk on her first week back. And she has been the best editor I could ever have wished for.

Her teammates at Harper are fantastic too – Liz Dawson in PR; Vicky Joss and Tanuja Shelar in Marketing; Morgan Springett in Editorial; Holly Martin and Harriet Walker in UK Sales; Angela Thompson and Ruth Burrow in International Sales; Ben Hurd and El Slater in Trade Sales; Laura Daley in Digital Sales; Fionnuala Barrett in Audio; Ellie Game in Cover Art; Melissa Okusanya in Publishing Operations; Sophie Waeland in Production; Frankie Gray, Managing Director and Publisher.

Also Kerr MacRae, the agent with a century of publishing experience (or so it always seems!). Great for a long lunch or a short conversation. Always plugged in. And I'm thinking of the popup book group that his late wife Jane kindly set up so I could get early views on my writing.

Others: my mum, always happy to help, always enthusing. My brother Tim and sister Sonya. My publishing friend Alan Samson. And a couple of heroes no longer with us: John Myers, who died at sixty on the eighteenth hole at St Andrews having inspired scores of radio people to take joy in the medium.

And above all Kenny Everett. I never met you, Kenny, but you're the reason I go into a studio every day.